SHALLOW GRAVES

Elise Noble

Published by Undercover Publishing Limited

Copyright © 2018 Elise Noble

v7

ISBN: 978-1-910954-79-9

Edited by Nikki Mentges at NAM Editorial

Cover design by Abigail Sins

www.undercover-publishing.com

www.elise-noble.com

The kiss of the sun for pardon,
The song of the birds for mirth.
One is nearer God's heart in a garden,
Than anywhere else on earth.
- *Unknown.*

CHAPTER 1

"YOU NEED TO bring a new...whatever that tree is. It's dead."

Mr. Flatts, the nitpicky office manager at law firm Rockett & Smith, pointed at the perfectly healthy *Calathea makoyana* on the shelf in front of us.

"The leaves are meant to be that colour—it's variegated."

He took a step back and appraised it critically. "No, no, no, Dove." His second chin wobbled as he shook his head. "I do believe it's sick."

My teeth ground together all of their own accord, making my fledgeling headache worse. What did Wes, my boyfriend and business partner, keep telling me? Ah yes. The customer was always right.

Even when they were one hundred percent wrong.

After all, which of us had spent three years studying for a degree in horticulture? A first-class honours degree, no less. I'll give you a clue—it wasn't Mr. Flatts.

I tried one more time. "It really is supposed to look like that. I brought it in to add a splash of colour."

He reached out one pudgy finger and flicked a leaf. "I want a replacement. Wesley guaranteed you'd replace anything we didn't love."

Damn Wes and his smooth talking. And to a lawyer as well. Mr. Flatts would probably sue us if a leaf dropped off. I'd overheard one of his lackeys threatening their cleaning firm with court over a dusty computer monitor last time I stopped by to water the plants.

"Then I'll bring you something new. Do you have any preferences?"

"Something green. Lively. I want vibrant."

Something vibrant? How about a damn triffid?

Half an hour later, with Mr. Flatts safely shut away on a conference call, I escaped the dingy offices of Rockett & Smith with my messenger bag of gardening tools slung across my body and the offending *Calathea* tucked under one arm.

"We get to ride on the Tube now, little one. You can suck all those nasty toxins out of the air."

Yes, I was talking to a plant, okay? Over the last six months, I'd come to understand they made better conversation than Wes. They didn't spout crackpot ideas for their next get-rich-quick scheme, nor did they ask why they'd run out of clean underpants.

The station attendant hovering at Blackfriars gave me a dirty look as I hurried through the barrier, highlighting another issue Wes hadn't thought of when he came up with the idea of starting our business to provide and care for office plants. In central London, we needed to carry the pots on the underground system or fork out for a cab. And when I said we, I meant me.

The *tsk, tsk, tsk* of the attendant followed me as I headed for the escalator. He could tut as much as he wanted—nothing prohibited me from taking a plant on the Tube, except common sense, perhaps, but I'd already proven I didn't have much of that. I mean, I'd stuck it out with Wes for three and a half years now.

Half an hour later, I shoved my way through the door of our tiny top-floor flat in Whitechapel. We'd chosen it not for its stunning decor or creature comforts, because it didn't have any, but rather because of the tiny roof terrace accessed by climbing out of the bedroom window.

That's where the spare plants for our business, Plants 2 U, lived in a makeshift greenhouse I'd knocked together out of wood battens and polythene, only hammering my thumb once in the process. The air-conditioning unit from the office next door vented right next to it, which meant the motley collection stayed warm even in winter. In summer I put my orchids out there to get some sun, but right now, in early January, they were spread along the windowsills in the bedroom and living room, much to Wes's annoyance. He liked plants when they made him money, but not so much when they graced his home.

My significant other glanced up from his spot on the couch as I walked past, surrounded by the holy trinity of laptop, TV remote, and beer. I noticed he flicked the screen on his computer to a spreadsheet, as he usually did when I came near. What had he been doing before? I'd bet on *World of Warcraft*, with an outside chance of porn. Sure, it irked me, but I'd got to the point I was past caring.

"Why have you brought that back?"

"Mr. Flatts reckons it's unhealthy."

Wes peered at the leaves. "Isn't it? It's gone a funny colour."

"No! It's supposed to look like this."

He shrugged. "Whatever. Just chuck it away and take him another one."

Grrrr! How could he talk about a plant so nastily? It was a living, breathing thing. Well, not breathing, exactly, but it definitely respired.

"I'll put it on the terrace."

"Not much space left out there."

"You need to find more customers, then." That was our deal. Wes put his business degree to good use by doing the accounting and marketing, while I did the dirty work.

"Yeah, I will. I'm thinking of branching out. What do you think of dog walking? The hourly rate's higher."

"And who would be walking the dogs? Me?"

"You like dogs."

"I also like lunch, and I didn't have time to eat any today."

The roll of his eyes said he thought I was being unreasonable. "Then we'll hire students or something. People are always looking for jobs."

And all the low-paid workers we'd employed had proven notoriously unreliable. I'd been through three assistants in four months, and the current girl called in sick every other day. What made Wes think walking dogs would be any different?

Nothing, probably, but as long as I stuck around to bail him out of each mess he got into, he didn't care.

"I'll get flyers printed tomorrow," he said. "You can give them out when you do the plants."

"I won't have time."

"Don't be silly. Just leave a pile in each office you go to." He slammed his laptop shut. "I'm hungry. Shall I order a pizza?"

"We can't afford it."

"What toppings do you want? Everything?"

It didn't matter what I said, did it? He already had his phone to his ear and, as usual, he'd do whatever he fancied.

The story of my life.

"Out of the way, amateur."

I fell back against the wall outside my first client's office as a neon-green bicycle sped past pulling a kiddie trailer. Except rather than children, the spiky leaves of a *Cordyline* poked out of the top. A groan escaped my lips as the slices of last night's pizza I'd packed in my bag for lunch got squashed between my body and the wall. I'd never been a fan of Hawaiian pizza anyway, and being flattened wouldn't make it taste any better.

"Hey! Watch out," I muttered.

Darren, my main rival in the office-plant-care stakes and the self-proclaimed "Queen of Green," smirked as he parked his bike up.

"Should have looked where you were going, shouldn't you? Or better still, you could stop trying to steal my customers."

"I don't..."

Oh, what was the point? Ever since we'd crossed paths a week into my new job, it had been secateurs at dawn. Darren never passed up an opportunity to bad-mouth me to my clients or anyone else who'd listen, and he didn't hesitate to insult me to my face either. I tried to block him out, but over the months, he'd worn me down.

"Sure you do. You poached the Scott Agency."

"They called us. I'd never even spoken to them

before that. Anyhow, you've been playing dirty tricks yourself."

Last month, although I couldn't prove it, I was sure he'd snuck into Marston's Accountants and sprinkled weed killer on the weeping figs in the lobby.

"Imagination working overtime again?"

"The receptionist saw you do it."

He'd come in pretending to be lost, and while the receptionist looked up directions on the internet, she'd glanced up and caught him pouring something into the decorative planters.

"No idea what you're talking about."

Of course he denied it. Exactly like he denied following me six months ago, then paying a personal visit to all the clients I'd attended that day. He'd undercut us, and we'd lost six contracts. Oh, how I longed to take a pair of shears to his private parts. Jail probably wasn't much worse than living with Wes, anyway.

Darren flounced off, and I carried on into the building. Streamline Software was the first of ten calls I needed to make that day, and I couldn't help yawning as I buzzed the door. I'd been awake half the night with my mind churning. Was this how I wanted to live the rest of my life? Dinner and TV with a man I didn't love, then days of trailing around offices stalked by the Queen?

Back at university, I'd dreamed of working in a huge garden attached to a stately home, carefully matching the flower borders to the setting. A job where I had a team of people I'd be able to call friends. When we moved from Nottingham to London because Wes craved the hustle and bustle of the big city, he'd fitted right in, but I'd never been more lonely in my life.

Now, as I flitted around another office snipping off yellow leaves and adding slow-release plant-food pellets to each pot, I took in the cheerful atmosphere. A couple of girls chatted about their dates for that evening, comparing outfits and destinations. I tried to remember the last time Wes took me out. Ah, yes, right after we arrived in London. We'd spent the evening in a sports bar, and he bought me a basket of chicken wings. Who said romance was dead?

"And how's the hunt for a new flatmate going?" the blonde asked the brunette.

She made a face. "Six applicants, and the last one turned up without shoes."

"As in couldn't afford them, or just didn't like wearing them?"

"He said having his feet wedged into the carcasses of dead animals made his soul weep."

The blonde giggled. "What about trainers? You know, made of synthetic stuff?"

"I didn't get that far. When he asked if I had a problem with nudity—sorry, expressing oneself through bodily freedom—I suggested we perhaps weren't a great match."

"Ouch."

"Who knows, if I get enough freaks applying, maybe my darling boyfriend'll take the hint and ask me to move in with him?"

They both laughed at that. Tempting though it was to keep listening, if I chopped much more off the bamboo palm it'd be another candidate for the reject pile, and besides, I shouldn't listen to horror stories about flat-sharing. If I ever got the courage to leave

Wes, that could be me stuck with a barefoot freak. I'd never be able to afford a flat on my own at London prices. Unless of course I found a job outside London, but all the positions at the Royal Horticultural Society and the other places I'd love to work had hundreds of applicants. After a year spent watering houseplants, I had little to help me stand out in the job market, my ability to carry two yucca plants and a *Dracaena* on the Tube without poking my eye out notwithstanding.

At least I didn't have spiky plants to lug today. The messenger bag slung over my shoulder didn't slow me down as I scurried out of the station at Lancaster Gate, heading for Hyde Park. I tried to find somewhere green to eat lunch every day, even in bad weather, and I'd scheduled my visit to the Mornington Hotel, just off Bayswater Road and next to the park itself, to end at noon.

"Copy of the *City Voice*, love?" A man in a red anorak shoved one of the multitude of free newspapers given out in London every day into my hands.

Something else to carry, but I always felt sorry for those guys as they tried to give out their huge stacks of papers and magazines to grumpy people on their daily commute. Few people ever smiled in London, something else I missed about living in a smaller place.

Still, I flicked through the rag as I nibbled on my mushy pizza. The pineapple I hated so much had squeezed its juice everywhere when Darren squashed me, but I didn't have the time or the money to buy anything else. Without thinking, I turned to the classified adverts at the back. How much would a London flat-share be? Most likely more than I paid at the moment, seeing as Wes had negotiated a good deal on the rent in lieu of the landlord doing any kind of maintenance. On days when the water ran cold in the shower, I cursed them both.

Single bedroom in Walthamstow, shared bathroom, use of kitchen... Ouch! How much? Suddenly, the bad taste in my mouth wasn't only caused by fruit that had no business being on a pizza. Pizza that tasted like prison food. Because unless I could find a job that, say, doubled my salary, I was stuck with Wes.

Adverts for get-rich-quick schemes filled the employment section. Did I fancy working from home earning sixty pounds an hour, with just a laptop and internet connection needed? Er, only if it didn't involve taking my clothes off or being a brick in a pyramid scheme. Or how about delivering flyers for seven pounds per thousand?

Then I saw it.

A few lines of text, squashed at the bottom of the page.

Neglected estate seeks capable gardener.

Do you have a love of village life and a flair for the beautiful? Know your peonies from your petunias?

If you'd like to get dirty, call me.

Did I want to get dirty? Well, yes, in a garden. Wait. Was the ad some kind of weird recruitment drive for strippers? Hmm. The first line definitely said they were looking for a gardener. Unless they were talking about lady gardens, and from the state of mine, I sure wasn't qualified for that job.

But what if it was genuine? A real estate looking for a gardener. That could be my dream job.

Did I dare to call?

CHAPTER 2

MY FINGERS HOVERED over the phone as I recited the number over and over in my head. The job probably wasn't suitable anyway. But I'd never know for sure unless I called, would I? And in ten years' time when Wes had me watering plants for sixteen hours a day with a pack of dogs in tow, I'd always wonder *what if*?

I dialled.

The phone rang for so long I thought no one was going to pick up, but just as I was ready to quit, an answer came.

"Good afternoon." The lady's accent was American, her voice a breathy whisper that reminded me of Marilyn Monroe.

"Hello, uh..." I really hadn't thought this through, had I?

"Sorry for the delay. I couldn't find my phone."

"That's no problem. Uh, I'm calling about the advert? In the *City Voice*? For a gardener?"

Boy, she might have sounded like a lady when she spoke, but her filthy laugh belonged to a lady of the night. "The *City Voice*?"

"The free paper in London?" Right now, I seemed incapable of speaking in anything but questions. "On page forty-seven?"

"Oh my goodness. Ivy must have placed that the

night we drank one too many sherries. What does it say?"

Who was Ivy? I read the copy back to her, cringing when I got to the "if you'd like to get dirty" line.

That laugh came again. "Oh, sweet Norma Jean. That explains the strange calls I've been getting this morning. One young lady offered to do something unpleasant with a bunch of tulips."

"So the advert was a joke? You're not looking for a gardener?"

She paused for an unbearably long time before she answered. Enough time for me to realise how much I wanted the job to exist. Whatever her answer, I needed to find a way out of my life with Wes. A desire to take the easy path in life had brought me to this point, but every day I spent in that relationship was a day wasted. A day I'd never get back. The time had come for me to woman up and grab what I wanted from life rather than gathering lint in the corner.

Finally, the lady spoke. "I didn't plan on looking for another month or so, when the tennis court's finished, but maybe it's fate. After all, I'm not getting any younger."

I struggled to picture her in my mind. When she first spoke, I imagined one of those young black-and-white-movie starlets, but now I wasn't so sure. Her words made her sound older. "If there's a job available, I'd be interested."

"Are you an experienced gardener?"

Oh dear. First question, and possibly the last if I didn't impress her. I really should have put some thought into this. The only job interview I'd ever attended was at the garden centre I worked in during my uni years, when the supervisor simply asked if I wanted the job, I said yes, and that was that.

I doubted this would be so easy.

"I completed my degree in horticulture a year ago, and since then I've been caring for plants on behalf of clients in London."

"Garden plants?"

"More houseplants. But I have a roof terrace at home and my own collection of orchids."

"Orchids? Such stunning flowers. The first gift my husband ever gave me was an orchid. Pink, like the dress I wore when we met."

"Was it a *Phalaenopsis*?" That was the most common variety, the kind supermarkets sold next to the checkout for men to bribe their way out of trouble with.

"Gosh, sweetie, I have no idea. Pretty, that's all I know. How about landscaping? Have you done landscaping?"

"Only at uni. But I was top of my class, and I also volunteered on a makeover project for the garden at the local hospital."

It wasn't much, but would it be enough?

Another pause. "It's hard to get to know a person over the telephone. Would you like to come and see the place?"

Freaking heck! "Could you tell me a little more about the job?"

"Sure I can. All my life I wanted to live in an old English country house, but my Richard, God rest his soul, he'd never leave Los Angeles. Now he's passed, so I finally decided to live out my dream before it's too late. I bought Arndale House a few months back, and it needs a whole heap of work. Nobody's touched the garden in years."

"I'm so sorry about Richard. Was he your husband?"

"For forty-five years. But don't be sad, sweetie. Life's too short for that. We had a good life together, and everybody has their time to move on."

Forty-five years? Even if she'd married at eighteen, that meant she was in her sixties at least. For a second, I envied her for finding a man to spend her life with so young, but now she was alone, and no matter what she said, it couldn't be easy. I struggled to think of something to say, but the lady carried on.

"Anyway, enough about me. What do you think of my little project?"

The chance to put my own stamp on a proper English garden? So tempting, despite the amount of work involved. "I'd very much like to see the place."

"Excellent! Tomorrow?"

That soon? "Uh, I'm not sure I can get time off work tomorrow. I could come next week?"

"Can you make next Thursday? I have yoga at ten, but I'm free after that."

I did some rapid calculations. If I shuffled half of my Thursday clients to Wednesday and the rest to Friday and worked from dawn to dusk on both those days, I could free up enough time.

"I can do Thursday."

"Wonderful. Northbury village is about an hour and a half outside of London." She rattled off an address. "Just ring the bell and ask for Marlene. What's your name, sweetie?"

"Dove Hallam."

"Dove? What an unusual name."

"My mum was stuck in bed most of the time she was pregnant with me, and there was a pair of white doves nesting in the tree right outside her bedroom window. She said watching them was the only thing that kept her sane, so she decided to name me after them."

"Such a sweet story. I was named after Marlene Dietrich—not nearly so interesting."

Really? I disagreed—being named after a film star sounded far more exotic to me. "I look forward to meeting you."

"Same here, Dove."

It wasn't until I hung up that I realised it had started raining. While speaking, I'd blocked out everything but the conversation that could change the rest of my life. I'd done it. I'd really done it, and I couldn't quite believe it.

Guilt set in as I jogged back to the Tube station. A part of me hated going behind Wes's back, but then I thought of the way he'd cancelled the trip to Madeira we'd spent two years saving for without telling me, and all because his Sunday League football team got to the next round of the Carlsberg Pub Cup.

I still seethed just thinking about it. Instead of a week in the sun, I'd been dragged to a drizzly football match to hand out energy drinks at half-time. And they bloody lost.

Besides, Marlene probably wouldn't offer me the job anyway. When she started looking properly, there were sure to be hundreds of applicants more qualified than me. No, I'd treat my trip to Northbury as a pleasant day out, a welcome break from the monotony of trekking around London.

One day to do what I wanted. One day.

Thursday came far sooner than I was expecting. The days flew by in a blur of repotting plants, being nice to idiots in suits, and walking two pet spaniels, a rottweiler, and a chihuahua. Out of the four, rottie was by far the nicest. He ambled along behind me, sniffing lamppost after lampost, while the spaniels barked at everything that moved and the chihuahua nipped at my ankles. The little sod had already bitten me three times. I needed to invest in chain-mail socks.

Of course, I didn't get much sympathy from Wes. He'd sprained his ankle at football practice on Monday evening, and since then, he'd been laid out on the sofa with his foot propped up on a cushion. It seemed having an injured leg also stopped him from ordering the groceries online, so I'd had to fit in a trip to Tesco on top of an extra half day of work yesterday, and now, as I sat on the train heading north, I couldn't stop yawning.

Sixteen stops to go. Did I dare to close my eyes? My body craved sleep, but if I gave in, the chances were I'd miss the tiny station that served the village and carry on to an unknown destination. I pulled out my phone and checked for messages. Eleven o'clock and still nothing. Wes had been asleep when I left, and seeing as he'd hobbled down to the pub last night and stayed there until the early hours, I figured I'd be safe until lunchtime at least.

A cup of overly bitter coffee from the onboard

trolley kept me awake until the tiled roof of Northbury Station came into view. Only two other people got off with me. One hopped into a waiting car, and the other walked off up the lane with the air of a man who knew where he was going. I'd hoped to find a taxi, but the place was deserted. Good start.

I called on my old friend Google, who'd already informed me Arndale House lay three miles away. I could walk, but arriving in a sweaty mess would hardly impress a potential employer, would it? A quick search found me the number of what seemed to be the only local cab company, where a lady with the hoarse voice of a heavy smoker informed me Bobby would be with me, "Right after he's dropped Mr. Milligan off at the doctor, love. His arthritis is playing up again. Must be this damp weather."

"Uh, I'm sorry to hear that."

"Happens to the best of us, duckie."

Thankfully, when Bobby arrived, he didn't have the same tendency to overshare. Although he did pique my curiosity.

"Where to, love?"

"Arndale House. It's—"

"I know where it is. Can't hardly miss it, what with all the goings-on up there. Like a bloody circus."

"What kind of goings-on?"

"Oh, you'll see soon enough."

Bobby drove so slowly a hearse overtook us, which meant the short trip to Arndale House took almost fifteen minutes. I used the time to get a good look at the village, not that there was much to see. A tiny high street with a handful of shops, a pub, and a few roads branching off to the side, mostly filled with the type of house that had to be inherited rather than bought. How could anyone afford to pay seven figures for a home?

"What's that place up on the hill?" I asked, spotting a behemoth of a mansion off in the distance.

"That's Northbury Hall. Belongs to the Earl of Northbury. The family's been here for three centuries."

The flat in London was my ninth home. My parents always thought the grass was greener, and we'd spent my childhood bouncing between terraced houses on the outskirts of London while my father commuted into the City each day to work as an accountant. It was hard to imagine staying in one place for so long.

"Here we are, love."

Bobby pulled up outside an imposing set of double gates, and I craned my neck to see through them. Wow. Marlene wasn't kidding about the garden being neglected. An impenetrable wall of green bordered the driveway on both sides until it disappeared around the corner out of sight. I couldn't help shuddering. The atmosphere was...foreboding.

I handed Bobby a tenner. "Keep the change."

"Good luck, love."

Luck? Why did I need luck? It was too late to wonder as I scrambled out of the car, and I'd never felt so nervous as I did when Bobby's Ford vanished in a cloud of exhaust fumes.

What was waiting for me at Arndale House? I reached up and pressed the buzzer on the intercom, a little nervous to find out.

CHAPTER 3

A MAN SPOKE through the intercom as I tapped my foot on the gravel.

"Yes?"

"I'm here for... I mean, I need to see... Uh, is Marlene there?"

"Who's asking?" His voice was smooth but had a Nordic edge to it.

"My name's Dove Hallam. It's about—"

"I know. The garden. Follow the drive, and I'll meet you at the front door."

The gates swung open with agonising slowness. I wasn't sure whether I wanted to go through them or not, because once I stepped inside, I'd be trapped. Oh, who was I kidding? I was trapped anyway. If not here, then back in London with Wes and a life I hated.

The driveway had to be half a mile long, and as I trudged through what was almost a tunnel where the trees met overhead, I kept my eyes peeled. Nothing jumped out from the bushes, but I did spot a cluster of Japanese maples coming into leaf and a majestic oak that had to be three hundred years old. I was so busy looking for more treasures among the trees, I barely saw the house until it was right on top of me.

Freaking heck!

Back in my first shared home at uni, when I'd

walked in one Saturday night to find my flatmate naked on the living room floor with a guy at each end and another in the middle, I'd been speechless. Now, for the first time since, my tongue was similarly tied, and once again, I didn't know where to look first.

The massive stone columns flanking the front door?

The cherry-red Rolls Royce parked in the driveway?

Or the amazing ass of the window cleaner halfway up a ladder to my left?

I was still trying to decide as the door swung open, revealing an impeccably dressed man. A butler? Or a model in the middle of a Saville Row photo shoot? His suit certainly looked made to measure. He stepped forwards, holding the door open with one hand and motioning me inside with the other.

"Ms. Hallam?" Yes, he was the Scandinavian on the intercom.

"That's me." My words came out as a high-pitched squeak.

"I'm Lars, Mrs. Grande's butler. She's asked that you wait in the drawing room."

Her butler? The only butler I knew was the one out of the Batman films, and Lars most definitely didn't fit that mould. He couldn't have been more than thirty, and his pale-blond hair and tanned skin looked out of place in what was practically a medieval castle.

The walk through the house took almost as long as the walk up the drive, and then Lars motioned me into a room bigger than my whole London flat.

"Please, sit down."

He closed the door behind me as I sank onto a rather expensive-looking leather sofa, set in front of a row of French windows that showcased a stunning view across the valley through a gap in the trees. If some more of that foliage was cleared, then...wow. Spectacular wouldn't even begin to cover it.

"Some view, huh?"

A woman's voice behind made me leap to my feet. I spun to find a girl my own age sitting at a table, surrounded by papers and magazines. Her eyes twinkled as she laughed at my reaction.

"Sorry. Didn't mean to make you jump. I'm Amber, the interior designer." She motioned at the rather bare room. "As you can see, I've got my work cut out."

I took a better look around, seeing more clearly the wallpaper that at first glance looked characterful but on close inspection was more shabby, and the stains on the elderly carpet. Amber followed my gaze.

"Don't worry, that lot's going just as soon as Marlene makes a decision on these samples." She waved a handful of paper swatches at me. "What do you think of this green for the sofas?"

Before I could answer, another voice sounded from the doorway.

"Now, Amber, don't be putting the poor girl to work when she's only just got here."

I swivelled around and tried to stop my eyes from bugging out of my head. When I'd pictured Marlene on the phone, knowing her age, I'd imagined a sweet little old lady with grey curls. Not a blonde Joan Collins in hot-pink yoga pants. This lady couldn't be in her sixties, surely?

She glided over, and instead of shaking my hand, she pulled me down to her level—all of five feet two at a guess—and kissed me on both cheeks.

"So good to meet you at last, Dove. You'll have to

excuse my attire. My yoga lesson overran again."

Close up, I took in her face. She had a few fine wrinkles around her eyes, but apart from that, her skin was firmer than mine. She had a better figure, too. I'd gone skinny since I finished university. Back then, my weekend job at the garden centre had kept me fit, but watering office plants didn't give me much of a workout.

"It's nice to meet you too."

Now what? This whole situation had me feeling off balance, as if I'd wandered through a portal into another world and I didn't quite understand their rules.

"Take a seat, sweetie. Lars will bring tea."

I settled back onto the sofa again and tried to wipe my sweaty palms on my trousers without being obvious about it. Even though I'd worn a white blouse and black slacks, I still felt somehow underdressed beside Marlene. Her clothes fit like a second skin, whereas mine were a little on the baggy side.

"So, has anybody shown you the estate?"

"No, but I saw bits of the house and garden as I walked past."

"You need a proper tour. I'll show you around, but I need refreshments first. Nobody does proper tea like the British. It's one of the things I love about this country."

"Have you lived here for long?"

"Only since I bought this place, so nine months now. But I spent plenty of time over here before that. My Richard was a movie director. Pinewood Studios isn't so far away, and he must have made a dozen pictures there."

A movie director? That made sense. Marlene

screamed old Hollywood. "Did you work in the entertainment business too?"

She preened and flashed a smile. Her teeth were as perfect as the rest of her. "I started off as an actress, but when I married Richard, I gave that up to travel with him."

Amber sighed behind us. "That's so damned romantic."

"Honey, you've got a good man too." Marlene turned back to me. "Amber's engaged to a soldier. A hero who fights for Queen and country." She leaned closer and dropped her voice to a whisper. "And he looks mighty fine in his uniform."

My eyes widened in shock, and she laughed then patted my arm.

"I may be seventy-one years old, but I still appreciate the finer things in life." Lars chose that moment to reappear, holding a silver tray aloft. "Like that man. Isn't he just divine to look at?"

What was I supposed to say to that? I could hardly deny it, but nor did I want to admit to having had a surreptitious ogle myself. "Er, he's not bad."

Lars smirked as he poured tea through a strainer with a steady hand. Meanwhile, Marlene's other words sank in. Seventy-one? My eyes must have given my thoughts away, because she laughed.

"I lived in Hollywood for most of my life. Anyone who's anyone there has a cosmetic surgeon on speed dial. Mine's the best, don't you think?"

"You certainly don't look your age."

"Maybe not, but I need to start acting it, and that means having fun in the years I've got left. I've got no kids, and I can't take my money with me." She shrugged. "So I might as well spend it."

"And that means doing up the gardens here?"

"Gardens and house. The place was a wreck when I first laid eyes on it, but I fell in love for only the second time in my life."

As I sipped my tea, I figured Marlene had the right idea. I might not be as old as her, but why waste what time I had left? I found myself nodding.

"What's that look?" she asked.

"I just agree with you, that's all. About spending your life happy." I hadn't mentioned my troubles with Wes to anyone, not even my own mum, but Marlene's infectious smile loosened my tongue. "That's why I'm looking for a new job. I'm not enjoying my time in London."

"You don't like your job?"

"It's not just that. I started the business with my boyfriend, but we don't really see eye to eye on things anymore. Every minute I spend with him seems like a chore nowadays."

"Then you need to let him go, for both of your sakes. When you find the person you're meant to be with, it'll be all pleasure." She gave me a wink as she sipped her Earl Grey.

The only thing that gave me pleasure at the moment required batteries. But that didn't matter—I was off men for the foreseeable future, and if I got this job, I'd have my hands full turning the chaos lurking in the grounds of Arndale House into something beautiful. But I didn't want to disagree with a potential employer, so I smiled and nodded.

Marlene put her cup on a side table and dabbed at her lips with a lace handkerchief. "Shall we go for a jaunt?"

"I'd love that."

It was an unseasonably warm day—something to do with the jet stream, according to the news anchors on breakfast television who gleefully reported stories of nutters swimming in the Serpentine in Hyde Park wearing only Speedos and a smile. I didn't even need a coat as we headed outside. I thought we'd walk, but when we got out the front door, Lars was waiting in a golf buggy. Marlene took his arm, and he helped her into the back seat. I slid in beside her.

"We can get a good way around in this, but we'll need to walk down the terraces at the rear."

Lars started the engine, and I tried not to get distracted by his well-muscled arms as we set off along the drive. Marlene chattered away, pointing out trees she liked and telling me more about the property.

"Parts of this place date back to the early seventeenth century. Used to belong to Lady Helena Wycombe, though she came to a nasty end. That story would've made a good movie."

"What happened?"

She leaned back in the seat, and her eyes sparkled. I got the feeling she'd told the tale many times before.

"Back in the time of the English Civil War, Lady Helena's lover, Sir Stanley Spenser, fought on the side of the Roundheads, and after his troops lost a battle, he was forced by the Cavaliers to run for his life. So run he did, right back to Lady Helena."

"That's kind of romantic."

"She hid him for months, in a chapel deep in the woods. Now, that's true love, sweetie."

"So they lived happily ever after?"

"No, tragedy struck. Lady Helena took him food every night, but the Cavaliers suspected her of helping him, and one night, they followed her to the chapel. The next morning she found him slain with a sword through his chest."

I gasped. What a horrible ending!

But Marlene wasn't finished. "Lady Helena was so devastated by his death, she came back to the house and poisoned herself. They say she makes that final journey every April nineteenth. The old caretaker swore he saw her walking across the lawn in a pale-green dress." She checked her watch, a fancy gold one with the date on it. "Three months to go. I'm planning a get-together around it."

"Like a seance?"

Lars sniggered in the front, and Marlene shook her head. "Oh no, sweetie. A party. I just love parties."

"Truth," Lars muttered.

Seconds later, Marlene tapped Lars on the shoulder, and the golf buggy drew to a halt next to the Japanese maples I'd spotted earlier.

"I simply adore these trees. Last fall, their leaves turned the prettiest colours. Do you think we could make them a feature?"

I ran through ideas in my mind, pictures I'd seen and gardens I'd visited. "Acers like acidic soil and shade, which is why they've done so well in amongst those conifers—their needles are acidic, so when they drop and rot down, they create the perfect conditions as well as blocking the sun. But they could be thinned a little." I pointed at one straggly-looking specimen near the middle. "That one could go. And playing on the Japanese theme would work. We could create a small clearing behind and put in a pool with a bridge over it. And perhaps a few giant bonsai trees on pillars to add interest in winter."

Marlene clapped her hands together. "I love it. A themed garden. We're having a Japanese room in the house, so that would fit right in. Maybe we could reflect some of the other rooms Amber's designing as well?"

My heart beat faster at the thought of it. What an amazing idea! "What other plans does she have?"

"There's the ballroom in Art Deco style that opens up onto the terrace. Old English decor in the kitchen. My sunroom's going to be themed on a temple, and we're filling the library with items from my travels. African masks, South American statues, little souvenirs from the Middle East."

"We could bring in plants from those regions. A lot of variants will survive in this climate with a bit of help in winter. Do you have a greenhouse?"

"Yes, but it needs to be renovated. Most of the glass is missing, and the doors don't open properly. Lars— let's go!"

As we drove around the estate, my head overflowed with ideas. A trailing mint plant for the wall nook by the old stable block. A reflecting pool in the hollow at the far end of the garden. Little box hedges around the borders in the kitchen garden, reminiscent of a French potager.

"And we'll need a path to Sir Stanley's chapel," Marlene said.

"The chapel still exists?"

Lars spoke up from the front. "The estate agent said so, but I doubt another human's been there for years."

Marlene nodded. "The grounds are full of little

surprises. The old owner told me there's an icehouse in the woods out the back somewhere, and a statue modelled on Michelangelo's *David*. Now, that I'd like to see."

The thought had me salivating, and not just over chiselled abs. This place was my dream project. Huge, yes, but the potential was almost limitless. "I wonder if there's a secret garden? Like in the book?"

Marlene's eyes took on a wistfulness I'd not seen before. "I loved that story as a child." She gripped one of my hands between both of hers. "If there is, we'll find it. When can you start?"

"You're offering me the job?"

"Of course I am, sweetie. You share the same vision I do."

"Well, uh, I don't know what to say." And I really didn't. I figured even if I got past the first interview, there'd be a second, and a few weeks in between to weigh up the pros and cons of making such a big change in my life. Now I'd been put on the spot, my stomach clenched in fear.

What should I do?

"Are you worried about that boyfriend of yours?"

I nodded.

"Take a day to think things over. I'd love for you to come here, but you need to do what's right for you."

And those words made up my mind for me. Since we'd moved to London, Wes had changed. Back at uni, he'd been kinder, more caring, and that was why I'd compromised and moved to the city with him when I was a country girl at heart. Now, he always put himself first. And I was sick of coming second. Or, in fact, at all, but that was a whole other problem.

"I don't need to think. I'd love to come and work here."

Marlene beamed at me, showing off her dental work. "Wonderful! We're gonna have so much fun with this place."

CHAPTER 4

I FIDGETED IN the front seat as Lars drove us back to the house, barely taking in the scenery as we trundled along. I almost couldn't believe it—I was moving to Northbury.

"I've got so much to do," I babbled. "Sort things out with Wes, tell my clients, find somewhere to live, pack, move my plants. Do you think there'd be space for some of my pots here? I'll probably end up renting a room, and I might not have enough space for them all."

"You bring whatever you want, sweetie," Marlene said. "But you don't need to worry about finding a home. You can share the cottage with Amber."

"Cottage? What cottage?"

She waved a hand towards the back of the property. "The guest cottage behind the stables. It's a work in progress, but Amber's done wonders with it. I'll get her to show you the place before you go."

A weight lifted from my mind, swiftly replaced by a tightening of my chest. Living here would definitely make life easier, but I'd barely met Amber. Would she mind a virtual stranger moving into her home?

"Are you sure? I could find somewhere in the village."

"Sure I'm sure. I worry about Amber out there on her own, but there are only two bedrooms finished in the main house right now—mine and Lars's. We had a problem with damp that took months to get fixed."

I tried to suppress my shudder at the thought of us being so isolated. I'd only ever lived in a flat or a shared terrace—never a cottage, and certainly not one where ghosts roamed the grounds. But I didn't have any savings, and if this job came with accommodation, I could hardly afford to pass it up.

"In that case, I'd love to live in the cottage. I'm sure it's wonderful."

"Welcome to the madhouse," Amber said cheerfully as she ducked her head under the low front of the porch. A narrow wooden bench ran along the edge with a pair of flowery Wellington boots tucked underneath it.

At five feet four, I had no need to bend. Amber was at least six inches taller than me and seemed to have been born into the supermodel gene pool given her long legs, slim figure, and pretty smile. The front door of the cottage opened directly into the lounge, and I wiped my feet on the mat as I followed her inside.

"Don't worry about mud. The whole place needs a good clean, and we're still weeks away from getting the carpets down."

The old flagstones looked cold, so I was thankful I didn't have to take my boots off seeing as I'd only worn a thin pair of socks. I followed Amber into the room.

"Well, we're going for rugs rather than carpet downstairs. I don't want to cover up these beautiful floors." She rubbed one with a toe. "Think of how many feet they've seen over the years. This cottage is as old as the mansion itself. Two decades ago, it housed the gardener, so I suppose it's fitting you'll be living in it."

"It's sweet."

Amber's laugh was deep and throaty. "Cosy, more like it, at least now that we've got the heating installed. People were smaller back when it was built, so the rooms are tiny. And there's only one bathroom."

"I promise I won't take up too much space."

"Oh, we'll be living in each other's pockets in a place this size. How are your cooking skills?"

She led me through to a half-finished kitchen. The units had been installed, but the walls were crying out for a coat of paint and there was a gap where the cooker should be.

"I can make the basics. I cooked most days at uni, but after we moved to London, I got lazy."

"We can share, then. I know how to make five things." She counted off on her fingers. "Pasta, jacket spuds, toast, scrambled eggs, and samosas. The cooker's getting installed the day after tomorrow."

"Samosas?" That seemed a little out of place.

"When I was little, I had an Indian babysitter. If I behaved for the whole week, she'd make them with me on a Friday afternoon. Once, I used the wrong type of chilli by accident and blew everyone's heads off."

She giggled at the memory, and I made a mental note to nibble a small corner first if she made them again.

"I've never made samosas, but I can grow all different kinds of chilli. We could put pots on the windowsill."

"And maybe some herbs? Chives and basil? I like the idea of old country charm. I can paint up a bunch of pots for you if you want?"

"I'd love that."

"This place'll look good one day, but it's taking a while because I spend most of my time over at the main house." She waved a hand at the empty space next to the back door. "I haven't even found a table and chairs yet. We'll have to eat off our laps on the sofa."

"I'm used to that. Our flat in London doesn't have room for a dining table."

Amber flashed me a sudden grin. "We're gonna get on great. It'll be nice having a roommate—it gets a bit lonely out here, and most of the other people Marlene hires are male."

"To do the heavy work?"

"You don't know Marlene very well yet, do you? No, she says at her age she needs to take pleasure where she can find it, so she employs all the men to give her something to perv over. Got to give the lady credit where it's due—she's got good taste. When she does the interviews, she picks out the hottest ones."

I almost choked. "She hires them based on looks?"

"It can get annoying sometimes, when she passes up on a better-qualified guy in favour of one who can bounce pennies off his ass cheeks, but having a load of pin-up boys to look at is unquestionably a perk of the job." Her voice dropped to a whisper. "I just don't tell my fiancé that."

"Does he live nearby?"

Her smile dropped. What did I say?

"No. He's away in Afghanistan at the moment, helping to train the Afghan security forces. He'll be out there for months yet. That's why I took this contract— Marlene might be bonkers, but at least she's around.

On my usual jobs, it's just me in the house all day."

Friendly company sure sounded like a bonus. In London, I was always the outsider in the offices I went to, the faceless minion to be ignored while the rest of the staff shared gossip and birthday cakes. Since uni, I'd never fitted in. Maybe now I'd have that chance?

"I'll be in the garden, but perhaps we could have lunch together sometimes?"

Amber's smile was wide and genuine. "I'd love that."

I'd done it. I'd really done it, and I was finally leaving. Funny how I always thought making that decision would be the hardest part, but now, travelling back on the train to London, I realised I'd been kidding myself. Telling Wes—that would be the difficult bit.

Should I speak to him right away? Or try to do some surreptitious packing first?

Marlene had invited me to start as soon as I wanted to, but she was happy for me to tie up loose ends in London first, thank goodness. Wes would undoubtedly take time to hire a new plant girl, and I didn't want them all to die. The thought of the ferns and trees I'd tended for the last year withering away made my heart sink.

By the time I put the key in the front door, I'd decided to take the coward's way out—sort out my belongings, clear out what I no longer needed, and repot any plants stuck in too-small containers so they were ready to go. That would take a week, and by then, I'd have worked out what to say.

My mouth was dry after my long train trip. I could have bought a bottle of water, but the train company always overcharged, and money promised to be tight until I got my first pay packet from Marlene.

"Wes, are you home? Do you want a drink?" I cut left into our tiny kitchen.

Of course he was home. Since we moved to London, he'd turned into a vampire, only he drank beer instead of blood.

"I'd love a cuppa. Can you make one for Magda too?"

Magda was here? My assistant? What about the plants she was supposed to water today? The schedule I'd written for her didn't allow time for tea with my boyfriend. I walked through to the lounge and found them both on the sofa.

"Magda's agreed to help with the new dog-walking business. Isn't that great?"

I narrowed my eyes. Magda might have come over to discuss the dogs, but why were the buttons on her top done up wrong? Halfway down, her blouse gaped, revealing a hint of red lace. Had I intruded on something I shouldn't? Or was I overreacting?

"Dove? That's good news, right? You said you couldn't do it all yourself."

"Yes, fantastic."

I thought back over the last few weeks, the weeks I'd spent running around from office to office while Wes lounged around at home, doing "marketing." And the calls I'd fielded from grumpy clients complaining Magda had missed yet another afternoon appointment.

What if she'd had other things to do? Like Wes?

No. No, that couldn't be right. Could it? I recalled

back to my parents' anniversary party last year, when I'd caught him kissing my cousin, Laura. He swore he'd been drunk and it was a case of mistaken identity, and I'd given him the benefit of the doubt as Laura and I did have the same colour hair at that time, but should I have been more suspicious? And when had I come home in the middle of the day before? I didn't know much about Magda, only that she was unreliable and had a penchant for overly tight trousers.

"Why don't you make those drinks and we'll go over next week's schedule?" Wes suggested. "I got talking to Tim in the pub yesterday, and his sister wants us to walk her bichon frise. Do you know what one of those is?"

"No." But I hoped it was something small.

"Magda?"

A shake of the head.

"Guess I'll have to look it up." He gestured towards the laptop sitting on our tiny side table, and as he turned his head, the light caught on something at the corner of his mouth. Was that... Was that lip gloss?

I took a step closer. Yes, it damn well was, and in the exact same shade as Magda's.

"Did I interrupt something?"

He held his hands out, nonchalant. "Like what?"

"Like, I don't know..." You snogging my assistant, maybe? "Something with you and Magda?"

"Dove, don't be ridiculous. We were having a business meeting."

Magda picked at her nails, unable to meet my eyes. As I followed her gaze downwards, Wes's fly caught my eye, the button undone and the zipper half-open. I *had* walked in on something, hadn't I? Five minutes later, and I'd have been washing my eyes out with bleach.

"You know what? I can't do this anymore."

"Do what? Look, if it's about the dogs, I'll make sure the owner leaves a muzzle if they're a bit dodgy."

"It's not about the bloody dogs, Wes. It's about the way I'm out working every hour of the day while you sit here on the internet."

"Somebody's got to sort out the advertising and the accounts."

"How can that take all day?"

"Well, there's other stuff too."

"Like what? *Call of Duty*? *World of Warcraft*?"

He didn't even try to deny it. "Maintaining my position in the league is important. It took ages to get where I did."

I'd been a schmuck, hadn't I? Slowly but surely, I'd let Wes turn into a lazy bum without so much as a murmur of complaint. The more I worked, the more tired it left me, and every evening I'd just crawled into bed, craving enough sleep to get me through the next day. Well, no more.

"I'm leaving."

That got a reaction. His eyes widened. "You're what? Leaving what?"

"Everything. You, the business, the flat. London."

"But you can't. We're in this together."

"The only thing you seem to have been in lately is Magda."

"Only because you're never here."

That little shit!

He must have realised what he'd said, because he leapt to his feet, pulled Magda up, and pushed her towards the door. "You should leave. I'll call you tomorrow, yeah?"

"Don't bother. Stay, by all means. I'll be out of your hair in a minute."

"I think it's best if I go." She hightailed it out without a backward glance, stumbling on her high heels.

In the lounge, Wes slumped back on the sofa. "I'm sorry, okay? But if you weren't always out working, it wouldn't have happened."

"So it's my fault you can't keep it in your trousers? I've been earning money so we could live and doing Magda's work too because she always lets me down."

"Fine, whatever. I won't do it again. But you've got to make an effort. There are supposed to be two people in this relationship."

I forced myself to take calming breaths. *Count to ten, Dove, before you throw something at him.* How could he have changed so much in the last year? How could I not have noticed?

"You know what? You're right."

His shoulders relaxed. "So we can sort things out, yeah? You'll get home earlier?"

"No, we can't. I meant what I said—I'm leaving. I refuse to share a bed with a man who I mean so little to."

"But what about the business? The plants?"

"I guess you and Magda will be working overtime." His spluttering followed me as I strode into the bedroom and kicked the door closed behind me. Turned. Opened it again. "And you'd better not forget to add the food sachets!"

Slam.

Oh hell, what had I just done? All my careful plans

to pack sensibly flew out the window as I shoved clothes into my suitcase. Jeans, T-shirts, a few jumpers. Toiletries. A painting my mum did. The Royal Horticultural Society's encyclopaedia. My grandma's rose necklace. When I was a little girl, sitting on her lap in the tiny garden behind my grandparents' cottage, she always used to tell me, "To plant a garden is to believe in the future."

And now I'd be planting a garden, and I finally had a future to believe in. Perhaps I'd get lucky and Darren would poach the rest of Wes's clients? Shaking, I sat on the case lid to zip it closed, then pulled out my phone and dialled Marlene.

"Hello? M-M-Marlene?"

"Dove? Why are you crying, sweetie?"

"I-I-I had an argument with my boyfriend. Ex-boyfriend. He's my ex-boyfriend now."

"Aw, and you want to come tonight?"

"Can I?"

"Sure you can. I'll send Lars to pick you up."

"You don't have to do that."

"I know, but I'm not having my new girl upset. Give me your address, and he'll leave right away."

"T-t-thank you." I garbled it out, guilty she was going to so much trouble, but unable to stand another train ride if I didn't have to. Silence descended, broken only by the slamming of the front door. Wes left? Without a word? Guess that told me just how much I really meant to him.

CHAPTER 5

"YOU HAVE ONE suitcase of clothes, and seventeen bags of plants?" Lars stared at the jumble I'd piled on the pavement below the flat.

"Do you think they'll fit?"

He looked from the boot of the Rolls Royce to the row of Tesco carrier bags I'd placed my beloved orchids into, then gave me a half grin, half grimace. "We'll make room. Some of them will need to go in the back seat." A resigned sigh. "I can polish the leather tomorrow."

"I'll help."

"I'm sure Marlene has other plans for you."

"Really? She didn't know I was even coming until two hours ago."

"And as I left, she'd already sat down at the table with her fancy fountain pen to make a list."

Lars ushered me into the front seat as he finished loading my life into the car. A bright pink *Phalaenopsis* flower dropped off its green stem and fluttered to the grey pavement, where it got crushed under his shoe. As I came to terms with the end of my relationship, my heart crumpled with it. When I looked back, Wes and I hadn't been in a good place for ages, but that didn't make his infidelity any easier to take. Deep down, I was still the girl who wanted to find that one lifelong partner, the same way my grandma found my grandad. He'd been a plumber, and when a leaky pipe behind her shower sent water cascading through her kitchen ceiling, he'd been the one to fix it. And then he installed a whole new bathroom suite. Six months later, they'd got married. I had a lot to live up to.

"I can't believe you came so quickly," Amber said as she helped to carry my belongings into the cottage. "Wow. You've got a lot of plants."

"I wasn't expecting to come for weeks yet, but... well, when I got home this afternoon, I found out my boyfriend hadn't been quite as faithful as I thought."

"Ouch. In your shoes, I'd have packed and left too. Do you want to talk about it?"

Talk? I'd never talked about my feelings before. The thought of doing so felt strange, alien.

"I don't even want to think about it."

"In that case..." She disappeared into the kitchen and came back a few seconds later holding a bottle. "I have wine."

Lars dumped the last of my plants on the living room floor. "All done. I'll see you in the morning."

"Thank you."

He gave me a small nod then closed the front door behind him. As soon as it clicked, Amber flopped onto the sofa. "Damn. I forgot to pick up the corkscrew."

"Shouldn't we tidy up before we sit down?"

"It'll still be here in the morning."

"I need to get my suitcase into my room at least."

"Okay, okay. I'll help."

I hefted the bottom end while Amber grabbed the handle at the top, and together we manhandled the thing up the stairs.

"What did you put in here?" Amber asked. "It weighs a ton."

"Everything I own."

"Wow." Her voice dropped to a whisper. "In that case, it doesn't weigh very much at all."

I huffed under the load, agreeing yet disagreeing at the same time. Shoving it down the stairs outside my London flat in anger had been so much easier. We'd almost got it to my room when Amber fell backwards and landed on the floor, the case popping open and spilling my life across the tiny landing.

"Oops." She held up the handle. "It fell off."

Well, it looked like I wouldn't be leaving anytime soon.

Or walking, if Marlene had anything to do with it. When we got downstairs again, she was standing in the lounge with a bottle in each hand.

"I've brought champagne to celebrate the end of a bad relationship, and sherry, because sherry cures everything."

"I'm not really much of a drinker."

"Nonsense, you just don't know it yet. I look good for my age, don't I?"

She looked bloody fantastic. "Er, yes."

She leaned in closer. "You know why?"

I shook my head. Fresh air? Moisturiser? Didn't she mention a bit of help from the surgeon's knife?

"I've pickled my insides." She popped the cork on the champagne. "Trust me, it works a treat."

"Uh, I'm not sure..."

Amber handed me a glass, the liquid fizzing over the rim onto my hand. "Stop talking and drink."

Oh, what the heck? It couldn't make my day any worse, could it?

It didn't.

In fact, it made it bloody brilliant. Two hours later, Marlene poured the last drop of sherry into my glass, and I hiccuped before taking a sip of it. At first, it had burned my throat, but now it slid down easily. Amber flicked off the TV as the episode of the dating show we'd been watching came to an end. We'd started off trying to have a conversation, but given up after we opened Amber's bottle of wine.

"I can't believe he chose the blonde," Amber said. "The brunette was more genuine."

"That's all relative, sweetie. The guy was no catch himself." Marlene waved a hand at me. "But don't worry, we'll find you a better one than that."

"Huh?"

"A man. We'll find you a better man."

Her words penetrated my addled brain, and I shook my head then thought the better of it as my skull throbbed. "I don't want another man. Girls are better."

One of her eyes widened, while the other struggled to focus. "You're a lesbian?"

"No! Not that there's anything wrong with lesbians. I mean, I'm sure it's very nice, but I meant I'm having more fun with you two than I did with Wes." Wow. That was a lot of words, and I was pretty sure I got most of them in the right order.

Marlene giggled. "Yes, we're the best. Just wait—we can do girlie nights. I'll invite Carrie and Ivy over and we can hire some of those revue dancers."

"Who's Carrie?" I whispered to Amber. "And Ivy?"

"Carrie's our age, and she lives next door. She's quite normal. But Ivy's a year older than Marlene and mostly bonkers." She smacked the arm of the sofa as she collapsed into laughter. "Ivy got sick of the chauffeur-driven Bentley last month and decided to buy herself a little run-around, but she came back with an Aston Martin DB11. Freaking awesome."

"Like a James Bond car?"

"Exactly! Her daughter went nuts."

"Cindy always did have a stick up her ass," Marlene informed me. "You got any more wine?"

Amber dredged up another bottle plus a box of chocolates she'd stashed in the cupboard for "emergencies." By the time Lars arrived to pick Marlene up in the golf buggy, it was almost midnight and none of us could stand without holding onto something.

"Toodles!" She waved as Lars rolled his eyes. "See you tomorrow."

I couldn't wait. Tomorrow was going to be awesome.

The next day dawned, bringing with it Satan and his marching band playing "Hit Me Baby One More Time" as they trooped around the inside of my head. Today was going to be hell.

I stumbled downstairs and found Amber in the kitchen, spooning coffee granules into a mug. She took one look at me and fetched a second from the cupboard.

"How are you feeling?"

"I left my paracetamol back in London."

"Don't worry—I've got loads. Marlene buys the economy-size packs."

"She sounded so...so classy when I first spoke to her on the phone."

"It's all an illusion, trust me. She's as nutty as they come."

"Does she do that often? Get properly drunk, I mean."

The kettle boiled, and Amber slopped water into the mugs. "Only once a month or so. When I first got here, Steve had flown out on tour the day before, and I was kind of upset. She and Ivy got me doing karaoke. Poor Carrie stopped by with a cake from her aunt and ended up sleeping it off on the living room floor."

"No Lars to take her home?"

"Lars hadn't arrived yet. He's only been here..." She counted on her fingers. "Five months, I think. There was another guy before him, Pierre, but Pierre keeled over halfway through a rendition of 'I Will Survive.' How do you take your coffee?"

"White, one sugar."

What had I landed myself in the middle of? I must have turned a delicate shade of green, because Amber patted me on the arm and gave me a reassuring smile.

"Don't worry—most of the time, we're quite sensible. Okay, maybe half of the time."

Oh dear.

A couple of headache pills, two cups of coffee, and a shower later, I felt ready to face the world. As I hurried down the overgrown path from the cottage to the main house, it hit me just what an enormous project I'd taken on. Yesterday, when I'd first looked around the garden, I'd seen all its potential. Today, I only saw a big mess.

I knocked on the back door and Lars pulled it open. "No need to knock. Marlene leaves the house unlocked in the daytime."

How different Northbury was to London. In the city, an unlocked door formed an invitation to every burglar, thief, and squatter within a ten-block radius. One of our old neighbours went on a week's holiday to Benidorm and came home to find six strangers cooking dinner in her kitchen.

"Where's Marlene?"

Lars glanced at his watch. "Just finishing up with her Pilates session. Do you want something to eat while you wait?"

How could she contemplate exercise after last night? I groaned at the thought of it as I considered breakfast. When I left the cottage, I hadn't been hungry, but I spied the plate of pastries on the table and my stomach growled.

"Maybe a small bite."

As I nibbled the corner of a melt-in-the-mouth cinnamon Danish, I stared out the back window at the jungle beyond. A themed garden? What was I thinking? And today, the image of Sir Stanley's chapel seemed more creepy than fascinating.

To avoid thinking about the horrors waiting for me outside, I turned to Lars instead.

"How did you come to work for Marlene? I don't want to sound rude, but you seem a bit out of place in Northbury."

He smiled sheepishly. "Same reason as you. I had to

get away from someone I once thought I loved. Turns out Northbury's a good place to run and hide."

"Where did you live before?"

"Manchester. I worked for a footballer and his wife." He blew out a breath. "No matter how awkward some of Marlene's requests are, nothing could ever be as bad as buttling for Terry and Tanya van Smith."

"Why? What did they do?"

"Let's just say the Shih Tzus lived up to their name and I got sick of rescuing drunk WAGs from nightclubs at three o'clock in the morning."

"I suppose at least Marlene doesn't stay up late. Have you always lived in England? Your accent isn't Mancunian."

"I moved here from Sweden when I was eighteen." He tilted his head to one side, listening. "Speaking of Marlene, here she comes."

Ten seconds later, she bounded in wearing today's choice of yoga pants—floral with a lime-green waistband. "Ah, I see you've become acquainted with Lars's pastries."

"He made these?" I put a hand over my mouth to save spitting out crumbs.

"He's a genius in the kitchen. And the gym, the parlour, and the rest of the house."

"They're delicious."

Marlene took one herself and ate it a lot more daintily than I did. "So, where do we start with the garden? This all happened a little faster than I expected."

"I'm sorry. Uh, I understand if you don't want to pay me for these first days."

Her peal of laughter would have made even the

grumpiest of people smile. "Don't be silly, sweetie. If you're working, I'll pay you, simple as that. But I'd suggest taking today to settle in and explore. I'll take you into the village after lunch and give you a tour."

Amber lent me a notepad and pen, and I spent the morning fighting my way through overgrown bushes and brambles while making copious notes. Writing everything down helped—if I broke the project into tasks, it meant that rather than climbing a mountain, I could traipse up flights of stairs. Approximately seven hundred of them.

"Going well?" Marlene asked when I half fell back into the kitchen. "You have a piece of..." She leaned forwards and plucked a sprig of privet out of my hair.

"Thanks. I need to draft a project plan, you know, to get things set in my head."

"Plenty of time for that later. I thought we could have lunch at the Northbury Arms."

"Not like this. I'm a mess." As well as my hair, I had a grass stain on my knee in the shape of Germany, plus a swollen toe from an argument with a fallen tree branch.

"Nobody'll mind." This coming from the woman who'd curled her hair perfectly since breakfast, dressed in a Chanel suit, and wore a strand of pearls that probably cost my month's salary. "You still look pretty as a picture, sweetie."

What was I supposed to say to that? Marlene was my boss—I could hardly argue with her. Besides, it was only a pub lunch. The place would probably be full of farmers and stable hands.

Or socialites and the landed gentry.

The first hint I got was when Lars parked the Rolls up between a Bentley and a brand-new Land Rover Discovery. The menu in the window gave me another clue. Twenty-seven pounds for the cheapest main course? If I ate more than a breadstick, I'd be bankrupt.

"The landlord turned this place into one of those gastropubs last year. Their lobster thermidor is to die for."

At sixty-three quid, I figured I might do just that.

"What can I get you ladies?" the host asked. "Marlene, you look particularly lovely today." Seemed they'd hired models to wait the tables as well.

I'd be having the soup with tap water, but I deferred to Marlene.

"Always a charmer, Eddie. Let me introduce you to Dove. She'll be working as my gardener. Dove, this is Eddie, the owner's son. He's single." She turned back to Eddie and whispered, "Dove's between boyfriends."

Aw hell, she made me sound desperate. Like when people said they were between jobs but in reality, they were un-hireable. Like I couldn't manage without a man.

Eddie met my eyes with a hint of panic, and I gave a small shake of my head. I couldn't believe her! I'd only been in Northbury for one day, and Marlene was already trying to set me up.

Eddie avoided looking at me while Marlene ordered surf 'n' turf for both of us, and my bank balance cringed. Or rather, my credit card, because my bank balance already matched the colour of my cheeks.

"And a bottle of Dom Pérignon," she added at the

end.

"No! I mean, I get sluggish in the afternoons when I drink at lunchtime." Oh, good grief, that made it sound as if I did it regularly.

Marlene giggled. "You heard her, Eddie. Just bring a glass for me."

Lunch was delicious, as it should have been at the Northbury Arms' prices. And Marlene only managed to mention my lack of a boyfriend twice more before she scooted off to the ladies' room. Eddie came to take the plates away, and I kept my eyes firmly fixed on the table. Boy, that wood grain was really interesting.

"Dove?"

I raised my head an inch. "Yes?"

"Don't worry—it's not the first time she's done it. Three weeks ago it was a friend of... What's her name? The designer?"

"Amber?"

"Yeah, a friend of Amber's. The poor girl only came to Northbury to upholster chairs. And before that, she tried foisting a whole selection of Ivy's clan onto me. Have you met Ivy yet?"

"I've heard about her."

He chuckled, and I had to admit he was really very handsome. "You've got a treat waiting there. Just don't get into a car with her."

"Why?"

"Let's just say she's on first-name terms with everyone at the local body shop."

I smiled in spite of myself. "I'll remember that."

"How long have you—? She's coming back. Quick, stop smiling."

I tried, but as Eddie walked away, I couldn't help

my lips forming a grin behind my hand.

CHAPTER 6

"YOU'VE GOT A leaf in your hair." Amber leaned over and removed not just one leaf, but a whole bunch of them and the twig they were attached to.

"Thanks. Everything's a little overgrown." That was the understatement of the year. At one point, I'd despaired of ever getting free from a particularly sticky shrub.

"How are the plans coming on?"

I flopped back onto the sofa. "I haven't got as far as actual plans yet. Right now, I'm looking at the jungle and wondering why I ever thought this was a good idea."

"I did exactly the same with the house when I arrived, but now I can see the light at the end of the tunnel. Spent three months tearing my hair out first, though. The best advice I can offer is to break each task down further into lots of mini-projects and tackle one at a time. Otherwise you'll cry."

"One at a time." That sounded sensible. "I should refine my list and prioritise."

I'd only got outside for an hour so far this morning before a heavy rain shower passed over and drove me back indoors. Damned British weather. If it wasn't chucking it down, you could barely stand upright because of the wind. With black clouds still hovering overhead, I borrowed a pad and pen from Amber before she returned to the main house, then sat at the table and began to write.

1. Terrace behind the house.

2. Clear path to chapel.

In between knocking back the alcohol over lunch yesterday, Marlene had set out her priorities, the main ones being outdoor entertaining space and tours to and from the scene of the historical crime at her ghost-themed party. We needed a route wide enough for the golf buggy because the guests wouldn't want to be stumbling over tree roots in their stilettos.

3. Prune trees along driveway.

4. Clear front courtyard.

5. Repair greenhouse.

6. Get back lawn into shape.

7. Start potager for the kitchen.

8. Dig pool for Japanese garden.

9. Walk of fame from terrace to lawn.

10. Build wall for secret garden.

11. Borders around lawn.

12. Hollywood-style sign on hill beyond house.

13. Yellow brick road to old stables.

14. Attempt to resurrect orchard.

15. Clear pond.

Honestly, the list went on and on. I stared at the top two. I could manage the back terrace myself with the assistance of a pressure washer, although if any stones had to be replaced, I'd need help as I couldn't lift those Yorkshire sandstone flags on my own. But clearing the path to the chapel? That would require a tree surgeon, plus some heavy machinery if we wanted to lay a surface. And what about the chapel itself?

Oh, sod it. I shuffled everything down one number. Before I could even start, I'd need tools and somewhere to keep them—a shed, perhaps, or a garage.

Of course, I'd also need to find the chapel in the first place. When I'd asked Marlene the location yesterday, she'd waved vaguely towards the woods at the back.

"The realtor said it was somewhere out there."

"Nothing more precise?"

She shook her head, but Lars had overheard the conversation. "There are some old maps in the cupboard in the study. Maybe they'll help?"

Today, as soon as the rain eased up for a few minutes, I tugged my coat on and ran over to the main house. Better to find a map than spend hours wandering aimlessly in the woods.

"Is Lars around?" I asked Amber.

"Day off. Can I help?"

"He said there were some maps of the estate in the study. Do you think anyone would mind if I looked through them?"

"Nah—I'll show you where the study is and you can rummage."

I found the maps rolled up on a high shelf, musty-smelling paper that made me cough when I unrolled them. The house took pride of place in the centre, and I recognised the cottage off to its left once I got my bearings. Ah, there was the chapel. I squinted closer. No, actually, that was the icehouse. The chapel was further into the woods. Was this map to scale? I sure hoped so.

The sky was still angry, so I drew out a smaller version of the map rather than taking the original outside. The chapel looked to be three hundred metres behind the house, slightly to the left like the cottage. I bet that once upon a time, there would have been a path that led past the cottage and into the woods, but of course that was long gone.

When I stood out the back after lunch, I couldn't even see the beginning of it, just a tangled wall of green, leaves rustling as water from this morning's deluge dripped from the branches. An old leylandii tree towered above, showering me with droplets each time the breeze moved its foliage.

"Well, no time like the present," I muttered to myself, climbing over the first fallen branch.

An hour later, I stood in front of a ruin. The chapel had once been a beautiful building—that much was clear from the elegantly carved stone columns peeping through the top of the ivy. But now the roof had caved in, and when I peered through the remains of the stained-glass window, the pews were mossy and rotten from years of exposure to the elements.

"What have I done?" I whispered. Now I'd got things organised in my head, I was ready to tackle the garden, but this? I didn't know much about buildings, and getting it into shape for visitors was beyond me. Was it even structurally safe?

My only answer came from the creaking roof timbers as the wind blew another dark cloud overhead. By the time I got back to the cottage, I was soaked through.

"So, how did your first day go?" Marlene asked. She'd

arrived at the cottage just after I got out of the shower, and water from my hair dripped down my back, dampening my jumper.

"Uh, a little prickly."

"Did you find the chapel? Amber said you came looking for the maps."

"Yes, I did."

"And? How does it look?"

Where did I start? "It could do with a bit of work. I'm not really sure—"

"You need help with it?"

"Yes! I mean, I think if you're going to have people visiting it, it needs to be checked out by an engineer. And it could do with a new roof. And clearing the route through will take a tree surgeon plus heavy machinery."

I'd expected Marlene to balk at the idea—after all, she'd just forked out for a full-time gardener. But she grinned instead.

"Excellent. I'll organise some suitable candidates."

"Don't worry. I can do that. I don't want to put you to any trouble."

"It's no trouble. Now, will you girls be coming over to the house for dinner? There's plenty for everyone."

"Of course we will," Amber said from the sofa.

When Marlene left, I made two mugs of tea and flopped down next to her. My muscles ached. Climbing through the woods was a far cry from watering office plants, and the hard graft hadn't even started yet.

"I didn't mean to create work for Marlene."

"Nonsense. She looks for any excuse to hire more eye candy. Did you see the team working on the tennis court?" She fanned herself. "I'm surprised she picked you, to tell you the truth. I'd expected another bloke, but I guess she felt sorry for me out here by myself."

"She's one interesting lady."

"Oh, definitely. Hurry up and finish your drink. I'm starving, and if we get lucky, Marlene'll spill some Hollywood dirt while we eat."

"Is Marlene cooking?" I asked Amber as we walked over to the house.

She doubled over with laughter, and we had to pause while she got her breath back.

"What's so funny?"

"The idea of Marlene cooking. Or doing anything, in fact. Don't get me wrong, she's a darling, but she never lifts a finger herself. Her husband was loaded, so she just hires people. Lars usually cooks, but it's his day off, so she'll order something in."

When we reached the dining room, the first thing I noticed was the four place settings laid out at the table.

"Is Lars joining us?"

Marlene's giggle came from behind me. "Lars always goes to London on his days off. I think he keeps a fancy man there."

"So who's the extra place for?"

"I thought Eddie could join us when he drops off the food."

I groaned while Amber rolled her eyes. "Does Eddie know this?" she asked.

"Not yet."

"Marlene, Dove's only just got out of a relationship. I'm sure she doesn't want to leap right back in."

"No, I really don't."

But Marlene was incorrigible. "It's just dinner, honey, with something pretty to look at."

"Honestly, I'm so sorry about this," I told Eddie's back as he carried Marlene up the stairs. After she'd quaffed three glasses of red and half a bottle of sherry, only Eddie's quick reflexes had stopped her from face-planting in the remains of her chocolate mousse.

He half turned and gave me a tired grin. "Nothing much ever happens in Northbury, so at least she's given me an interesting evening. Are you really an ex-rhythmic gymnastics champion?"

"No, she made that up."

"You got off lightly," Amber muttered from in front of us. "Before she realised I was committed to Steve, she told one of the roofers I was an ex-Vegas showgirl. I mean, look at these thighs—do they say dancer to you?"

Eddie reached the top of the stairs, barely out of breath. "I'm not quite sure how to answer that."

"No. The answer's no. I've got far too many wobbly bits."

Amber shoved open the door to Marlene's room, and Eddie laid her on a four-poster bed that had enough frills to make a princess go green with envy. I tucked her in while he took a step back and appraised the scene.

"Do you think we should put her in the recovery position or something? I mean, she's unconscious."

Amber herded us out of the room. "Oh, she's done this plenty of times before. Lars'll have a Bloody Mary waiting for her in the morning and she'll be good as new."

Marlene was already snoring softly as we trooped along the landing, and I marvelled at the woman's strength. A mere mortal's liver would have given up years ago, but she looked better than women half her age. Me included, after my adventures in the garden earlier.

"Do you want a coffee before you go?" I asked Eddie. A caffeine-laced apology, if you like.

"I wouldn't say no."

"Do you mind if I turn in?" Amber asked. "I've got a meeting with the curtain lady at eight, and I need to look through a bunch of fabric samples before that."

Wonderful—I'd be left alone with Eddie just as Marlene intended. "Not at all. Sleep well."

I didn't know my way around the kitchen in the main house, and even less so around the barista-quality coffee machine on the counter. After I'd rooted through the cupboards for a few minutes, though, the culinary gods looked on me favourably and I unearthed a jar of Nescafé.

"Instant okay?"

"Instant's fine."

"Milk? Sugar? Although I'm not sure where the sugar is."

"No sugar, and I drink it black."

An awkward silence ensued while we waited for the kettle to boil. Eventually, I figured I'd apologise again, only for Eddie to start speaking at the same time.

"You go," I said.

"No, you—it wasn't important."

"I just wanted to say I was sorry for landing you up in this mess. If I hadn't been here, Marlene wouldn't have forced you into staying."

"Don't worry about it. She and Ivy have tried their tricks plenty of times before, only it's usually an invite to a party at Northbury Hall, and one of Ivy's relatives is the hapless victim."

"Just so you know, I'm really not interested." I clapped a hand over my mouth. "Oh! That came out totally wrong. I mean, it's not you, it's me."

"Isn't that speech supposed to come at the end of a relationship?"

I forced a laugh and avoided eye contact as I poured boiling water into a couple of cups. Marlene didn't have mugs in the main house, just fine bone china with delicately painted flowers and matching saucers. "What I meant is that I recently broke up with a long-term boyfriend, and I'd rather stay single for a while."

"Same. Well, it was a girlfriend, and we split just over a year ago."

"Really?" Eddie seemed like such a nice guy, and he certainly wasn't lacking in the looks department. "I mean, I'm sorry to hear that."

"Yeah, well, it wasn't meant to be."

"Does it get easier?" I whispered.

"A little. That life burned me out. I was an investment banker in London—started right after I finished uni—but it's not a kind world to be in. Greed, greed, everywhere, and everything's disposable. My friends...my ex-friends...they picked up a different woman every night and couldn't understand why I didn't want to be like them anymore. So I quit. Left it all and moved back in with my parents at twenty-seven."

"I ran too."

His lopsided smile tugged at my heart. "Northbury was supposed to be a temporary solution, but my mother had some health problems, so I stuck around."

"I'm so sorry. Will she be okay?"

"She had a heart bypass four months ago, and she's well on the road to recovery." He shrugged. "Working at the pub isn't too bad. The pace of life here suits me, and now I don't need to get into a contest over who scores the biggest bonus."

"Well, I need to earn money, but being here's more than that. I get the chance to put my stamp on this place." I waved an arm at the darkness beyond the windows. "And it's more sociable than Whitechapel."

"Yeah, it is."

We fell silent again as we drank our coffee, but this time it wasn't an awkward chasm between us. Once Eddie put his cup down, I loaded it into the dishwasher alongside my own and walked him to the back door.

"Thanks for being so understanding about this."

His kiss on my cheek was unexpected but...nice. "We all need friends. Call me if you ever want to hang out."

"Nothing more?"

I got a proper smile that time. "Nothing more."

CHAPTER 7

"I LOVE THESE designs!" Marlene exclaimed. "Especially the little bridge over the pool in the Japanese garden and the tropical borders. Can banana trees survive in this climate?"

Oh, thank goodness. I'd spent three days sketching and measuring outside, as well as collecting pictures of plants and landscape features to show Marlene the details of what I wanted to do with the place. To hear she was as enthusiastic as me about my designs made me sag in relief.

"*Musa basjoo* can. We'll just need to cover it with fleece in the winter to protect it from frost."

"And those plants with the giant leaves—what are they?"

"*Gunnera manicata.* They do well near water, and I'm sure that dip at the back of the lawn used to be a pond. If we dig it out and reline it, we could make it into a feature, maybe with a waterfall at one end and stepping stones across the middle. It depends how much you want to spend."

"Can't take the money with me, and I never could have children." She gripped my hand tight, her papery skin dry. "So you make this place look beautiful, okay?"

As the word "children" left her lips, her voice hitched, and I felt sorrow over what never happened for her and her husband. "I will, I promise." I smiled, trying to lighten the mood. "A waterfall it is."

"Wonderful. And I hired a tree surgeon. He arrives tomorrow morning at nine, so you'll need to have a think about where you want him to start."

"Is he from the village?"

"No, I heard the local guy isn't that good. He's coming from the next town."

When Marlene said the village tree surgeon wasn't that good, I think she meant he wasn't that good-looking. There were no such issues with Vince, who turned up in one of those sexy crew-cab pickups that made a girl want to get in the back seat rather than the front and dressed as though he were on his way to a calendar shoot. Loose jeans, checked shirt, well-worn work boots —hello Mr. July.

"I wonder if he knows what he's doing?" I whispered to Amber, who stood next to me on the front steps as he strode across the drive.

"Does it matter?"

"Nope. I'm thinking I might need to supervise him."

"From behind?"

"Obviously."

He stopped in front of us and dazzled us with a smile. "Hey, ladies."

Amber twirled a lock of hair around her finger, and I made a concerted effort to keep my mouth shut.

"Hi," Amber said.

"I'm Vince. Is Marlene around?"

"Right here, sweetie."

We turned in time to see her skip out the front door in a velour tracksuit with BABE written across the ass in diamanté. Clearly, last night's sherry hadn't had any lasting effects, because she bubbled with energy as she skidded to a halt in front of Vince and offered up a cheek for him to kiss.

He obliged with twinkling eyes, and she took his hand and led him into the house.

"You'll be working with Dove this week. She's got big plans for this place, but everything's too much, so she needs a man to help her."

Oh good grief, she made me sound like I was incapable of doing anything. "It's just some of the heavier work I need a hand with."

Marlene turned and raised a finger to her lips in warning.

"Get used to it," Amber whispered. "You might as well. Besides, look at the muscles on those thighs. And the arms! Can't you just imagine them wrapped around you?"

"I won't get any work done if I think that way."

"I doubt Marlene will mind."

But I did. I'd always been at my happiest in a garden, ever since Gran and Grandad Hallam gave me a small patch of dirt to play with at their house in Somerset. I'd only been six years old, but that summer I'd grown tomatoes, radishes, spring onions, and green beans. I could still remember Grandad lifting me up to pluck the pods off the canes, followed by the sickening realisation that I'd have to actually eat them. Up until then, I'd never much liked vegetables.

As we walked through the house, Lars emerged from the kitchen and gave Vince the once-over, followed by a nod of approval. At least somebody was happy about Marlene's meddling.

She led us out onto the terrace then melted back inside with Amber, leaving me, Vince, and a whole swimming pool full of awkwardness. Hmm... A swimming pool. Maybe I should work one of those into the plans somewhere. You know, to go with the tennis court.

"So..." he said.

"So."

"Where do you want me to start?"

"Out there"—I pointed towards the rear jungle —"are the remains of a chapel, complete with a ghost. Marlene wants it to be the focal point at a party she's planning for three months' time, but at the moment, you need to be in the SAS to get there."

His lips twitched. "I was only in the marines, but I'll see what I can do."

"Seriously? You were a marine?"

"For six years. Why?"

Because ever since I watched Tom Cruise in *A Few Good Men*, I'd had a thing for men in uniform? Nope, couldn't exactly admit to that.

"Uh, it's an interesting change of career."

"Being a marine isn't a job you can do forever. They were having cutbacks and offered a group of us voluntary redundancy, and I leapt at the chance. Gave me enough cash to start my own business, and now I employ a couple more former services guys too."

"Will they be coming to help?" I asked a tad too quickly.

He chuckled, and I suspect he knew precisely what was going through my mind. "Maybe."

"Right, okay, I'd better show you where this chapel is." I marched off, and he sauntered along behind, still laughing, while I wished the ground would open up and swallow me.

Which it did fifteen minutes later.

I'd just made an ungainly scramble over a fallen tree when the earth disappeared from beneath me and everything went dark. Vince's, "Holy fuck," sounded from behind as something soft brushed over my face. What was that? I reached a hand up, only for it to get covered in cobwebs too. My shriek echoed off the walls as I thought of the eight-legged freaks closing in on me.

"Get me out!"

As my eyes adjusted to the gloom, I spotted the set of wooden steps I'd tumbled down, but when I tried to clamber back up, they gave way beneath my weight and I fell again, landing in a heap of rotten wood and, worse, something squishy.

Vince's silhouette appeared in the light above me, and he crouched down, offering me a hand. I was shaking as I grabbed it, and when he lifted me clear, I did the grown-up thing and burst into tears.

He clutched me to his chest as he peered into the hole. "What is that? An old root cellar?"

I recalled the map in the study. "I th-th-think it's an icehouse."

"Are you okay?"

"My ankle hurts." I stretched out each limb, testing, then leaned into him again. "But apart from that, I'm okay."

"You know, if you'd wanted a piggyback, you could just have asked."

A laugh bubbled out of me. I couldn't help it. "That

wasn't—"

"I know. Let's get you back to the house and see to that ankle. I can check out the chapel later."

When Marlene saw Vince carrying me bridal-style across the patchy lawn, I thought she was going to pee herself. Her face lit up and she practically danced a jig, at least until she realised I was hurt.

"What happened?"

"I fell down a hole."

"Great idea, but it looks like the execution could have gone a little better."

"I didn't do it on purpose," I hissed.

Ever the model of efficiency, Lars appeared at the back door holding a bag of ice and a tea towel. "You'll be needing these?"

Vince nodded. "Where can I sit her down?"

"There's a chaise longue in the parlour."

I felt far more elegant than I deserved when Vince set me onto the overstuffed red velvet seat next to the French windows. A soft groan escaped my lips as he straightened. Having been pressed up against a wall of muscles for the past five minutes, I sure would miss them.

"Thanks."

"You rest. I'll go out and look at the trees along the driveway, and then I can plan what needs to be done." He winked as he walked towards the door. "You know, organise for extra manpower."

Be still my beating heart.

Amber scurried in a minute later, looking pale. "Oh my gosh! What happened? Marlene said you hurt your foot?"

"My ankle. I think I sprained it."

She peered closer and made a circular motion in front of her face. "You have a few little smudges."

"What? Where?"

"Uh, wait a second. I'll grab a mirror."

She came back with a compact, and I stared in horror at the ghoul looking back at me. Black streaks covered both cheeks, and... "Aaaaah! There's a spider in my hair. In my freaking hair!"

"Hang on, hang on. It's okay, I think it's dead."

Oh, that was so much better. "Can you just get it out?"

She rifled through my mess of dark-brown hair. At least it was almost black so it didn't show the dirt as much as my face. "Gone now."

I leaned my head back and closed my eyes. Not only had I fallen on my ass in front of Vince, twice, he'd also played the white knight while I looked like an extra from a horror film. The sexiest man I'd met in ages, and I'd come off like a fool.

"Could you bring me some wet wipes? Or a washcloth? Tissues? Anything?"

She gave me a mock salute. "Aye aye, ma'am. Be right back."

Except before she returned, I heard voices in the hallway and Marlene led three strangers into the room —an elderly couple and a girl around my age. Fantastic. My humiliation was now complete.

"This is the sweetheart I've been telling you all about. Dove, my new gardener."

The older woman squinted at me, while the man's gaze wandered to the window. The girl stared for a moment, then averted her eyes.

"I don't look like this normally," I said, trying to

sound chipper. "I had a tumble in the woods and got a bit dirty."

"What were you doing out there?" the old lady asked. "Surely they're dangerous for a young girl?"

"Auntie, we're not living in the nineteenth century. Women do everything that men can do now." The younger woman's brown curls bounced in the sunlight streaming in as she gave me a shy smile.

"So they say, dear, but she shouldn't have to. Looking after the grounds is a man's job. That's why we have Bertie."

The brunette crouched down beside me. "Bertie doesn't really garden anymore, just pushes the mower around once a week and sits on the bench by the back door the rest of the time. I'm Carrie, by the way."

"I've invited the Hearsts to stay for lunch," Marlene said. "They live next door, and Carrie and her aunt make the most divine cakes."

"I daren't eat too many." Carrie patted her stomach. "Or they end up here."

Mrs. Hearst gave me a sad smile. "I used to bake every day until my eyesight went. Now it's two or three times a week with Carrie helping."

Marlene refused to let her be miserable. "But those scones you made last week were divine. You'll have to give Lars the recipe."

Carrie stayed with me while Marlene led Mr. and Mrs. Hearst to the cluster of sofas on the other side of the room, calling for Lars to bring tea and biscuits as she did so.

"Marlene says you've just arrived?"

"Yep. It's been a busy few days."

"I can imagine. She likes to get things done. You

wouldn't have recognised this place last year. It was practically a shell."

Her accent was cute, but it wasn't English. "Where are you from? Australia?"

"That's right—near Perth. I moved here just over a year ago to take care of Auntie and Uncle." She lowered her voice. "Uncle's got Alzheimer's, and Auntie's in denial. She just pretends everything's fine."

"That must be hard for everyone."

"It's worst for her, especially with her vision problems. We don't have any other relatives left alive, and I couldn't just leave them to fend for themselves."

Wow. It took a special kind of person to uproot themselves so selflessly like that. "I bet they're grateful."

"Auntie is, but Uncle forgets my name from one day to the next. Not that we were ever close in the first place. My family emigrated when I was a toddler, and last year was only the second time I've come back."

"So you're here permanently?"

"I'm not sure. I agreed to visit because I thought it would be an adventure, and this place has kinda grown on me. Except for the weather, anyway."

"At least it's not raining today. That would have made my trip in the woods ten times worse."

Imagine the icehouse with an inch of mucky water in the bottom as well as all the dirt. Although it might have drowned some of the spiders, I suppose.

"What were you doing out there?"

I explained about Lady Helena, the chapel, and Marlene's plans for the party, and Carrie shuddered.

"I'm not convinced I believe in ghosts, but I can't say I love the idea of traipsing through those woods at night. What if there's another pit waiting?"

"Honestly? I'm not too thrilled at the prospect either, but you know Marlene. If she's determined to do something, it's gonna happen."

"I do know Marlene. And her parties are legendary. A few months back, she and Ivy organised a hen party for Ivy's goddaughter, and it was wild. Ivy almost got arrested when she got a real cop confused with the stripper cop and asked him what he could do with his truncheon."

"Oh dear."

"Yeah, exactly." She grinned. "Still, I'm intrigued to see how much havoc she creates with this ghost thing."

Visions of panic and elderly partygoers needing CPR filled my head. Could an ambulance even get down the path to the woods?

"I'm more nervous than intrigued. Someone will have to clear up the mess."

CHAPTER 8

"WELL, THERE IT is." I pointed ahead.

Overnight, the swelling in my ankle had gone down enough for me to strap it up and hobble out to the woods with Vince. And when I say "hobble," I mean he carried me half the way. Oh, the hardship.

"I see what you mean about it being in bad shape." Vince sat me on a log and ventured forwards, peering through each window as I had the other day. "Those roof timbers need removed or replaced. Marlene can't let anyone near the place in that state."

"That's what I thought. And as well as clearing a path, we'll need to check all the ground in case of any more unexpected obstacles." I recalled Carrie's words from yesterday.

"True. Do you have people lined up for that?"

"I'm not sure. I don't think so. I mean, Marlene picks out the contractors."

"I bet she does. This was the first time I've been asked for a topless photo instead of references."

"Surely she didn't...?"

"She did. I sent one of me in combat trousers and dog tags." He turned and winked. "Thought she might like that."

"Well, she definitely seemed to. She wouldn't stop talking about you over dinner yesterday."

"My girlfriend certainly found the story amusing."

His girlfriend? I didn't know whether to laugh or cry. After a moment's consideration, I doubled over. "Marlene's trying to find me a new boyfriend, and I think she was hoping you might be it." I tried to smother my giggles. "She went to all that trouble for nothing."

Vince joined in with hearty guffaws that boomed through the woods. "She's a character, that old lady."

"She is, but I can't help wishing she'd let me get on with my job without all these distractions."

He smiled playfully. "So I'm a distraction?"

"No, I mean... Of course you are. Surely you must know that?"

"Always nice to hear a lady say it."

"Shut up."

He joined me at the log and motioned for me to scoot over so he could sit down. "You know, we could have some fun with this."

"What do you mean?"

"Wind meddling Marlene up a bit. It might take the heat off you, at least."

My lips curved into a grin all of their own accord. "I think I like that idea. Won't your girlfriend mind?"

"Trust me, she'll see the funny side."

"In that case, I love the idea. But first, we need to sort out the plans for this place."

"I know a decent builder if you need one. He's not cheap, but he'll do a good job."

"I'll speak to Marlene about it. Uh, what does he look like?"

"Possibly not model material."

"Oh dear. Perhaps we could just not tell her that

bit?"

"Good plan."

In keeping with our new-found fakery, Vince slung an arm around my shoulders as we walked across the lawn, and I did my best not to giggle. A shadow moved across one of the windows at the back of the house, and a curtain twitched. Was that Marlene watching us? Or Amber, or Lars?

"You seem to be getting on well," Amber said as we walked in the back door.

"Is Marlene here?"

"No, she went out for lunch."

Vince dropped his arm, and I sighed. Foxed again. "We're trying to play Marlene at her own game. Vince is already spoken for."

"Nice idea, but if the amount of men she tried to set me up with is any indication, you'll have to hump him on the dining table for her to get the hint. Oh, don't act so horrified."

Lars poked his head around the door. "Your tools have been delivered. I've stacked them in the old wood store next to the cottage."

"Thanks."

"Would you like something to eat? I've made a selection of sandwiches and a fruit cake."

All three of us replied in the affirmative. After this morning's exertions and only a slice of toast for breakfast, I was starving, and even though Lars played down his efforts, the sandwiches were dainty crustless affairs with four different fillings, and the fruit cake was actually more of a flan, complete with kiwi, pineapple, and strawberries, all served up with fresh cream.

"Glad I got this job now," Vince said as he stuffed a third slice into his mouth. "Worth it for the food alone."

The front door slamming made everyone jump, and Vince shuffled his chair closer while Amber sniggered. When Marlene came into the dining room and saw us, the small gap didn't go unnoticed, although she didn't look as pleased as I imagined she would.

"You kids getting on well?"

I pasted on a smile. "Sure are."

"That's good, that's good. And I have news. The veterinarian came out to give Ivy's cat her shots this morning, and he'd like to take you out for dinner tonight."

"But..."

She leaned over and picked out a sandwich, taking the opportunity to whisper in my ear. "Make Vince jealous, honey."

I thunked my head back against the chair. Foiled again.

"So, anyway, the bull's scrotum was inflamed, and that's why it charged at me."

"Fascinating."

I tried to block out Peter's words as I pushed most of an individual Key lime pie around my plate. My appetite had deserted me during the starter when he told me all about the morning he'd spent with his hand stuck up a cow's arse. That was it—I'd had enough. As soon as I woke up tomorrow, I'd tell Marlene I really was a lesbian. If she tried to set me up with one more man, I'd scream.

Eddie paused by the table. "Everything okay with that?" He gestured at the mess I was stirring.

"It's good. I'm just full, that's all."

"You should eat more, Dove," Peter chipped in. "I like a woman with a nice rump on her."

Had he considered dating a heifer? He seemed to spend half his time with parts of his anatomy stuffed inside one.

"No, honestly, I'm not very hungry."

He grabbed his spoon and helped himself to a mouthful. "Not bad. Could use more cream, though."

Asshole. He gulped down another bite before he went back to smearing Stilton on a cracker. I'd never been a fan of blue cheese. Any food that had mould in it was a no-no in my eyes, and it smelled bad too.

"Grape?" he offered, holding one out between his finger and thumb.

"No, thank you."

"As I was saying, I've got this bull to operate on tomorrow. From the puffiness, I think there's a lot of pus in there. Sometimes it squirts out when I make the first incision." He chuckled around a mouthful of cheese. "That's always entertaining."

Please, somebody kill me now. All this talk of wounds, not to mention the particularly ripe Brie Peter had just cut into, made me want to vomit.

"And after the bull, I'm going to..." His phone rang, and I mouthed a silent thank you to whoever called it. Peter held up a hand. "Excuse me... Yes?... Hmm... Colic, you say?... Okay, fifteen minutes."

He pushed his chair back. "So sorry, got to go and see to a sick horse. It's having trouble defecating." He rifled through his wallet and dropped fifty pounds onto the table. "That should cover my half. I'll give you a call tomorrow, and we can rearrange."

Before I could tell him not to bother, he'd disappeared out the door, leaving me staring open-mouthed after him. He'd lumbered me with half the bill for a meal I didn't want or eat, made me feel ill the entire evening, and thought I'd want to do it again? Men were from Mars, women were from Venus, but Peter came from Uranus.

A tall glass sliding across in front of me made me jump, and I looked up to see Eddie smiling at me.

"You look as if you could use a G&T. On the house, and don't worry about the other half of the bill either."

"You don't have to do that."

"Did I seriously overhear him describing how he gave a show dog a fake testicle after it got cancer down there?"

"Yup."

"I'll bring you another drink when you've finished that one."

Eddie was overly generous with the gin the second time around, but I'd downed half and choked on a lemon pip before a middle-aged couple stopped by the table.

"Are you that new gardener from London?" the woman asked.

"Yes, at Arndale House."

She turned to the man. "Told you." Then she looked back to me with narrowed eyes. "That job should have gone to Percy. He does all the gardens around here. Moving in from the big city and stealing his work—that's not fair."

What? Who was Percy?

"But that wasn't my decision—" I started, but she was already halfway to the door, tightening the belt on her Burberry trench coat.

With a heavy sigh, I necked back the rest of my drink. After this evening, I deserved it.

"How many times has he called?" Amber asked.

I glanced down at my phone again. "Seventeen missed calls and eleven texts. No...actually, make that twelve."

"I'm so sorry, sweetie," Marlene said. "I'd never have given Peter your number if I knew he'd start stalking you."

Amber snatched the phone from me and scrolled through the messages. "You've got to give him points for creativity. I bet not many men ask women to join them for an evening of canapés and dissection."

I didn't want to watch Peter cut up a horse's leg any more than I wanted to watch him eat cheese again. Marlene had apologised profusely over the affair and promised not to set me up on another blind date, but Peter didn't seem to be taking the hint.

Carrie raised her glass of wine from the other sofa. "I wish I'd known you were going out with him—I could have warned you."

"You knew he was a weirdo?"

"When I took Auntie's dog for his shots last year, Peter got our number off the computer system and kept calling the house. Auntie got really confused about it all."

"What happened? Did he stop?"

"Only when I told him I was a lesbian."

Amber giggled. "Maybe you should go out for dinner together. You know, pretend you're a couple?"

"And I'll pay the bill," Marlene said.

I helped myself to another handful of crisps—the expensive, hand-fried kind. They'd always been my weakness, more so even than chocolate. "Thanks for the offer, but I'm just going to ignore him."

After what that woman said to me after dinner, I didn't feel like venturing out again in a hurry.

"Carrie?" Marlene asked.

"Oh, don't worry about me. He hasn't called for ages, and I'm sort of seeing somebody now."

Marlene and Amber both squealed. "Who?" Amber asked. "You never said anything."

"It's just casual. A few meals out and one trip to the cinema in Great Haseley."

I'd learned Great Haseley was the next town over, where Vince lived.

"You'll be bringing him to the party this weekend, though?" Marlene asked.

"What party?"

"Ivy's Super Bowl party at Northbury Hall."

The three of us choked on our drinks.

"I didn't realise Ivy liked football," Amber said.

"She doesn't, sweetie, not really. We never did understand the rules, but those men wear tight trousers and they don't hide much. You all have to come."

"I'm not sure..."

"She's organised organic beef burgers and gourmet tortilla chips. You can't turn those down."

"Okay, we'll come. Right, girls?"

Carrie and I nodded. Even though I hadn't been at

Arndale House for long, I'd already learned that Marlene would win any argument.

Chapter 9

"I CAN'T BELIEVE I have to go to a Super Bowl party,"
I said to Vince the next morning as we grabbed a coffee
before work. "Isn't that in the middle of the night?"

"I believe so. The half-time show'll be okay, though.
I hear the Ghost's doing the music."

"I'm sure I can get you an invitation."

"Washing my hair that night. Besides, I'm more of a
rugby man myself. None of that fannying around."

Vince's hair was half an inch long. "Ivy's organising
it. I haven't met her yet, but people have told me
stories. I bet she'll have it on a big screen, and I'm sure
there'll be wine involved."

"So I'll be carting you around in the wheelbarrow
on Monday morning, then?"

I didn't know whether to giggle or groan. "That's a
definite possibility."

Once we'd finished our drinks, Lars took our cups
before we could put them in the dishwasher.

"You don't have to do that," I told him.

"Please, I have a system."

"Oh, okay. Thanks."

Vince headed to the front of the house to get his
truck, which had his tools in it as well as an industrial-
sized chipper attached to the back. Once he'd chipped
the branches he cut, he'd leave the pile by the old

kitchen garden for me to use as mulch on the borders. I'd lay seep hoses underneath, and it would keep the weeds out and the water in.

While he worked on the path to the chapel, I planned to make a start on the back terrace. The whole area needed weeding then washing, and the mortar between the stones begged for replacement. At least the weather wasn't looking too bad today. The air was chilly, but every so often the sun peeped through a chink in the clouds.

I rubbed my gloved hands together as I walked towards the old wood store. I'd need the wheelbarrow, a trowel, a hand fork...

"What the...?"

The barrow lay on its side, dented, and the tyre hung shredded from its rim. Alongside, the shaft of the spade had been broken in two and the tines of the fork were bent. I'd ordered hand tools—secateurs as well as the trowel and a small fork—and I couldn't see those anywhere.

I sank down on my knees, mouth open. Who had done this?

The rumble of an engine sounded then stopped, and heavy footsteps crunched towards me on the gravel path, followed by Vince's voice.

"I forgot to... Hey, what's all this mess?"

He picked up the corner of a new tarpaulin that had been slashed in a dozen places.

"I don't know. This stuff got delivered yesterday and now look at it." The first tear trickled down my cheek, swiftly followed by another as Vince knelt beside me. "Who would do this?"

His mouth set in a grim line, his voice flat. "I don't

know, but I'd like to find out."

I tried to get up, but my legs refused to work. To me, this wasn't just broken tools. It felt like a personal attack on my hopes and dreams. When my legs wobbled, Vince helped me to my feet and steadied me there with an arm around my waist.

"Come on, let's get you back inside."

"No, I need to work."

"You can't, not without tools. You need a chair and a hot drink."

When I didn't move, he picked me up, and I didn't struggle as he carried me back into the kitchen in the main house.

"What happened?" Lars asked. "Not another accident?"

"No, somebody's vandalised Dove's tools."

"Are you serious?"

"Afraid so. Everything's trashed."

Lars's eyes flashed. "Someone trespassed on the estate last night?"

"What?" Marlene's voice came from the doorway.

Vince explained again, and when Marlene turned pale, I got a little worried about her, what with her age.

But then she stamped one Converse-clad foot. "Nobody does that and gets away with it. I'm calling the police."

Before any of us could utter another word, she stomped off along the hallway and we heard her voice in the next room, first sweet, then cajoling, then angry, and finally saccharine.

"A constable will be with us in half an hour," she informed us when she reappeared. "They tried to tell me it wasn't a serious incident at first. Those idiots."

Nope, nobody argued with Marlene.

"Thanks for helping with this."

Vince flashed me a grin. "Kids or not, we don't want this happening again."

Kids. That had been the policeman's guess when he visited earlier.

"Since the youth club closed down last year, we've seen more petty crime like this," he'd said. "There's not much for them to do in Northbury. Unless you know of anyone else who might bear a grudge?" He'd looked at each of us in turn. When he got to me, I shifted uncomfortably.

"I think some people in the village aren't too happy about me getting the job here."

"What makes you say that?"

I explained what happened at the end of my date, and Marlene's nostrils flared.

"I heard Percy starts drinking at eight and doesn't quit until he passes out after lunch. Hardly the type of man I want working in my garden."

Considering Marlene had been known to do the same thing, her statement left me a bit surprised, but I guess she wasn't trying to operate hedge trimmers or a shredder. Alcohol sure didn't mix well with heavy machinery.

The policeman scribbled in his notebook. "I'll make some enquiries. Anybody else?"

Given that Peter went out on an emergency call right after last night's date, I figured we could rule him out, and even though Wes wasn't happy about me leaving, I couldn't see him trekking all the way to Northbury to break a few tools. I shook my head, as did everybody else.

The forensic investigator who'd accompanied the policeman straightened up. "I've got prints, but don't get too excited. They could have got there during manufacturing or delivery."

"Thanks for trying," I said.

He gave me a tired smile. "That's my job."

After the police had departed, Vince and Lars abandoned their plans and drove to the big garden centre in Great Haseley, then the DIY store. When they got back, they spent the afternoon fixing up the door on one of the old stables, and as I shone a torch, Vince screwed in the final corner of the padlock hasp. My new tools were already stacked inside, where they'd hopefully be safe from whoever paid last night's visit.

Marlene appeared with Amber, the older woman wearing sparkly pink wellies topped off by a fur coat. Amber draped a shawl over my shoulders.

"I can't believe this," she whispered.

"I've ordered food in," Marlene said.

"But—" Lars began.

"Honey, when you've been slaving away out here for the whole afternoon, I'm not having you start in the kitchen." She turned to Vince. "Are you staying?"

"Sorry, I've got something on tonight."

"Maybe another time?"

He cut his eyes in my direction then smiled at Marlene. "Yeah, that sounds good."

"And we all appreciate you helping out today. Nobody's going to ruin my plans for this place and get away with it."

"I like her," Vince whispered to me as we trooped back to the house. "Feisty."

"I like her too."

I'd never met a woman quite like Marlene before. While life at Arndale House might be challenging, nobody could ever claim it was dull.

Chapter 10

BY THE TIME dusk fell on Friday, the woodchip pile was taller than me, but there still wasn't much of a visible path through the trees.

"I've marked everything that needs to come down," Vince said. "Now I'm organised, I should be able to get through the rest quickly. You given any more thought to the builder?"

"I gave his name to Marlene, and he's coming in for a chat on Monday."

"That's good. If she wants people walking through those woods, we'll need to put some sort of surface down on the path as well. At this time of year, it won't take much to turn it to mud."

"What would you recommend?"

"If she's after a temporary fix, she might get away with a layer of woodchips, but those aren't gonna be kind to high heels. The other option is to put more effort in upfront and go for road planings, gravel, or even slabs."

"I'll talk to her about it. Did you take the pictures of the chapel?"

"Sure did. What's your number? I'll send them to you."

I read it out, and he typed it into his phone. At least the messages from Peter had slowed to a trickle. Today,

I'd only had one call and two texts. Would I like to go to a lecture on worm counts? No thanks.

"Thanks. Have a great time this weekend."

Vince was taking his girlfriend for a last-minute minibreak to the Peak District. I couldn't help feeling a little bit jealous.

"You too. Enjoy your party."

"Please, don't remind me. It's going to be carnage."

Marlene was sponsoring the champagne, and it had arrived by truck yesterday.

"I won't expect you out early on Monday morning."

"How many people are going to this party?" I asked Marlene as she painted black stripes on my face. She'd bought us football jerseys with our names printed on the back to wear over our leggings. Apparently, we'd be supporting the Baltimore Ravens. Lars had cried off, saying he'd pick us up when we were done and besides, somebody needed to look after the house.

"Ooh, one or two hundred."

I did a double take. "That many?"

"Ivy likes parties. Her daughter complains if she holds too many, though."

"And you're sure Peter isn't going?"

"Ivy assures me she didn't invite him. Is he still bothering you?"

"Three texts and two calls today." And I'd ignored them all. How long would it take him to stop completely?

When we arrived at Northbury Hall, I could kind of see Ivy's daughter's point. The Rolls Royce was famed for a ride so quiet you could hear the ticking of the clock, but the clock was drowned out by the thumping bass coming from the mansion at the end of the driveway.

"Wow. That's some place."

It made Arndale House look like a bedsit.

"Isn't it?" Amber said. "And it's stunning inside, although I'd love to redo the main lounge. It's just too dark at the moment."

Lars pulled up outside then helped us out of the car, and an elderly butler opened the front door as soon as we set foot on the steps. I thought I caught a hint of resignation on his face as he eyed up Marlene.

"Good evening, Mrs. Grande."

"Hi, Albert." She handed him her cape. "You've met Amber, and the new girl is Dove."

He nodded in our direction. "A pleasure."

Marlene knew where she was going, and we followed her through to a ballroom. Seriously—a ballroom. I thought those only existed in fairy tales, but there it was, complete with ornately panelled walls and a huge chandelier in the centre. Except there was no dancing being done tonight. Sofas and beanbags dotted the room, and three...no, four men dressed as football players wove in and out with trays of beer and canapés held aloft.

"Oh, honey, would you look at the ass on that one." Marlene's eyes tracked the nearest of them. "Ivy's done well tonight."

"Where is Ivy?" I asked.

Marlene glanced around the room until her gaze rested on two women by the door. A grey-haired lady dressed in a football jersey and a younger brunette wearing a twinset and pearls. "Oh dear. Looks as if Lucinda's on the warpath again."

"Lucinda's her daughter?"

"Yes, although how they're genetically related, I've never quite been able to work out."

A dark-haired man walked through the door next to them, and my breath hitched. He wasn't just hot, he was incendiary, but in a dangerous sort of way. And sweet, as he leaned down and kissed first Lucinda, and then Ivy on the cheek.

"Who's that?" I asked Marlene.

"Ivy's grandson." She giggled. "But don't get any ideas about Nye. He's taken."

A petite blonde appeared next to him, and he slid an arm around her waist. I couldn't help sighing. Yes, that was the kind of girl who got a man like him. Pretty, curvy, and with a smile to cut through the darkest of days.

Another man came in, and Marlene gave a small jerk of her head. "But that one, he's free."

I glanced at the newcomer—the same height as Nye but a lighter build. Although that was relative, because judging by the way his grey T-shirt stretched over his chest, he clearly worked out.

"And who's he?"

"Zander Graves. A friend of Nye's."

I tried not to stare as I drank him in. Thick light-brown hair, clean shaven, a dimple in his chin. I couldn't quite see the colour of his eyes, but when he focused in my direction, I quickly looked away.

Then looked back again as a blur of turquoise flew past me.

"You asshole!" The blonde in the bright blue dress

slapped Zander hard enough to turn every head in the room.

He held both hands up. "Hey, I never said I'd call."

"How can you show your face here tonight?"

"I was invited." He tried to take her by the elbow and lead her out of the room, but she shook him off. "Melissa..."

"My name's Clarissa," she snapped, hands on hips.

Nye burst out laughing. "Smooth, mate. Real smooth."

Clarissa flipped her hair over her shoulder and stormed out as Nye's mother gave Zander a filthy look, but he grinned in return, and she followed Clarissa.

Marlene wrapped my fingers around a glass of beer. "On second thoughts, maybe give that one a miss, sweetie. I'm gonna catch up with Ivy."

Beside me, Amber waved at Nye's girlfriend, and she wriggled out from under Nye's arm and hurried over. She and Amber embraced before Amber introduced us.

"Dove, this is Olivia Porter. Olivia, meet Dove Hallam, Marlene's new gardener."

She hugged me too, and I nearly spilled my drink.

"Lovely to meet you, Dove."

"And you," I got out.

Olivia grabbed a redhead walking past with a tray of cakes, and the football player-slash-waiter beside her stopped too. "This is Cherry. We run a bakery together."

Cherry held out her tray. "Cake? And it's Olivia's bakery. I just work there."

"We run the bakery together," Olivia said firmly. "If anything, you do more than me. And this is Lachlan, her boyfriend. One of Ivy's models called in sick, so she press-ganged Lachlan into helping."

"It was easier to carry a tray than argue," he muttered.

I helped myself to a cake iced like a miniature football. "Thank you. These look delicious."

"Better go," Cherry said. "If I leave him on his own, old ladies keep pinching his bum."

"Occupational hazard," Olivia said, turning a snort of laughter into a cough. Once they'd departed, talk returned to the garden. "I don't envy you, trying to get that wilderness into shape." She waved down another passing footballer so we could all help ourselves to mini hot dogs. "I wouldn't know where to start. I even managed to kill off a cactus once."

A cactus? But those things were practically indestructible.

"I'm looking forward to the job, actually. I've always loved gardening."

"I can't wait to see it when it's finished."

"That'll take years, but Marlene wants enough done to throw a ghost-themed party in two and a half months."

Olivia gestured at the football-waiters and rolled her eyes. "I can just imagine it—sexy spectres. More drama, especially if Ivy helps with the planning."

Amber nodded towards Nye and Zander. "Ivy didn't even get involved in tonight's most entertaining spectacle. Reckon Zander will strike out after that?"

Olivia giggled. "Oh, not a chance. Zander's skills in the bedroom are well known around these parts. He'll have them queuing up by the end of the evening."

"But what about Melissa?" I asked. "Sorry,

Clarissa?"

"I can't feel too sorry for that girl, not after she hit on Nye when she knew we were engaged. Besides, Zander may be a cad, but he's always upfront about his total lack of commitment. Ooh, look—there's Carrie with her new guy. Let's go over and say hello."

Why were so many hot men let down by their personalities? Mind you, Wes wasn't exactly God's gift, and he'd turned out to be even uglier on the inside, so perhaps looks weren't much of an indicator. Maybe I should stick with plants? After all, if the video I caught Wes watching on the internet one day was anything to go by, there was a lot a girl could do with a courgette and her imagination.

An organic courgette, obviously, because otherwise the pesticides... *Stop it, Dove!* Vegetables belonged in the garden, Wes belonged in the sewer, and men like Zander belonged with other girls.

CHAPTER 11

I FOLLOWED OLIVIA and Amber via a waiter carrying a platter of mini-burgers, then wished I hadn't. When the man on Carrie's arm looked me slowly up and down, it made me want to bring my food straight back up again.

Carrie didn't seem to notice as she gestured in my direction. "Neil, this is Dove."

He dipped his head, but I didn't want his lips anywhere near my face, so I stuck my hand out and accidentally-on-purpose jabbed him in the chest instead. That forced him to take half a step back, but when he shook, he held onto my hand for too long.

"Very pleased to meet you."

I didn't like his smarmy smile either, and I gritted my teeth. "Same."

"Do you live around here?"

"Next door to Carrie."

His smile grew broader, and this time it was me who backed away.

"That's great," he said. "I'm sure we'll see more of each other, then."

Was he seriously flirting with me in front of his girlfriend? I hadn't had a whole lot of experience with that kind of thing, but it sure seemed like it. I glanced at Carrie, but she was talking to Amber and Olivia.

"Sorry, but I'm really busy with work."

"You know what they say about all work and no play."

"Hey, ladies." Oh, thank goodness. Saved by Nye. He'd come over with a plate of mini-donuts, plus Zander in tow. "Gonna introduce us, babe?"

Olivia helped herself to a chocolate creme. "This is Neil, Carrie's boyfriend, and Dove, who works for Marlene."

He shook Neil's hand, then mine. "Nye Holmes. My deepest sympathy. I imagine being in Marlene's house is hard work."

"Well, you've got Ivy."

"Only in small doses. I spend most of my time in London."

Beside me, Zander greeted Neil then rested a hand on the top of my arm as he leaned in and placed a feather-light kiss on my cheek. "Zander Graves."

Up close, his eyes were soft amber with a darker ring around the iris, and when he ran his gaze from my head to my feet, a flush of heat followed. Olivia said he'd have girls queueing up? Based on that reaction, I was afraid I might be one of them.

But my heart didn't have the capacity to cope with a man like Zander, even if he was interested in someone like me. Clarissa and her type? They were all front of house, while I was more back office.

I murmured, "Nice to meet you," with no idea what to say next, but luckily Ivy saved me by blowing an air horn.

"The game's starting!" she shrieked.

"So who are the Ravens playing?" I asked nobody in particular.

Zander smirked. "It's the Denver Broncos versus the Carolina Panthers."

I looked down at my shirt. Nope, it clearly said Ravens. "Why did Marlene get us Ravens shirts?"

Olivia looped her arms through mine and Amber's. "She probably liked the colours. Come on, let's grab a sofa for the girls. The guys can go and do their own thing."

I soon found myself squashed between Amber and Carrie as they whooped and hollered. Well, Carrie clapped politely, but she still showed enthusiasm I couldn't work up.

"How do you know what's going on?" I asked Amber. "I mean, when to applaud?"

"I've got no idea what's going on. I think we're just clapping for the asses."

Okay, I could live with that, especially once I'd drunk another beer or two. Before I knew it, it was time for the half-time show, and people leapt up and began shoving sofas out of the way.

"Now what's happening?" I whispered to Olivia.

"Now we dance, and then we eat donuts again. And..." She hiccupped. "Cupcakes."

Oh no. Not dancing. I was the least coordinated person on the planet, the one who'd snuck off and sat on my own at the back during birthday discos. The last time I ventured out to a nightclub with Wes, I'd trodden on his foot and his toe turned blue. He'd complained about it for weeks.

"Uh, is there a bathroom I can use?"

"Out of the main door, turn left, and it's along the corridor."

Right, I had a plan—lock myself in until the music

stopped. And as toilets went, it had to be the poshest one I'd ever been in with its white marble floor and gold taps. Even the moisturiser was by Bvlgari. I closed the toilet lid and sat down with my head against the cool wall, wishing I was in my bed at home.

At least, until banging on the door startled me out of my slumber.

"Hurry up in there, would you?"

Oh, dammit. Somebody needed to pee. I hastily pretended to flush the toilet and wash my hands, then slunk out as Clarissa barged in, clutching the hand of a lanky guy with his shirt untucked. Seemed as if she wasn't so hung up on Zander after all.

Now I needed to find a new hiding place, only I didn't want to go sneaking around Ivy's house uninvited, especially if there were more Clarissas around doing things I'd never dare to do in semi-public.

Perhaps I could find my way to the garden? Even if it was chilly, I'd rather be outside.

"Hey, Dove, come and dance!"

Before I could get my bearings, a hand grabbed mine and dragged me towards the ballroom, and worse still, it was creepy Neil.

"No, I don't want to."

"It's a party—you have to dance."

"Where's Carrie? Shouldn't you be dancing with her?"

"Dunno. Anyway, I'd rather dance with you." He got behind and propelled me forwards, right into a wall.

"Oof." A wall that spoke.

"I'm sorry."

Zander looked down at me, and then his gaze

flicked to Neil, assessing the situation.

"There you are, gorgeous. Thought I needed to send out a search party." He wrapped an arm around my waist, plastering me against his side as he addressed Neil. "Thanks for keeping an eye on her, mate. Think I saw your girl over by the buffet table."

Neil mumbled something and turned tail, leaving me hard against a man who took my breath away. I meant it. I couldn't breathe.

"Could you just...loosen your arm a little?" I wriggled in his grasp.

His hand slid to my hip, which was worse in a lot of ways. All my blood rushed south, and my brain went blank.

"You looked like you needed a hand," Zander said.

"He was being a bit pushy. I don't know how to thank you."

His fingers stroked over my hip. "I can think of a way."

A jolt of electricity surged through me. Surely he didn't mean...? I raised my eyes from the floor, pausing on an admittedly impressive bulge as I dragged them up to his face.

"I'm not that sort of girl," I snapped.

For a moment, he looked shocked, and then he roared with laughter. "Bloody hell, even I'm not that forward. I was talking about a dance."

My cheeks burned, and I was sure I'd just gone an alarming shade of puce. "I'm so sorry, I mean, I just assumed after earlier, and what Olivia told me..." Dammit, now I'd brought her into my mess too.

"If, by the end of the evening, you decide you are that sort of girl, I'm not going to say no. But for now, all

I want is a dance."

"But I can't dance."

"Every girl can dance."

"Not this one."

"Prove it."

"Fine. If you want to get your feet hurt, that's up to you."

He smiled, eyes twinkling, and my feet nearly forgot how to work. But then we were on the makeshift dance floor and Zander slid his hands up my sides, all the way along my arms until he'd wrapped them around his neck. His own arms went to my waist, locking me against him as he began to move.

And hot damn, the man could move. His hips swayed in time to the beat, taking me with them, and I must have been drunker than I thought because I was actually enjoying myself. I mentally catalogued my alcohol intake—two beers, one Coke-and-something, and a worryingly garish cocktail. Was that enough to make a girl lose her mind?

I didn't know, but I sure as hell had fun finding out.

Then the music stopped, and an involuntary groan escaped my lips as my eyes met Zander's.

"I told you so," he whispered, his lips close enough that they brushed my ear.

"Just a fluke."

He chuckled as he pressed a kiss to my cheek, not just a polite peck but a definite lingering smooch this time. For a moment, while he seared my skin, I began to think that maybe I *was* that sort of girl.

But then he pulled back, and the moment was lost. "See you around, Dove."

I spent the rest of the evening sneaking glances at

the boys' sofa, where Zander was drinking beer with Nye and a few others, and mindlessly stuffed popcorn into my mouth as I tried to concentrate on the big game.

Except I totally lost my appetite ten minutes before the end when a skinny blonde wearing a diamond tennis bracelet that probably cost my annual salary slid onto Zander's lap, and he wrapped both arms around her. She leaned back against him, and by the time the final whistle blew, he was nibbling on her earlobe.

"Great game, huh?" Amber said, chomping on a last handful of tortilla chips.

"I got kind of lost."

"I don't even know who won, but I'm sure it was the guys in the white trousers."

"Weren't they *all* wearing white trousers?"

"There you go."

Marlene bounced over with streamers in her perfectly coiffed hair, waving a pompom. "I used to be a cheerleader back in the day, did you know that? Lars is on his way to pick us up, so if you want another cocktail, best to drink it quickly."

I looked across at the buffet table, just in time to see Zander walk in front of it with the blonde firmly in his grasp, past the empty plates, around the piles of discarded party poppers, and towards the door.

"I don't want anything else to drink this evening."

I already felt ill enough as it was, although the nausea was tinged with hurt now. How could he move between girls so quickly? That hurt turned to full-on anger when he got to the door and turned back to the room. The bastard caught my eye, glanced at the girl on his arm, then looked back at me and quirked an eyebrow. Was he seriously suggesting a threesome?

That...that... Olivia was right—he was a complete cad.

I feigned nonchalance and shrugged, tamping down the pain in my chest that threatened to bubble over into tears. What a cold-hearted bastard.

Zander just grinned, tightened his grip on the blonde, and left.

CHAPTER 12

"SEEMS I WAS right not to expect you before eleven."

Vince looked better than should be allowed on a Monday morning, whereas I'd glimpsed myself in the mirror before I left the cottage and bore more than a passing resemblance to a scarecrow.

"We didn't get back until late. Or rather, early."

And when we did, I'd wasted entirely too much time thinking about Zander and his man-whorish behaviour and not enough time sleeping.

"Have you reminded Marlene about the chapel?" Vince asked.

"It's on my list of things to do, but she's not up yet."

When I'd stumbled over to the big house with Amber, only Lars had been awake, waiting in the kitchen with a jug of coffee and fresh croissants. My hero.

"Didn't think she would be. When I spoke to Lars earlier, he reckoned she wouldn't show her face until mid-afternoon." He grinned and hefted his chainsaw. "Which gives us a few hours to get started."

By the time Marlene shuffled outside next to Lars, wearing a pair of oversized sunglasses, I was counting down the minutes until my next paracetamol. Unsurprisingly, Vince's chainsaw didn't mix too well with my headache. Or Marlene's hangover. The next moment there was a lull in the din, she stuck two fingers in her mouth and let out a piercing whistle, then winced.

"Ouch."

When Vince looked up, she beckoned him over.

"You called?"

"Why don't you leave that alone for today, sweetie? I'll still pay your full rate."

"What were you drinking?"

"Everything."

He chuckled. "You shouldn't mix the grape and the grain."

"It was the hot dogs that disagreed with me. Too many carbs."

I caught Marlene's arm before she could escape back to the house. "Don't forget the builder's coming this afternoon to discuss the chapel."

"Can you handle it? I'm going back to bed."

"But I'm not sure what you want. I mean, in terms of budget, and how much work you want done. Just a tidy up? Or a full renovation?"

"I want it beautiful. Make it look like it did when it was built, and don't worry about the cost. Oh, and I want the path wide enough to drive the golf buggy down—that way I can use it for my morning meditation in the summer."

She looped her elbow through Lars's and leaned on him as she shuffled towards the house. It was the first time I'd seen her look her age. I let out a thin breath as she disappeared.

"Well, that was easier than I thought," I said, then smacked my palm on my forehead. "'Make it beautiful'? What sort of brief is that?"

Vince shrugged. "Better than making it ugly."

The builder, Hal, agreed with Vince when he turned up forty-five minutes later. We all took a trip out to the chapel, and Vince narrowly stopped me from cracking my head off a tree branch. The lack of sleep was getting to me. I sat on a log as the men discussed the project, grateful that Vince had stuck around rather than going home.

"Lot of work, isn't there?" Hal said.

"Yeah. Reckon you can do anything with it? We've got two and a half months."

"You say the lady's basically given us free rein?"

"Make it beautiful," I mimicked.

Hal turned to me, and I raised my bleary eyes to his face. Even that took an effort. Vince was right about him not being a calendar model, but he had kind eyes, and I loved his Scottish accent.

"I'd much rather have the choice over how we renovate than a client who micromanages. I just finished a job where the woman even specified the brand of tiling grout we had to use. Nearly bricked her up behind a wall, I tell you."

Ouch. That was like being told what variety of seeds to plant, or which compost to buy.

"Marlene's more of a concept person from what I can tell. Give her an overview, and if she likes it, she writes a cheque."

"Then I think we'll get along just fine."

"You'll take the job?"

"Yeah. In all honesty, I don't have much choice. I

was due to start building an extension next week, but the couple split up and cancelled it."

Oh, thank goodness. I mean, how terrible. "How long do you think it'll take?"

"First, your man here's got to clear the path." He nodded at Vince. "We'll need it wide enough to bring the equipment in and out. After that, we'll strip everything back to the stonework, repair the broken parts, and get the roof on. Reckon it'll take a couple of months if we start right away, as long as we can get the right stones to match."

"Where do we get those?"

"I know a guy."

"So it's all organised?" Amber asked as we sat down to a semi-healthy dinner of pizza with salad.

"I wouldn't go as far as that, but the builder's starting on Monday."

"Any good? I only caught a glimpse."

"No! I mean, he's very nice. But I'm not looking for a new boyfriend, no matter what Marlene might think."

"I saw you dancing with Zander last night."

I waved a hand dismissively even as my heart sped up. "That was nothing. Neil wanted to dance with me and I was trying to get rid of him, and then Zander noticed and intervened."

"Carrie's Neil?"

"Yeah. What did you think of him?"

"Honestly? Not a lot. Even less if he was bothering you at the party."

I was glad it wasn't just me. Having spent the last

three and a bit years with Wes without realising what a slimeball he was until right at the end, I no longer trusted my own judgement. Best to stick with gardening. Plants mostly did what I expected them to. And pizza. I could quite happily spend my evenings with pizza.

"Did you make this?" I asked Amber. Dinner had been ready when I came in.

She spluttered a laugh. "Of course not. Lars did. If he weren't gay, I swear I'd marry him in a heartbeat."

Okay, so in that particular instance, I might relax my newly implemented "no men" rule.

"You'd have to fight me for him."

"Better than Peter. Is he still messaging you?"

"We're down to three messages and only one call today." And a text from my mother, which was almost as bad. When was I coming to visit? Never, if I could get away with it.

Lars's cooking put both Amber and me into a food coma, and we didn't stir until we'd watched an episode of *EastEnders* and a romcom that turned out not to be "com," nor particularly "rom" either.

"I can't believe we wasted two hours of our life," Amber mumbled as she stretched her arms and legs out.

"Did you lock the doors earlier?"

"After those tools got vandalised? Too right."

Even so, I couldn't help peering out into the darkness after I'd turned off my bedroom light. A sliver of moonlight reflected off the sludgy water in an old stone birdbath nestled amidst the tangled brambles out the back. Another project for the future. I'd add it to the list.

Hey, what was that? A shadow moved outside, and my chest seized. Where was my phone? I snatched it off the nightstand, then returned to the window in time to see a huge fox stalk across the garden. Phew. False alarm. I watched for a few minutes longer, but apart from the whisper of the breeze through the evergreens, all was still, and I slid between my chilly sheets. It was nights like this I missed Wes. I made a mental note to buy an electric blanket, which would serve the same purpose as well as being more reliable and cheaper to run.

By the early hours, I'd had a dirty dream about somebody I shouldn't have and a rethink on the electric blanket position. I was quite hot enough now, not to mention slightly sweaty and wide awake. Damn that man. I'd danced with him once. Once! What gave him the right to invade my dreams like that?

By six, I gave up on the idea of getting back to sleep and headed for the kitchen. At least I'd have time for a leisurely breakfast and two cups of tea before I had to face the outside world. Although if the sound of rain on my window in the early hours was any indication, I didn't want to set foot outside the door.

Amber peered at my notepad as she wandered into the kitchen at seven, yawning. "Up early?"

"I couldn't sleep."

"What's that?" She pointed at my doodles.

"My plans for the tropical borders behind the house in, say, a year's time. I can't wait to get started on them, but I've got so much other stuff to do first."

"You'll get there. I feel that way about the house too. I really want to work on the bedrooms, but downstairs takes priority. The spiders get to keep their digs for a bit longer."

"That makes me feel a little better." I glanced outside, where daylight was beginning to win the battle against the darkness. "Still, I need to get going. Vince'll be here at eight, and he's lending me his pressure washer to do the terrace."

"Let's hope it doesn't freeze tonight, then, or we'll all be going ice skating tomorrow morning."

"Weather forecast reckons it'll stay above zero until the end of the week."

But only just. I shivered as I pulled on an extra pair of socks to wear inside my wellies. At least my feet would stay warm and dry, which was more than could be said for the rest of me. I'd only used a pressure washer a handful of times, and the fine spray clung to everything.

I slipped out the front door and sat on the bench to pull my boots on. Then screamed.

Amber wrenched the door open behind me. "What? What's happened?"

I pointed silently at the eight-inch carving knife embedded in the toe of one of her wellies, the shiny blade horribly at odds with the Cath Kidston florals.

"Holy shit," she whispered, collapsing beside me on the seat. "Did you put that there?"

"Of course not!"

"Sorry. Just clutching at straws."

Amber reached out, and I smacked her hand away.

"Don't touch it. We need to call the police."

"Oh, yeah."

I got up, but she slumped back on the bench and began trembling.

"Come on, we can't stay out here."

She didn't move, and I tried to work out the best option—lock ourselves back inside or sprint to the main house. I longed for Lars's steady words or Marlene's take-charge personality, but there was no way Amber was up to running anywhere, and I wasn't leaving her alone or going by myself either.

"We have to go back into the cottage. Please. Can you stand?"

"I-I-I..."

"What's up, ladies?"

A shriek had already escaped by the time I realised it was only Vince coming towards us, and his smile quickly turned to worry.

"What happened?"

"S-s-someone put a knife through Amber's boot."

It only took him half a second to assess the situation. Thank goodness he'd arrived early.

"Back inside. Now."

I tripped over my feet trying to do as I was told, and when Amber didn't move, he picked her up and half threw her in after me. Only when the door was securely bolted behind us and he'd settled Amber on the sofa did he speak again.

"Are you okay?"

"Yes. I mean, nobody hurt me. I didn't even see anyone, just went to put my boots on and the knife was there beside them."

He stared towards the front window. "I bet whoever did it is long gone. Amber, when did you last wear the boots?"

"Uh... Th-th-the day before yesterday." She'd lost all her colour, and I reached out to tug her dressing gown closed.

"Shit. I was hoping it could have happened at the same time as the tools."

"It must have happened last night," I said. "I wore my boots yesterday, and they were right next to Amber's. I'd have noticed the knife if it was there then."

"Did you see anyone last night? This morning?"

"No, nothing. Well, I saw a shadow in the garden before I went to bed, but I thought it was a fox."

He pulled out his phone. "Right, I'd better call the main house, and then the police."

A tear rolled down Amber's cheek as I fought against the bile that rose in my throat. The tools being vandalised was bad enough, but I'd more or less convinced myself that was kids. This was different. A knife? That was a threat, and one I didn't think I'd ever get out of my head.

CHAPTER 13

VINCE TOLD MARLENE to stay at the house with Lars, but she was having none of it. Five minutes later, she turned up in a jogging suit with Lars in tow.

"Are the police on their way?" she asked Vince.

"Yes, they promised to send someone out again."

"Good. Nye's coming too. Nobody threatens my girls and gets away with it."

"Nye? Why Nye?" I asked.

"He works at some detective agency in London. Ivy says he's very good at his job."

I bet he was. I'd certainly confess to committing a crime if it meant he'd frisk me. No! *Dove, stop thinking that way.* This was a very serious problem.

"When will he be here?" Vince asked.

"Late morning, Ivy promised."

"And the cops reckoned a couple of hours until they arrive." Marlene tutted, but Vince laid a hand on her shoulder. "They say it's not a priority as nobody's hurt, and I can see their point. The knife isn't going anywhere. In the meantime, you, Amber, and Lars need to stay in the main house. I'll keep Dove near me in the garden."

Amber shook her head, bottom lip quivering. "What? You think we can carry on as normal after this?"

"We have to. Whoever broke Dove's tools and left that knife in your boot is looking for a reaction, and the best thing you...we can do is not to give them one. So yes, we get on with life."

"He's right, sweetie," Marlene said. "Don't give that monster the satisfaction."

I nodded, hoping nobody noticed my hands shaking.

"Come on," I said to Amber. "Let's get you dressed, and I'll walk over to the house with you." Inside, I didn't feel much braver than her, but I couldn't make the situation worse by showing that.

She allowed me to help her upstairs, and I waited on the landing while she dressed in leggings and a woollen tunic. Usually, Amber looked perfectly put-together with impossibly neat eyeliner and not a hair out of place, but this morning, she hadn't bothered with make-up at all and just shoved her hair up into a messy bun. Although even that looked hipster rather than pitiful.

"It'll be okay," I said as we walked downstairs. "It's probably just some weirdo messing around."

"What if it isn't?"

I didn't have an answer for that.

"Why do you think this is happening?" I asked Vince as we headed for the woods. He'd said I needed to stay in sight, so rather than working on the terrace as I'd planned, I'd be spending the morning hauling branches to the wood chipper.

"The world's full of sick people."

"But it started right after I arrived."

"Could be a coincidence."

"It was my tools that got broken, and that knife could have been meant for me. I mean, what if someone thought those boots were mine and not Amber's?"

Vince wrapped an arm around my shoulders. "Don't think about it, at least for this morning. It's what he wants."

Vince certainly tried his best to keep my mind off things with the amount of work he gave me. Branch after branch fell to the ground, and by the time I'd shredded all the bits I was able to pick up, I could barely lift my arms. At eleven, Vince climbed down from an old oak tree and unhooked his climbing harness.

"You've done well. We'll stack the logs for firewood later."

"Can't move."

"It's good exercise."

"How do you do this every day?"

"Practice." His phone rang, and he held it to his ear for a moment. "That was Marlene. The police are here."

As was Nye. My heart did a little skip when I walked in and saw him sitting at the kitchen table. The man was perfect—great body, sexy smile, and friendly too. And best of all, he was taken, so there was no temptation. I could admire him safe in the knowledge that he was off limits, which fitted in perfectly with my new policy on love.

Constable Newington, as he introduced himself, was in his mid-forties at a guess, and wore the jaded look of a man going through the motions with little hope of a positive outcome.

"So, you say you didn't hear anything or see anything concrete until you went to put your boots on in the morning?"

"That's right."

He sucked in a breath. "Well, we'll check for fingerprints and the like, but..."

He trailed off, and I knew not to get my hopes up. "What about the lady in the Northbury Arms? She said the villagers weren't happy I was here. Or Percy, the gardener? Maybe he's holding a grudge?"

Newington shook his head. "Old Percy's always drunk by evening. I doubt he'd have enough faculties to pull a stunt like that. You'd be more likely to find him passed out on the lawn."

"But..."

"I'll ask around, don't worry."

Marlene slammed the door after him, her lips pursed into a thin line. "Well, that man doesn't deserve to wear a badge."

Nye knocked back a mouthful of coffee. "It's the same everywhere. The police are overworked, underpaid, and drowning in a sea of paperwork. I can't blame them for getting demoralised, especially once they've been on the force for a while. Once they get to forty, it's all downhill to retirement."

"So, Sherlock, what can you do to help?"

Nye glared at her. "Nothing, if you keep calling me Sherlock."

"Ivy calls you Sherlock."

"Yes, and I hate it, but she says she's got grandmother's rights."

Marlene laughed. "Okay, Mr. Holmes. No

Sherlock."

Did she ever stop? Even though Nye was less than half her age, she couldn't help flirting with him and did a far better job than I would have.

He picked up one of Lars's homemade cookies and bit off a chunk, then chewed slowly.

"The motive bothers me. Both incidents have been at the cottage, not the house. Marlene, if someone wanted to get your attention, they'd have hit closer to home. Which leaves Dove and Amber. Dove, Marlene said you'd split up with a boyfriend recently. Amicable?"

Oh, wonderful. My failed love life rehashed for an audience. "Not amicable, exactly, but we didn't scream and throw things. I found out he was cheating, he stormed out of the flat, and then I packed and left."

Nye raised an eyebrow. "If he was the one cheating, I'm surprised you *didn't* scream and throw things."

Putting into words what I'd only just found the courage to admit to myself was difficult. "To be that upset, I'd have needed to love him, and all that had been gone from our relationship for a while. I'd already planned to leave before I found out about the other woman. I just brought it forwards a bit."

"Was he upset when you left so suddenly? I understand you ran a business together as well."

"We had different ideas there too. He wanted to expand into dog walking, and I preferred to focus on the plants. Sure, me leaving probably caused him inconvenience for a while because he'd have had to do some work himself, but long-term? I can't see him being devastated."

"What about the money he needed to spend on

buying out your share?"

"Huh? I didn't ask for any money."

"Really?" Nye shook his head like I'd missed a trick. "Okay, so I'll move him down the list. Did you have problems with anyone else in London?"

"Only Darren. He calls himself the Queen of Green. But he was a competitor, and with me leaving, I don't see how he'd gain from following me here. It's not as if he'd want to scare me into going back to London."

"Understood. I'll have a poke around and also look into that woman from the pub. Any idea who she was?"

I shook my head. "Eddie might know." I closed my eyes. "Or Peter. I was having dinner with him."

"Peter Griffin from Bell End Farm?"

"I never knew his last name. Marlene arranged the date for me."

Nye burst out laughing and turned to her. "Dove and Peter Griffin? What were you thinking?"

"He's a veterinarian. They make good money."

"I went to school with Peter Griffin. When he was fifteen, he brought a girl in our class a slow worm on St. Valentine's Day. I can still hear her screams now."

"Ivy didn't tell me that."

A freaking slow worm? I'd got off lightly. "Uh, he's called me a few times since then, but it seems to be tailing off now."

"Sounds about right," Nye said. "He never was good with girls. Always preferred cows. He's got a herd of Friesians on the farm, and they've all got women's names."

"Do you think he'd do anything odd?" Marlene asked.

"Like the knife?"

She nodded.

"I doubt it. I'll take a closer look at him just in case, but there are other avenues I think are more likely to be fruitful, and I need to speak to everyone else in the household first. Amber, have you noticed anybody strange recently? Here or in the village?"

"I need to use the bathroom."

Before any of us could say another word, she hurried from the room, head down.

Marlene and Vince watched her go, Nye watched Marlene and Vince, and I watched Nye. Lars carried on eating half a grapefruit.

"Is she always that nervy?" Nye asked.

"Well, no," Marlene said. "But it's not every day a knife-wielding maniac comes to visit."

Nye spun his phone in his fingers, paused to check the screen, then spun it again. "True. But Dove isn't shaking, and from what I've seen of both girls, if I was a betting man, I'd have put money on Amber holding up better than Dove."

"Thanks," I said.

"Just an observation."

"So, what? You think she's hiding something?" Marlene asked.

"Yeah, I do."

Footsteps on the tiled floor outside the door heralded Amber's return, and everyone except Nye desperately tried to look as if we hadn't been discussing her behind her back.

"Everything okay?" he asked as she slid back into her seat. He kept his tone light, but now he'd revealed his thoughts, I detected a layer of granite underneath.

"Y-y-yes."

"Did you think about my question?"

"I haven't seen anybody odd around."

"Heard any rumours? A stranger in Northbury? A newcomer?"

She shook her head, eyes fixed on the table.

Nye thumped the wooden surface, making everyone jump, not least of all me. Lars's coffee slopped over the edge of his cup and formed a puddle in the saucer.

"I don't believe you."

"But I didn't see anything!"

"Nye..." Marlene warned.

He held up a hand. "You might not have seen anything, but you know something. I want to know what."

Tears trickled from Amber's eyes and splashed onto the table. I longed to give her a hug, but when I started to get up, Nye glared at me and shook his head.

"I-I-I did something bad. Before I came here."

"Like what?"

"When I met Steve last year, it was love at first sight. I know that sounds corny and all, but trust me, I never believed in it until that moment in the Garrison pub either. One look, and we knew we wanted to be together, but the problem was, we were both already involved with other people."

"And?" Nye asked. I wasn't sure I wanted to hear the answer, even if I'd already guessed.

"We spent that night together."

Her face crumpled as she wept, and even though her distress made my heart ache, I couldn't bring myself to comfort her. Cheating didn't sit well with me, especially after what Wes did.

"We didn't mean to," she sobbed. "It just happened.

I told my boyfriend the next day that we were over, and he didn't seem all that bothered. It was more of a casual thing, anyway."

"And Steve's girlfriend?"

Something else flashed in Amber's eyes. Fear. "She was supposed to be away on a work trip."

"Supposed to be?"

"She came back early and walked right in on us." Amber's voice dropped so we could hardly hear her. "She said she'd kill me."

Nye remained dispassionate, cold even. "You think she was serious? Or did she say it in the heat of the moment?"

"Steve tried to calm her down, but she wouldn't stop shouting. Over and over again. She'd kill me. She'd kill me." Amber put her hands over her ears. "I'll kill you. I'll kill you."

Nye's face softened as Amber collapsed forwards, and no matter what she'd done, I couldn't leave her like that. I shoved my chair back and went to her side.

"It'll be okay," I whispered into her hair.

"Did she do anything?" Nye asked.

"Spread rumours about me. Sent text messages telling me what a horrible person I am. Tried to hit me with her car once."

"Is that why you moved?"

She nodded. "When Steve got posted to Afghanistan, I was scared to stay near the base alone. Natalie's got too many friends."

Marlene pressed her lips together, eyes narrowed. "So you decided to bring your trouble here instead?"

"I didn't mean to, I swear. I didn't tell a soul from that area where I was going. I'll leave. Please, just give me time to pack."

"No, missy, you won't leave. Many women have been scorned over the years, and while I can't condone what you did, threatening violence isn't the answer, especially when it involves coming onto my property and upsetting Dove too. Nye, I want to hire your company to solve this problem."

"You don't have to—" Amber began, but Marlene waved her quiet.

"I'm not starting again with a different designer. You've done wonders with this house. Nye?"

"I'll get a contract drawn up. What do you want?"

"What do you recommend?"

"I'd suggest ramping up security at the house and cottage—burglar alarms, movement-activated lights, improved door and window locks, CCTV. And until we can get that lot installed, a man on-site to keep an eye on things."

"Do it. Nobody messes with Marlene Grande."

Chapter 14

"DO YOU WANT something to eat?" I asked.

Amber sat on the sofa, knees drawn up to her chin, exactly the way she'd been for the last half hour. At least she'd stopped crying now.

With no answer from her, I poured coffee granules and hot water into two mugs anyway, taking comfort in normality for a few minutes. I suppose I should have been relieved at the prospect that the attacks weren't aimed at me, but it was impossible to relax, not with my friend still in danger.

"When does Steve get back?"

"Three months. Marlene said he could stay here while he's on leave, and then he's off on deployment again." She looked up at me with worried eyes. "Are you okay with him sleeping in the cottage?"

Short term, I could cope with anything. Surely Steve wouldn't be messier than Wes?

"Of course. And it'll be summer by then. The terrace'll be finished and we can barbecue rather than having to squash into the kitchen."

She managed a weak smile. "I've got a good recipe for marinade."

"I can do coleslaw. Who knows, if I get my act together I might even be able to grow the vegetables to put in it."

I'd need to get seeds first, and without the greenhouse being in a useable condition at the moment, I'd be restricted as to what I could grow because any seedlings outside would get killed off by the frost. But I could germinate plants on the windowsills next to the orchids and buy cloches to protect them outdoors once the weather got a bit warmer. Hopefully, Lars wouldn't mind giving me a lift to the garden centre sometime over the next few days.

A knock on the door shook me out of my thoughts, and I peeped through the lounge window to see who it was. Nye. I realised my heart was hammering in my chest. *Calm down, Dove. Calm down.* Nobody was going to attack in broad daylight.

"How is she?" Nye asked once I'd let him in, keeping his voice low.

"Talking again, which is good. Did you have any luck with organising things?"

"My go-to guy for security systems is up north until Thursday. We'll send him a layout for the house so he can think things through, and he'll start work on Friday."

Three days away. "So we're on our own until then?"

"No, of course not. I'll shuffle our teams around and have someone come this evening to stay until Spike's got the security system up and running." He sighed. "Grandma's insisting I charge Marlene mate's rates."

"Thank you for doing this."

"Believe me, if I didn't pull out all the stops for Marlene, I'd never hear the end of it."

In a way, we were lucky. Even though Amber and I were living on edge, Marlene took the situation seriously and Nye would send us a babysitter. Tonight, we could sleep again.

Eight o'clock, and I forked off a corner of Lars's lasagne and stared at it. I loved Italian food, but my stomach turned at the thought of eating any more, not when it was dark out and we were still on our own in the main house. Even Marlene seemed subdued.

"Are you sure someone's coming?" Amber asked.

I attempted a reassuring smile. "Nye called half an hour ago to apologise for the delay. Apparently, they needed a lot of manpower for another job today."

"If he doesn't turn up, I'm sleeping on the couch in here tonight."

And I wasn't going back to the cottage alone. "Me too."

My phone beeped, and I fished it out of my pocket, expecting a message from Nye or perhaps Peter even though his communications had dwindled, thank goodness. But it was my mother.

Mum: Dove, when are you coming to visit? You didn't reply to my last message.

Dammit, why? Whenever I trekked across to Somerset to see my parents, I came back feeling like a failure, and with Wes and me not having worked out, she'd have more ammunition than ever to convince me to get a "proper" job, which to my mum and dad involved staring at a computer for ten soul-destroying hours a day.

Dove: I'm really busy with work at the moment. Will try to come soon.

Even though we'd been waiting for it, the *crack* of

the huge iron knocker on the front door made us all jump, and we stared at each other for a moment before Lars shrugged.

"I'll go." His unspoken words: "Nobody's got a beef with me."

Hushed voices drifted through from the hallway, followed by footsteps—Lars's clipped brogues on the tiled floor plus another softer set, barely audible.

Lars was smiling as he came through the door, but any relief that our saviour had come was short lived as my chest seized.

"At least Nye sent us a cute one," Marlene said.

Zander grinned and gave her a salute as he dropped a duffel bag next to his feet. "Always happy to oblige, ma'am." He turned to Amber and me. "Evening, ladies."

Oh, hell. This was who Nye had sent to stay in the cottage with us? Like we didn't have enough problems without a walking ball of testosterone kipping on the sofa. A shiver ran through me at the mere thought.

"Have you eaten?" Lars asked.

"I grabbed a sandwich at the airport."

Marlene preened a little, looking happier than she'd been all evening. "What were you doing at the airport, sweetie?"

Zander bent to kiss her on the cheek. "I was supposed to be working in Edinburgh for a few days, but I got called back."

"Well, we'll do our best to make you feel at home. Amber, Dove—do you want to show Zander the cottage?"

No. No, I didn't. I wanted to show him the door then watch his tail lights recede into the distance as he drove off back to wherever he came from. But I could hardly do that with my employer watching, and besides, Amber needed his help.

She pushed back her chair and got awkwardly to her feet, stumbling against the table. Zander steadied her with an arm around her waist.

"You realise she's got a boyfriend, right?" I said to him.

He levelled his gaze at me. "Yes, I've been briefed."

I stared at his hand, resting on her hip.

"What? Would you rather I let her fall over?"

"I'm sure she can walk by herself."

He leaned down and murmured something in her ear, and she nodded. Zander didn't take his eyes off me as he lowered his arm to his side. "Happy?"

"Delirious."

Marlene clapped her hands and let out a false laugh. "Now, now, kids, you all play nice. Remember, Zander's here to help."

I gritted my teeth. "In that case, let me show you to the cottage."

His eyes burned into my back as I led the way along the path. Shadows danced in the light from my torch, but as a fox ran out in front of me, I barely flinched. Anger fuelled me tonight, enough that if a crazy man did jump from a bush, he'd be the person who needed to watch out, not me. Why Zander? Of all people, why did Nye have to send the only man who'd made me feel something and nothing in one short night?

The instant I opened the cottage door, Amber yawned and headed for the stairs. "I need to sleep. You don't mind, do you?"

"No, you go." I could hardly force her to stay awake,

could I?

"So, where do I sleep?" Zander asked.

I pointed at the sofa, decorated with a couple of coats over the arm and my breakfast plate on the seat. Fingers crossed, I'd dropped toast crumbs all over it.

"And the bathroom?"

"Middle room upstairs. The lock doesn't work, so you'll have to wedge the door closed."

It hadn't mattered when I was only sharing with Amber, but the prospect of doing my business without a solid barrier between me and Zander made me shudder. What if he walked in while I was in the shower? The thought of dragging him into it with me flitted through my mind, and I grabbed the plate and hurried through to the kitchen before he saw me blush. I needed to stop thinking of him that way. A cad. He was a damn cad.

The plate bore the brunt of my frustration as I bent over the sink and scrubbed at the Marmite stains so hard a little bit of the pattern came off the china. I'd have kept going too, if a hand hadn't appeared on the counter either side of me.

"Trying to wash away your dirty thoughts?"

The sound of the plate cracking as I dropped it in the sink covered my gasp. "How dare you?"

"Am I wrong?"

That...that asshole. "No! I mean, you're wrong. I wasn't having dirty thoughts."

"Really? I notice you hesitated before you answered there."

I writhed around to face him, then gave his chest a hard shove. He didn't move, not even an inch.

"Get off me!"

"You're the one touching me."

"Well, get un-around me."

"What's wrong, Dove? We got on so well on Sunday night, and now you're channelling a sulky teenager."

I folded my arms. "Am not." He started laughing. Dammit, he was right. "You drive me to it."

"How? I've only met you once before."

"You're a womaniser."

"I won't deny I enjoy women's company." He closed his eyes and let out a slow breath. "In very small doses. But they know exactly what they're getting into."

That was more or less what Olivia had said, but it still didn't sit right. "You use them."

"And they use me."

"Melissa didn't feel that way."

He grinned. "Clarissa."

Whatever. "You hurt her." And me, I didn't add. "Any time a woman gives a piece of herself to a man like that, it means something."

I jumped as he reached out and tucked a lock of hair behind my ear then leaned in closer. "Ivy was right —you're a sensitive girl, Dove. I'm sorry somebody hurt you."

"Ivy talked to you about me?" What had she said?

"Warned me, more like, although I suspect that came via Marlene. If I want to get invited to Northbury Hall again, I have to keep my hands off." He shuffled forwards until he pressed against me with everything but his hands. "Even so, for a night with you, being banished would be worth it. But you're not that kind of girl."

I was speechless. Could he hear my heart hammering in my chest? Feel it? Any second now, I thought it would smash out of my ribcage.

"And you're in luck," he continued. "Because I've got two rules. Firstly, I never spend more than one night with a woman."

I'd worked that one out. "And the second?" I whispered.

"I don't fuck clients." He dropped his hands and took two paces back. "So congratulations, Miss Hallam. You're now untouchable."

Zander was already dressed when I got up in the morning, working at a laptop on the sofa. Even after what he said last night, I'd still piled six towels behind the bathroom door as I showered, as well as the scales, the stool from next to the basin, and Amber's industrial-sized bottle of hair conditioner.

"Did you hear anything last night?" I asked when I made it downstairs, vowing to keep our conversations about work. Work was safe.

"Nope. I set up motion sensors at the front and back before I went to sleep, but nothing tripped them."

"That's good. What will you do today? Go out and interview people?"

"Maybe. But I'll take a wander around the estate to get a feel for the place, then do some research first." His expression softened. "You feeling better this morning?"

"Fine."

Amber appeared, and today she looked a bit more like her normal self. Her hair was still a bohemian mess, but she'd put on make-up—eyeliner, mascara, and red lipstick. I rubbed my own lips together self-consciously. All I ever wore was a touch of lip balm, and not for the first time in my life, I felt inadequate.

"Shall I make coffee?" she offered.

"I'm gonna go to the main house and get the proper stuff from the coffee machine." I deserved that much at least.

"Then we're all going," Zander said. "I'm supposed to keep you both safe."

"Don't worry. Vince'll be here in a minute, and I can go with him."

"Vince is the tree surgeon?"

"That's right." And not a reprobate like Zander.

"I want to meet him before you go anywhere alone."

"You can't seriously think this was Vince? You're supposed to be looking at Steve's ex-girlfriend."

"In my eyes, everyone's a suspect. How long have you known Vince?"

"Not long," I admitted.

"Precisely. I prefer to keep an open mind. Natalie's one possibility, but there are a lot of other people in the village you've both come into contact with, and I understand from Nye you already received a warning in the pub."

True, but Vince? Just then, I saw him approaching up the path and pulled my coat on. Zander could do what he wanted, but I was getting coffee with Vince and then I was going to work. Did Zander plan to investigate everyone in the village? Where would he stop? Vince? Lars? All the people in the Northbury Arms? Neil? The Hearsts? Everyone on Ivy's guest list? Peter? Eddie? Hey, perhaps while he was at it, he could drive to London and drag Wes in for questioning. And

Magda.

"What's up with you?" Vince asked as I bolted out the door. "You look as if you want to gouge someone's eyes out."

"Sorry. It's not you. Nye's sidekick arrived last night, and he's already driving me crazy."

Vince settled an arm over my shoulders. "I'm sure he's only doing his job, and speaking of which, are you okay to help me out in the woods again today?"

My back and shoulders still ached from yesterday, but anything was better than being near the house with a man who preferred to investigate women's underwear rather than actual cases. "Of course."

Speak of the devil. Zander strode out of the cottage, making a beeline for Vince, and he didn't look happy.

Marvellous.

CHAPTER 15

"OKAY, I'M OFFICIALLY dead." I sank onto a tree stump and stretched out my limbs one by one, grimacing at the burn.

Vince looked up at the sky. "Don't think that matters today. Looks as if we're in for a storm this afternoon."

"I mean it. You're gonna have to carry me back to the house."

"I could call Zander if you want? He seemed awfully protective of you earlier."

"Don't you dare." The first meeting between Zander and Vince had been like two stags fighting, with neither of them wanting to give up their territory. I was waiting for them to lock horns, but thankfully, Lars had stepped in with croissants and calmed everybody down. "I can't believe he suspects you've got something to do with this."

"He wouldn't be doing his job properly if he didn't ask questions. It was the part where he tried to make you stay inside I objected to. He needs to realise your passion lies outdoors, and that's not something you can ignore."

"Why don't you take a week off, Dove?" I mimicked.

"He only suggested that because he cares. That much is obvious."

He did? "Well, he's got a funny way of showing it."

Vince picked up the last two logs we'd chopped and stacked them on the pile. We'd filled up the small log store beside the cottage and the bigger one next to the main house, and we hadn't quite worked out where to put the rest of them. I'd jokingly suggested having a really big bonfire, and Marlene had latched onto the idea. Now she and Ivy were planning their fireworks party for November the fifth, something they hoped would go with a real bang. Amber's expression of shock had mirrored my own when Marlene suggested it, but as Lars whispered, we still had the best part of a year to change her mind. Either that, or we'd get a whole posse of firemen turning up, which admittedly had its plus points.

"Cut Zander some slack," Vince said. "He works for Blackwood Security, and if he didn't know his stuff, he wouldn't have a job there. The people who run it don't mess around."

"You know them?"

"Only by reputation. They do government work as well, and when I was in the marines, I heard stories. Trust me when I say you don't want to get on their bad side. Now, do you want me to carry you to the truck?"

Didn't want to get on their bad side? Oh, that sounded reassuring. "You're leaving?"

"It's not safe clambering around in a tree with a chainsaw in the rain. I heard of a guy who chopped his arm off that way. Since Zander's here, I thought I'd head home and spend the afternoon with my girlfriend. She's been giving me grief lately for working too many hours."

Dammit, why were the good ones always taken?

Vince was right about the storm. Just after lunch, a rumble of thunder heralded the arrival of a deluge from the heavens. Amber was stencilling a pattern of leaves on the dining room wall, working in silence and concentrating on every brushstroke as I ran inside to shelter. "Where are the others?" I asked.

"Marlene's gone to see Ivy, Lars is cooking, and Zander's in the living room."

I peered out at the rain again. The garden was a washout, but if Lars took me to the garden centre, I could buy the seeds, compost, and trays I needed to start off some seedlings. And judging by the smells coming from the kitchen, I suspected he was making cookies, so even if he didn't have time to take me, it was well worth a visit to his lair.

"Are those chocolate chip?" I asked him.

"Yes, but you'll have to wait five minutes until they're cooked, and then they need to cool. If you want the double chocolate, I'll be putting those into the oven after."

"So you'll be busy cooking all afternoon?"

"Yes, that's the plan. I've also got a birthday cake to make for a friend of Ivy and Marlene's."

"Oh." On the plus side, at least I'd get two kinds of cookies.

"Why do you ask?"

"I need to go to the garden centre at some point, but it can wait."

A voice came from the hallway. "I'll take you."

Zander leaned on the doorjamb, wearing a black

jumper that looked so soft I wanted to steal it. Minus its owner, of course, even if he did have a smile that made my insides go funny.

He raised an eyebrow, waiting for my answer. Yes or no? Well, the only thing worse than being stuck in a house with Zander while it rained would be sitting in a car next to him.

"Thanks, but it's fine. I can go another day."

"I'm driving Marlene to London tomorrow," Lars said. "Soonest I can do is Friday."

"Aren't you supposed to be looking after Amber as well as me?" I asked Zander.

"She'll be fine in here with Lars for a couple of hours."

If I didn't get the seeds planted soon, it would be too late, especially for the onions, which took so long to grow. Tradition dictated I should have planted them on Boxing Day, so I was already a month late. Dammit, if I refused a lift, I'd look like the unreasonable one, and what did Vince say to me this morning? Cut the guy some slack?

"In that case, thank you. When will you be ready to go?"

"Now's as good a time as any."

"I'll just grab my handbag from the cottage."

"There's an umbrella by the door," Lars told me.

Wonderful. Now all I needed was a canoe to get up the path, and I'd be set.

"Is this your car?" I asked as Zander led the way to a BMW 5 Series. The rain had eased from torrential to merely pissing it down.

"Whose else would it be?"

"I thought perhaps it was a company car. I mean, it's a bit 'salesman.'"

He bleeped the locks and opened the door for me, brows knitted together. "Salesman? So what sort of car did you think I'd drive?"

"Something flashier, I guess." Something that matched his looks. "A Porsche? An Aston Martin?"

"We're not all James Bond, you know. I rarely get into car chases, and I've never shot anyone. And do you know how difficult it would be to follow someone covertly in an Aston Martin? I'd rather blend in."

I stared at him. "Blend in? I bet every woman within a hundred-yard radius watches when you walk past."

Dammit, I couldn't believe I'd just said that out loud.

The corner of Zander's lip quirked, but he didn't reply until he'd got behind the wheel and started the engine. "The question is, Dove, are you one of them?"

That wasn't the sort of question I could answer without sounding like an idiot, so I opted for the silent treatment, at least until we'd cleared the outskirts of the village. When that got too painful, I turned on the radio and fiddled with the buttons until I found a station playing old pop songs.

"Do you know where you're going?" I asked, mainly because I didn't.

"Lars gave me directions to the garden centre while you were getting your bag, and I programmed the satnav. Could have built the thing too, with the amount of time you took."

"I needed to change my jumper," I mumbled. And possibly I'd stopped to brush my hair and put on a touch of lip gloss.

"Are you planning to buy much?"

I leaned back into the leather seat, thinking through my list as the trees whipped past on either side of the lane. The countryside was so different to London—it was almost like driving in a tunnel where the boughs met overhead, and big dollops of water plopped onto the windscreen.

"Nothing big. Well, except a bag of compost. Mostly packets of seeds and trays to plant them in."

Zander changed down a gear as we approached a side turning, and a triangular sign warned of a steep gradient. From the top of the hill, the view across the valley was stunning, and for a few seconds, even Zander glanced across to enjoy it. Then the trees closed in again.

"Will the compost make my car boot dirty?" he asked. "Fuck!"

Honestly, was there really any need for that language? It was only a bag of compost. "Look, if it bothers you, we can buy some rubbish sacks to line the boot with." But Zander wasn't listening. "What's wrong? Why are we speeding up? You're going too fast for the bend!"

"The damn brakes have stopped working."

"Are you joking?" I asked, but the way his knuckles turned white as he gripped the steering wheel told me he wasn't. A shriek escaped as I grabbed onto the door handle with one hand and the seat belt with the other.

Zander pulled on the handbrake, but that barely made a difference to the vehicle's pace. Another "fuck" left his lips as he steered to the left, scraping the side of the car along the earth bank beside the road to try and scrub some speed off. The wing mirror nearest me popped into the air, and I screamed again as the window behind my ear shattered.

"Hang on."

"I am hanging on!"

The smell of rubber filled the cabin as the tyres scraped against rocks and tree roots, and I didn't know whether to close my eyes or keep them open. Did I want to see death coming?

Then it got worse. A little green hatchback appeared around the bend, and the lane was too narrow for both of us to pass even if we'd been going a sensible speed rather than—I glanced over at the speedometer—fifty miles an hour. I just caught sight of the shocked expression on the lady's face as Zander jerked the wheel to the side and launched us up the verge. Then we were flying through the air, as gracefully as two tons of rather battered metal could, just as the opening bars of Queen's "Who Wants to Live Forever?" played on the radio.

Twigs crackled as the BMW flew through a hedge, then...nothing.

CHAPTER 16

"DOVE? DOVE!"

"WHAT...?" I tried to open my eyes, but they'd been glued shut and didn't want to cooperate. Why did everything hurt? My muscles had been sore after Vince made me carry an entire tree, but this was a whole other level of pain.

"Dove? Are you awake?"

I didn't know. Was I? I tried again with my eyes and got one to crack open. White curtains blew in the breeze. White with streaks of red on them. Then a hand clamped around my wrist, and I screamed.

"Thank goodness. Are you okay? What hurts?"

"Everything." I put my free hand up to my face and tried to pull my eyes open properly. They resisted for a second, and then I rejoined the land of the living, although I kind of wished I hadn't. Zander's car was wrapped around a tree, broken glass filled my lap, and the tattered remains of airbags hung limply from the wreckage. "What happened?"

"BMWs weren't designed to fly."

I tried to reach for my seat belt, but Zander held me still.

"Don't move. I've already called the office, so help's on its way, and if you've damaged anything, I don't want you to make it worse."

"Are you okay?"

"I'll live. Can't get out, though, not with that tree wedged against my door."

"Did you say the brakes stopped working?"

His mouth set in a grim line. "Yeah, I did. Up until we got to that hill I'd barely used them, but the moment I tried to apply them strongly, the pedal went straight to the floor."

"We could have died."

He let go of my arm and twined my fingers between his instead. "But we didn't. Stay positive and don't dwell on what might have happened."

A tear rolled down my cheek, mingling with blood that trickled from my nose before it dripped onto my shirt. "But—"

"Dove, don't." He released my hand to fish around in his pocket, then passed me a handkerchief. "Here."

"I'm sorry. I'm so sorry. If I hadn't wanted to go to the garden centre..."

"It would have happened next time I drove the car." He squeezed my hand again. "I'm only sorry you were with me. Usually when I give a girl a wild ride, it's a whole lot more pleasurable."

I couldn't help giggling at his crudeness in spite of the situation. "You're an asshole. Did anyone ever tell you that?"

"Many times. Melissa, for one."

"Clarissa."

"Whatever." He began to laugh, then stopped abruptly.

"Are you okay?"

"My side hurts. I'm sure it's nothing."

Footsteps crashing through the undergrowth made

us both turn our heads, and a second later, Nye's head appeared in Zander's window.

"Fuck me. Are you okay?"

"More or less."

"And Dove?"

"Shaken."

"Not much of a first date, Zee."

"We were going to the garden centre," Zander told him.

"You? In a garden centre? You've only got one plant, and it's made of plastic."

"Dove needed stuff for work, only someone had other ideas."

"What do you mean by that?"

"The brakes failed. Do you know how likely that is to happen?"

Nye's black expression told me it wasn't very likely. "You reckon our mystery person's been testing out their automotive knowledge?"

"I left the car out front in the driveway last night. Fuck. It was wide open."

"We had no indication things would escalate this way."

"I should have anticipated—"

"Zander." It was my turn to grip *his* hand. "Don't blame yourself. Please. Like you said, we need to stay positive—we're both more or less okay."

His fingers wrapped tighter around mine, but he wouldn't make eye contact.

"I want this car checked thoroughly."

"I'll make sure of it," Nye said.

It took the fire brigade another hour to cut us free from the car, and even though we both protested we could walk, they insisted on strapping us to spinal boards. I went in the first ambulance with Nye as a paramedic assured me Zander would follow on shortly.

"Do you think we'll have to stay in the hospital?" I had a killer headache, but at least my nose had stopped bleeding.

Nye shrugged. "We'll see what the doctors have to say."

Wonderful. Just as long as nobody called my parents. If Mother found out, she'd be there in no time to lecture me on the dangers of gardening, riding in cars with strangers, and taking too many antibiotics.

Two hours later, I'd been poked, prodded, and X-rayed, and a nurse who reminded me of my Grandma Kathleen pronounced me ready to leave. "Just take it easy for a few days, lovey. You've got awfully banged up."

"Do you know where Zander is?"

"That nice young man who came in after you?"

Something like that. "Yes, him."

"The doctor's just finished fixing up that nasty hole in his side. Twenty-three stitches." She shook her head. "Not many men would have been walking after that much blood loss."

"What? He said he was okay."

"Maybe you misheard him? He certainly needed medical attention."

Bloody hell. Zander had been talking to me, making me laugh, and all the time he was badly hurt. With the black jumper he was wearing, I hadn't noticed the blood.

"Can I see him?"

The nurse gave me a kind smile. "Of course, lovey.

If I had a man like that, I wouldn't want him out of my sight either."

"Oh, we're not—"

"He's in the end cubicle to your right."

As soon as she left, I rolled off the bed and slipped my trainers on. The bloodstains decorating the tops of them were a reminder of the earlier horrors that I didn't need. They'd be going in the bin the moment I got home.

The end cubicle on the right, the nurse said. I crept along the corridor until I reached the closed curtain, praying I hadn't got the wrong bed. The last thing I wanted to do was to walk in on a stranger.

Oh, for heaven's sake. "Don't you ever stop?"

A pretty nurse perched on the edge of Zander's bed, his hand resting on her thigh. Medical attention. Right. She looked at me and pouted, then slowly stood up. "Call me," she said, before sashaying off along the corridor.

"I can't help it," he said.

"Try." I took her place, minus Zander's hand. "You and me, we've got to have a serious talk about communication."

"I thought we were getting on better. You haven't called me an asshole for a couple of hours now."

"Asshole. The nurse said you had a nasty cut. Why didn't you mention that?"

"Didn't want to worry you. Being trapped in the car was quite bad enough."

"But—"

"What could you have done? Nothing. The ambulance was on its way, and it wasn't bleeding fast enough to be life-threatening."

"You're impossible."

"You like me that way, admit it."

Never. "No, I don't. Most of the time, I don't think I like you at all."

He clutched at his chest. "Now I'm hurt."

"Good thing you're in a hospital then, isn't it?"

"Not for long. I'll be out of here as soon as Nye brings me new clothes. The nurses insisted on cutting me out of my other ones. I offered to undress myself, but there were four of them and they were enjoying themselves."

Yes, totally impossible. "Do women ever not fall at your feet?"

"You haven't. Yet," he added under his breath.

"Don't get your hopes up, pretty boy. Besides, I thought I was untouchable?"

"A guy can dream. Reckon Lars is making something good for dinner?"

Was he serious about the dreaming part? Or just messing with me? Mind you, even if he did mean what he said, being one more on top of the other 364 other women he undoubtedly slept with every year wouldn't exactly make me feel special.

"Is that all you think of? Sex and food?"

"I'm a man. You expected something more?"

I recalled Vince's words about Blackwood, and I also suspected Nye wouldn't foist an idiot on his grandma's best friend, not if he wanted to stay in Ivy's good books. Not to mention the way Zander had stayed cool as liquid nitrogen when the brakes failed. His attempts to slow the car down undoubtedly saved us from worse injuries.

"Oh, I think you've got more, and I'm waiting to see

it."

CHAPTER 17

NYE DROPPED US back at the Arndale estate. I thought he'd head off up the driveway afterwards, but he surprised me by carrying on around the house and pulling into the double garage next to the Rolls Royce.

"Are you staying for dinner?"

"Until Spike's finished installing the security system, you've got Zander in the cottage and I'm camping out in the lounge to keep an eye on Marlene."

"Don't you have work to do?"

"I also have a grandma I love dearly, even if she does try my patience at times."

Lars had done us proud again with... Well, I couldn't pronounce the name, but it was fish wrapped in pastry. I ate until I was stuffed, then finished off with three cookies seeing as I'd missed out at lunchtime. While I ate, I snuck a glance or two over at Zander. Despite his insistence everything was fine, he looked stiff and uncomfortable, and that only got more pronounced as he walked Amber and me back to the cottage.

"You're not okay."

"I only need another painkiller."

"You should be at home resting, not working."

"I can sleep here just as easily. Besides, I need to do research for a couple of days, and if I go to the office and do that, I won't be able to move from all the get-well-soon chocolates and sympathy cards."

"You have a lot of women in the office?"

"A few. And they come under rule two. Call it an addendum."

A part of me I didn't care to admit existed sagged in relief at hearing that. Zander had some morals to go with the pheromones he trailed out everywhere.

Amber gave me one last hug before she retired to bed. "I'm so sorry you got hurt."

"We got off lightly under the circumstances."

"I hate this. I hate the idea that I could have brought this on you."

"We don't know that you did. That's why Zander and Nye are here—to find out."

"If it is Natalie, I'll... I'll... I don't know what I'll do, but it won't be pretty."

I hugged her back. "Go to sleep. We'll talk about it tomorrow."

She went upstairs, leaving me with Zander in the lounge. I eyed up the sofa then looked at his side. When I'd rated him one hundred percent asshole, I'd been glad he had to sleep on lumpy cushions a foot too short for his height, but now I'd dropped that percentage by a few points, I felt slightly guilty.

"I can sleep on the sofa tonight. Why don't you take my bed? It'll be more comfortable."

"I'm not leaving you down here alone. You'll be too vulnerable. Unless you want to share, I'm the one sleeping on the sofa."

Share? I thought about it. Hell yeah, I thought about it. What red-blooded woman wouldn't? But in the end I just couldn't. We'd settled into a truce, one where he kept his hands mostly off me and I called him out on his lewd behaviour as I saw fit. It kind of worked. If he planned on sticking around until we caught whoever was trying to hurt us, I didn't want to cause any awkwardness, and sleeping in the same bed, even if nothing exciting happened, would doubtless make things weird.

"Sorry, Zee." I used Nye's nickname for him. "Looks like you're sleeping here, but I can lend you an extra pillow."

"You're all heart, Dee."

Morning brought sunshine, a light frost, and a knock at the door.

"It's Lars," Amber called out. Her bedroom was at the front and overlooked the path from the main house.

"I'll go."

I rushed downstairs, only Zander beat me to it. Wow. If I'd known he slept shirtless, I'd have asked Lars to visit yesterday morning too.

"This came for you and Dove," Lars said, handing over a package.

Zander shook it. "Any idea what it is?"

"Nope. One of the ladies from the village brought it and wished you both a speedy recovery."

"She knew about the crash?"

"The Women's Institute have their weekly meeting on Wednesday evenings. Believe me, the whole village knows about the crash."

Zander closed the front door and turned around, but I barely saw the lumpy parcel wrapped in

Christmas paper. My gaze went straight past it to the jagged line of stitches gracing his right-hand side. A crust of dried blood still clung to the line down the middle.

"Bloody hell."

"Don't dwell on it." He winced as he bent over to rummage in his bag for a clean T-shirt. "It'll be good as new in a couple of weeks."

"What if it leaves a scar?"

"Then it leaves a scar. Who knows, maybe it'll put some of the women off?"

He also had a taut stomach and a six-pack. I couldn't help noticing while I looked at the damage, just because I was checking for bruises, you understand.

"I doubt that."

A smile flickered on his lips, and I also noted he was wearing glasses.

"So, what do you think of men with scars?" he asked.

"I guess it depends."

"On what?"

I was beginning to understand Zander a little better now. At least, I thought so. He flirted outrageously and followed through a lot of the time, but he was also self-deprecating and kept me at arm's length. I had a feeling it wasn't just because of his rule two. And rule one? Something stopped him from getting close to women, and the more time we spent together, the less I thought it was because he was just a man-whore.

So perhaps that was why I said what I said.

"It depends on whether those scars are on the inside or the outside."

He froze, and for a moment, his good-natured mask slipped, replaced by an agony he hadn't shown even with his side sliced open. Today's pain ran deeper. But a second later, his smile ratcheted back into place.

"Don't suppose you'll be too keen on me, then. Shall we open this parcel?"

In those seconds, the ones when I saw Zander raw and true, I wanted to hug him until he healed, but how could I when he hid that side of himself so much of the time? Instead, I forced a smile of my own.

"Sure. It's sweet of her to send a gift. What's with the glasses?"

"I haven't put my contacts in yet."

He didn't have to. The thin wire frames only had the effect of making him look even hotter. Sexy chic. Dammit, I needed a glass of water. Not to drink, but to pour over myself.

Zander ripped the paper open and held up a lumpy woollen pile. "Socks?"

"They look hand-knitted."

"We're supposed to wear them?"

"What else do men do with socks?" We both had the same thought at the same time, and I'd looked at Zander's crotch before I could stop myself.

"Don't need any socks there, Dee."

No. No, he didn't.

And the gifts kept coming throughout the morning, piling up in the dining room at the main house. By eleven, we had a mountain of knitted items, crocheted stuff, and even a needlepoint picture, not to mention enough baked goods to feed an army battalion. After the accident yesterday, Lars and Marlene had cancelled their trip to London, and now Lars hung up his oven mitts in disgust.

"I don't think I'm needed today."

Marlene eyed up the trays of jam tarts. "Sweetie, I don't think you'll be needed for the entire week. Maybe we could donate this to the homeless?"

"I haven't seen many homeless people in Northbury."

"What about London? Nye, could you take some of this in your truck?"

Nye looked up from his laptop. "I'm kind of busy, I'm afraid."

"The fruit cakes will keep," I said. "Perhaps we could freeze the other stuff?"

Zander, now back to wearing contacts, held up a scarf so long the ends reached his knees when he wound it twice around his neck, together with the matching gloves. "I'm more worried that we might be expected to wear these things. Look, those hats have got our initials knitted into them. Were they up all night making this shit?"

I picked up mine, hot pink with a yellow "D" and a pompom on the top, and pulled it on. The edge reached the bottom of my nose, and Zander rolled it up until I could see again.

"Cute," he said. "Wonder if we can get you the matching jumper?"

"You mean dress."

Nye chuckled then smiled. "Look on the bright side —if there was any bitterness in the village about Dove being here, it's been eclipsed by sympathy now."

I'd stiffened up after a night in bed, and my neck ached from mild whiplash despite the airbags, but my injuries paled into insignificance beside Zander's.

"I'd rather they still disliked me."

"Is there anything from forensics yet?" Zander asked.

Nye shook his head. "Not yet. I called in a favour and the police have bumped it to the top of the list, so we should get something preliminary by tomorrow at the latest."

"Have we spoken to BMW?"

"No reports of unexpected brake failures on the new five series. The last known issue was a recall on some 2012 models because of a problem with the vacuum pump, but that caused the brakes to become hard and you said yours went soft."

"I've got a bad feeling about this."

"Me too."

The room fell silent until a knock at the front door startled us.

"I'll get it," Lars said. "Let's hope it's not more cake."

It was more cake. Carrie sheepishly slid a Victoria sponge onto the dining room table and looked around. "Sorry. Auntie heard about the accident and insisted I bring this, but it seems like you've got quite enough food already."

"Why don't you stay and help us to eat it?" Marlene suggested.

"I could be tempted by a slice. The kitchen smelled delicious all morning, but Auntie banned me from sampling the goods."

"Let's have a girls' day. You, me, Dove, and Amber. I think after this week, we need it. The boys can do their thing while we watch a movie."

"What about work?" I asked. "We need to get the

chapel ready for your party, and we're behind already."

"Another day won't make much difference. Just relax."

CHAPTER 18

ZANDER'S FOOTSTEPS ECHOED through the empty room behind me. One day, it would be a proper study, but fixing it up was somewhere near the bottom of Amber's list of priorities, so for now, I'd borrowed it to use as a makeshift plant nursery. The big French windows at the back would allow enough light in, and I'd set up racks next to them to hold the trays of seedlings.

While the other girls watched movies yesterday, I'd multitasked on the internet and ordered everything I needed by express courier. Lars had taken delivery of my goodies first thing this morning, along with a pair of lace doilies, a pot of jam, and a dozen Cornish pasties from a handful of latecomers.

Now, I crouched next to three trays resting on a protective layer of spread-out newspaper with a scoop of compost in my hand, watching as Zander approached.

"Forensics have come back. It was definitely sabotage. Someone damaged the brake circuits, both of them to override the fail-safe, and enough to ensure that they'd give out the first time I hit the pedal hard."

We'd suspected as much, but it still didn't make it any easier to hear. Or any less confusing. I straightened up, careful to keep my head still, as any sudden movements caused pain to shoot along my neck.

"I don't get it. What is this person trying to achieve?"

Zander sat down, back against the wall and legs stretched out in front of him. As he hit the floor, he winced, and I saw how much his side hurt despite the handful of pills he'd eaten with breakfast. I knelt beside him and wiped my hands on a piece of paper towel.

"You're not the only one who can't work out what's going on. I've got no idea, and neither does Nye. The brake lines were obvious—someone wanted to stop me from looking into this mess—but until then, everything was minor. Why draw attention to themselves?"

"The knife in the boot wasn't minor."

"Nobody got hurt. It was designed to scare you, and it worked. If they'd stopped there, I'd have spent a week babysitting and asked a few questions to keep Ivy happy, Spike would have installed a burglar alarm and some lights, and we'd all have gone away. But now? Now I'm pissed."

"I'm sorry about your car."

He laughed. "I don't give a shit about the car. It was insured. I'm angry because you could have got hurt and I'm supposed to be keeping you safe."

"But you *did* get hurt." I sniffed back tears and reached out for his hand, but he drew it away.

"Untouchable goes both ways, Dee."

"I only—"

"Please, just don't." He pushed up the wall to his feet. "I also came to say Spike's here. He's going to look at the cottage first, and he's got some associates coming in over the weekend to help."

"Does that mean you won't be staying with us

anymore?"

Zander closed his eyes for a moment. "Do you want me to stay?"

I looked up at him, and the sensible thing would have been to say no. Five days ago, I definitely would have. But today? So much had changed. There was more to Zander than his womanising ways, and with rule two firmly in place, I felt safer trying to find out what.

"We'll need to find you a better bed."

I'd overslept on Friday, but on Saturday, I got downstairs by six thirty only to find Zander had still beaten me to it. Rather than giving me a glimpse of his chest again, he offered a poor alternative.

"You want a cup of tea? Or coffee?"

"I'd love some tea, but I can make it. Why are you up so early? Is your side sore again?"

He ignored my offer, wandered through to the kitchen, and put the kettle on. "We've got a lead on Natalie. I'm gonna dig into it a bit more."

"Are you planning to speak to her?"

He shrugged. "Maybe."

"Please don't. What if she tries to hurt you? Can't you just do whatever investigating you do, then leave it to the police?"

"Stay calm. Don't get your knickers in a twist." He snaked a hand down and cupped my ass, pulling me closer than I ever wanted to be. "Thong. Nice. I like a girl who avoids VPL."

If I'd managed to regain my senses before he

stepped back, he'd have needed another trip to A&E, but as it was, my knee met thin air and instead of howling in pain, he chuckled.

"You... You... What happened to being untouchable?" I snapped.

He stared at his hand in mock disgust. "Sometimes this does its own thing."

"On second thoughts, go talk to her. With any luck, she'll chop bits off you."

He fished two teabags out of the caddy and dropped them into a pair of mugs. "Lighten up, Dee."

"Just when I start to think you might not be a complete asshole, you go and prove me wrong."

"I'm sorry, okay? I've... I've never tried being just friends with a girl. It's harder than I thought."

"You don't have a single female friend?"

He considered my question then shook his head. "I've got a bunch of phone numbers and a few female colleagues. And some of my guy friends have got girlfriends."

"And if you touched, say, Olivia that way?"

"Nye would kill me."

"Right. And how about if you touched one of your female colleagues that way?"

"I did. She grabbed my junk and we called it even."

Okay, bad example. Although, the idea of grabbing his bits... *No, Dove. Stop it.* What kind of women did he work with?

"Let's stick with Olivia. Next time you're about to do something or say something, first imagine doing it to Olivia. If you think Nye might not like it, then don't do it to me. Got it?"

He looked so sheepish I felt slightly guilty. "Got it."

"Good. Now, shall we start this conversation again? You're going to see Natalie?"

"I'm not sure if we'll find her today. She moved to Birmingham after the bust-up with Amber, but we haven't confirmed whether she's still at the last address we have for her."

"So you're going there to check?"

"Nye's coming with me. Although I'm not convinced it's her who's behind the sabotage. Maybe the tools and the knife, but my brakes? Natalie trained as a hairdresser, not a mechanic."

"Someone could have shown her how to do it. Or she could have looked it up online. I mean, you can find out how to build a bomb on the internet, can't you? Surely there's a diagram of a BMW's brakes available?"

"Undoubtedly, but can I see her creeping under my car in the dark with a hacksaw in one hand and a printout in the other? My gut's telling me to look elsewhere, but we can't afford to pass up any lead, no matter how slim. It's not as if we have many others."

I saw his point even if I didn't like it. "Be careful, okay?"

He took a step forwards and dipped his head, then hesitated and straightened up again. Thinking of Olivia? "I will, I promise. Save me one of those pastry things for dinner."

"Which pastry things? There's got to be seventeen different kinds now."

He flashed me a grin over his shoulder. "I'll trust you to sample them all and pick out the nicest for me."

Gah! He really could be impossible.

By nine in the evening, I'd finished planting my seeds—vegetables galore, six pots of herbs for Lars to use in the kitchen, plus a dozen varieties of flowers to add some colour—and they were all neatly installed in the study-slash-nursery. I'd also sampled more varieties of carbs than I dared to think about and collapsed into a food coma on the sofa between Amber and Marlene. They were watching a reality show, but I couldn't concentrate.

"Why aren't the guys back?"

"One of them would call if there was something wrong," Marlene said. "Hey, this girl can really sing."

"I like her dress too," Amber added.

I looked to Lars for help, but he'd fallen asleep in the corner. Only the fact that Spike's team was still out working in the cottage kept me from panicking as darkness closed in around Arndale House.

I'd nearly chewed my nails to the quick by the time the front door clicked open and Nye and Zander strode in, looking far more relaxed than I felt. I half ran towards them, checking for damage as I went, and remembered at the last second that throwing myself into Zander's arms was a really bad idea.

"You're okay?"

Nye raised an eyebrow. "You sound surprised."

"I thought Natalie might have been dangerous." As Zander stepped under the Art Deco chandelier, his hair gleamed under the lights, shining in shades of copper and blond. "Hang on—did you do something to your hair?"

"Apparently the highlights complement my eyes."

I sagged back against the sideboard. "I've been worrying all day and you've been to the bloody hairdresser?"

"Hairdressing is what Natalie does, and boy does she love to talk. I heard about her new car, her asshole of an ex-boyfriend, the bitch who stole him from her, and the holiday in Ibiza she and five friends got back from the day before yesterday that she took to get over him."

That sank in. "So it couldn't have been her who cut the brakes?"

"No. And they were away for two weeks, so she didn't do the other stuff either."

Amber scrambled off the sofa and came over. "What if she was lying? She might have said that to cover her tracks."

"She's tanned the colour of a conker, and besides, we got someone to check with the airline while we stopped off for a curry."

"But I was so sure it must have been her. I mean, she was so hung up on Steve."

"I think that's passed. If the photos she posted on Facebook this afternoon were anything to go by, she's replaced him with a DJ, a holiday rep, a pair of twins from Wolverhampton, and a guy with a second-rate tattoo of Pocahontas on his arse. Oh, and when she gave me my receipt, she also gave me her phone number."

"Are you going to call it?" I blurted, then immediately wished I could pluck the words out of the air and burn them. Everyone turned to stare at me.

Zander looked at me over the top of his glasses—

new ones, I noticed. Thick black frames that went with this afternoon's preppy look. I could tell he was trying not to smirk, although I wasn't sure if that was because yet another woman had thrown herself at him or because I'd put my foot in my mouth once again.

"Please, Dee. I do have some standards."

Nye raised an eyebrow. "No, mate, you don't."

"Can we stop talking about Natalie?" Amber asked. "And if it wasn't her, who's been causing all the problems?"

"That's a question for tomorrow morning. We need to get some sleep, and Spike and his crew want to get back to Northbury Hall for a rest too." Nye yawned, and it was contagious. I clapped a hand over my mouth as it opened wide of its own accord. "Zee, take the girls back to the cottage, will you?"

"Can't we finish watching this?" Amber asked.

"I'll walk you over after," Lars offered.

Zander moved towards the door. "Dee, are you staying or coming with me?"

I didn't particularly want to be alone with him, but I did want my pillow and my duvet. Plus, I didn't have a clue what was going on with the TV show, and now a really screechy girl was up on the stage.

"I'll come."

"I wish," he said, and I glared at him. "Shit, I forgot again."

Zander held the torch as we picked our way among the puddles on the path. Another rain shower had passed over earlier in the evening, and a damp, earthy smell hung in the air as tentacles of moisture wrapped around us. Spooky, but at least I wasn't alone.

Spike and two more guys were sitting in the lounge

when we got back, but Zander just nodded to them, and they vanished out the door with barely a murmur. No doubt they were as tired as we were, seeing as they'd been working for over twelve hours.

"What's this?" Zander asked, pointing at a large box next to the sofa.

"I ordered you a better bed—only a fold-up one I got on next-day delivery from Amazon. Marlene's quite generous with her credit card."

"If I didn't know better, I'd start thinking you cared."

"I did it for purely selfish reasons. I figured if you spent another night on the sofa, you'd start moaning about a backache, and I don't have any earplugs."

That's what he said, and that's what I said, but we both knew we were lying. No matter how much I tried to pretend otherwise, I did care.

Chapter 19

"ARE YOU WORKING today?" Zander asked.

"Huh?"

I'd got up early again, and this morning my efforts were rewarded. Zander's back muscles rippled—freaking rippled—as he made us each a cup of tea.

He turned around, and I quickly looked away.

"I said, are you planning to work today? Or are you taking some time off? Do I need to come out and sit with you?"

"I should do a bit." I hadn't taken much time off since I got to Arndale House, but I also seemed to lose hours every day due to problems beyond my control. If the garden was ever going to look like a garden again, I needed to catch up. "Maybe I could weed outside the front of the cottage while you keep an eye on me through the window?"

"Suits me. I've got computer work to do. Is Amber around today?"

"She's going to the cinema with Carrie, and then they're planning to shop. I guess she figures it's safe now that she knows Natalie isn't stalking her."

"She's probably right. I doubt our perp will do anything in public. Don't you want to go with them?"

"I've never been fond of shopping." I looked down at my jeans and the jumper I'd bought on sale two years ago. "You can probably tell."

"Better to be pretty on the inside."

Although it was a kind way of telling me I wasn't pretty on the outside, it still stung. I took one last look at his chest then walked back into the lounge.

"I'm going to get started."

"Don't you want your tea first?"

"No, I'll get it later."

I took my misery out on the border under the cottage window, and by the time Zander appeared two hours later, I had a patch of bare dirt and a big pile of weeds. Oh, and a cut on my arm and a backache.

"Your tea got cold, so I made you a fresh cup."

"Thanks."

"You've got dirt on your face."

Oh dear. "Where?" I fished a tissue out of my pocket, ready to wipe.

"Pretty much everywhere."

Zander tried to keep a straight face, but his smirk just couldn't keep itself hidden. Wonderful. *Way to go, Dove. He's already promised not to touch you without the need to make yourself even more unattractive.*

"If I hear a single comment about you liking dirty girls..."

"Hey, I didn't say a word."

"You're thinking it. I can tell from your expression."

"What I'm thinking is that I need to go into the village and get more of a feel for the place. Are you up for a walk?"

Despite the size of the estate, I was beginning to feel claustrophobic stuck there. "I'd love a walk, but I'll have to take a shower first."

"Excellent plan." He wrinkled his nose.

I threw a handful of dirt at him, but he danced backwards out of the way.

"You drive me crazy."

He just laughed. "Good thing I'm sexy, huh?"

"Shut up."

"So, why exactly are we going into the village?"

This afternoon, Zander had dressed from the L.L. Bean catalogue in spotless boots, jeans, and a dark grey down jacket. My look could best be described as "lived in."

"Because I'm stumped. Nothing about this case fits. We've done background checks on half the people in Northbury, and Nye grew up with most of them. Anybody with anything close to a motive has an alibi for at least one of the crimes, and whoever took out my car brakes needed decent mechanical knowledge. Sometimes, taking a step back shakes something loose in my head."

"Who had a motive?"

"Percy. His sister-in-law, the woman who warned you off in the pub. A developer who was in talks to buy Arndale House before Marlene came in with cash. There was some animosity there." He shook his head. "Peter, but he had his hand stuck up a mare's backside."

"How long have you been doing this?"

"Working for Blackwood?"

"Yes."

"Eight years."

"Really?" He didn't look that old.

"I started there straight out of school. Well, I bummed around in London for three months, then joined the real world."

"Didn't you want to go to uni?"

His face clouded over. "Once, but I changed my mind."

Better tread carefully there. "Well, uni didn't get me very far, did it? Everything I own fits in one suitcase."

"Money isn't everything."

"But I bet you don't usually sleep on a camp bed in a half-renovated cottage, do you?"

He shrugged.

"Do you?"

"I bought a flat a few years ago."

Bought it, not rented? The whole investigations thing must pay better than I thought. Zander cut down a narrow footpath, and I paused by the faded sign announcing its existence.

"Do you know where we're going?"

"I've studied satellite maps of the area. This is a shortcut."

Maybe so, but there was something the satellite maps didn't show. Mud. Slimy, sucking mud a good few inches deep. Mud, mud, mud everywhere.

"I'm sure it'll get better in a minute," Zander said.

"You reckon?" I tugged at one foot and almost lost my boot. "Because it's looking worse to me."

"Come on." He held out a hand, and I grabbed it, only for him to nearly pull me off my feet. "Hey! Watch it."

He began laughing, then stumbled, fell out of one of his boots, and landed on his arse. That made me giggle until I realised I was going down too. When I sprawled over him, his "oof" was tinged with pain.

"Shit, that hurt."

"Your side?"

He nodded, then grimaced as I tried to lever myself off him. In the end, I rolled sideways, getting even muddier before I stood and helped him up.

"Are you okay?"

"Doubt that helped the healing process." He stared at me for a moment before his laughter got louder. "You should see the state of yourself. Good thing I like my girls filthy."

"I'm not one of your girls. And if you cared to look in the mirror, you're pretty damn dirty yourself, Zee."

I walked off and he stumbled along behind me, still chuckling. "You're cute when you're pissed, Dee."

"Shut up."

He didn't. He kept sniggering even as we made our way back the way we'd come, looking like a pair of swamp monsters. Then without warning, there were three of us. Zander shoved me behind him as the newcomer bounded around, woofing and leaping as we tried to stay upright.

"What the hell...?" Zander asked.

"It's a dog."

"I can see that, but where did it come from? Where's its owner? It should be on a lead if they can't keep it under control."

I pressed closer and peered over his shoulder. "It's not wearing a collar."

We stood still for a minute, and the dog stopped jumping and sat, staring at us. Waiting?

"What does it want?" I whispered.

"At a guess? Food. See how thin he is?"

I patted my pockets and found a lump. "I've got a flapjack. Do you think he'd like a flapjack?"

"Why on earth have you got a flapjack?"

"In case I get hungry. One of the ladies in the village brought them over. They're really nice."

"Sometimes you're hilarious, Dee. Give it here."

I passed it over, and he unwound the cling film and broke a corner off. "Here, puppy. You want this?"

The dog grabbed at the food and Zander snatched his hand back, letting the flapjack fall into the mud. The dog wolfed it down anyway. Zander held out another chunk, and this time, the dog was more gentle. Within seconds, he'd eaten the entire thing.

"That's it. All gone." Zander held out his empty hands, and the dog sniffed them and then whined. "Ask her. She's the one who carries snacks in her pockets."

"I haven't got any more." A shiver ran through me as a gust of wind rustled the trees. "But I'm getting really cold."

"Let's get you home, then. It's not as if we can walk into the pub looking like this."

Zander offered his hand, and I shook my head. Not only did I not want to get pulled into the mud again, I was also worried I might actually start to like him if he kept being nice.

"I'll take my chances alone."

I managed to keep my boots on as we waded back towards Arndale House with our shadow following. He'd got muddier than us, probably because he was shorter, but he seemed more cheerful. When we reached the main road, we all stopped and stared at each other.

"Go on, off you go," Zander told the dog, but he

inched closer.

"I think he likes you."

"He likes flapjacks."

"Perhaps if we carry on walking, he'll go back home," I said.

"I don't think he's got a home. No collar, and what kind of owner would let their dog get so thin? Maybe we should call the dog warden and report him as a stray?"

"At least then he wouldn't be r-r-running around in the r-r-road."

Zander looked me up and down. "Fine, I'll do that, but after I've got you home. No point in you surviving a car crash only to get taken out by hypothermia. I'd give you my jacket, but it's soaked." He settled an arm around my shoulders, and this time I didn't complain as he pulled me close. It was better than freezing.

The march home helped to warm us up a bit, and when we got to the gates, the dog was still hot on our heels. Zander opened the little pedestrian gate beside the main ones and let me slip through, leaving our companion on the other side as he followed. As soon as we began walking away, the mutt let out an anguished howl.

"Aw, he's sad."

Zander squeezed my shoulders. "I'll call the dog warden as soon as we get to the cottage. Come on."

The dog carried on howling for a few seconds, then stopped, and I looked back in time to see him wriggle under the gate and bound after us. "I don't think he wants to be on his own."

"Good grief."

At the cottage, the dog darted between our legs and

into the kitchen. After a quick sniff, he shook muddy water everywhere and sat in front of the radiator looking ever so pleased with himself.

I stared at the splashes and groaned. "What a mess."

"It's not just him. We're both dripping on the floor." Zander shrugged out of his jacket and dropped it by the washing machine, then pulled his jumper over his head. When his fingers went to his fly, I held up a hand.

"Stop. Too much."

"What? You've never seen a man in pants before?"

Yes, but not such a hot one. "What if Marlene walks in?"

"She'll get her camera out and ask me to pose by the window."

"Her magnifying glass, more like."

"Ouch."

He dropped his trousers, and I almost reached for my own camera. His thigh muscles matched the rest of him, he didn't have an ounce of fat anywhere, and his legs were bronzed to perfection. At least I wasn't cold anymore.

"You don't have to pretend you're not looking, you know."

I smiled sweetly and made an effort to focus on his face. "I was just wondering whether you use a spray tanning booth or sleep on a sunbed?"

"My mother passed on her skin tone." He turned towards the window and muttered under his breath, "About the only good thing she ever did."

I quickly marked her off my list of potential conversation topics. "Sorry."

"It doesn't matter."

"If it's any consolation, you look nice from the back too."

He glanced over his shoulder and gave me a tired smile. "Blessing and a curse, Dee. You need to get out of your stuff too."

"I'll change upstairs."

"No, you'll drip muddy water all over the place. Hang on." He walked into the lounge, then came back seconds later and threw me one of his T-shirts. "Put this on instead. Promise I won't peek."

Zander went out again, and I quickly dumped my soiled clothes on top of his and tugged the shirt over my head. It fell to mid-thigh, so at least I was decent.

"What do we do about the dog?" I called.

He'd curled into a ball now. When he looked up at me with soulful eyes, the tip of his tail twitched, almost as if he knew I was talking about him.

"Just searching for the dog warden's number."

I wandered into the lounge and found Zander in front of his laptop, still half-naked. *Dammit, Dove, don't drool.* He punched a number into his phone then set it on speaker.

"Yes?" a woman answered.

"I'm trying to get hold of the dog warden," Zander said.

"That's me."

"We've found a loose dog running around Northbury. Quite thin, doesn't have a collar on. I'm not sure what colour he is under all the mud. Maybe brown."

"I know the one. Someone saw him get chucked out of a car a few weeks back, but I haven't been able to catch the little sod. If you've got him, I'll take him off your hands and he can do his seven days in the pound."

"Seven days?" I asked. "Then what?"

"He might find a rescue space, but if he's the dog I'm thinking of, he's a Staffie-cross, and there are far too many of those at the moment."

"And if he doesn't find a space?"

"He might get an extra day or two if he's lucky."

"And then you put him to sleep?"

"Sorry." She didn't sound sorry. She sounded cold, matter of fact, like killing a dog was an everyday occurrence. Probably it was.

"What else can we do? How can we help him to find a home?"

"The other option is for him to stay with you for twenty-eight days, and if nobody claims him, he's yours."

Beside me, Zander shook his head. "You don't need a dog, Dee. We've got enough going on."

"I can't let him die," I whispered, then told the woman, "Put me down for the twenty-eight days."

Once I'd hung up, Zander put his hands on his hips. "Have you lost your mind?"

"Probably."

"We've got a maniac on the loose, the cottage is full, and we don't even know if he's house-trained."

"You're cute when you're pissed, Zee."

CHAPTER 20

I LEFT ZANDER in the lounge and walked back through to find my new friend. A muddy puddle had spread out underneath him on the tiles, and I hoped it was only water.

What the hell was I supposed to do with a dog? I was pretty sure I couldn't keep feeding him flapjacks. He cracked an eye open and looked up at me before curling into an even tighter ball against the radiator.

"It's okay, boy. You can stay."

A hand on my waist made me jump. "Dee, if you're serious about this, he needs a bath. He stinks, and he could have fleas or something."

"I guess." I looked at the lump of dog, then the stairs. "Uh, could you help me?"

"Bloody hell. How did I end up in this mess?"

Ten minutes later, we'd manhandled a slightly cheesed-off hound into the shower, and both of us were filthy again.

"Seeing you mud-wrestle with the dog made all this worth it, though," Zander said.

"Shut up and pass the shampoo."

The water ran brown while we scrubbed at the dog's fur. It wasn't long enough to be matted, but it sure was caked in mud, grass, and... "Ugh. I don't think I want to know what that was."

"Then don't think about it. Does he need conditioner?"

"Why not?"

Twenty minutes later, we admired the fruits of our labour. The dog turned out to be a reddish-tan colour with a white patch on his chest and a long, slurpy tongue he used to lick us at every opportunity. I fell back against the wall while he attacked, holding up my hands to protect myself against the slobber.

"Get him off!"

Zander just laughed. "Can't blame you, fella. I'd do the same if it wouldn't get me a kick in the nuts."

"Please, stop being an asshole and help me."

"Okay, okay. I'll take him downstairs while you have a shower."

Boy, the hot water felt good. I stood under the stream so it hit between my shoulder blades and warmed my aching muscles, replacing a little of my energy. What a morning. Not just the dog, but Zander. My skin still tingled from his every touch, and there'd been a lot of those, plus my retinas burned from him in that pair of tight black Calvin Klein briefs. I'd set aside my feelings while we washed the dog, but now I was alone, my mind ran riot and my blood ran south. I looked over and checked the bathroom door. Yes, the stool was still wedged against it.

Oh hell, I hated myself for what I was about to do, but at the same time, I needed it. Zander had turned me into a walking ball of lust, and I hadn't had a release since I got here. Sod it. I loosened the shower head, leaned back against the wall, and thought of the man downstairs while I aimed that jet of water exactly where I needed it.

When I walked into the lounge, the dog was happily ensconced in a pile of knitwear next to the couch, and a freshly showered Zander was lying back on it, examining his side as a pair of sweats rode low on his hips. How did men shower so fast? He'd cleaned up in the time it took me to get dressed, although granted, I'd spent a while hunting for matching socks. And also cooling down.

"You made him a bed?"

"Neither of us was actually going to wear that stuff, were we?"

"At least it's been put to good use." I nodded at his side. "Are you okay?"

"The dressing fell off in the shower. I need to put something else on it. It's looking a bit red around the edges, but I'm hoping the antibiotics will fix that."

I took in the array of medical supplies on the coffee table. "You need help?"

"I wouldn't mind. A guy needs three hands to do this neatly."

I held a gauze square against him while he cut and taped the edges. He'd just pulled a shirt on when the door opened and Marlene and Amber walked in.

"Good day?" Marlene asked.

Zander grinned at her. "Sure. I spent the afternoon frolicking in the shower with Dove, and now it's time for dinner. Couldn't be better."

"We did not frolic."

But we'd lost Marlene's attention as she spotted the dog lying next to us. "Ooh, who's this?"

"We went for a walk and he followed us home. The dog warden says he's a stray."

Dog put on a soppy face and wagged the tip of his tail.

"Isn't he just adorable? Are you keeping him?"

"I hadn't thought that far ahead."

"Well, every country estate should have a dog, right?" She perched on the edge of the sofa and spread her arms wide. "Come to Marlene, sweetie."

Dog ambled over and leaned against her legs, then rested a paw in her hand. I had to hand it to him—he sure knew how to suck up.

"He's so thin," Marlene exclaimed. "What's he had to eat?"

"Uh, a flapjack."

"Sweetie, he needs proper food. I believe Lars has some steak in the fridge. I'll have him cook it up for... What's his name?"

"He doesn't have one yet."

"Then we'll have to think of something appropriate. And buy him a proper bed and accessories. And a leash. He needs a leash. There's a dog thief around here, and we don't want him getting stolen."

Zander shook his head. "I doubt someone would want to steal him. He's been wandering around for a while."

"Mrs. Hearst's West Highland Terrier got stolen last year. She let it out to do its business one morning and poof! Nobody ever saw it again. Carrie put up fliers on every lamp post offering a reward and hunted all over the countryside."

"Was it a pedigree?"

"Yes, and Mrs. Hearst had owned her for almost

eight years. Even now she still leaves a bowl of biscuits out just in case."

That must have been devastating, to have loved something so dearly only for it to vanish. "Zander, we need to get a leash."

"I need new boots as well," Zander said on Monday morning. "Dog ate one of mine."

"But Lars fed him steak and roast chicken last night."

Zander pointed to the mangled mess by the back door. "Guess he was still hungry."

"In that case, we need to get him a bone and some of those squeaky toys. And proper dog treats."

"I can borrow Nye's truck if you want to risk another trip out with me."

Weirdly, after seeing the way Zander reacted in a crisis, I felt safer with him behind the wheel than anyone.

"Can we go this afternoon? The builder's starting today, and we're already behind on the clearing, so I need to spend the morning outside."

"Sure. You need a hand?"

"Aren't you supposed to be detecting?"

"Unless something else happens, we're kind of at a dead end."

"So you're leaving soon?" My insides lurched at the thought, which was stupid considering I hadn't wanted him there in the first place.

"I figured I would be since Spike's nearly finished installing the security system up at the main house, but

Nye talked to Marlene last night and she wants me here to—quote—keep her girls safe." He shrugged. "If she wants to carry on paying my day rate, I'm fine with that."

And so was I, even if it pained me to admit it. "In that case, I'd love a hand."

The woods were already a hive of activity when I got out there. Vince had brought a colleague to help, and Hal came with a team of three. Lars, Marlene, and Amber were outside as well.

"Why are you here?" I asked Amber.

"Marlene and Lars wanted to check out the men, and Spike's drilling holes in the walls up at the house. I can't hear myself think."

"I'm pretty sure they're all straight," Lars said. "Disappointing."

Despite the grey weather and the early hour, Marlene rivalled Amber in the hair and make-up stakes. "But that means more choice for Dove. Three of them are single. I checked."

"I'm not interested—" Hot breath on the back of my neck made me jump, and I found Zander standing far too close for comfort.

"What's the plan, boss?"

"Stop sneaking up on me."

"Nah, it's fun." Dog was with him, and he licked my hand as if he agreed. Honestly, two against one wasn't fair. I'd have to find a way to get my own back, but meanwhile, I planned to put Zander to work.

"Right, we're starting off by building a decent path through the woods so we don't end up neck-deep in mud."

"You didn't like that? I thought the part where you

landed on top of me was fun."

"Stop talking. We're having a path. Vince has cleared halfway, and Hal's going to follow up with the mini-digger. Once he's taken six inches off the surface, we'll put down a layer of sand with slabs over the top. The slabs and sand are arriving at ten."

"How far does the path need to go?"

"All the way to the chapel, and it's going to widen out at the top so there's a small terrace. After that, we can start on the chapel itself. Repairing the walls and replacing the roof are the priorities."

Beside me, Marlene clapped her hands in glee. "This is so exciting."

Exciting yet terrifying. I wasn't just gardening now, I was project managing too, and I couldn't afford to mess things up.

Amazingly, the morning went smoothly, and I began to appreciate Marlene's penchant for filling her life with fit men. Watching them work certainly brought a little sunshine into my day. At least until lunchtime. That was when Monday made its presence known.

My phone rang, and distracted by Zander shovelling sand, I answered it without thinking.

"Dove? Where on earth are you?"

Oh shit. "Hi, Mum."

"You keep ignoring me. I was beginning to worry you were dead."

"Not dead, just busy."

"Busy doing what? Not watering office plants, that's for sure. When you didn't get back to me, I called Wesley, and he said you'd upped and left him. Have you gone quite mad?"

I'd been trying to avoid having this conversation with my mother. Confessing I was not only single but that I'd got another gardening job would doubtless add to my parents' disappointment in me.

"Dove?"

"Yes, Mum?"

"Where are you living? Have you got a new job? Laura's got a new job, working as a PR assistant for a fashion label. And she's still with that lawyer. A real go-getter, your father says."

I was convinced my cousin and I had been swapped at birth. She got parents who loved their country home in Somerset and went hiking on the weekends. When my parents retired and moved into Gran and Grandad's old cottage, they paved the front garden, AstroTurfed the back garden, and spent every spare moment complaining about the village where Mum grew up. I couldn't work out why they didn't just move back to London and be done with it.

"Good for Laura."

"It's a shame you struggle so much with meeting men. Maybe if you made a bit more effort with your face and wore better clothes..."

Grrr. I saw red every time I spoke to my mother.

"Actually, Mum, I've got a boyfriend. I moved into his flat in Chelsea after I broke up with Wes, and now I've got a very good job working as a project manager. Now, if you'll excuse me, I've got projects to, er, manage."

I hung up and stared at the phone. *Please don't ring. Please don't ring.*

"What's up, Dee?" Zander asked. "What did the phone ever do to you?"

"Huh?"

"You're giving it a death stare."

"Oh. It's nothing. Just that my mother phoned me."

"You don't get on?"

"We get on better when she's in one county and I'm in another. It's not that I don't like her—I mean, she's my mum. It's just that every time she calls, she manages to make me feel totally inadequate."

And why had I made up such a stupid lie? Now she'd invite me and my imaginary boyfriend to all her painfully dull parties, and I'd have to make up even more fibs to get out of them.

"Sounds like my mother. Don't think about it, that's my strategy. Are you ready to go to the pet store? Dog's put in a request for one of those balls on a rope."

Zander looked so serious I laughed in spite of myself. "Fine, let's go to the pet store."

Anything to take my mind off my bloody family.

CHAPTER 21

MARLENE LOOKED AFTER Dog while we went to buy him food that wasn't steak, caviar, or salmon, and something to chew that wasn't an item of clothing or piece of furniture. He'd had a quick nibble of the table leg while we ate lunch.

When we got to the pet superstore in Great Haseley, I picked out a trolley while Zander headed for the nearest aisle.

"So, we need a bed, a collar, some food..." he said. "Hey, look at this. We can get him a water fountain."

It looked kind of fun until I saw the price. Sixty pounds! "He doesn't need a water fountain. He was drinking out of a puddle quite happily this morning."

"Not much of a fairy dogmother, are you?"

"What does that make you? The dogfather?"

Zander picked up a plastic gun and squeaked it at me. "I'm gonna make him an offer he can't refuse."

"Oh please, stop it."

"Why? Am I embarrassing you?" He found three tennis balls and began juggling. "How about this?"

"I can't take you anywhere."

He tossed the tennis balls into the trolley, as well as the gun, a fluffy monkey, a knotted rope, and a bone designed for a canine twice Dog's size. Meanwhile, I tried to behave sensibly and picked out tins of food and a big bag of kibble. Even though Zander was four years older than me, I was clearly the grown-up here.

"Are you done?" I asked.

"I think so."

"This lot's going to bankrupt me."

"I'll pay."

"You don't have to do that. It was me who wanted to keep him."

"And it was me he snored next to all last night, so that makes him at least partly mine."

"No, he's my dog. We can't share him. You'll leave soon, and what'll happen then?"

Zander stared past me. "I don't know. I hadn't really thought about that, but he's a neat dog. Maybe I could visit? Or he could stay with me sometimes?"

The harlot in me jumped up and down and clapped her hands in glee, but the realist told her to shut up.

"That's a commitment, Zee."

"Yeah. And?"

"You measure your relationships in hours. Have you ever taken any kind of responsibility for another living creature before?"

"Yes."

"Like who?"

"My sister."

He walked off to the checkout and dumped everything onto the counter, then practically threw his credit card at the checkout girl. I hurried to catch up, trying to fit the latest piece of Zander-jigsaw in with everything else I knew about him. It didn't want to slot into place.

"You never said you had a sister."

"Yeah, well, I don't like to discuss my family."

I'd gathered that. I shoved a bunch of dog toys into a bag, bundled the bed up under one arm, and tried to keep up as he strode back to Nye's pickup.

My mind was still churning as I slid in beside Zander and buckled my seat belt. Should I leave it? Or ask for more? I still hadn't worked him out—how he could joke around one minute and turn black the next. The sensible option would have been to turn the radio on or chat about Dog, but the girl who couldn't resist the lure of a man more complex than her tax return opened her big mouth.

"Are you close to your sister?"

He stayed silent as he concentrated on pulling out into traffic, then sighed. "Yes."

At least he didn't bite my head off. "Does she—"

"Dove, drop it. Please."

Okay, now it was time for the radio. I found a station playing cheesy pop songs and turned it up enough to drown out the awkward silence that filled the truck as Zander drove us back to Arndale House.

Dammit. Would I ever fully understand him?

That evening, I stuck with safe topics of conversation like food and the weather. It was blowing a gale outside, with rain hammering off the windows and wind howling past the chimney.

"Do you reckon the roof will be okay?" I asked Zander.

"This cottage has got to be two hundred years old, and it hasn't caved in yet."

Amber put a bowl of spaghetti in the middle of the

table to go with the bolognese sauce she'd made.

"We had a storm like this a few months back, and nothing blew off. A tree fell down next door, though. Carrie couldn't get out of the driveway for three days, and Lars had to take her to the supermarket."

"Perhaps we should have got Vince to start at the front of the house rather than by the chapel."

Zander broke off two pieces of garlic bread, put one on his plate, and gave the other to Dog. "Relax, Dee. It'll be fine."

"You shouldn't feed him garlic bread."

"Why not? He likes it. Right, Dog?"

"Well, it's you he'll be breathing garlic over all night."

"Hmm. I wonder if he likes Trebor mints?"

Only once again, I was wrong. Dog huffed over both of us as we tried to quiet him later on in the evening. Every time the thunder rumbled, he growled, and lightning made him bark. Then the alarm panel by the front door joined in with a chorus of beeps.

Zander got up to take a look. "I'll have to take the motion sensors offline. All the branches blowing around are playing havoc with them."

"What if someone tries to break in?"

"We've still got contact sensors on every door and window."

Amber stayed in her bedroom with cotton wool stuffed in her ears and her pillow over her head while I lay on the couch and took it in turns with Zander to stroke Dog's head.

"We could try distracting him with food again," Zander suggested. "He was quiet earlier."

"That's your answer to everything? Food?"

"Unless you want to find him a lady dog."

"The two of you deserve each other."

Even a block of cheddar didn't keep Dog quiet. He took a nibble and then scratched at the door, whining to get out.

"Maybe he needs to pee," I said.

"Maybe. You should take him out."

"What happened to sharing?"

"I had a think about that, and I figured when it's wet, he's your dog."

Thanks, Zander. I looked down at my pale-pink pyjamas, then out at the darkness. No, I didn't remotely want to go outside, but I didn't fancy clearing up a puddle inside either.

"Okay, fine. I'll take him."

Zander burst out laughing. "Whoa, you gave in so easily. I was just messing with you. I'll take him. Can you put his leash on while I find my spare boots?"

Rain blew in and splashed me as Zander opened the door and went out, head down against the driving wind. I fetched a towel from the bathroom for his hair, then watched his torch beam from the window as it swept over the garden, back and forth. Hurry up, Dog. How long did it take to pee?

Zander's torch beam suddenly cut towards the woods and he began jogging. Had he seen something? I stuck my face right up to the glass, but he soon disappeared out of sight.

Now what? I checked my watch as a minute passed, then two, still with no sign of Zander. I opened the front door and shouted his name, but it was pointless— I could barely even hear myself over the wind.

Oh, sod it. I couldn't leave him out there alone. I

grabbed my jacket, shoved my wellies on, and headed after him, praying nothing bad had happened.

Fear coursed through me with every step away from the cottage, as the lights from the lounge grew fainter and darkness closed in. Clouds covered the moon, and I could barely see the path.

"Zander!"

A branch came out of nowhere and nearly took my eye out. I ducked under it, fell over a rock, and got tangled in a bramble. Only an arm snaking around my chest kept me from face-planting in the mud.

"Dee? What the fuck are you doing out here?"

"I was worried about you."

"Get back inside. Now!"

He moved his arm to my waist and half carried me back to the cottage with Dog pulling the other way, still barking.

"What happened? Did something happen?"

Dog ran to the window as Zander locked the door and reset the alarm, and Zander didn't speak until he'd wrapped the towel around my shoulders and sat me on the sofa.

"Someone trashed the digger. Judging by the amount of water inside the cabin, it happened recently, but I couldn't find anyone."

"You went looking?" Was he crazy?

"Of course. It's my job."

"You could have been hurt."

"I'm trained to avoid that, but you aren't. You should have stayed in here." He closed his eyes and breathed in deeply. "If something had happened to you..."

"It didn't."

"Never, ever go out on your own like that again. Promise me."

"But—"

"Promise me."

"Okay, I promise." I slid out of my wellies and left them by the front door. "Now what?"

"Now, I call for backup."

"Did you find anything?" I asked the next morning as I made tea.

Zander had insisted I stay in the cottage with Dog while he went back out to search the woods with Nye, two other colleagues, and the police, and I'd drifted off on the sofa. Someone must have carried me upstairs, because I awoke in bed.

"Nope. The rain washed away any footprints, and it was too wet for a tracking dog to be any use." He reached down to scritch Dog behind the ears. "This boy gets extra biscuits today, though. He knew somebody was out there."

"Is the damage bad?"

"All the windows are broken, and it looks as if someone took a rock to the controls."

I shuddered at the thought. What if that had been someone's head?

"I hate that somebody got so close."

Zander gave me a quick hug, then looked surprised at himself. But not as surprised as me.

"Don't worry," he said. "I'll be here, and now we've got a guard dog as well as the burglar alarm."

I tried to make light of it and cracked a smile. "My

heroes."

But Dog's halo slipped at lunchtime when he ran through the main house and left little muddy paw prints all over Lars's clean kitchen floor. Had he been digging? Lars glowered, but Marlene only laughed.

"That dog is so darn cute, but he needs feeding up. Here, sweetie, you want some roast beef?"

Dog's chewing drowned out my groan. Honestly, Zander and Marlene were as bad as each other.

"You can't keep calling him Dog," Amber said, helping herself to a sandwich. "He needs a proper name."

"Cujo," Zander said around a mouthful of food.

"No way."

He was too cute. Dog, not Zander. Okay, Zander was cute as well, but I wasn't about to admit that.

"Arnold," Marlene suggested. "I once knew an Arnold who had a mouth like that. Sort of droopy at the corners."

"Arnie," Zander said. "Could work."

"Beauty?" Amber asked. "Because there's beauty in everyone."

"Almost everyone," I said. "I don't see much in whoever's terrorising us."

"Okay, almost everyone. How about Scrappy? Like in the cartoon?"

"Scooby," Zander countered.

None of those names suited him. He needed something fun yet sensible.

"What about Bear? Like a teddy bear, but it's kind of tough as well."

Zander shrugged. "I'll go with Bear."

Marlene squealed and clapped. "I love it. We can

get him a bow for his collar and some of those little T-shirts."

"Bear it is," Amber said.

"Bear. But he doesn't need clothing. He's already got a fur coat."

By mid-afternoon, I was already having a rethink on the name. Houdini, perhaps?

"Zander, where's the dog?"

He looked around from where he was talking with Vince next to the chapel. Someone had collected the broken digger on a trailer before lunch, and until the new one was delivered tomorrow, all the men were working with Vince to clear the trees. Hal had been furious this morning, but he'd calmed down when Marlene offered to pay the insurance excess.

"He was here a few minutes ago. I tied him to..."

I followed Zander's gaze and saw an empty collar hanging from a leash wrapped around the trunk of a nearby sapling.

"Maybe I should have done the collar up tighter."

Excited woofing told me Bear was nearby. "I'll take him back to the house with me. I need to rotate the seed trays in the study."

Except I'd have to wash his paws first because the little sod was digging again. How about we change his name to Digger? Or Dozer? Or Mole? Those would certainly fit.

"Come on, Bear. If you leave quietly, I'll even give you cheese."

His whole head was underground, and he sprayed me with soil as I got close. What had he found? A rabbit hole? I made a grab for him, but without his collar on, my fingers slipped off his fur.

"Please, dog. What's so exciting?"

I peered into his hole, now a good foot deep and twice as wide.

Then I screamed.

CHAPTER 22

I STUMBLED BACKWARDS away from the hole and tripped over a tree root. My arms windmilled as I tried to stay upright, but I couldn't stop myself from falling. Bear leapt after me and began licking my face.

"Urgh! Get off!" I shoved at him because I knew where that tongue had been.

Zander ambled over, laughing. "Easy, Dee. It's just mud."

"It's not! It's not just mud! Look in the hole."

"What are you on about?"

"Look in the damned hole!"

I closed my eyes and fought back vomit as the horrible image of what I'd just seen filled my mind. Matted brown hair. Greyish-cream bone. And worst of all—a sightless eye socket staring up at me.

"Fuck me! Vince, get over here."

Heavy footsteps clomped past then stopped. "Fuck me."

"It's human, isn't it?" I asked.

"We need to call the police," Vince muttered, bending to take a closer look.

"Isn't it?" I shrieked.

An arm wrapped around my shoulders, and I recognised the smell of Zander's aftershave.

"Open your eyes, Dee."

"I don't want to. Not again."

"Vince, I'm taking her back to the cottage. I'll call out the cavalry, but do me a favour and catch the damn dog."

Zander cradled me against his chest as he walked along the path, his steps soft on the humus in the woods then louder as he crunched over the gravel. He held me on my feet as he fumbled with the door lock and alarm, and I felt as if my knees were going to give way.

"Easy, Dee. I've got you."

He pulled my boots off, helped me over to the sofa, and pulled me into his lap, wrapping one arm around me as he held his phone to his ear with the other.

"Janelle? I need to speak to Nye... Then get him out of the meeting. It's urgent."

Zander crushed me tighter as he waited, and I burrowed into his chest, desperate to get away from the horror lurking in the woods. If only I hadn't looked into that bloody hole. Now I'd never unsee that...that... I didn't even know if it was a man or a woman.

"Nye, it's Zander. There's a body in the woods. We just found it.... No, it's been buried a while, I reckon... No, I'm in the cottage with Dove. She saw it first... Can you call them?... Okay, see you soon."

Zander tossed the phone onto the coffee table and put his other arm around me too. A tremor started in my belly, and soon I was shivering from head to toe. I could still smell it. The body. The rich soil was tinged with a rotten undertone—the stench of death—and it crept down my throat and made me gag.

"Do you need to go to the bathroom?"

I shook my head, willing myself not to throw up.

Not in front of Zander, anyway, especially when he was so damned calm.

"Can you open your eyes yet?"

"Do I have to?"

"Eating lunch might be tricky otherwise."

Lunch? The mere thought of food turned my stomach, and I scrambled off his lap and ran for the stairs. In the bathroom, I stared at the clean porcelain bowl of the toilet and willed myself to keep breakfast down as Zander stood behind me holding my hair back.

Downstairs, the front door slammed and I heard Bear barking. Vince's voice floated up to us a minute later.

"I've wiped the dog's paws, but he'll have to stay in here. He got out of his collar again, and he won't leave the body alone."

Oh, yuck. The way he'd slobbered on me made my face screw up in disgust. He'd been right there, in the hole, touching...

"I need a shower. I've got to get it off me."

Without thinking, I pulled my jumper off, and then my T-shirt.

"Unless you want to give me a show, you need to close the bathroom door." Zander backed away. "I wouldn't say no to watching, though."

I smiled in spite of everything. "You're a pig."

"Worth a try."

I kicked the door shut and tore off my remaining clothes. The shower was hot, too hot, but I didn't care. I needed the heat to wash the putrefaction off myself. Steam billowed as I scrubbed at myself with a loofah, even my face, and only when the water ran cold and my skin was too sore to touch did I stop.

When I stepped out of the shower, the door was cracked open a few inches and somebody had draped my bathrobe over the radiator. Zander? More and more often, he surprised me with his sweetness.

And I nearly tripped over him when I walked onto the landing. He was sitting on the floor with his legs stretched out.

"You okay?" he asked.

"I'm not sure."

"Come on downstairs. I've made you a cup of tea. Plenty of sugar." He got up and held out a hand, but before I could take it, he reached forwards, pulled my robe together, and tightened my belt. "You were gaping."

"It's odd when you act all gentlemanly."

"Oh, I snuck a peek. I just don't want the other men who'll be arriving soon to see the good bits."

"I should slap you."

"Go ahead. I'd probably enjoy that."

"Pig."

"Oink."

Despite Zander's lecherous ways, I pressed against him on the sofa as the lounge filled up. I felt comfortable around Nye, Marlene, Amber, and Vince, but six police officers and another half-dozen men in black who Zander introduced as his colleagues left me feeling overwhelmed. And desperately wishing I'd put some underwear on.

"It's safe to say we've found our mystery man's motive," Nye said. "If I were him, I'd have wanted to stop anyone from finding that body too."

"Do you think it was all the same person?" Amber asked.

Nye nodded. "It makes sense... Dove arrived to work on the garden, so someone vandalised her tools to stop her, and when that didn't work, he tried again with the knife. He probably thought the boots with the flowers on them were hers. Except rather than you lot being scared off, the situation got worse because Zander arrived to poke around. So our culprit tried to take him out of the picture."

"And when we got ready to dig up the woods, he must have really panicked," Vince put in.

"Only Bear got there first."

"The dog did less damage than the digger would have, so we got lucky," one of the policemen said. A sergeant, from the bars on his epaulettes. "Well, not lucky, exactly..."

I tuned out the details as they talked about forensics, investigations, time since death, suspects, identity. Zander stayed businesslike, the consummate professional apart from the arm that slipped around my waist, his hand resting lower than I should have been comfortable with.

"How are you feeling?" he whispered as another of the policemen launched into a speech detailing the step-by-step process for removing the body.

"Okay."

But I'd lied. With his body heat seeping into me, I really, really wished I'd remembered to put my knickers on, because I was making a mess.

"I hate the thought of someone out there watching us," Amber said on our way back to the cottage after dinner.

We'd given up on the idea of cooking and ordered a pizza. The man on the phone complained about delivering to the middle of nowhere, but Marlene offered to pay double and suddenly it wasn't so much of a problem anymore.

"I mean, he must be watching, right?" she continued.

"I'd put money on it," Zander said. "This place was tangled up in an inheritance dispute and stayed empty for almost ten years before Marlene bought it. Whoever buried the body must have known that. It's not the kind of place you stumble over by accident, even without a proper boundary fence. So yes, I reckon he's local."

"But it's more than that. He knows what we're doing," I said. "He smashed up the digger the same day it arrived."

"Half of the village knew the chapel was being rebuilt. Marlene and Ivy went to the rotary club that afternoon, and Marlene told everyone there about the nice new men working on her garden. Why do you think three women stopped by with cake this morning?"

"I didn't notice."

He blew out a breath. "I can understand that. It's been a hell of a day."

"I wonder if he's out there now?"

The prospect made me shiver as we walked into the lounge.

"Not tonight. Not with the pair of coppers camped out in the chapel." Marlene had made sure they got a pizza too. "Right now he's in bed, wondering what the fuck to do now. Probably thought those woods would be overgrown forever."

"I doubt I'll sleep either."

"I will," Amber said. "I'm knackered. See you guys tomorrow."

"I need a glass of wine first."

Alcohol was one thing we had plenty of, thanks to Marlene, and I poured myself a generous glass of red. Zander declined, saying he was on duty.

"Do you think things will get better or worse? I mean, now we know the body's there, the murderer's got nothing else to hide."

"Only his identity. It'll be interesting to see how he reacts when we start getting close." Zander spoke in a cool, detached tone, tinged not with fear but with curiosity.

Me? I was terrified. "What do you mean? He might try to hurt us again?"

"Some run, some fight. It won't be aimed at you, though. He'll want to stop Blackwood and the police."

My stomach lurched into my throat. "What if he hurts you?"

"He won't. I'll be careful." Zander gave me a two-fingered salute. "Scout's honour."

"Will you still be staying here?"

"Good a place as any. Marlene's quite excited about the whole thing. She said it's like being stuck in an episode of *Midsomer Murders*."

Trust Marlene. To her, everything was a drama.

"And Nye? Doesn't Olivia mind him staying at the

main house so much?"

"Olivia understands. That's how she and Nye met, anyway. She had a sick freak after her, and Nye took care of the problem."

"She was a Blackwood client?"

"Nye gave her a good discount."

"So this rule two, it's not a company-wide policy?"

He chuckled. "No, more of a personal thing. If I didn't have rules, I'd never get any work done." He took my empty glass and carried it through to the kitchen. "Time for bed, Dee. You want me to tuck you in?"

He waggled his eyebrows, and I didn't know whether to accept gratefully or slap him. In the end, I settled for turning on my heel and marching up the stairs.

"I can manage by myself, thank you very much."

CHAPTER 23

DESPITE THE DRAMATIC events at the Arndale estate, life continued more normally than I thought it would. Obviously, we couldn't go near the woods as the police had festooned them in blue-and-white crime scene tape, but the back terrace and its cracks and algae still awaited me.

Vince began chopping back the trees that lined the driveway, and Marlene felt bad about Hal and his team having nothing to do, so she came up with the marvellous idea of renovating the old stables.

"Wouldn't it be fabulous to look out the windows and see a herd of ponies grazing?" She waved an arm at the paddocks in the distance. "Those fields are all mine. Do you girls ride?"

Amber and I looked at each other and shook our heads.

"Don't horses smell yucky?" Amber asked.

"I'm sure we could shampoo them."

Hal tried and failed to keep a straight face as she led him outside. What next? Goats? Giraffes?

I barely saw Zander for the next few days. He worked from dawn to dusk and crawled into the cottage to sleep once I'd gone to bed, disappearing before I got up in the mornings. With the police poking around all over the estate, we figured I'd be safe enough on my own as long as I stuck near the house, so I spent the days pressure washing the terrace and filling in the gaps between the stones with a mixture of sand and cement. We'd decided to leave the cracked ones where they were in the end—Marlene thought they added character.

"Everyone's got lines, sweetie," she said. "No matter how much we try to get rid of them."

On Friday afternoon, I stood back to admire my work. No more green, just a relatively smooth expanse of sand-coloured flagstones with a low wall separating the terrace from the tatty lawn. It needed some pots to jazz it up, and selecting plants to go in them would be my favourite part of the job. An involuntary snort escaped. As long as I could get to the garden centre and back in one piece, that was.

"Looks good." Zander's voice made me jump.

"Do you have to do that?"

"What?"

"Sneak up on me."

"Sorry. I didn't mean to."

I let out a long breath, trying to release some of the tension in my stomach. It had crept up on me over the last few days, tightening a few notches when the black coroner's van trundled out with the body, and a few more when the police questioned me. Not that I was able to help.

"Sorry, I shouldn't have snapped. I'm just on edge at the moment."

"We all are. Are you done for the day?"

I nodded, then pressed a hand to my mouth as I yawned. "Tired and hungry."

"Then let's get dinner."

"Do you know what Lars is cooking?"

"He's not. He's gone with Marlene and Amber to see Ivy."

"Oh, I forgot." They'd asked me at breakfast if I wanted to go as well, but I knew I'd be too tired after a day in the garden. The stress of the week had left me drained. "I can make something, but I'll warn you now, I'm not a great cook. I used to live on ready meals and sandwiches."

"You probably won't fancy my burnt offerings either. You want me to pick something up or take you out for dinner?"

He was offering to take me out? Not like a date, obviously, but I couldn't help being secretly thrilled at the prospect of being seen out in public with a man so far out of my league.

"To the Northbury Arms?"

"Best not. I've already been in there once today, and we'll never get a quiet dinner. Strangers insist on talking to you every thirty seconds. It's not the same as London."

"Where then?"

"You get changed. I'll come up with somewhere."

Changed into what? What was a girl supposed to wear for a non-date? I hadn't felt these nerves with Peter when I yanked on a pair of smart-ish black trousers and a polo neck without a second thought, so why was I frantically cataloguing the contents of my wardrobe like a fashion intern getting ready for a job interview?

And dammit, why didn't I own anything pretty?

What was Zander wearing? *Think, Dove, think.* Uh, soft grey flannel trousers and a navy-blue crew neck.

Not too smart, but not jeans either. Should I wear a skirt? I had two—a frilly thing I'd always considered a bit short and a knee-length one I'd worn to my grandma's funeral. Neither of those said "fun dinner with a friend."

Okay, trousers. I needed trousers. I briefly considered Amber's wardrobe, but anything of hers would be too long for me.

"Dee? What are you doing up there? Knitting yourself a new outfit?"

"No, uh, I'm looking for matching socks."

Matching socks? Could I sound any thicker? I pulled out a pair of black jeans that looked vaguely smart and yanked them on, finishing off with the top Laura bought me last Christmas. I'm pretty sure she meant it as a joke, seeing as I never normally wore anything that flouncy.

Now, make-up. Yes or no? Perhaps I could take a leaf out of Amber's book and go simple, with black mascara, a touch of eyeliner, and red lipstick. I scurried into her room and borrowed her make-up bag—she always said to help myself if I wanted to.

Oh shit. It looked as if spiders were crawling out of my eyes and I'd been punched in the mouth. Quick, where were the tissues?

"Dee? You okay up there?"

"Just coming."

I attempted to act nonchalant as I walked down the stairs. Just your everyday dinner with an incredibly hot friend, nothing special. Good thing I hadn't tried hard, really, because Zander barely looked at me.

"Pizza place in Great Haseley?"

"Suits me. Are we borrowing Nye's truck again?"

"No. I bought a new car. Don't worry—it's parked up next to the police surveillance van."

He gave Bear one last scritch on the head and held the door open for me. As we neared the main house, I wished I'd thought to put on a jumper, but it was too late now. Zander bleeped his car open, and I did a double take.

"What's this?"

He grinned, teeth white in the moonlight. "You said the BMW made me look like a salesman. Does this one meet with your approval?"

Hell, yes. "What is it?"

"An Audi R8."

Otherwise known as sex on wheels. Low, black, and sleek. At least I'd be getting one kind of hot ride tonight.

Zander settled into the driver's seat, looking quite at home. I, on the other hand, felt like an imposter. Maybe I should have gone with the shorter skirt? Oh! And the roar of the car was doing strange things to my insides.

"How are you holding up?" Zander asked. "I've hardly seen you since the other morning."

"Okay. Keeping busy to take my mind off things. You?"

"Keeping busy, but with my mind very much on things."

"Is there any news? Do you know who the body is?"

"No good news. You'd think in a close-knit village like Northbury, she'd be easy to identify, but nobody's been reported missing here since 1983, and our girl's been in the ground for considerably less time than that."

"How long?"

"The medical examiner's still trying to narrow it down, but she had a train ticket in her pocket from the December before last, so not more than fourteen months. But from the post-mortem results, at least ten."

"The way she looked, I thought it would have been longer."

"Time wasn't kind."

"Do they know how she died?" I wasn't sure I wanted to know, but I felt compelled to ask.

"Blunt force trauma to the head. A hammer, most likely." Zander glanced over. "You're not gonna puke, are you?"

I breathed in the new-leather smell and shook my head. "No, but I'm not sure I'm hungry anymore."

He chuckled. "Cheap date." His words had barely registered in my brain before he backpedalled. "Well, not a date, but you know what I mean."

I did. I was well and truly friend-zoned. Which should have helped me relax a little, but the knot in my stomach wouldn't undo.

"More of a business dinner?"

"We can go with that, although I'd rather not dwell on business too much this evening. Not after I spent hours chasing a wasted lead."

"What kind of lead?" All my knowledge of investigations came from watching crime dramas on TV. What did Zander do in real life?

"We widened our search of the missing persons records and found a girl who disappeared from Great Haseley last January. She looked like a possible, but I tracked her down in Coventry this afternoon. The only good part of today was the drive back on the M6 toll road."

"So going out for dinner isn't good?"

"That depends on whether they serve tagliatelle with tiger prawns."

The menu in the little Italian restaurant listed king prawns, which appeared to be close enough, as it left Zander smiling.

"Bruschetta to start with?" he asked.

"Why not? I deserve carbs after the amount of work I did today."

"What are you having for your main course?"

"Pizza." Bread and bread. Perfect.

We certainly got good service, although the waitress's smiles were aimed at my dining companion rather than me. As she drizzled chilli oil on my Margherita, she missed the plate completely and seasoned my lap instead.

"I'm so sorry! Here, let me wipe it off."

She swiped at my jeans with a napkin and made the mess worse.

"It's okay—just leave it."

"I'll discount your bill by fifty percent and pay for the dry cleaning. Gosh, this has never happened before."

I could kind of understand it—I bet not many of her customers looked like Zander.

"Honestly, it's okay."

She gave me one last apologetic glance and scuttled off.

"A really cheap date," I said to Zander.

"I'll have to bring you with me again."

We kept to safe topics over dinner, and Zander

conversed with an easy charm that let me see why his little black book had so many numbers in it. But I tried to push that out of my mind as we discussed current affairs, TV shows, and our favourite foods.

Speaking of which, I spotted mine on the dessert menu the waitress dropped in front of me after she cleared our plates away.

"I'm having the profiteroles. How about you?"

"I don't eat dessert."

"What, never?"

"Three courses for me goes starter, main course, sex."

Whoa. Sometimes he could be incredibly blunt. I stared at the table to hide the blush that crept up my cheeks.

"Inappropriate?" he asked.

"Definitely."

"Sorry. Still struggling with this whole girl-as-a-friend thing."

I took a deep breath. "Shall we start again?"

"Okay."

"Zander, what are you having for dessert?"

"I'll try the profiteroles."

"Better."

Those pastry puffs were better than any sex I'd ever had, anyway. Wes was more of a dollop of plain vanilla ice cream, melted slightly around the edges. Although as Zander opened the car door for me outside the restaurant, I couldn't help wondering what he had on his menu. At a guess, homemade tiramisu garnished with chocolate gelato, profiteroles with fresh cream, and a helping of panna cotta, served with enough espresso to keep him going all night.

CHAPTER 24

"DOVE?" CARRIE'S VOICE crackled through my mobile as I pressed it to my ear. I'd hoped it might be Zander telling me he'd finished work, but no such luck. I hadn't seen him since we got back from dinner yesterday.

"Yes?"

"Oh, thank goodness. Nobody's answering the house phone. Uncle had a funny turn, so I took him to the doctor, and he collapsed in the waiting room. They suspect he's had a stroke."

"I'm so sorry..."

"I didn't think I'd be long, but now I've got to go with him to the hospital, and Auntie's on her own. Is there any chance one of you guys could keep her company until I get back?"

"Of course. Do we need to do anything in particular?"

"This evening's pills are marked up in the box next to the fridge, and if you wouldn't mind helping her with something to eat? She can't read the packets anymore, and I don't like her going near hot things in case she burns herself."

"That's no problem at all. I hope your uncle's okay."

Marlene shared my sentiments when I found her decorating the table in the dining room, bopping around to the sound of Britney Spears. No wonder nobody heard the phone—she'd turned the music up to deafening.

I dialled it down a few decibels. "Mr. Hearst's ill, and Carrie's taken him to hospital. Can one of us keep Mrs. Hearst company until Carrie gets back?"

"Oh, that poor girl. As if she didn't have enough on her plate. Would you mind going? I've got six ladies arriving in a quarter of an hour for a game of poker, and it's too late to cancel. They'll be on their way by now."

I thought back to what Zander said about the killer losing interest in us now the body had been found.

"Sure, I'll go." But I wasn't quite brave enough to walk there on my own in the dark. "Could Lars drop me off?"

Lars could, and fifteen minutes later, I knocked timidly on the door of Fernleigh House. The seconds ticked by, and then I heard the shuffle of Mrs. Hearst's feet and the tap of her walking stick.

As she welcomed me in, I waved Lars off in the car.

"See you later," I called.

"Come in, dear," Mrs. Hearst said. "Carrie said you'd be coming around. So very kind of you to give up your evening for an old lady like me."

"I don't mind at all."

Fernleigh House was about half the size of Marlene's place, but inside it felt homely. I glimpsed a living room filled with a comfy-looking overstuffed sofa and matching chairs as Mrs. Hearst shepherded me through to the kitchen.

"Would you be able to lend a hand with dinner? I know the ingredients, but I'm not so good at putting them together anymore."

"I'm not very good at following recipes."

"Neither was Carrie when she first got here, but now she's a fine cook."

I'd thought spending the evening with a person I barely knew might be awkward, especially with the age difference, but Mrs. Hearst was such a sweetheart she made it easy. She sat on a stool at the counter and directed me from memory, first to get all the ingredients from the cupboards, then to put everything together. Before I knew it, I was placing two quiche bases into the oven.

"I've never made pastry before."

"It's easier the more you practice. Will you be joining us for dinner? Carrie and Fred shouldn't be long."

I wasn't convinced her husband would be coming back this evening, but I wasn't about to have that conversation. Far better for the news to come from her niece. It also had the potential to make dinner a bit uncomfortable, but I could hardly decline.

"Thank you, I'd love that."

"We'd better set the table."

"Where's the crockery?"

"In the sideboard."

She led me through to the dining room, which doubled as a picture gallery. Three of the walls were lined with paintings and photos, while a fourth held shelves filled with books.

"Wow. These are amazing." I stopped next to a stunning watercolour landscape—a view I recognised from one of my trips into the village. "Did you paint this?"

"Before my eyes went. I miss having a brush in my hand."

"And the photos?"

"Fred took most of them. It's how we met—I was out painting one day, and he stopped to take pictures of the view, or so I thought. He snuck in half a dozen of me without me noticing. One of them's over by the window."

How beautiful—rolling hills blurred in the background as a young Mrs. Hearst became the focal point of his lens. And next to it? "This is your wedding day?"

"It is. There are more in that cream album on the end shelf if you'd like to see."

I flipped through the pages, lost in somebody else's memories. Those pictures showed how love should work—smiles, happiness, shared interests, and a lasting companionship as two matched souls grew older. I said a silent prayer Mr. Hearst would be okay.

The *ding* of the oven timer shook me out of my thoughts, and back in the kitchen, Mrs. Hearst instructed me on how to make the filling for the quiche.

"We'll not bake them yet. Best to wait until Carrie and Fred get home. Let's tidy up, then make a salad while we wait."

I'd just picked up the bag of flour to put it back in the cupboard when a *gong* loud enough to wake the dead echoed through the house. Next thing I knew, the flour hit the floor and exploded, covering me, Mrs. Hearst, and half of the kitchen.

"Oh shit. I mean, oh sugar."

She let out a peal of laughter. "I keep forgetting the effect that doorbell has on newcomers. We had to make it loud because of Fred's hearing."

"Uh, I'll see who it is while you change."

"Don't forget to look through the peephole in the door first. Carrie always lectures me about that."

I did so and swore under my breath as I unlocked the door.

"Zander? What are you doing here?"

His eyes widened as he took in my appearance. "Shouldn't that be my question? Is Pablo Escobar hosting a party in there?" He leaned forwards and swiped his tongue up my cheek. "Yuck. Is that flour?"

"Ugh. Get off! Yes, you made me jump when you rang the doorbell, and I dropped the bag."

He burst out laughing. "Hang on; I've got to get a photo of this."

"Don't you dare."

He pulled his phone out of his pocket. "This is too good to pass up."

I made a grab for it, but he held it out of my reach. "Give that here."

"No chance."

Even on tiptoes, I couldn't reach, but I quickly thought of an alternative solution. This time, it was Zander's turn to yell.

"Oi! Get off me."

I stepped back and admired my handiwork. Yep, half of my flour was now on him.

"You'll pay for that."

"Whatcha gonna do, spooky?"

He clapped his hands together, and a cloud of flour puffed into the air.

"I don't know yet, but when I do, it'll be good." Before I could protest, he squashed his face against mine and took a selfie. "Maybe we could convince Marlene to make her ghost party fancy dress."

"You think she'll go ahead with that?"

"Marlene's the queen of bad taste—of course she will." Headlights turned down the drive, and Zander unwrapped his arm from my waist. "Who's this?"

"Carrie, probably."

It was, and I blushed as she looked us over from head to toe.

"What on earth happened?"

"The doorbell rang, and I dropped the flour."

She giggled. "When I first heard it, I dropped the eggs, but this might actually be worse."

"I'll clear it up, I promise. How's your uncle?"

"He's awake, and he doesn't seem much different to before, but they've got loads of tests still to run."

"Is that good?"

"It's as good as we could have hoped for. He's eighty-three now." Her eyes flicked to the doorway. "I just need to explain to Auntie."

"She went to change."

Zander helped me to clear up the mess in the kitchen while Carrie talked to Mrs. Hearst and finished off the quiches. By the time she pulled them out to cool, we'd vacuumed the floor and wiped the surfaces, but the pair of us were still covered.

"Are you staying to eat these? I could find some plastic bags to go on the chairs."

"I think it would be better if we went home and took a shower," I said.

"In that case, let me put a quiche and salad into tubs for you to take along. At least then you won't need to worry about cooking."

With dinner sorted, we soon found another problem, in the form of Zander's brand-new Audi, complete with black seats, black carpet, and black accessories.

"We can't get in it like this," he said. "The valet'll have a heart attack."

"You have a valet?"

"I hate washing cars."

I jumped up and down, but not much flour fell off. "So, what's your suggestion?"

He took the food boxes out of the carrier bag Carrie had put them in and stacked them in the passenger footwell, then pulled his jumper off and put it in the empty bag. I came to my senses as he began unbuckling his belt.

"What the hell are you doing?"

"Solving the problem. Come on, your turn."

"I'm not taking my bloody clothes off!"

"Why?" His sodding smirk came back. "I have seen a woman in her underwear before."

"Not this woman. I'd rather walk."

He pointed along the dark driveway. "Be my guest. I'm not leaving the car out here on its own. I'd cry if I crashed this one."

"Did you plan this?"

"You were the one who rubbed yourself all over me earlier." He gave me a cheeky grin. "Quite enjoyed that bit."

"Pervert."

He sighed, popped the boot, and pulled out a black sweatshirt. "Fine, put this on. Spoil my fun."

"You're incorrigible."

"Would you want me any other way?"

Much as I hated to admit it, no, I wouldn't.

"You promise you won't look?"

"Cross my heart."

He turned around and so did I, keeping the car between us. As fast as I could, I stripped off my powdery clothes and dumped them in a pile, then pulled on Zander's hoodie, complete with Blackwood Security logo on the left breast. As I spun back to face him, he quickly jerked his head away.

"Did you look?"

"Of course I did. I've been celibate for over two weeks now."

That...that asshole!

"What happened to crossing your heart?" I screeched.

"I crossed my fingers too. Shall we call that payback for the frottage episode?"

"It was not frottage!"

"Yeah, yeah."

"You're a pervert."

"You already called me that earlier. Would it help if I said I liked what I saw?"

I picked up my bundled clothes and threw them at him.

"No, it bloody wouldn't. Pig."

CHAPTER 25

THANKFULLY, EVERYBODY WAS still engrossed in the poker game as we crept past Arndale House on the way to the cottage. I spied them through the dining room window, and the dim glow cast enough light for me to admire Zander's arse again.

Hey, I never crossed my heart, fingers, or anything else, okay? But I did need to press my legs together on the way back in the car because him being nearly naked in such close proximity did funny things to my nether regions.

"At least they've scaled back the police presence," he said. "Would have been interesting explaining these outfits, and I'm cold enough already."

"Me too."

He turned back and glanced at my chest.

"I can see that."

I walked right into that one, didn't I?

"Do you always think with your dick?"

"When I'm not working? Pretty much, yeah."

"But I thought I was a client? Do you speak to all your clients like this?"

We got to the cottage, and he held the door open for me.

"Dee, you fall into some weird category of your own. You're kind of a client, and sort of a friend, except all my other friends have testicles, so I'm still not quite sure how to talk to you. I'm experimenting."

"How about your sister? Why don't you think of me like that?"

He made a choking sound. "If I had these thoughts about my sister, I'd get arrested."

"What thoughts?"

"Standing there in not much more than your underwear—trust me, you don't want to know."

"Should I get dressed, then?"

"That's probably for the best."

The way I felt at that moment, he was right. If I stuck around, I might have been tempted to try and convince him to break rule two, and that could only have been a bad thing. Instead, I skipped the clothes and went straight for my pyjamas, then climbed into bed. Even when I lay back and closed my eyes, all I could see was his six-pack and well-toned thighs.

And he'd been having dirty thoughts too, not to mention spying on me while I changed. That comment about celibacy? Was he getting so desperate he'd sleep with anyone to get his rocks off? Because under normal circumstances, where he had his pick of all the girls in London, I couldn't see him giving me a second glance.

Which, in his words, was for the best. Because under rule one, I'd get a single night, and I strongly suspected that night would ruin me.

When I got downstairs for breakfast the next morning, Zander looked as if he'd got considerably more sleep than me. He was already working, seated on the couch with his laptop balanced on his knees and half a croissant on a plate next to him. I stifled a yawn as I stumbled to the kitchen, my body craving caffeine.

"I made you tea," he said. "Heard you get up."

"Thanks, but I need coffee this morning."

"Make a cup for me, would you?"

The kettle took a few minutes to boil, long enough for me to make toast too. Two slices of wholemeal with Marmite—a good start to the day, one I hoped would go a little more smoothly than yesterday.

I shoved Zander's legs off the sofa and put the mugs and my plate on the table as I sat next to him.

"What's that for?" I pointed at the tree on his laptop screen. "Spinning gum?"

"Huh?"

"Spinning gum. Its leaves are unusual because they're round with the hole in the centre. When they die, they spin around the twigs when the wind blows— that's how it got its nickname."

"What else can you tell me about it? I should have woken you up and asked you earlier."

"Not unless you wanted to be wearing your coffee. Why does it matter, anyway?"

"Because they found one of those leaves in the victim's pocket. The police's forensic botanist is dragging his heels on getting back to us, so anything you know would help."

I racked my brain for everything I'd learned in my second-year botany class. The lecturer had shown great affection for all seven hundred and something species of eucalyptus, but his droning voice meant I'd been guilty of drifting off on occasion.

"Okay. Spinning gum, botanical name *Eucalyptus*

perriniana. Originally from Australia, but now it's common throughout the world as an ornamental. Only juvenile plants have those round leaves—the leaves on mature specimens are long and thin."

"When you say common, how common?"

A picture popped into my head, of a spinning gum blowing in the breeze. "I've seen one recently, but I can't remember where."

"On the estate? In the village?"

"I don't know. Shh. I'm thinking." I bit into my toast, taking in Zander's look of distaste. "Not a Marmite person?"

"Marmite was created in the fires of hell."

"You don't want a bite, then?"

"Stop talking and think harder."

I did, but it was no good. I could picture the tree and the overgrown rosemary bush next to it, but not its location. My lack of familiarity with the area didn't help.

"Can we take a walk into the village and see if we can spot it?"

The moment Bear saw us putting our boots on, he leapt around the front door, then grabbed his leash from over the bannister and dumped it at Zander's feet.

"Looks as if this is a family outing," he muttered.

A dry laugh escaped before I could swallow it down. "What?"

"Nothing. Just the idea of my family going for a walk together. It would never happen." Even in London, they'd taken cabs everywhere.

"That makes two of us."

"Your parents don't like the great outdoors either?"

"No, my parents didn't like the idea of having a

family." He opened the door and stepped out before I could say another word. "I'll let Marlene know we're going out," he called back over his shoulder.

Shit. Every time I found out a snippet of Zander's past, it made my heart ache more for him. And I burned with curiosity about the sister he'd mentioned. What age was she? Where did she live? Why didn't he like to talk about her? All questions I didn't dare to ask.

And he didn't bring it up again when I met him at the front of the house.

"Where to, kemo sabe? Left or right?" he asked.

"Might as well flip a coin."

"I don't carry coins, just notes and condoms."

"Pig."

"Coins ruin the line of my trousers." He produced a slim wallet from his back pocket. "Logo for left or no logo for right. You call it."

"You can't flip a condom."

"A ten-pound note'll blow away. Besides, I don't have any other use for the condom at the moment."

"Can't you find yourself another...Clarissa? Or that other girl you went with at the Super Bowl party?"

"Petronella?"

"You remember her name, then?"

"Only because she keeps texting me pictures of her body parts."

I stifled a giggle. "Are you serious?"

In return, he pulled out his phone, scrolled to the messages, and flipped it over. I immediately wished he hadn't, that I could unsee the image of a pigtailed socialite with her legs spread while seated on a...

"Is that a real tiger rug?"

Petronella made Peter the veterinarian look almost

normal.

"Apparently it's a family heirloom."

"Yuck. Nye's right. You have no standards."

He fell silent for a few seconds. "Maybe that's changing," he whispered before looking me in the eye. "Come on, logo or no logo?"

"Fine. Logo."

The Durex packet flew in the air and landed at his feet.

"Right it is."

"But I wanted to go left."

He grabbed my hand, and Bear tugged both of us right along the lane. Overruled, but with Zander's palm warm against mine, I couldn't be too upset. Let the eucalyptus hunting begin.

"My feet hurt," I grumbled around midday. "Tell me again why we didn't drive?"

"Because my R8 would have got stuck on that rutted track."

"At least we'd have been sitting down rather than standing."

"How about I take you to the pub for something to eat? Hopefully, the lunch crowd'll be thinner than the dinner crowd. I'll even buy you dessert."

"Can I get a piggyback?"

"Nope."

"Vince gave me a piggyback."

Zander stopped dead. "He did?"

Oh, did I detect a teeny hint of jealousy? "Sure. It was like he hardly noticed my weight at all."

"Here, hold this." He handed me Bear's leash. "And hop up."

This walking lark was a lot easier when Zander was doing it and not me. He was barely breathing hard by the time we'd covered the half mile to the pub, which certainly vouched for his stamina. Bear bounded alongside, full of energy too.

"We'll have to hide him under the table," Zander said.

"And order him a steak sandwich. Marlene's been spoiling him. Did you know he refused to eat his kibble last night?"

"At least he's not so skinny now."

"Wait. Wait! Stop! Put me down."

He dropped me so fast I nearly fell on my knees. "Thought you were never going to ask. Finally decided to take some exercise?"

"No, look." I pointed at the spinning gum in the car park of the Northbury Arms, right at the far end near the bin store. "That's what we're looking for."

"Are you...? No, stupid question. Of course you're sure."

"At least we found it."

"Yeah, we did. In a place where everyone in the village goes. I'd hoped we'd find it in somebody's garden." He closed his eyes for a second. "Then again..."

"What?"

"Leave it with me. I need to think. Let's get lunch."

"I've eaten too much."

"You're the one who couldn't choose between two desserts."

"But they both sounded so good."

Chocolate fondant versus sticky toffee pudding—how could a girl be expected to decide?

Eddie stopped by the table to clear our plates away. "Do you want me to pack that up to go?"

"Better not. I might be tempted to eat it all."

"Coffee?"

"Coffee sounds good—anything to beat that mid-afternoon slump."

"Zander?"

"Make it two."

Eddie had just put the coffee on the table when my phone rang. I expected Marlene, Amber, or even Carrie, but "Mum" flashed up on the screen.

"Shit."

The word left my mouth before I could stop it.

Zander glanced down at the screen. "Aren't you going to answer that?"

I tried for a smile but didn't quite manage it. "I'll call her later. Better not interrupt lunch."

"I don't mind."

"But I do." I blew out a thin stream of breath. "The last thing I want to do is talk to my mother. If I wanted a lecture on my career choice, I'd go to the job centre."

"She doesn't approve of your job?"

"My parents offered to pay all my uni fees and living expenses if I did an economics degree like my father. I earned a modicum of respect when I started the business with Wes, and when they heard I'd packed that in, they weren't happy. She'll only be calling for an update on my life, and I don't want to discuss it."

"You want something stronger than the coffee?"

"I can't let them drive me to drink."

"Then you're a better person than me."

"But I've never seen you drink."

"I rarely do anymore. Since my father died, I haven't felt the same urge."

Shit. I'd wanted Zander to tell me about his family, but I hadn't expected that. "I'm so sorry."

"Don't be. He wasn't much of a father."

I'd had my differences with my own dad, but it would still hurt if he wasn't around. What had happened to make Zander so bitter?

Chapter 26

WE ALL SPENT the weekend under house arrest, or at least that's how it felt. The police presence had dwindled, Vince, Hal, and their guys weren't working, and Zander and Nye were off doing their thing in the daytime.

Then there was the rain. Oh, the rain. Early on Sunday, I could have sailed from the cottage to the house rather than walking. The only joy came from my seedlings—which were sprouting nicely, especially the three varieties of tomatoes—and the fourteen episodes of *Gossip Girl* we watched, complete with a smorgasbord of snacks and enough nail polish to start our own salon. Mine would be chipped by the end of Monday, but having a girlie day was fun. Even at uni, taking time for myself had been rare, and I'd all but lost touch with those acquaintances now.

An interruption came on Sunday evening with a phone call from Zander, at exactly the wrong time because the coat of purple I'd just put on my nails was still sticky. I jabbed at the screen with a knuckle to answer.

"Helloooo?" I giggled.

"Dove? Have you been drinking?"

I looked at the bottle of Moët et Chandon with the straw sticking out of the top. "A little."

"You're still at Arndale House, though?"

"Yup. With Marlene and Amber and Lars and Carrie and chocolate."

He blew out a breath. "Good. Look, promise me you won't go into the village. Any of you—tell the others."

A modicum of sense broke into my fuzzy mind. "Why? Have you found something?"

"Maybe. Nye and I won't be back tonight, but we'll send someone else to keep an eye. His name's Max Tian —black hair, part Chinese, always looks grumpy. Make sure you ask for his ID before you open the door."

"What's wrong? Will you be okay?" My voice rose in panic.

"Nothing's wrong—we just need to spend a bit of time with the team at the office."

"On a Sunday evening?"

"Blackwood works twenty-four seven."

"Will you be back tomorrow?"

"I hope so." His voice softened. "Sleep tight, Dee."

Max duly turned up, and Zander was right—he had one facial expression, which fell somewhere between a scowl and a frown.

"Is everything all right?" I asked.

"Fine."

Well, okay then. Max had brought his own sleeping bag, which he unrolled on Zander's bed, and although having him downstairs was better than being by ourselves, I didn't feel the same pull to get up in the morning and make him a cup of tea as I did with a certain brown-haired Blackwood employee who looked deliciously geeky before he'd put his contact lenses in.

When would Zander be back?

Not Tuesday, or Wednesday either, and on Thursday the rumours started.

Lars got back from breaking the rules and visiting the butcher's shop in the village in time for lunch, with two chickens, a pheasant, half a cow, plus the latest gossip.

"Did you hear Eddie got questioned by the police?"

"Eddie from the Northbury Arms?" Marlene asked. "Nye mentioned they'd made some progress, but he didn't say what."

"The one and only. He spent yesterday afternoon at the police station."

"Like, arrested?" Amber asked.

"I'm not sure. He was back at the pub this morning. The butcher heard it was routine questioning, Mrs. Potter from the post office thought he'd been accused of murder, and according to the lady behind me in the queue, he's out on bail."

Eddie? I could hardly believe it. I may have only met him a few times, but he'd been nothing except nice, helping me out of that jam with Peter, and even on Friday when I went to the pub with Zander, he'd been smiling and joking. Eddie?

A sick feeling balled in my stomach as I recalled that visit. The *Eucalyptus perriniana* in the car park and Zander's comment about needing to think. Did he know something about this?

I turned to Max, glowering in the corner behind his laptop. "Do you know what's going on?"

He shrugged. "I'm executive protection, not investigations."

"Aren't you going to wait for lunch?" Marlene asked as I got off my stool at the breakfast bar.

"I've got a headache. I think I'll lie down for an hour and see if it clears."

"Try a cool washcloth on your forehead. That always helps me."

Washcloth my ass. The only thing, or rather person, causing me a headache was Zander. Apart from Sunday's all-too-brief phone call, he hadn't spoken to me since last Friday, and it didn't occur to him to mention that the police might have a suspect? *Eddie*?

I called Zander, but his voicemail picked up, and an impersonal message told me Zander Graves from Blackwood Security was unavailable but would phone me back at his first opportunity.

"It's Dove. Can you call me?" I hung up and immediately dialled again.

This time he answered, sounding far from happy to hear my voice.

"It isn't a good time."

"What's happening? You disappeared, and Max knows nothing, or so he says."

"Things are moving quickly. I really can't talk right now."

"When, then?"

"Not sure."

A shiver ran through me. "Zee, I'm getting nervous here. Are you safe?"

"I'm fine." A long sigh came down the line. "Look, I'll come back tonight, okay?"

"Really?"

"I promise. It'll be late, though."

"Doesn't matter." He hadn't planned to come back,

had he? He was only doing it because I'd made a fuss. "Thanks," I whispered.

Promises, promises. Zander's didn't mean a lot, did they? Eleven o'clock came and went with no sign of him, and Max looked even more pissed off than usual as he sat on the sofa watching *Orphan Black* on his laptop. I checked my phone for what seemed like the millionth time, but there was no reply to any of the three text messages I'd sent, or my recent voicemail. I'd turned into bloody Peter.

"Have you heard anything?" I asked Max in desperation.

"No."

"Can't you call Blackwood? I'm worried about Zander." He'd claimed to be safe, but what if he'd only been trying to make me feel better? "What if he's hurt?"

Max didn't answer, just turned back to his laptop and began typing. Rude as well as grumpy. I tried to follow the TV program, but anger took over as I came up with some choice words to say to Zander if he ever deigned to bother calling me.

"He's fine," Max said.

"What?"

"Zander's fine. I've checked our monitoring system. He's with Nye, and they're both lit green."

"Do you know where they are?"

"In the City. At Rewind. It's a—"

"A nightclub, I know."

So rather than coming back to Northbury, Zander had gone out on the prowl instead. If nothing else, the knowledge acted like a bucket of cold water on my libido.

"Are you going to bed now?" Max asked. "I need sleep."

Well, I might as well. Not much point in staying awake to wait for a lying bastard, was there?

At first, I thought I'd imagined the dip of my bed, but when I opened my eyes, the silhouette of the man in front of my window was sure as hell real. I screamed, but no sound came out because of the hand he clapped across my mouth.

"Shh, it's me."

"Zander?"

"You get many other men creeping around your bedroom in the middle of the night?"

"No, but... What are you doing here?"

"I promised I'd come."

"What time is it?"

"Three o'clock. I said I'd be late."

I flicked on the lamp beside the bed in time to see him yawn.

"There's late, and there's ridiculously late."

Yes, I sounded pissy, and then I felt guilty when I realised how tired Zander looked.

"I had to work."

"Max said you were with Nye in a nightclub. I figured you'd gone hunting for a girl."

"I was, but not in the way you think."

"You mean you didn't get sick of the whole celibacy thing?"

"Believe me, the celibacy thing is beyond old now. My balls feel like they're about to explode. But I don't ditch work to get a quick fuck."

He sounded angry, and rightly so after what I'd accused him of.

"I'm sorry. I thought you weren't coming back."

He tucked a lock of hair behind my ear, and his voice softened. "I don't break promises either."

"I'm sorry," I whispered again.

"I'd better tell you what's going on."

"We can talk in the morning."

"No, it has to be now. I need to leave first thing and go back to London."

Shit. He really had come all the way to Northbury just to speak to me. "Okay, now."

He leaned over and took his boots off, then lay down beside me, yawning even wider than last time. "We began background checks on almost everyone in the village at the start of this thing—we skipped kids and anyone over eighty, plus Nye's family because he knows their secrets already. Stuff trickles in slowly, but early on, we found Eddie moved to Northbury the December before last from the City."

"He already told me that—it's hardly a secret."

"Did he tell you he split with his girlfriend right before?"

"He mentioned it, yes."

Zander propped his head up on his hand and stared at me. "And you didn't think that might be important?"

"I kind of forgot up until now. It was just something he said in passing."

"I see. Did Eddie also happen to tell you nobody's seen her since? Or that the night before she was last seen in London, the neighbours heard shouting coming from his apartment?"

"No."

"I thought he might have left that part out."

"But Eddie's so nice."

"So was Ted Bundy."

"I can't believe it."

"I've met the man a few times, and he's never pinged my radar either, but I watched him being questioned yesterday, and the man's definitely hiding something."

"Did he say anything about his girlfriend?"

"Only that she left of her own free will and he doesn't know where she is."

"Perhaps that's the truth?"

"Innocent men volunteer every bit of information they can think of to help clear their name. They don't call in a high-priced lawyer and refuse to discuss the girl in question."

"So the body next to the chapel could be hers?"

"I've spent the last four days looking for Isabelle Fontayne, and so far she's a ghost."

I lay thinking of all the times I'd spoken to Eddie, and how open he'd been. He'd told me he quit his job because of the greed in the profession, not because he ran scared, and he'd sounded so honest, so casual when he said it.

"Maybe I'm just a terrible judge of character."

Nothing but silence.

"Zee?" I rolled over, but his eyes were closed, the only sound his rhythmical breathing. Dammit, he'd fallen asleep. Now what? After he'd driven to Northbury especially to see me, I'd feel guilty waking him up again, and besides, Max was in his bed. Oh, sod it, let Zander stay there. I fetched a spare blanket from the cupboard and tucked it over him, feeling a little sweaty as I crawled back under the duvet next to his warm body.

Calm down, Dove. It's not like he'll molest you in your sleep.

"Zander, get off me!"

Far from heeding my words, he pulled me tighter against him and nuzzled my neck. And if what I could feel against my bottom was any indication, then yes, the enforced celibacy thing was causing him big problems. Really big problems.

I elbowed him in the ribs. "Zander!"

"Mmm. Dee, you're hot."

"That's because you're draped all over me, you pig." I gave him one last shove and rolled upright. "I can't believe I took pity on you and let you sleep in my bed."

He groaned as he sat up. Where had his jumper gone? Last night, he'd been wearing a soft wool crew neck, tight enough to show a hint of his pecs. Now I got the full show.

Hot damn, that chest was so lickable I forgot to even be mad.

"Tired," Zander mumbled.

I picked his jumper up off the floor and resisted the urge to bury my nose in it before I threw it back to him.

"Get dressed, would you?"

Were those his trousers next to the door? Bloody hell, yes. And the bulge in his underwear as he climbed out of my bed sent a flood running between my thighs.

"I don't have the energy to get up. I've only slept ten hours in the last four days."

"I'll make you a coffee."

"You drive a hard bargain, lady."

Nope, he'd got that wrong. The hard part was all his.

Thankfully, Amber's door stayed closed as we went downstairs, because if she'd seen us, that would have led to a whole bunch of questions I didn't want to answer. Max cracked an eyelid open as we walked through the lounge, but Zander merely grinned at him. "As you were, mate."

"I hope he doesn't think..."

"Of course he does. This is me we're talking about."

"Set him straight!"

"Nah. This is much more fun, don't you agree?"

"No, I don't."

The kitchen door closed behind us, and Zander got a gleam in his eye that made me nervous.

"Dove, please, not in the kitchen." He made kissy noises loud enough for Max to hear and probably Amber too. "You wore me out already."

"Stop it!"

"Feisty. I like that."

"That's it. No coffee."

He got down on one knee and held both hands out to me just as Amber walked in.

"Whoops. Sorry, I'll come back."

"It's not what it looks like."

Except Zander clasped one hand over his chest. "Dove, I realise I've been an idiot, but I need to tell you..."

"Shut up! And get up."

Amber had beaten a hasty retreat by the time he finished his sentence. "I need to tell you I just can't live without caffeine."

"Be still my beating heart."

I wanted to be cross with him, but the dark circles under his eyes reminded me of the effort he'd made to keep his promise last night. Instant didn't seem good enough, so I dug out a bag of Colombian roast Lars had brought and spooned coffee grounds into the cafetière I'd unearthed from the back of the cupboard the other day. And while Zander leaned against the counter trying to keep his eyes open, I buttered two slices of toast and slid them over.

"No Marmite," I said.

"My hero. Heroine."

"Will you be okay to drive back to London?"

"Max can keep me awake. He needs to go home for a bit, anyway, before his fiancée comes looking for him."

"Max is engaged? Like, to a woman?"

"Yeah, I know. It surprised us too."

"Will you be back tonight?"

"I'm not sure. Somebody will, but it might not be me." He reached out and squeezed my hand. "I'll call and check in with you this evening."

Chapter 27

THAT WEEK, I got to see the ugly side of life in a small English village. Back in London, I used to joke we could have a serial killer living one side of us and a drug dealer on the other without ever noticing. In fact, I was fairly sure we had a brothel at one point, but in the spirit of any good Londoner, I avoided eye contact with the strange men in the hallway and ignored the grunting noises in the early hours. If I didn't tell anyone, it didn't exist.

Not so in the country. Eddie's name didn't just get dragged through the mud; the good people of Northbury submerged it in boiling tar and did so gleefully. Everyone from Marlene's cleaning lady to the old guy who took it upon himself to pick litter off the pavements each morning had an opinion on the subject. When the postman knocked on the door one lunchtime, I thought he might have a package to sign for, but no, he just wanted to tell me that someone Eddie went to school with remembered him burying his pet hamster in the woods behind his house after it died, so maybe he'd been planning his crimes even then?

And the rumours only got wilder as the week progressed.

"I heard from Margie in the bakery that Eddie got a girl pregnant and threatened to kill her and the baby if she didn't get an abortion," Amber said on Friday.

"No, no, no," Carrie argued. "June in the grocery store said they went into rehab together."

"You've both got it wrong," Marlene said. "He was about to get fired from his job for embezzlement and turned to alcohol."

"Have you heard anything juicy?" Amber asked me.

Only that Eddie was adopted and his real father had been jailed for murdering a prostitute, from Bridie at the hair salon. My split ends had made me book an appointment in desperation.

"No, nothing."

How much of it was true? I didn't want to participate in the whole "guilty until proven innocent" game, but at the same time, I couldn't help feeling curious. One person would know the answers, but he'd been in London all week while our new guard, a cross between the Terminator and the Incredible Hulk, slept in our lounge instead. The others carried on gossiping as I slipped outside and sent Zander a text message.

Dove: What's really happening with Eddie? Is it as bad as everyone's saying?

Zee: What are they saying?

Dove: Where do I start?

Zee: Shit. Don't listen. The Northbury gossip tree is more of a triffid.

Dove: Will you be back soon to give me an update?

My phone rang a second later as I peered at the buds on a lilac bush outside the front window.

"Dee, I'm just going into a meeting."

And I bet that meeting would carry on all afternoon and most of the evening. "You're not coming back soon, are you?"

"I'm still trying to get to the bottom of a few things."

The words "I miss you" balanced on the tip of my tongue, but I hastily swallowed them.

"That's okay, it doesn't matter."

I thought we'd been cut off, Zander stayed quiet for so long. "Zee?"

"It's Saturday tomorrow, and Bryson's coming back to London. Get him to give you a ride. We can catch up over lunch."

"What, like just the two of us? Who's Bryson?"

But Zander had already gone.

I pulled open the front door of the cottage and found the Hulk sitting in front of his laptop.

"Are you Bryson?"

Bryson barely fitted behind the wheel of his Range Rover, and he drove down the M40 at five miles an hour under the speed limit the whole way. If he didn't get a move on, I'd be late. *Dammit, Dove.* Why had I taken so long to decide on what to wear? It wasn't as if I'd had a lot to choose from, and I already regretted my choice of indigo jeans and a plain maroon V-neck jumper.

My nerves didn't ease any when Bryson pulled into the basement car park of a six-storey office building in King's Cross. This was where Zander worked? It seemed so...so...professional. Even the stone-faced receptionist who peered up as Bryson pointed me over to her desk looked as if she had a master's degree in posh.

"Can I help?"

"I'm Dove Hallam, here to see Zander Graves."

"Do you have an appointment?"

"Not exactly. He's taking me out for lunch."

Her practised smile slipped as she picked up the phone. "Zander? Your 'date' is here."

"It's not a—"

She gestured towards a leather chair on the far side of the atrium. "Wait over there, please."

I drew curious glances as people hurried in and out of the building, and more than once, I caught the receptionist looking at me with an expression of mild disgust. What had I done? Unsure, I used a copy of *Vogue* from the table next to me to hide my face until Zander emerged from the lift behind the security gates.

He'd almost reached me when another man paused to shake his hand.

"A booty call at lunchtime, Zander? Bold move, even for you."

"Not what it looks like, Tim."

"Sure, mate."

So that's what they thought I was? A number from his little black book? Tears prickled the corners of my eyes as I realised I must be the laughingstock of the building. For some stupid reason, I'd really been looking forward to catching up with Zander, spending a little time with him over a sandwich or a burger. Now I wanted to hop on the nearest train and go back to my plants. At least they didn't make me feel like a cheap hooker.

"Dee?"

"I shouldn't have come."

"You heard that?"

I was pretty sure Tim intended me to. "Always did have good ears."

"He didn't mean—"

"Yes, he did."

"I'll set him straight."

"You'll have to set the whole building straight. I'm sure everyone knows about the tart waiting in reception by now. Blondie over there probably sent a memo around."

Zander motioned at me to get up, placing a hand softly on the small of my back as he steered me over to the reception desk. "Marie, I'm taking Ms. Grande's personal assistant out for lunch to give her an update on the Northbury case. Have Tim pull together a summary of the case notes and email them over to me."

"Now?"

"Now."

"I think he's having lunch."

"Now, Marie. His lunch will have to wait." He smiled down at me. "Ms. Hallam, I've booked a table at La Croisette. I trust that meets with your approval?"

"Very much so, Mr. Graves."

He gestured towards the door. "Shall we?"

I managed to keep a straight face until we got onto the pavement, then a smile crept across my lips. "You didn't have to do that."

"Yes, I did. You're not a booty call, Dove. You'll never be a booty call."

"You confuse me when you're sweet."

He slid his hand down my back...lower...lower. "Unless, of course, you want to be. Not like I'd decline."

Normal service: resumed. "Get your hand off my arse."

His chuckle sent vibrations through my insides. "At least you're smiling now. So, what do you want for lunch?"

I pretended to pout. "What, you don't really have a reservation at some fancy French place?"

"Sandwich? Burger?"

"Burger. And I want fries with it."

"As I always say, Ms. Hallam, you drive a hard bargain."

Zander pushed the boat out and bought me onion rings as well. He sure knew how to show a girl a good time.

"You spoil me, Zee."

"Do you want apple pie? Ice cream? A donut? Or is the pleasure of my company enough?"

For that, I reached over and snagged his last chicken nugget. "Oink oink."

"You crush me, Dee."

"Yeah, right. You're back in London now, and I bet your phone is just bursting with numbers. Do you alphabetise the girls? Or categorise them by hair colour?"

"Bra size, actually. Look, if you must know, I've been so busy working I'm thinking of getting one of those priest collars and being done with it."

"Your balls must be blue."

"More of a deep purple." We stared at each other for a second, and heaven help me, I did picture two hairy purple walnuts before I burst into laughter with Zander. "But we're not here to discuss me and my exploding tackle. You wanted an update on the case?"

"I did."

"I think I can safely say that anything being talked about in Northbury is bullshit. The reality's quite dull. Eddie's hiding behind a lawyer, and Isabelle's still missing. She was living in his apartment, but apart from a stack of boxes in his wardrobe that he brought with him when he moved into his parents' annex, there's no sign of her."

"You could have told me that on the phone."

"I could have." He took a sip of cola and sighed. "But then I wouldn't have had an excuse to...get out of the office."

"I guess it's nice to escape Northbury for a few hours too. Not that I don't like living there, because I do, but sometimes I miss the city. Now I'm here, I think I'll pop to Oxford Street before I catch the train back. I could do with more clothes."

"Need some company?"

"You want to go shopping with me? You?"

"It's either that or listen to Tim ramble on about yesterday's golf tournament."

"Oh, my heart bleeds."

He tilted his head to one side and made his lip go droopy.

"No, don't do that. You look like Bear when he wants another cocktail sausage." Dammit, he looked so cute. "Okay, fine. You're carrying the bags."

Turned out shopping with Zander wasn't so bad, because rather than walking to the Tube station, he waved down a black cab.

"I don't want you complaining your feet hurt, because I'm not giving you another piggyback."

"Can't take the strain?"

I shrieked as he picked me up and carried me into the back seat, and while I should have scrambled off his lap and probably kneed him in his blue-slash-purple balls while I was at it, I didn't. Instead, I dropped my head onto his shoulder as he rested his hand on my thigh, both of us silent as the driver pulled away from the kerb. I didn't know about Zander, but I was afraid that talking would break whatever weird moment we were in.

Luckily, I could always rely on my mother and her impeccable sense of timing to do it for me.

"Aren't you going to answer that?"

I pulled my phone out of my pocket and checked the screen. "Nope." Reluctantly, I shuffled over to my own seat.

"Your mother?"

"Yup."

Usually, she took the hint and left it a day or two before she tried again, but my phone rang a minute later. And again right after that.

"Please, put me out of my misery," Zander said. "If I hear that song once more…"

"What's wrong with Beyoncé?"

"The thought of putting a ring on it scares the shit out of me. Just answer, would you?"

"Fine." I jabbed at the screen. "Hi, Mum."

"I thought for a minute you were ignoring me."

"Sorry, I had my phone on silent and missed your call."

"It doesn't matter. You've answered now, just in time for your surprise."

"What surprise?" And why did I have a really bad feeling about it?

"Your dad and I came to London to meet Laura for lunch to celebrate her promotion, and we thought we'd stop off and have dinner with you while we were here. I'm dying to see your new home."

Shit. Shit, shit, shit. "Now's not a good time. In fact, I'm out."

"But you're in London?"

"Uh, yes, I'm in London."

"Then we can meet a little later. We're just taking Laura shopping in Oxford Street first."

"I already have plans later."

"I'm sure you can postpone them. We're your parents, Dove, and we hardly ever see you."

"Hello? Hello? Mum, you've gone all crackly. Uh, you're..."

I hung up and tried to slow my breathing.

Beside me, Zander chuckled. "That was real grown up, Dee."

"My parents wanted to come over for dinner."

"Over where? Arndale House? I'm sure Marlene would be thrilled—she'll use any excuse for a soirée."

Oh, if only. "Not exactly. I did something so, so stupid."

"Really? You surprise me."

"I've had enough sarcasm for one day. Please."

His tone turned from teasing to serious. "What did you do? It can't be that bad, surely?"

"You remember how I said Mum and Dad never approved of my career choice?"

"Yeah."

"Well, they found out I'd broken up with Wes and quit the business we started, and rather than admit I'd followed my heart and become a gardener, I kind of..." I took a deep breath. "I kind of told them I'd become a project manager and moved in with my new boyfriend in Chelsea."

I'd hoped for sympathy, but I should have known I wouldn't get it. Zander roared with laughter until I wanted to slap him.

"Don't look at me like that, Dee. This is the best laugh I've had in ages."

"It's not funny. What the hell am I supposed to do? And we can't go to Oxford Street either because that's where they are right now."

He leaned forwards and spoke through the partition to the driver. "We've changed our minds. We need to go to Soho, not Oxford Street."

"What are you doing?" I asked.

Zander's arm around my shoulders offered me a touch of comfort as his thumb came up to wipe away the tear that rolled down my cheek.

"Good thing I live in Chelsea, Dee."

CHAPTER 28

"YOU LIVE IN Chelsea?" I asked Zander.

"Don't sound so surprised. Where did you think I lived?"

Oh, marvellous, another jam to get myself out of. "Uh, I hadn't really thought about it."

"Deeeee..." Zander ran his fingers lightly up my side, and I squirmed away. "Oh, so you're ticklish."

"Don't. Just don't." He reached over again, and I squashed myself into the corner of the seat. "I thought you'd live somewhere a little more...seedy, I guess."

Was that hurt that flickered in his eyes? The corners of his mouth flattened, and I groaned inside.

"Zee, I didn't mean it. I'm sorry."

"Yeah, you did. And what's more, you're probably right. I'm hardly a poster boy for Chelsea's high society."

"Is that where you grew up?"

"Partly. We moved around depending on who my mother was married to that year."

"How many times?"

"Five husbands, eight homes. She made a career out of it."

"And now?"

"She lives in Monaco with some prick twenty years older than her. We haven't seen each other since I got drunk at the wedding and she had security escort me onto a plane."

I had no idea what to do or say, so I did the only thing that seemed sensible and hugged him. "I'm so sorry, Zee."

"Don't be. It's not your problem."

"I wish it wasn't yours either. Does your sister live with her?"

"Half-sister, and I think it's safe to say our mothers hate each other. No, Alana lives with me."

Today just brought shock after shock, didn't it? "She lives with you? For how long?"

"Six years."

"How old is she?"

"Twenty."

Two years younger than me, and that meant she'd moved in with him aged fourteen. "That's... I don't know."

"Odd? Strange?"

"Difficult?"

Zander tapped on the Perspex partition to get the driver's attention and dropped a twenty-pound note into the tray. "We'll get out here."

"Zee..."

He wrapped an arm around me. "Just know that right now, I've got three things in my life I care about. My sister and my job are two of them."

I stepped onto the pavement. "What's the third?"

"You. Come on, fake girlfriend. We've got an outfit to buy you for tonight."

Zander steered me into a boutique while confusion whirled through my mind like a spin dryer on overload. Zander cared about me? He'd just admitted it. But in what way? In the same way he looked out for his sister?

Or something more?

And if it was something more, how did I feel about that?

Hold on, what sort of boutique were we in? I took in the rails of deliciously dirty underwear lining the walls, and the mannequin in front of me brandished a riding crop that matched her leather corset.

"What sort of dinner do you think this is?"

He ignored me, marched up to the counter, and kissed the girl behind it on both cheeks. Tell me she wasn't another of his conquests?

"Lily, this is Dove. We're having dinner with her parents tonight, and it'd be best if she wore something that wasn't jeans."

Her jaw dropped. "You're meeting her parents? Are you feeling okay?"

"It's not like that. Dove told a tiny fib that means they think she's dating a guy who lives in Chelsea, and I'm helping her out."

"Hang on, hang on. Dove? Is this the same Dove Max has been looking after?"

"Yeah."

She rushed around the counter and hugged me, catching me off balance so I stumbled back against Zander. "You poor thing. It's awful not feeling safe in your own bed at night."

"You know Max?"

"I'm engaged to him."

Oh, bloody hell, this was Mr. Grumpy's girlfriend? But she seemed so normal, apart from being cinched into a satin corset. And sweet. And beautiful.

"I, uh, see."

The stunning diamond on her finger didn't lie.

"Lily, we need help here."

"Give me two minutes to change, and I'll come play personal shopper."

She disappeared into a fitting room, and I sank onto a velvet stool. "You don't have to do all this."

"If I'm going to do something, I do it properly." Zander smiled. "This girl-as-a-friend thing's getting easier, huh?"

"I guess."

But for me, the "just friends" part got harder with each sweet word and every kind gesture.

"The difficult part will be explaining the arrangement to my sister. She's too smart to believe an excuse if I try to get rid of her for the evening, which means I need to tell her the truth. Wish me luck."

"Good luck."

Thankfully, Zander held the phone away from his ear, because I heard his sister's scream from three feet away when he announced he planned to bring a girl home.

"It's not an actual girlfriend, you understand that?... No, just friends... No... No way, not now... Can you throw some of your girl shit into my room so it looks like she sleeps in there?... I'll explain later... And go to the florist and get a few orchids. We need plants... And dinner... Yeah, love you too."

When I heard Zander tell his sister he loved her with such affection in his voice, the butterflies in my stomach flapped in competition with my fluttering heart. Only an idiot could fail to understand how much he cared for her, and the realisation he was capable of love, even though it was for a family member, stirred a hope in me I'd never let see the light of day before.

And fear, because what if she didn't like me?

"Will I meet your sister later?"

"It was all I could do to stop her rushing over to help you shop."

Lily skidded to a halt beside us. "Nope, that's my job. Come on."

Zander trailed behind us to a boutique down the road, talking on the phone as Lily and an assistant she obviously knew piled up dresses for me to try on. In the fitting room, I rifled through their selection in a search for price tags, but I couldn't find a single one. That scared me.

"I'm not sure any of these are right."

"Have you tried the grey one?" Lily asked. "Let us see it on."

The grey dress easily outdid any item of clothing I'd ever worn, but a maroon silk number eclipsed it. The skirt flared out as I twirled in front of the mirror, and the keyhole neckline hinted at cleavage I'd never dared to show off.

"That's it," Lily said. "Perfect. Now we need to find you some accessories. Actually, I've got a ruby necklace you can borrow."

"I'm pretty sure I can't afford this one."

She jerked her thumb at Zander, who was hovering by the door. "Don't worry, he already paid. I think he's bored now."

"He what? He can't."

She laughed. "He just did. Look, he's got the same stubborn streak as Max. There's no point in trying to talk him out of it."

"Watch me."

I stomped over to the door, hands on hips, and Zander tore his eyes away from his phone.

"What?" he asked.

"You can't buy me a dress."

"It was surprisingly easy. All I needed to do was hand my credit card over and like magic, the assistant put it into a bag."

"That's not what I meant and you know it."

"No, I think you should explain." His trademark smirk crept onto his face.

"All right. Fine. You're a friend, at least sometimes, when you're not being really, really annoying. And friends don't buy me expensive dresses like that."

"Your logic's flawed because one just did."

"I can't accept it."

"Well, otherwise you're wearing jeans because according to Alana, now we have to swing by Nicolas and pick up the champagne she's ordered."

"Maybe I *will* wear jeans."

"And I was looking forward to admiring your legs all evening."

"Or I'll find a fancy dress shop and pick up a nun costume."

"Aww, honey, listen. We're having a tiff exactly like a real couple."

Arrrgh! This man made me want to throw things. Heavy things. At him. "You're impossible."

"Not impossible, Dee. Just difficult." He offered an arm to me. "Shall we?"

Nerves set in as we drove across Chelsea Bridge, getting

closer to Zander's flat and possible doom. I'd texted my parents with the address earlier, but I still wasn't sure what to expect.

"Are we near?"

He pointed to an apartment block right next to the river. "Up there."

Inside, my panic increased as the lift rose one floor, two floors, three, four, five, six. The fear Alana would hate me threatened to turn me into a quivering mess. Even my own cousin always looked at me with the kind of disdain usually reserved for chewing gum stuck to the bottom of her shoe.

"After you," Zander said, motioning me out along the hallway.

"You really think this is a good idea?"

"No, it's a terrible idea, but I know what it's like to have difficult parents."

"I meant about meeting your sister."

"That's a bad plan too because she'll talk for the entire evening."

Before I could come up with another reason to run back to Northbury, he slotted his key into the door to flat 607 and swung it open. A girl appeared in front of me, three inches taller, with long blonde hair and the slender body of a supermodel. Vivid blue eyes looked me up and down, assessing.

"Oh, Zee. Where did you find her?"

"Work. She's sort of a client."

"She's not like one of your usual efforts."

"Lanie..."

"Don't. How can I not be excited?" She broke into a smile, showing her perfect white teeth. She and Zander must have shared the same orthodontist. "Do you know how many girls he's brought home with him? None. Not. A. Single. One."

"Never?"

"Never. And you look so...normal. Not at all what I was expecting."

I wasn't sure whether to take that as an insult or a compliment. "Uh, I work as a gardener in Northbury."

Might as well get that out of the way.

"So that's why we've got plants now?" She looked to Zander.

"Her parents won't believe she lives here otherwise."

"Well, I bought the orchids, and a palm tree, and a weird thing with spiky leaves. The guy who delivered them said something about cutting the stems off once they've flowered, but I got distracted by his ass...istant's phone call asking whether the plants were everything I hoped for." She turned to me. "Can you help?"

"Sure."

Alana stepped over, gazelle-like, and looped her arm through mine. "Lovely. You can give me plants-101 while we sort out dinner. I'm sure Zander's got things to do."

He shrugged helplessly as I got dragged through to the kitchen, away from him and into the bear pit. Alana scared the crap out of me.

"Sit." She pointed at a high stool, and I perched on the edge as she fetched a bottle of white wine from the fridge and pulled out the cork. "We might as well start with this now."

"Don't we have to make dinner?"

"The caterers delivered it half an hour ago. Lasagne, and it comes in one of those big earthenware dishes so we can pretend we made it ourselves. Neat, huh? Anyhow, tell me about you and my brother. Is it serious?"

"No! There's nothing going on between us. He's just doing a favour to help me out."

"No way? I thought he was kidding about that."

I told Alana the whole story of my day in London, including how I'd stupidly lied to my parents but carefully leaving out the part where I sat on Zander's lap in the cab. I still didn't understand that bit myself.

"So, let me get this straight. Your parents worship your cousin, who has a really dull job in an office, but they're disappointed because you chose to do something you love?"

"That's about it." Yup. While I'd got dirty in the garden as a kid, she'd played boss and secretary with her Barbie dolls. "I'm convinced me and Laura were switched at birth. I'm sure they'd much rather she'd been their daughter."

"Well, tonight your star's gonna shine brighter than hers."

CHAPTER 29

THE DOORBELL RANG just after seven, and I hurried to let my family in. Alana had given me a tour of the apartment earlier so I knew where everything was, and I couldn't help rolling my eyes at the negligee she'd draped across Zander's bed.

"You don't think that's a bit much?"

"Every girl needs sexy undies."

"I usually sleep in pyjamas."

"Shh! So do I. Come on, let's do your hair and make-up before your folks arrive."

Now, I tucked a few stray strands behind my ear and took a deep breath before I opened the door. So much could go wrong tonight—my parents were fond of interrogation as an ice-breaker, and Laura's bitchy side was bound to make an appearance when their backs were turned.

"Mum, Dad, lovely to see you. Laura, I'm glad you could make it too."

Mum took in my appearance while Dad peered into Zander's home.

"You look very...elegant." Mum sounded surprised, and I couldn't deny that hurt.

"Where's this lad, then?" Dad asked, his voice a mixture of curiosity and disbelief.

"I'll fetch him—he just went to change."

I left them in the lounge, an airy, modern space fronted by a full-length balcony. Zander's bedroom door was closed, and I knocked quietly.

"They're here."

"Door's open."

I pushed inside as Zander finished buttoning up his shirt. He'd put on another pair of those soft flannel trousers, the ones that hugged his ass and made me want to squeeze it. Dammit, tonight would be difficult enough without that added temptation.

"Are you done?" I asked.

He patted aftershave onto his cheeks from a bottle on the chest of drawers. "Now I am. Ready to do this, pseudo-girlfriend?"

"No."

The arm that slid around my waist made me tingle all over, especially when his fingers came to rest right over my hip bone. And when he softly kissed my cheek, I slumped right into him.

"Got to get in some practice, Dee. You want a turn? No tongues."

"Shut up and pretend."

Together, we walked out into the lounge, where my family had gathered by the window. Mum's eyes widened slightly, Dad's narrowed, and Laura went white.

"Everyone, this is Zander. Zander, this is my mum, Valerie, my dad, Robert, and my cousin, Laura."

He and my father shook hands, and I noticed Dad pull the idiot move of gripping too tight. Once Zander extricated himself, he leaned forwards to kiss my mum on the cheek, and she blushed. When he pulled the same move on Laura, she turned an alarming shade of scarlet.

"Pleased to meet you all," he said, giving them a smile that could melt steel.

"You too," trilled my mother.

Laura muttered something that sounded suspiciously like "bastard."

What was her problem? Jealousy? She'd always gone for his type, but why couldn't she even pretend to be happy for me for once in her life?

"If you'll excuse us, we'd better check on dinner. Back in a moment," Zander said.

"Do you mind if we step out onto the balcony?" Mum asked. "The view's very impressive."

I'd barely noticed it apart from a quick glance out the window when I arrived, but lit up, the banks of the Thames certainly looked stunning.

"Of course. Let me unlock the doors," Zander said.

He let them out, and we retreated to the kitchen, but I didn't realise until the door flew open behind us that Laura had followed.

"What the hell are you playing at?" she spat at me.

"Sorry? You're the one who invited yourself over for dinner."

She turned on Zander. "Is this some sort of cruel joke to rub my face in it? You left my bed without a word and now this?"

Holy shit.

Alana appeared behind me. "You mean you two…? Oh, you couldn't make this up."

Zander's face was a mask of confusion as he squinted at Laura. "Hang on, did we…?"

If I'd thought Laura was angry before, now she was in danger of exploding. And she'd probably suck the rest of us into the mess like a dying star.

"You mean you don't even remember? Last July at the Luna Bar?"

The smart thing would have been for him to nod and make up some platitude, but for a clever guy, Zander could be incredibly dense.

"Sorry. But look on the bright side—that gives you a free pass for a second go."

He caught her fist before it made contact with his nose, but he missed her knee coming up between his legs. Alana leapt forwards as he doubled up in agony.

"Don't you hurt my brother!"

She wound her hand around Laura's hair and tugged, but rather than her head snapping back, an entire hair weave came away in Alana's hand, leaving Laura's newly dyed platinum tresses waist-length on one side and bobbing around her shoulder on the other.

"You bitch!"

False nails flew, along with a bowl of mixed salad and a glass of red wine. I grabbed Laura while Zander recovered enough to haul Alana off to the far side of the room. She stared daggers at my cousin while I tried to calm my breathing and process what had just happened.

"Laura, I think you should leave." I should have told her that a long time ago—I didn't need her toxic presence in my life.

"With pleasure. You and your sick little friends can carry on playing mind games on your own."

"Don't let the door hit your skanky ass on the way out," Alana called, and it took all my strength to stop Laura from going back for another try.

As the slam of the front door echoed through the flat, I traipsed back to the kitchen.

"That went well."

"Sorry," Zander said. "I honestly don't remember her."

Alana grinned. "Told you being a man-slut would get you into trouble one day."

"Please, that's not helping," I said. "Should I ask my parents to go?"

Zander limped over and sat on a stool. "You reckon Laura will tell them anything?"

I thought for a few seconds. She'd said last July?

"No way. She's been dating her boring lawyer since last February, and I can't imagine he'd be happy to hear she cheated with you."

His face blackened. "She cheated? If that's true, she's an even bigger bitch than I thought."

"It's true."

"Fuck it." He slumped over the table. "She lied to me. I always, always ask girls if they're single first."

"It's not your fault." He looked so crestfallen I went over and hugged him. "I caught her kissing Wes too."

"Your ex cheated on you with your cousin? Was he insane?"

"I think it was just a kiss, and they were both drunk."

"That doesn't make it okay, Dee."

"I know. But back then, I... I was scared of being alone."

He wrapped his arms around my waist and pulled me close. "You won't be alone."

My mum's voice calling from the living room interrupted our thoughts. "Dove? Is everything okay in there?"

Zander blew out a long breath. "Give me a couple of minutes and a packet of ibuprofen. Lanie, you need to sort out your hair."

"We're still doing this?"

He handed me a bottle of wine and two glasses. "Take this out to your parents."

Once I'd announced Laura's sudden departure due to a headache, the evening went more smoothly. In fact, as I relaxed against Zander's side on the sofa after dinner, I began to feel more comfortable than I had a right to. His warmth, combined with two glasses of wine and the rich chocolate mousse I'd eaten for dessert, left me feeling really sleepy.

My dad had thawed out as they talked business over dinner, and Zander surprised me by admitting he held an investment portfolio. They carried on their discussion over coffee until Dad announced they'd better head off.

"We've got a long drive to Somerset." He'd turned down the wine I'd brought out earlier in favour of sparkling water. "Perhaps we should move back to London one day."

"I don't know," Zander said. "The city's always so busy—a place in the country holds a certain appeal, especially for Dove. Right, sweetheart?"

"What? Uh, yes."

"I'm just glad she's seen sense for the moment and found herself a proper job. No more messing around with flowers."

"There's a lot to be said for doing a job you love."

"That doesn't pay the bills, son."

When the door closed behind them, I picked up the empty glasses from the coffee table and carried them through to the dishwasher. Zander followed with the remains of the wine.

"I'd better head off too, if I don't want to miss the last train," I said.

"You're not going back to Northbury by yourself tonight."

"I'll be fine. I texted Lars earlier, and he said he'd pick me up at the station."

"And I called Marlene and said you were staying here."

"You've already helped enough without me camping out on your sofa overnight. Besides, I didn't bring a change of clothes."

Alana came in behind us. "No need to sleep on the sofa. I've got a pull-out bed in my room for when friends stay over, and you can borrow clothes from me."

"I'm not sure they'll fit."

"We'll find something. You're not riding on the Saturday night train with all the drunk people, and besides, we can hang out tomorrow."

Being honest, running for the Tube didn't hold much appeal.

"Are you sure that's okay?"

"Positive. Do me a favour and open another bottle of wine while I find a spare duvet."

With my parents gone, I expected Zander to sit in one of the armchairs, but he squashed onto the sofa next to me again and picked up his glass of red.

"Thanks for tonight," I said softly.

"Weirdly, I kind of enjoyed it. Apart from getting kneed in the bollocks. Obviously, I'd rather have avoided that part."

"I'm sorry."

"And I'm sorry I slept with your cousin."

I'd thought about the situation constantly during dinner, and yes, it stung. Okay, it more than stung. It felt like Laura had thrust a stake through my heart. But it happened before I knew Zander, and even if it had happened last week, it still wouldn't have mattered, because I didn't have any claim on him. But yes, it hurt.

"Can we just not mention her again?"

"Suits me."

Alana came back in and picked up her wine just as Zander's phone rang.

"It's the office. Better take it."

She shook her head. "He works too much, but that's our cue for bed. We need sleep so we can do something fun in the morning."

The pyjamas she'd left out for me stretched a bit tight across my chest, but I loved the flowery pattern. As I climbed into the low bed across from Alana's, I smiled to myself at how the day had gone from bad to good, and best of all, I'd made a new friend.

"I meant what I said earlier about you not being the kind of girl I expected," she told me.

"What kind of girl were you expecting?"

"Honestly? More of a Laura. Zander's always gone for polished but prickly, and I'm so happy you're not one of those."

"I was really nervous about meeting you today."

"Why?"

"Because I know how much Zander cares for you."

"He's acted that way since I met him."

"Met him? You didn't grow up with him?"

She fell silent, and for a minute I thought she'd fallen asleep.

"We first met at a golf club barbecue when I was thirteen."

"Sounds like fun," I guessed. It wasn't as if my parents were members of a golf club or anything.

She snorted out a laugh. "Our mothers got into a fight in the bar."

"A fight? Are you serious?"

"That episode with Laura in the kitchen tonight? Let's just say I learned from a pro."

"What happened?"

"Blood and champagne went everywhere, and while we were waiting for the police to arrive, Zander and I got talking. I'd never had anyone I could talk to before. Not who'd listen. We swapped email addresses before our mothers got arrested and kept in touch even when they tried to stop us."

"Why did they try to stop you?"

"Because they're both bitter and twisted, just like our dad's other four ex-wives. He sure knew how to pick 'em. Mind you, he cheated on every single one, which only made things worse."

"Zander said you moved in with him when you were fourteen? I'm surprised your mum agreed."

"She didn't have a choice."

"Why not?"

Alana fell silent again, and I worried I'd been overly nosy. After all, we'd only known each other for a few hours, even if it felt like much longer.

I listened to the sound of Alana sniffling in the darkness, a girl in pain trying to cope with it alone. Should I give her a hug? As an only child, I'd never had much practice at playing the sister role, and I wasn't sure how to approach it.

"This thing with you and Zander—what is it, exactly?" she asked. "You said it was pretend, but that's not how he looks at you."

"I'm not sure what you mean. We're friends, most of the time. Sometimes he drives me around the bend and sometimes... I don't know."

"When you're not looking, he watches you. As if he doesn't ever want to stop."

"He does?"

"I think he likes you. I mean, really likes you."

"No, I'm pretty certain he doesn't, not in that way. He's never made any kind of move, and besides, he's got rule one and rule two. Has he told you about those?"

"Rules, schmules. He already broke rule three tonight."

"Rule three? What's rule three?"

"Never bring a girl home."

"Oh."

"Right. Oh. Has he told you much about his past? Our past?"

"He never wants to discuss it. He... He mentioned that your father passed away. I'm so sorry."

"Don't be. He wasn't much of a father."

"That's what Zander said."

Bedclothes rustled in the darkness, and the side of my mattress dipped as Alana lay down beside me. I scooched over to make room for her as she choked back a sob.

"I'll tell you because I like you, and my brother does too. I'm sure you think our living arrangements are weird."

"No, I—"

"They're weird. We all know that."

She sighed, a long, tortured exhalation, and my heart seized because I knew what she had to say wasn't good.

"We don't have to talk about this," I said. "Not if you don't want to."

"Oh, hell. Am I oversharing? Zander always tells me I talk too much."

"No, no. I mean, it's fine. If you want to talk, I'm here to listen."

"That's what my therapist says." A pause. A sniffle. Then Alana spoke again. "When I was thirteen, my mother got a new boyfriend, ten years older than her, but it turned out she still wasn't young enough. He used to come into my room at night to play his sick games. Pet the pussy. Suck the sausage. He bribed me to stay quiet with clothes and toys and even a bloody pony, but I knew it was wrong and I told my brother."

"Oh my..." I was lost for words. "How old was Zander? Nineteen?"

"Yeah. He wanted to kill the pervert, but if Zander went to jail I'd have been screwed, so we made a video instead."

"Of the—"

"Exactly that. We told Mother that if she didn't let me move in with Zander, we'd go to the police, and if the pervert ever went near another child, we'd make sure he got prosecuted. Seeing as she liked money more than her own daughter, it wasn't a hard decision."

Turned out I knew what to do after all. Alana wept into my hair as I held her tight, and I had a feeling she'd been waiting to get her secrets off her chest for a long time.

"For what it's worth, I think you made the right decision too."

"I know. It was tough at first. Zander had just failed his first semester of uni because he kept going to parties, so Father cut him off. That's when he started working at Blackwood, and we lived in a crappy bedsit in Sydenham. I went to school, cooked, and cleaned while he worked all the hours he could."

"He did well to buy this place."

"Nah, it was Daddy's guilt that bought this place. He got diagnosed with cancer three days after my seventeenth birthday, and he only lived a fortnight after that. He had an attack of conscience on his deathbed and left all his money to Zander. You know what his final words to my brother were?"

"What?"

"Don't ever get serious about a woman, son. If you fuck them more than once, they'll fuck you over."

"Wow."

"Zander's never let a girl in. Not one, until now. He's changed over the past few weeks, and I believe it's because of you."

"Or just because he hasn't been getting any." I clapped a hand over my mouth in the darkness. "Shit, I'm sorry. You're his sister, and I shouldn't say things like that."

"Don't worry about it. I noticed he hasn't been going out to bars lately. But there's more. He's been distracted, kind of spacey, and the Thursday before last he let me stay out past midnight without texting every half hour to check I was okay."

A week last Thursday? "He was working late, and then he drove to Northbury to see me."

"Precisely. You take some of the pressure off. I love Zander, don't get me wrong, but he can be so overprotective."

"It's good that he cares."

"He background checks all my friends. Once, he even banned me from catching a lift home with a guy from my communications seminar because he found out he got a speeding ticket. Oh, hell, I shouldn't have told you that. I don't want to scare you off."

Better to have a man who cared than one like Wes who acted totally disinterested then slept with my assistant, although the speeding ticket thing was perhaps a little harsh. "I'm not going anywhere."

"Apart from brunch tomorrow?"

I couldn't help giggling. Maybe it was the wine, or maybe it was the relief of finding out what made Zander tick. "Brunch tomorrow. I look forward to it."

CHAPTER 30

ZANDER WENT INTO work on Sunday morning with a hug for Alana, a kiss on the cheek for me, and a promise he'd be back in the evening to drive me to Northbury.

"Be good. Don't do anything I wouldn't do."

Alana grinned at me. "That means we can do practically anything. Do you fancy going out to a bar for a quick beer, then catching the Eurostar and waking up drunk under the Eiffel Tower with a boy whose name escapes you?"

I stared at Zander. "You did that?"

"It was a long time ago. And not with a boy, for fuck's sake."

"He had his passport and a twenty-pound note. I had to cancel his missing credit cards and *aller à Paris* to rescue him."

"I love your sister," I said, sliding an arm around her waist.

"I should have known getting the pair of you together was a bad idea."

But he was smiling, and so were we.

Zander kept his promise and arrived back at six, just

after we did. Brunch had turned into a trip to Oxford Street, safe again now my family had gone back home, and I'd bought six bags of clothes.

With Alana along to help, I'd stepped out of my comfort zone with a couple of pretty skirts and a pair of high heels. Nothing expensive, just Topshop, but they still made me feel more grown up. I'd never needed "date" clothes before, but I was keeping everything crossed that Alana was right and I might need something nice to wear in the future.

Last thing, we'd made a quick stop in Selfridges, which, according to Alana, was where Zander liked to buy his cufflinks.

"You don't have to get him a gift," she said.

"But I want to. He didn't have to help me out yesterday, and neither did you." I'd tried to pay for brunch, but when she insisted on splitting the bill, I'd bought her a scarf she liked later.

"I keep telling you why he did it—he likes you. Just tell him you feel the same, and you can stop this weird courtship ritual."

"And I told you I don't think you're right."

The last thing I wanted was to scare Zander off, not when I'd grown to enjoy his company so much. I'd rather have him as a friend than not see him at all.

"We'll see. Ooh! You have to get these ones. Look, the tops unscrew so you can keep aspirin tablets in them. A perfect reminder of last night."

"I'm not sure that's a good idea."

"It's perfect. He'll see the funny side, trust me." She handed them to the assistant. "Could you wrap these, please?"

Now Zander and I were in the R8 barrelling up the

M40, and I still hadn't found the right moment to give him his gift. He'd spent the first part of the trip discussing CCTV footage with the office through an earpiece, then put the music on. I'd wait.

Or fall asleep. That was a good option too.

Zander's hand on my thigh woke me as we drove past the "Welcome to Northbury" sign on the outskirts of the village.

"Tired, Dee? Are you asleep?"

"I was, but now I'm awake."

Even more awake when his hand didn't move.

"Do you want to stop and pick up a takeaway?"

"I already ate out with Alana, but if you want something, then stop."

"Nah, Lars'll have something in the fridge."

We drove along the high street and turned left, heading for Arndale House, our beds, and more uncertainty over what was or wasn't happening between us. Only...

"Why aren't the street lights on?" Zander asked.

"I don't know. Maybe someone forgot to push the button? Or the bulbs have blown?"

He slowed as we passed a handful of driveways, peering down each one. "Everything's dark. Reckon we've got a power cut."

"Great. I'll probably walk into things and end up with bruises."

"Good thing I've got a torch in the boot, isn't it?"

"Were you really a Boy Scout?"

"No, but you've seen my wallet. I'm always prepared."

"Asshole."

Luckily, the doors on Marlene's garage were the old

type that swung open manually rather than electric, and Zander parked the Audi inside then clipped the padlock back on.

"Want me to take some of those bags?"

"I can manage. I've been carrying them all day."

He shone a torch on the path as we headed for the main house. Flickering light glimmered in a single window—the TV room at the side, although nobody would be watching tonight.

That was where we headed.

"Where's Marlene?" Zander asked.

Amber put her book down next to the candle. "She had a headache, and she said if she couldn't watch *Strictly Come Dancing*, she might as well go to bed. Lars took her up just after the lights went out."

Lars lay on the leather sofa, snoring softly. "When did the power cut start?"

Amber checked her watch. "About an hour ago. I called the electricity company, and they said they were looking into it."

"Half of the village is out," Zander said. "Dee, will you hold the torch while I make a sandwich?"

"Sure. I really fancy a cuppa, but I guess I'll have to make do with wine."

I trailed him towards the kitchen, and the torch cast eerie shadows on the walls. A candlestick turned into Slenderman, a china dog turned into Cerberus. And what was that at the bottom of the stairs? I grabbed Zander's arm and swung the beam in that direction.

"Bloody hell!"

I dashed towards Marlene's crumpled form, lying motionless on the parquet floor.

"What do we do? What do we do?"

Zander thrust the torch into my hand. "Hold this and call an ambulance."

My hands shook as I dialled 999, and Zander leaned over Marlene.

"She's breathing, but it's shallow. Get my phone out of my back pocket and call Blackwood too. Speed dial one."

The ambulance took fifteen long, long minutes to arrive, and Nye turned up with a stoic Ivy before it left. Amber and I stood with her while Nye and Zander made a quick trip upstairs then conferred quietly in one corner. While I couldn't hear what they were saying, their body language left me even more worried.

Finally, the paramedics got Marlene loaded onto a stretcher, swaddled in blankets and hooked up to a heart rate monitor. The *beep-beep-beep* should have offered me some comfort, but what I really needed was the man standing by the door.

"Are you going to the hospital?" I asked Zander when he finished his conversation.

"Nye's taking Ivy. I'll stay here with you, and we've got a couple more people coming."

My teeth began to chatter, and Zander took off his jacket and tucked it around my shoulders.

"You okay?"

"Yes."

"Really?"

"Okay, no. I'm scared for Marlene."

"Me too, but she's in the best place. Nye'll make sure she gets top-notch care."

"But what if—"

"Don't think about it.

"Why couldn't she have just stayed in bed? I mean, she already knew there was a power cut, so why wander around in the dark? If she'd wanted water or something, she only had to go to her bathroom. Then she wouldn't have fallen down the stairs."

Zander stepped closer, using his body to push me into the study. "I'm not convinced she did."

"Did what? Of course she fell. We found her at the bottom of the stairs."

"Did she fall? Or was she pushed?"

It took a few seconds for his words to sink in.

"You can't seriously be suggesting Amber or Lars..."

"At the moment, I trust two people in this house: you and Nye. I'm worried someone's been in Marlene's bedroom, and Bear's not right. Kind of groggy."

"Oh my..." The thought of someone hurting Marlene made me shudder. "Now what?"

"Blackwood's forensics team is on its way, and until we know what's going on, I want you by my side, okay?"

"I'm not going anywhere."

Zander gripped my hand as he led me back to the lounge, where somebody had lit a whole bunch of candles. The blue lights of the ambulance disappeared off down the drive as he deposited me in an armchair and stood staring out the window.

"The paramedics said Marlene's vital signs were stable," Amber offered.

"So I heard," Zander said. "Let's have a little chat about what happened, shall we?"

"Isn't it obvious? Marlene fell down the stairs."

"And neither of you heard her?"

"What are you saying?" Lars asked.

"Just that in a silent house, I find it odd that nobody heard a woman fall down a flight of stairs and land on a wooden floor."

"Wait a minute—"

"It wasn't that quiet," Amber interrupted. "I called the power company, but they took ages to answer, and I put them on speaker so I could read my book. They played the same Cyndi Lauper track over and over for half an hour."

"Can I talk to you separately?" Zander asked.

"Why?"

"You know why."

Amber and Lars looked at each other, and then she shrugged. "I've got nothing to hide."

"Do you want me to leave?" I whispered to Zander.

"Stay. Like I said, I want you near me."

When the doorbell rang an hour later, we didn't know much more than before. Amber claimed to have gone to the TV room while Lars put Marlene to bed. When he came back, they'd gone to the kitchen together to find more candles, and although Amber couldn't be sure Marlene wasn't lying at the bottom of the stairs then, she hadn't seen her. Lars told the same story.

"Do you believe them?" I asked Zander as we went to let his colleagues in.

"Either they're telling the truth or they're working together."

"You really think they could have done all this? And the girl? Neither of them were here the December before last."

"Honestly? No, I don't. I might suspect them if Bear wasn't acting weird. If somebody drugged him, it wouldn't have been Amber or Lars. Besides, we've already dug Amber's skeletons out of the closet, and Lars's background check was clean. Nothing suspicious came up in the UK or Sweden."

"Lars said Bear was tired from a long walk this afternoon."

"He'd still have barked. And the power cut at the same time? I don't believe in coincidences like that."

Zander used a handkerchief to open the front door by the very end of the handle, and six men walked in, four of them carrying hard plastic cases. Another held a camera, and the sixth looked as if he ate steroids like candy.

"Right," Zander said. "We need to pay particular attention to entrances and exits. Everyone else has come and gone through the side door tonight. Look at Marlene's bedroom too. Her handbag, the chest of drawers, and the nightstand in particular. And take a blood sample from the dog."

"You really think somebody came in?" I asked after we'd shown the team which bedroom to look in.

"The power cut took out the alarm, Bear's sleepy, and then there's Marlene. Nye and I have both put her to bed in the past few weeks, and even if she's raging drunk, she carries her handbag upstairs and puts it on the chair by the dressing table. Now it's on the dressing table itself, and when I asked Lars where she'd put it tonight, he was ninety percent certain it was on the chair."

Zander's phone rang, and he put it to his ear.

"Yeah?... They're sure?... Fuck it."

"Bad news?" I asked once he'd hung up.

"The police have been watching Eddie, and they reckon he's been home all evening."

"Could he have snuck out?"

"Possibly, but he doesn't feel right either. He's hiding something, I'm sure he is, but the Isabelle thing feels off."

"In what way?"

"Her stuff being in his wardrobe. If you've killed a girl, you know she's not coming back and you get rid of it. You don't keep her electric keyboard, her collection of recipe books, and her fucking yoga mat unless you're expecting her to come back and pick them up."

"How about the girl's body? Nobody's identified her?"

"Nope. We can't find any of Isabelle's relatives to get a DNA sample, and her dentist wasn't so good at record-keeping. The police are considering facial reconstruction, but that takes time. Dammit. This is one of the most frustrating jobs I've ever worked on. Everybody's got a secret."

Including me. Because as Zander stood in front of me, upset and passionate about his job, all I wanted to do was wrap my arms around him and kiss his frustrations away.

CHAPTER 31

AMBER DECIDED TO sleep on the sofa in the TV room that night, and after the way Zander had interrogated her, I understood why she didn't want to be in the cottage with him. With us.

Bear ambled along the path behind us, stopping occasionally to sniff and once to pee on a bush. Zander was right—the poor pooch didn't look as sprightly as usual. When we got into the lounge, he flopped onto his bed and promptly fell asleep.

I should have been tired, but visions of the paramedics wheeling Marlene into the ambulance swam around in my head and kept me wide awake. Zander didn't seem to share my problem as he climbed under his duvet fully clothed.

"Aren't you going to change?" I asked. He usually slept in boxer shorts.

"If I do, it's a sure bet I'll have to get up in the middle of the night. Tempting fate and all that."

"Perhaps I should stay dressed too, just in case."

"No, you need to get some sleep."

I tried, but every creak and groan of the house made my heart beat faster. Twice, scratching noises at the window caused me to leap out of bed, only to find a twig scraping the glass. At three o'clock, I gave up, gathered my duvet around me, and went downstairs to the sofa.

Zander opened one eye as I stretched out along the cushions. "What's wrong?"

"I can't sleep on my own upstairs. The house makes noises."

I'd figured he'd laugh at my worries, but he snaked a hand across the gap between his bed and the sofa and twined his fingers in mine. "It'll be okay, I promise. Sleep."

And with his hand clutched against my heart, I finally did.

"Rise and shine, Sleeping Beauty."

Zander's voice filtered into my consciousness, and I squinted into the sunbeam shining through the window.

"It's too early."

"It's eight thirty. I left you as long as I could, but the forensics team needs to take your fingerprints before they leave. Just for elimination purposes."

Instantly, dark clouds threw a shadow over my mood as I remembered last night's events. Marlene in hospital, the main house full of Blackwood employees, Lars and Amber pissed off over Zander's questions. At least Bear was wagging his tail.

"How dressed do I need to be?"

He pulled back my duvet. "If you put your bathrobe over the top of your pyjamas, you'll be fine. They're at the door."

I expected them to dip my fingers in ink and print them onto a card like I'd done at school once when the local bobby came out to tell us all about his job, but the Blackwood technician got me to press each fingertip in turn onto a digital pad. It only took a minute.

"Can I go back to bed now?" I asked Zander.

"Nope. We should go and visit Marlene, and then I want to take a look at what she was doing yesterday."

"Have you heard how Marlene is?"

"Nye called. She's in a coma."

"Oh, shit. Did he say anything else?"

"Her vital signs are stable, but she's shown no signs of waking up."

"When are visiting hours?"

"Whenever we want them to be—Nye's already charmed the nurses."

Of course he had. And when Zander arrived too, they'd probably set out snacks and bring in the really comfy chairs.

"Give me five minutes to take a shower, and I'll be ready to go."

Whenever I'd seen Ivy before, she'd belied her age with her colourful choices of clothing and a cheeky glint in her eyes. This morning, she looked every one of her seventy-two years as she gripped Marlene's hand, a hand sprouting tubes in every direction.

"Grandma, would you like a cup of tea?" Nye asked.

No answer.

"She's barely spoken a word since we arrived," Nye murmured as Zander and I got close.

"She's probably in shock."

"Yeah. The doctors are keeping an eye on her. I'm

going to fetch her a drink, anyway. It can get cold with all the others." He motioned at three cups lined up on one of those wheeled tables. "Do you want anything?"

"We wouldn't say no to a couple of coffees," Zander said.

"Keep an eye on her?"

"Of course."

When the door to the private room swung shut behind Nye, Zander crouched beside Ivy.

"I'm so sorry. We both are."

"People always said my driving would do her in, not a tumble down the stairs."

"Your driving's not that bad."

Ivy looked up at him for a beat.

"Okay, it is, but you've got airbags."

"The doctors won't say much. Whether she'll wake up, or if she'll...if she'll..."

"She'll wake up. She's got a party planned, and you know Marlene never misses an opportunity to break out the canapés."

"I can only hope. I wish she hadn't drunk all that wine in the afternoon, but she was so upset."

"What are you talking about? Why was she upset?"

Ivy sighed and looked up at Zander. "We, uh, got into a little argument in the pub."

He closed his eyes for a second and pinched the bridge of his nose, a gesture that spoke of hidden frustration. "Did you tell Nye this?"

She glanced over at the door and dropped her voice to a whisper. "No, because he told us to avoid the Northbury Arms, but Marlene said nobody stood between her and the pan-fried fillet of sea bass."

"So, what happened?"

"We sat down and the waitress took our order—you remember, the young girl with the red hair?"

"I know her."

"Ever such a darling, isn't she? Anyway, we'd just taken a sip of our wine when Marlene said she wanted to show me something—a photo of a young girl taken at Arndale House, a few years ago judging by the state of it. She wanted to know if I recognised her."

"And did you?"

"No, and then the Griffins came to say hello. Peter and his parents. You remember Peter? The vet? I think you met him at one of my parties."

"He's not a man you forget."

"They didn't know her either. We'd just waved Mr. and Mrs. Thompson over to take a look when Eddie's mother stormed out from the kitchen and started yelling at Marlene."

"Dare I ask why?"

"She said Marlene was stirring up trouble by bringing you and Nye in with all your questions."

"And what did Marlene do?"

"Told her that somebody had to get justice for the poor dead girl. Then they started arguing about everything from Eddie's love life to the burnt bits on last Wednesday's shepherd's pie, and we both got thrown out."

Zander took several deep breaths as he kept himself calm. "And what then? You went back to Arndale House?"

"No, to Northbury Hall. I had my housekeeper make us club sandwiches, and we shared them over a bottle of wine. Usually, a tipple calms Marlene down, but she was still furious after we got on to the petit fours, so I gave her some of my Valium." A tear rolled down Ivy's cheek. "What if that made her lose her footing on the stairs?"

Unlike me, Ivy was a dainty crier. She sobbed quietly into a lace-edged handkerchief until Nye arrived back with a cardboard tray of coffee cups topped with plastic lids. He took one look at her, abandoned the drinks on the table, and pulled her into a hug.

"What happened?"

"Apparently there was an incident in the Northbury Arms," Zander said, and recounted the story for Nye.

Ivy dabbed at her eyes throughout, and once Zander finished, Nye looked down at her and groaned.

"What am I going to do with you?" he asked.

"I'm sorry. It's just that we always go out for lunch there, and we were hungry."

"Did Mrs. Cochrane make any threats? Or was she full of bluster?"

"I-I-I don't really remember. It was so confusing. Mostly, she just kept telling us to get out."

"I'll have a word with her. And this photo you were looking at—what happened to it?"

"I don't know. Marlene didn't mention it again, only groused about Mrs. Cochrane all afternoon until Lars drove her home. If she didn't put it back in her bag, I guess she left it in the pub."

"It's not in her bag. Can you tell me anything more about the girl in it?"

"I only saw it for a few seconds before Mrs. Griffin took it." Ivy flicked her eyes up at me. "Around Dove's age, but with lighter hair all pinned up on her head, and not so pretty. Why? Does it matter?"

"I don't know, but Marlene seemed to think it did.

Any idea where she got it?"

Ivy shook her head. "You could try Maude Hearst. Marlene went to visit her in the morning before she picked me up."

The heart rate monitor next to the bed kept up its monotonous beeping as Nye and Zander stepped out into the corridor to confer. I found myself feeling a bit awkward—after all, I barely knew Ivy, Marlene was unconscious, and now I'd been pulled into the middle of more drama.

"Are you okay? Is there anything I can do?" I asked Ivy.

"Living to a good age is a blessing and a curse, Miss Hallam. Fifteen years ago when my husband passed, I swore I'd live the time I had left to its fullest. Look at me—I'm still going strong, but too many people I care about have left this earth."

"Marlene won't give up. She's too stubborn."

"Her husband always said that about her as well."

"She'll be back, you'll see."

I sincerely hoped I was telling the truth.

"Now what?" I asked Zander once we'd settled back into the car.

"Nye gets the Cochranes, and we get the Hearsts."

"We?"

"As I said, I want you by my side. I can't concentrate on the investigation if I'm worrying about you all day."

I considered protesting, saying I'd be fine at home in the cottage, but the truth was I didn't want to be on my own either. "Are we going straight there?"

"No time like the present."

Carrie answered the door when we arrived, red-faced. "Excuse the state of me—I was vacuuming upstairs when I saw your car out the window. Dove, I tried to call you earlier. One of the ladies at Auntie's coffee morning heard Marlene had an accident?"

Zander answered for me. "She fell down the stairs."

"Strewth—is she okay?"

"She's in a coma."

Carrie's hand flew to her mouth. "No way! I can hardly believe it—Uncle only got out of the hospital yesterday, and now Marlene's taken his place. Can I do anything to help?"

"We've got the medical situation under control, but I understand Marlene came to visit yesterday morning?"

"Yes, to keep Auntie company while I collected Uncle. Why?"

"She picked up a photo from somewhere, and we're trying to find out who was in it."

"Hmm, she didn't mention any photo to me, but I only saw her in the driveway for a moment while I got Uncle out of the car. Do you want to ask Auntie? I think she's in the living room."

"If it's not too much trouble."

"No trouble at all. Do you want coffee?"

Please, Zander, say yes. With the drama at the hospital, neither of us had drunk ours there, and I desperately needed a caffeine hit, not to mention some breakfast. I had a sudden craving for junk food—an egg-and-bacon muffin with hash browns and a big dollop of ketchup.

"Black for me, white with one sugar for Dove."

We found Mrs. Hearst sitting in the chair by the window with her eyes closed, plugged into an MP3 player. Zander tapped her on the shoulder, and she jumped.

"Sorry."

She squinted in his direction. "Who's that?"

"Zander. I'm working for Marlene."

"Oh yes, she's mentioned you. Told me you're a handsome young man. Is she all right? Hilda Armstrong said she'd been taken to the hospital."

"That's right, but we're hoping she'll be back home soon."

Mrs. Hearst patted Zander's hand. "I'm sure she will. The nurses in that hospital looked after Fred ever so well. I'd best send a card and flowers. Maybe some fruit?" She addressed me. "Does Marlene eat much fruit?"

Only in wine. "Not a lot."

"Chocolates, then."

Yes, liquor chocolates. "I'm sure she'd love that."

Zander sat on the sofa opposite, and feeling like a spare part, I perched beside him.

"Ivy tells us Marlene stopped in to see you yesterday morning?"

"Oh yes, we had a lovely chat and a slice of lemon drizzle cake. Would you like a piece? I'm sure there's some left. Or a cheese scone? Carrie made those yesterday afternoon."

"Better not. Don't want to ruin lunch. Did Marlene say much in the morning?"

Dammit. Didn't he realise how hungry I was? The thought of cake made my stomach growl.

"Later," he mouthed at me.

"Marlene's always so chatty," Mrs. Hearst said. "She told me all about the police investigation into that poor girl's death. Such an awful thing to happen in the village, and so close to us. Just think—we could have been in here watching television just like we were last night while the killer buried her. Well, I say watching television—Fred and I fell asleep in the middle of an episode of *Midsomer Murders* and didn't wake up until the lights came back on after that power cut. Did you watch *Midsomer Murders*? I want to know what happened at the end."

"Have you tried the ITV Hub?" I asked.

Zander tried to steer the conversation back in the right direction. "Did Marlene talk about anything else?"

"She was interested in the history of the Arndale estate. We've lived here for almost forty years, you see, since Mrs. Pearlman was the lady of the house. Now, that's a heartbreaking story. Her husband went out to play golf on his sixtieth birthday, had a heart attack at the eighteenth hole, and left her all alone. He'd won the game too."

"She died, what, five years ago?"

"In body, yes, but her spirit departed long before that. She never left that house until she moved into a nursing home a decade ago, and the place went to wrack and ruin. I dug out some of the old photo albums and showed Marlene the place in its heyday. The Pearlmans used to hold a soirée on the last Saturday of every month. Not like Marlene's shindigs—proper cocktail parties where the men wore tuxedos and the ladies dressed up in their finery."

When Mrs. Hearst mentioned the word "photo,"

Zander and I looked at each other, both having the same thought. Did Marlene get her photo from here?

"Marlene had a photo with her at lunchtime, according to Ivy. Did she borrow one from you?"

"Not that I know of, dear. She didn't ask to."

"Did anything catch her eye?"

Mrs. Hearst's brow furrowed as she stared towards the window. "She looked at a few of the old chapel, back before the roof fell in, and mentioned getting copies made, but she said she'd like to look through the rest of the albums when she had more time before she did that."

"That's it? The chapel? Nothing of a person?"

"Now I think of it, she did say there was a picture of a girl stuck to the back of one of the estate photos."

"Do you know who it was?"

"She showed me, but I couldn't make out the details. Brown hair, that's all I saw. A big pile of brown hair." She sighed. "Those albums have ended up in such a jumble over the years. People rummage through them, and I can't see to put them straight anymore. Do you want to have a look?"

Zander glanced over at the wall of photo albums and his shoulders slumped. "That might be useful."

"Did Marlene take the photo from here?" Mrs. Hearst asked.

"Maybe."

She tutted. "I don't know why she didn't ask me first."

"Perhaps she thought she had and forgot?"

"Quite possibly, dear. When you get to our age, your mind's not what it once was. Did I offer you some cake? I can't remember. Or we've got cheese scones, haven't we, Carrie?"

"On second thoughts, cake sounds like a good idea."

CHAPTER 32

"WHAT A WASTE of a day." I slammed the door of Zander's R8 perhaps a little harder than I should have.

"Not a waste, Dee. At least we know there's nothing useful in those albums now."

The engine roared to life, and the headlights illuminated the steady drizzle. It had begun raining around lunchtime and showed no signs of letting up anytime soon.

"How could one man take so many photos? There must have been ten thousand of them."

"I guess he enjoyed his hobby."

Most of them had been landscapes or nature shots, but we'd still taken each one out of its plastic sleeve to check for other pictures hidden in behind, as Mrs. Hearst thought Marlene had found. Even with Carrie helping and the piles divided into three, checking took all afternoon and part of the evening. And it had been pointless. Most of the pictures of brown-haired girls were early photos of Mrs. Hearst herself, a few of Carrie she said were taken in Australia and posted over, plus a couple of girls from the village that Zander recognised. From the way he spoke, I suspected he had intimate knowledge of them too, and that made me even more peeved as we pulled out of the driveway.

"Aren't we going home?" I asked as he whizzed past

the gates of Marlene's place.

"I thought we'd pick up a takeaway. With everything up in the air at the moment, I don't want to be reliant on Lars's cooking."

True, Lars hadn't been in a great mood last night, but the idea of sitting by myself in Arndale House for a bit without having to make small talk or deal with Zander's penchant for shagging everything that moved suited me just fine.

"Can you drop me off?" I asked.

"Why would you want me to do that?"

Because I was sick of always being the bridesmaid, never the bride. "I'm tired, that's all."

"We'll get a pizza, and then you can go to bed."

Alone. Always alone. "Fine. Just make it quick." He glanced over at me, and I knew I was acting pissy, but I couldn't stop myself. The day had been horrible from beginning to end. "What?"

He kept his eyes fixed on the road. "Nothing. I'll call ahead and order."

Only before Zander could dial, Nye's name flashed up on the car's dashboard display as he phoned in.

"Well, that was a wasted day."

Nye echoed my thoughts, and he sounded almost as cheesed off as I felt.

"Nothing?" Zander asked.

"The Thompsons didn't get a good look at the photo before the altercation started, Mr. Griffin thought she was kind of plain with brown hair, and Mrs. Griffin described her as honey blonde and quite pretty. Peter reckoned she had eyebrows like tiger moth caterpillars and lips like a sow's vulva. I googled that on my phone, and the shrink from the office called to ask if I wanted to talk about anything."

Zander barked out a laugh, and even I couldn't help smiling. "No wonder the asshole's single," he said.

"Then I tried speaking to Mrs. Cochrane, and she chucked a glass of red over me. Threatened to throw the bottle too if I didn't leave her family alone."

"Nice to hear you haven't lost your touch with the ladies."

"Luckily, I found that redheaded waitress before I left—you know, the one you fucked after Ivy's summer ball last year?"

The knife cut through the air and plunged straight into my heart.

"Dove's in the car with me, and you're on speaker."

"Shit. Sorry. To both of you."

Zander spoke. I couldn't. "Don't worry about it. Dove knows what I'm like."

I did, and as he used the present tense, the blade twisted through both ventricles. Over the last couple of weeks, when he'd slept next to me in bed, taken me home to meet his sister, entertained my parents, and comforted me, I'd dared to hope he might have changed. But I'd been wrong, hadn't I?

"Yeah, but still..." Nye cleared his throat. "The waitress cleared up the mess after Marlene and Ivy left, and she's sure there wasn't a photo kicking around, which means Marlene must have taken it with her."

"It wasn't in her bag."

"So, either she took it out and put it somewhere, or somebody else did."

"Any news on Bear's blood test?"

"Forensics expect the results tomorrow, but we heard back from the power company. Someone threw a branch at one of the overhead lines. It could have been kids, or it could have been—"

Zander tapped his fingers on the steering wheel as he paused at a crossroads. "Our culprit. I don't believe in a coincidence like that. And the fingerprints?"

"They're still going through those, but they've found over forty sets. Hardly surprising with the number of visitors Marlene has, but it's not going to help our case."

"Any signs of forced entry?"

"No, but the deadbolts weren't engaged, and the other locks are relics from a time when people left their doors open all day."

As Marlene had done until the problems started. Security hadn't been her prime concern when I'd first moved to Arndale.

"So someone could have picked the locks to get in," Zander said. "The question is why? What was their aim? Looking for that photo, or to push Marlene down the stairs?"

"Whatever it was, they took a huge risk with Lars and Amber in the house."

"You're telling me. And if they wanted the photo, did they find it? We should go through Arndale House again, starting with Marlene's room."

"Agreed. Want to start now?" Nye asked.

"Where's Eddie?"

"Still in the pub. The cops say he hasn't left for days."

"Hiding behind his mother. Boy, it takes a big man to do that."

I'd once considered Eddie a friend, and it was difficult to admit I may have suffered another lapse in judgement.

"Maybe he's hoping it'll all blow over," I suggested. "I'd probably hide too if the entire village was spreading nasty rumours about me."

Zander shook his head. "I don't trust the man. He's cagey as hell."

Nye agreed with him. "Me neither, but we're stalled on that for the moment, and we can't afford to ignore other avenues."

"Meet you at Arndale in half an hour?"

"Works for me," Nye said.

"Want a pizza?"

How could Zander still think of food?

"Large with everything and a side of chicken wings," Nye requested.

Seemed he didn't have a problem with *his* appetite either.

When Zander parked on the corner near Perfect Pizza, he opened my door for me, but I stared studiously at the dashboard and didn't move. Acting like a statue seemed a better option than slapping him or bursting into tears. After a few seconds, he closed it again and went into the restaurant.

What was wrong with me? I didn't have any claim on Zander, and if I was honest with myself, he'd never done anything to suggest I did apart from being too damn sweet on occasion. So why was I being such a bitch? I mentally counted through my calendar—still just over a week to go until my period was due. Could it be early onset of PMS?

Headlights of a fast approaching car bounced off the rear-view mirror and made me blink in the glare. Who was in such a hurry? As the car slowed for the junction, I glanced over at the driver and did a double take. Eddie? Didn't Nye say he was supposed to be in the pub with a police surveillance team outside?

Shit!

He accelerated up the road and I fumbled for the door handle, then almost fell into a puddle next to the kerb in my hurry to get out. Rain stung my face as I sprinted across the pavement to the door of the takeaway and yanked it open.

"What happened? Did you forget a topping?" Zander asked as I gasped for air.

"No! Eddie just drove past."

"Are you sure?"

"If it wasn't him, it was his double."

Zander chucked a couple of twenty-pound notes on the counter, shouted, "Pick that up later, mate," and followed me out the door.

"Which direction did he go?"

"Right."

The R8 roared as Zander swung the wheel to the right and raced up the road with me desperately trying to clip my seat belt into the socket.

"What car was he driving?" Zander asked.

"Uh, a black one? Or maybe green? Or maroon? Blue? It was dark."

We accelerated through the curves of the lane, tree branches whipping past on either side. At least with it being dark, we'd see headlights of any cars coming in the opposite direction, which was just as well seeing as Zander didn't seem bothered by the whole "drive on the left" concept.

"Let's hope he didn't turn off," Zander muttered.

Let's hope we didn't spin off. Another minute passed before I glimpsed a set of tail lights ahead of us, turning into a left-hand bend. Zander must have seen them too, as he eased off the accelerator.

"Better hope that's him and not some other sod on his way back from the pub. I can't get close enough in this beast to check."

"But you were gaining on him."

"And loud enough to wake the dead."

Good thing one of us was trained in this sort of thing, wasn't it? Zander hung back as the car ahead turned onto the main road, and then he called Nye.

"Where's Eddie?"

"I assume he's still at home. The surveillance team promised to call if he moved."

"Check. Dove reckons she just saw him drive past us in the high street."

We drove on in silence until Nye phoned back a few minutes later.

"Son of a bitch—his mother said he was in bed, but when the cops insisted on checking, all they found was a pile of pillows and the window cracked open. I'll send the nearest car to help you."

"Hang on, he's slowing down. Call you back."

The car turned off the main road onto a side street, and Zander pulled to the kerb as it stopped outside a convenience store a hundred yards ahead. A shadowy figure climbed out and walked inside, but we were too far away to make out who it was.

"Come on," Zander said.

"We're getting out?"

"I want to check it's actually Eddie. Otherwise, we're wasting our time here."

Zander flipped up the hood on his jacket with one hand as he pulled me tight against him with the other arm. To anyone watching, we were just another couple hurrying to get out of the rain on a stormy night. With the adrenalin coursing through my veins, I'd pushed my earlier upset to one side because if Eddie was behind all the trouble, I wanted him to go down as much as Zander did. And if he'd snuck out tonight, who was to say he didn't do the same last night when Marlene took her tumble?

We got closer to the store, one of those with a glass front and dusty goods that nobody would ever buy arranged in the window like an advert for days gone by. I peered inside, but I couldn't see Eddie among the racks of sweets and birthday cards.

Without warning, Zander shoved me back under the awning and pressed me against the brick wall of the shop next door, squashing the breath out of me.

"What are you—"

I didn't get to finish my sentence before his lips were on mine, a hard, closed-mouth kiss at first, but as Eddie hurried past two feet away from us, Zander licked along the seam of my lips and they opened of their own accord. My head told me to push him away, but my body melted against his and my arms wrapped around him as I gifted him whatever he wanted to take from me.

But even as his mouth gave me my first taste of sin with a hint of cherry ChapStick, his eyes were watching Eddie as he got into his car and drove off. Zander didn't pull back right away. He blinked for one long second as he sucked on my lower lip, a move that caused sparks to burst in my belly and fire to ignite in places that had been lacking attention for far too long.

"Good spot," he finally whispered. "You okay?"

No, because you've just set the bar so high any other man will need the space shuttle to get over it.

"Never been better. Are we following?"

Only Zander's arm around my waist kept me upright as we half ran back to the car, and once I'd collapsed into the passenger seat, I couldn't stop trembling. *Zander kissed me.* Sure, it was only work-related, but bloody hell, the man knew what to do with his mouth.

I lost track of time and distance as we followed Eddie's car into a housing estate, one where the Audi looked like an opera singer at a pop concert among rows of small family hatchbacks and the occasional moped. Zander kept well back as Eddie parked outside a bungalow at the far end of the street, and we waited until he went inside.

"What do you think's happening?" I asked.

"Don't know, but I need to call Nye. I've got no idea whose car that is, but it's not Eddie's."

Five minutes later, Nye came back with the news that both the car and the house Eddie had gone into belonged to a Dalton Wendall, twenty-four years old, no criminal record, not even a parking ticket.

"Eddie's a named driver on the insurance and has been for six months."

"Before all this started. Interesting."

"Any thoughts?" Nye asked.

"I think I know Eddie's secret. Give me a few minutes."

Zander hung up and reached for the car door again.

"What's happening?" I asked. "What's his secret?"

"Give me a few minutes," he repeated.

"No way. I'm not staying here, especially when it was me who spotted Eddie in the first place."

"Dee, please."

"Don't you 'Dee' me. I'm coming." Although not quite in the way I almost had earlier.

"Fine." He cracked a grin. "But if someone sees us, you know what's gonna happen."

"Fine."

Maybe I was wrong about the coming part.

CHAPTER 33

ONCE AGAIN, ZANDER held me close as we walked along the pavement. I was beginning to like this surveillance lark. Perhaps I could get a job at Blackwood when this was over? After all, with Marlene in a coma, my position at Arndale seemed somewhat uncertain.

The house next to Dalton's lay in darkness, a "For Sale" sign standing crookedly in the front garden. Judging by the state of the lawn, almost a foot long in patches and bare in others, selling the place came low on the owner's list of priorities. But it did give us the perfect place to spy from.

Keeping low behind the chest-high fence, we crept along the path and into a back garden as neglected as the front. Even the side gate had given up trying to cling to its hinges and lay rotting on the ground.

Oh, shit. "I think I just trod in something."

"Have fun walking home."

I wiped my shoe along the grass, and I was about to jab Zander in the ribs when he paused next to a *Ceanothus* bush with enough leaves to give us cover and slowly stood up. A light glowed from a solitary room next door, giving us a perfect view of a bedroom done out in muted creams with a hint of maroon. A vase of roses sat on the windowsill, but that wasn't what caught my attention. I'd never watched anybody having sex before, let alone two men, and while the logistics kind of fascinated me, I didn't want to stay for the full show.

"Always nice to be right," Zander whispered. "Got down to it pretty fast, didn't they?"

"You knew this was what they were doing?"

"A man doesn't stop off to buy a bottle of rosé and a box of chocolates unless he's planning to get lucky." He pressed a button on his watch, and the dial illuminated. Just gone nine. "Now, do we let them finish before we knock on the door?"

"Knock on the door? You can't be serious?"

"I like to catch people off balance. Let's go."

"I'm not sure..."

"You can wait in the car if you want. Make sure you lock it."

"No! I'm coming with you."

Bile rose in my throat as Zander rang the bell, and when nobody answered, he pressed it again and knocked for good measure. Footsteps sounded on the other side before the door was yanked open.

"Evening, Eddie. Does your mother know you're here?"

I'm not kidding, Eddie went as white as his carelessly tied bathrobe.

"W-w-what do you want from me?"

"How about the truth?"

Eddie looked from Zander to me, and I clutched Zee's hand tighter. Finally, Eddie sighed and seemed to shrink before my eyes—a man defeated at a game he hadn't wanted to play in the first place.

"You'd better come in."

His friend walked into the hallway in a pair of jogging bottoms and an inside-out T-shirt, and I almost felt guilty for ruining their playtime. Almost, but not quite.

"What's going on?"

"This is one of the detectives I told you about and his girlfriend."

I shook my head. "Oh, we're not..."

My words fizzled out as Eddie's gaze dropped to our joined hands, and I hastily let go.

He looked Zander in the eye. "What were you saying about the truth, mate?"

"Just get on with it."

Oddly enough, nobody offered us drinks as we took a seat on the sofa in the lounge, with Eddie sitting in the chair opposite and Dalton perched on the windowsill. Was Zander's mouth as dry as mine? He seemed so calm, as though he did this every day. Who knows—maybe he did.

"What's going on, Eddie?"

"I stepped out to visit a friend."

"Cut the bullshit. We're dealing with a murder here, and possibly another attempted one."

Confusion showed in Eddie's eyes, and his brow furrowed. "Attempted murder? What are you talking about?"

"Your mother didn't tell you?"

"I've been avoiding my parents as much as possible. Every time I see Mother, she complains I've brought shame on the family."

"As of last night, Marlene Grande's in a coma. We're not sure if she fell down the stairs or someone pushed her."

"Well, it wasn't me. I was here."

"All night?"

Eddie looked towards Dalton, who shrugged. "From around this time until four thirty."

"And what about Isabelle? I know you haven't told us everything there."

"That wasn't me either. She's not even dead."

"So why not tell the police everything?"

"Just tell him," Dalton said. "We can't keep living like this."

Eddie slumped back in the chair. "If I do, will it get back to my parents?"

"Your parents? That's who you're worried about?"

"Have you ever talked to my dad? I mean, really talked?"

Zander shook his head.

"I love my mother. She's the one who brought me up, who drove me to school every day and arranged my birthday parties. And my father? I guess I love him too, but he's also a bigoted, homophobic asshole when it suits him." He glanced over at Dalton. "If he finds out I'm gay, he'll make sure I'm cut off from the entire family."

"So you'd rather he thought you were a murderer?" I blurted.

"That'll blow over when the police work out the girl's not Isabelle."

"Who is she?"

"No idea. I only know who she isn't."

Zander sighed. "Start at the beginning, would you? I'm not going to tell your parents, although I can't guarantee they won't find out some other way."

"Fuck. I need a drink. Dalton, could you get that

wine? Actually, something stronger."

Dalton slipped from the room as Eddie began his tale.

"I worked for an investment bank in London. Money ruled, big money. I had plenty, but the place was full of men like my father, and after I'd been screwing people over for a few years, I realised money wasn't everything. I also began to question my own views. We'd go out to a strip bar in the evening, and my colleagues would be lusting over the tits while I snuck glances at their asses."

"How does this tie in with Isabelle?"

"I'm getting to that. I met her in a bar one evening, and she had the sweetest damn smile, and I wondered if I'd been mistaken. Maybe I'd just been waiting for the right girl to come along, after all? We started dating, and when Isabelle's lease ran out, she moved in. But they didn't go away—the feelings—and as work got shittier, the only thing that kept me sane was a little experimentation. That's what Isabelle walked in on."

Bloody hell! She walked in on him with a man? Ouch.

"Who were you with?" Zander asked. "Dalton?"

"I don't even remember his name, and he legged it pretty fast when Isabelle started yelling. I yelled back, and we both said some pretty nasty things."

"She threatened to tell all Eddie's friends," Dalton said, walking back in with a bottle of Scotch and two glasses.

Eddie glared at him.

Zander shrugged. "Sounds like a motive for murder to me."

Dalton balled his fists up, and Eddie gave Zander a

look that said *fuck you*.

"I didn't kill her. We both ran out of steam, and I knew deep down it was all my fault. I wasn't capable of loving her the way she wanted me to, and anyone would have been upset if they saw what she just did. No, we sat at the dining table and hashed out a deal."

"Which was?"

"She'd always wanted to take a cruise—one of those big ships with stops in every port—but I'd been putting it off for ages because work was so damn busy, and truthfully, I hated the idea of being on a boat with a bunch of strangers. So, we got on the internet, and I booked her a damn cruise."

"On her own?"

"You don't know Isabelle. You could throw her to the wolves and she'd make friends with every single one of them. To her, it was one big adventure."

"So she went on a cruise?"

"A hundred and eighty nights, all the way around the world. If she was on the boat, she wouldn't be talking to our friends, would she?"

"But that was over a year ago."

"Yeah, I know. She called a couple of months in and said she'd met a guy. Some artist from Canada. Wanted me to hang onto her stuff until she could pick it up, but told me not to hold my breath."

"I don't understand. Why didn't you just tell us this?"

"And risk stirring up the whole hornets' nest again? Most of the time Isabelle was sweet, but she had mood swings that made Medusa look friendly. Get her on a bad day and everyone would know what I did. And like I said, this murder bullshit will blow over sooner or later."

Zander narrowed his eyes. "While you've let the police chase their tails, the real killer has been walking free."

"I'm sorry for that. Really, I am. But I care about my mother too much to drop a bomb on her."

"So, what's your plan? You're gonna keep Dalton hidden away here forever?"

Dalton walked over and sat on the arm of Eddie's chair, and they looked at each other. Really looked. You'd have to be blind to miss the love between them, and I felt angry on their behalf that they had to hide it.

"I've almost finished my PhD," Dalton said. "Then we're moving to Paris. With the money Eddie saved by living with his parents, we can afford to buy a decent apartment. I've got an assistant's position at the Louvre waiting for me, and Eddie's writing a cookbook."

Beside me, Zander sighed. "I'll need to check all this out. I don't suppose you can remember the artist's name?"

"Sorry. I'm not sure Isabelle ever told me, but she did mention he was staying in the cabin next to hers."

"Can you send me details of the cruise?"

"I'll email them over if you give me your address."

Zander did so, then sighed. "So, if the girl in the ground isn't Isabelle, and you didn't kill her, who the hell is she and why did someone bury her there?"

"Like I said, it beats me. Do you want my advice?"

"Go on."

"Look for somebody outside the village. I grew up in that pub, listening to the gossip every night, and when folks get a drop of alcohol in them, it lets their true character show. I can't see any of our neighbours committing murder. They moan, they bitch, and they'll drag your name through the mud with the mere hint of a rumour, but killing a woman? No way."

"I'll take those thoughts on board." Zander got to his feet. "For what it's worth, I hope you'll both be happy."

"You too, with your non-girlfriend."

Back in the car, Zander didn't start the engine right away. Instead, he leaned back in the seat and closed his eyes. "Fuck it. Another lead gone."

"But at least we know now, and I'm glad you went easy on him at the end, even though he wasted so much time. This isn't pleasant for anyone."

If I'd been in Zander's position, I'd have been tempted to let Eddie have a few choice words, then regretted it later.

"I'm well aware of the problems that arise from dealing with a difficult father."

I didn't even think before I pulled Zander's hand into my lap. "I'm sorry."

"It's all in the past." He gave my fingers a squeeze before wrapping his hand around mine on the gear stick. "Do you still want that pizza?"

I didn't feel angry like I had earlier. Zander was right. The past was the past, and even if we had no future, we could still enjoy the present.

"Pizza sounds great."

Chapter 34

THE NEXT MORNING, I attempted to un-crick my back as I walked to the main house with Zander. Another night on the sofa hadn't done it any favours.

In the kitchen, Amber and Lars sat on one side of the breakfast bar while Zander and I took the other. Vince and Hal leaned against the counter. Tension ruled, and Nye's arrival with Ivy did little to ease it.

Nye helped his grandma onto a stool then hovered protectively behind her, a sweet gesture, and one that made me feel a rare pang of sadness that children didn't appear to be on the horizon for me. Not when I couldn't even manage to find a suitable man.

"Tea?" Lars offered, ever the gentleman where visitors were concerned.

"English breakfast with a twist of lemon, please," Ivy requested.

"I'd prefer coffee," Nye said.

Once everybody got settled with their drinks, we stared expectantly at Ivy. After all, it was she who'd requested this little meeting, and I'd lain awake half the night worrying over what she wanted to discuss. A word about Marlene's estate, that's all she'd said.

"I'm sure you're wondering why I gathered you here," she began. "I thought it best to do this sooner rather than later. As I'm sure you all know, Marlene doesn't have any living relatives, and we've been close friends for a number of years. This situation was something she worried about, enough to set up a Lasting Power of Attorney with regard to her finances and health in case she ever became incapacitated in this manner."

Right then, Ivy didn't sound like the slightly bonkers old lady I'd grown to know and love. She was all business, and I realised that underneath her quirky exterior, she still hid a shrewd mind and an intelligence most people only dreamed of.

"As of now, I have control over all of her affairs, including any decisions to be made concerning the Arndale estate. And I say this: I believe she will wake up. Marlene isn't a quitter. And when she comes back home, I want this place ready for her damn party. You'll be paid as usual, and if you need extra manpower, find it. Marlene's never missed a social event, and she isn't about to start now."

Nye grinned. "That's my grandma."

She turned her attention to him. "And you can stop standing around. Haven't you got a murder to solve?"

He gave her a salute. "Yes, ma'am."

After Ivy's decree, we got back to work. The garden wouldn't weed itself, and I needed to order pots, plants, and all the accoutrements that went with them. Ivy gave me her accountant's number and promised he'd take care of the cost.

Zander and Nye spent the day turning the house upside down in search of the missing photo, and although truthfully nobody expected it to turn up, we were still disappointed when it didn't.

And Bear's blood test results didn't help either.

"Diazepam? The dog took Valium?" Zander asked whoever was on the other end of the phone as we ate our sandwiches for lunch.

Apparently, the answer was yes, because he hung up shaking his head.

"Valium?" I asked.

"Apparently it works as a sedative in dogs."

"Didn't Ivy say she gave some to Marlene?"

"Yes. And according to Nye, she's done it more than once, so we can't be sure Bear didn't find a couple of spare pills rattling around and decide to snack on them."

"So we still don't know whether her fall was an accident?"

"Exactly, but this missing photo's bugging the hell out of me, especially if more people in the pub heard her talking about it."

"And the power cut."

"That too. The power company said they had a similar incident in Great Haseley six months back, and it turned out to be teenagers, but still..."

"It's a mess, isn't it?"

"Everything's a mess at the moment."

"Any luck with Isabelle? You don't have to go to Canada, do you?"

"I've got hold of the passenger manifest and found a possible name for the artist. Our Quebec office is trying to track him down, but apparently, he doesn't have a phone. Go figure."

Three days later, Zander located Monsieur Langevin and his new wife, Isabelle, living in a log cabin in the wilds on the north-east shore of Quebec. Apparently, the nudes he painted of her sold for big money at auction, and she rarely felt the need to wear clothes anymore.

"Our boys got quite an eyeful," Zander said. "Especially when she uncrossed her legs."

I choked on a mouthful of cornflakes. "What, she didn't get dressed when they visited?"

"Apparently neither of them did. I quote, 'Being liberated from the fabric of society frees the mind as well as the body.'" He waggled his eyebrows. "Want to try it sometime?"

With Zander? Oh, yes.

"Absolutely not."

"You sure about that?"

He was only teasing, but my heart still lurched.

"Positive. I need to get outside. Some of us have work to do today."

His chuckles followed me out the door, and I slammed it behind me. How did that man get me so riled up with just a few words? Okay, and a sexy smile?

And riled up enough to forget to put my gloves on, too. I tried to manage without them, but after half an hour of measuring out new vegetable beds, I kept dropping the tape measure because I could no longer feel my fingers. With any luck, Zander would have gone out.

Or almost as good, be in the shower.

I heard the water running as soon as I got in the door, and I thanked my lucky stars I wouldn't have to face his hotness until lunchtime, when he'd promised to make me grilled cheese with my tomato soup.

Now, where did I leave my gloves? On my bedroom radiator if I remembered rightly.

I got halfway up the stairs before I realised I had a problem. Zander may have been in the shower, but the bathroom door had swung open, and I could see everything. Ev-ery-thing.

And Zander wasn't just washing himself. He was touching himself. Hot damn!

The sensible thing, the smart thing, the right thing for me to do would have been to quietly back down the stairs and erase all images of that particular act from my mind. The way he leaned his head on one arm as it rested against the side of the shower, angled away from me. The way the water ran down his muscled torso and over his tasty ass. The way he fisted his cock in his hand and stroked, slow and steady, his grip firm.

Yes, that would have been the smart thing. But when had I ever been smart? My legs wobbled, and I sank to my knees on the stairs, unable to tear my eyes away.

A minute ticked past, then two, and the ache between my legs grew to a steady throb. How I longed to unzip my jeans and find my release, but I didn't dare. If he turned his head... Oh, hell, I couldn't back away. I shifted a little, and the seam of the denim rubbed in precisely the wrong spot, or the right spot, depending on how you looked at it. I just couldn't help myself. My hand inched downwards, fingers pressing through the fabric as Zander's movements grew faster, jerkier.

And when he came hard against the shower tiles, I did too, so violently I slid halfway down the stairs.

"Hello?"

His voice floated from the bathroom, and I crawled behind the sofa, flattening myself against the floor so he wouldn't see me if he decided to poke his head out.

Please, don't be a detective all your life.

Time slowed, and I swear my heart stopped beating as I waited for footsteps on the stairs, but nothing came. Except Zander and me, of course. Bloody hell.

Slowly, so slowly, I backed out of the cottage, careful to pull the door gently so the *click* of the lock was barely audible. What on earth had I been thinking? Oh, that's right—I hadn't. I'd pulled yet another stupid Dove move and somehow got away without being caught, but the result meant that while I should have been considering the depth and angles for my raised beds and how much timber I'd need to order, all I could see was a naked Zander, climaxing over and over again every time I blinked.

"Dove, you've really done it this time," I told myself.

"Done what?" Zander asked from behind, causing me to drop a trowel on my foot. I hopped backwards and almost fell, but he caught me, holding me against his stomach so I could feel every one of his abs and his... Dammit! Not helping.

"Uh, I've taken on a lot with this vegetable garden. It's wild."

"Wish I could lend a hand, but I've got to head out for a bit. Do you want me to make your lunch first?"

No, because then I'd have to look at him for longer, and I'd end up replaying the water running down his chest, lower and lower...

I forced a smile. "It's fine. I'll make something in a minute."

"See you later, then."

I couldn't wait.

CHAPTER 35

"JUST LEAVING LONDON. I'll be back by seven as long as the traffic's okay."

Hurrah. I'd half hoped Zander would stay in town overnight, even if it meant sleeping in the cottage by myself. Amber had moved most of her stuff into the main house on the pretence of getting an early start each morning, but it didn't take a genius to understand she was still cross about being questioned over the Marlene affair.

"I'll see you soon."

"Stay in the house until I get there."

"I'm already in the cottage. I'll keep the door locked, I promise."

"Alarm the perimeter."

"Yes, sir."

I hung up, and Vince, who was sitting across from me with a cup of tea, chuckled.

"I give him a week before he goes full alpha."

"What are you talking about?"

"Zander, and his tendency to get all protective over you."

"It's his job."

He drained his cup and put it in the dishwasher. "You keep telling yourself that."

Before I could interrogate Vince further, he slipped

out the door with a cheery, "Don't forget the alarm."

Men. They confused the hell out of me.

By the time Zander opened the front door, I'd managed to make a passable imitation of spaghetti bolognese, aided in no small part by a ready-made sauce I found in the freezer.

"Honey, I'm home," he called.

Oh shit. "I've made dinner. It might be edible."

"Don't do yourself down. A client sent me a crate of wine, so I've brought a couple of bottles."

"That was nice of him. Or her?"

"Him. He does it every year—I found his missing daughter, and today's the anniversary of the day she went home."

And what did I do for my job? Dug holes and pruned things. A man like Zander played in a different league to me. I fetched two plates from the cupboard and put them in the oven to warm while I drained the pasta, and tried once more to overwrite my mind with a fully clothed version of hotness. It didn't work.

"You look stressed," he said. "Here, have a glass of red."

"Thanks." I gulped half before it occurred to me I should slow down or risk looking like an alcoholic. "Uh, it's good. Full-bodied and all that jazz."

What was I even saying? Thoughts of naked Zander made my words go totally random.

He tilted his head to one side. "Are you feeling okay? Tired?"

"Tired! Yes, I'm tired."

I grabbed onto the word and used it as my shield.

"Why don't you sit down? I'll finish dinner and bring it through."

Usually, I'd have waved him away, but tonight I practically sprinted into the lounge with a hasty, "Thanks," over my shoulder.

This would wear off, right? At some point, I'd have to look him in the eye again.

As he carried through my plate on a tray, complete with cutlery and the wine I'd forgotten to pick up, I focused on the TV and a soap I didn't enjoy and never watched. Next time my hands got cold, I'd deal with it a different way. In fact, dying of hypothermia looked like an attractive option at the moment.

"Are you watching this?" Zander settled beside me with his own dinner.

"Feel free to change it."

Thank goodness, he found a movie he wanted to watch. Something with plenty of shooting and explosions and not enough plot to matter. Me? I found wine.

And sleep, it turned out. When I stirred, the TV was still flickering with an advert for a miracle juicer that promised no waste, extra vitamins, and easy cleaning. Or—I eyed up the empty bottle on the table—I could drink a different fruit-based beverage that didn't require any of that faffing around. One with interesting side effects, like waking up draped over Zander in the early hours of the morning.

What?

Oh, bloody hell. He stirred underneath me, tightening his arm around my waist as he did so. I tried moving a little to relieve the pins and needles in my right arm, only for his eyes to pop open and stare right into mine.

In the semi-darkness, I felt rather than saw him looking at me, drinking in feelings I'd intended to keep hidden for both our sakes as I lay plastered against his chest with our lips mere inches apart.

When I was nine years old, I ate seven choc ices in a row because the sun was shining, the birds were singing, and I could open the freezer door all by myself. At twelve, crisps were my weakness. The teacher told me off at school one day, and when I got home, I troughed down an entire multipack to cheer myself up. Four flavours, twelve bags, and one hell of a stomach ache. Today, at almost twenty-three years old, I once again displayed that same remarkable lack of common sense or self-control as I lowered my head and touched my lips to Zander's.

For a few wonderful seconds, he kissed me back in a repeat of our surveillance-related experiment yesterday. Heat rushed through me, only for a fire hose to hit me square in the chest as he pulled back.

"Dee, don't. We shouldn't."

"Why not? We're both adults. Last time I checked, kissing was allowed."

Or had I misread things that badly? No, not unless he was in the habit of carrying an economy-sized salami around in his pocket.

"I have rules."

"Maybe you should break them?"

"And with you, it would be so fucking easy. Dee..."

"What?"

"If we started something, I'd never want it to stop, and... I'm scared."

He ended on a whisper and looked away, but before I could think of something to say about the way he'd just bared his soul to me, he got up and lifted me with him.

"I'll put you to bed."

"Wait, we should talk about this."

"Those five rules have kept me safe over the last ten years."

Five rules? What were the other two? "So take a risk. You already broke one of them."

"And I shouldn't have."

We were halfway up the stairs, and the set to his mouth grew grimmer with every step.

"Zander..."

He deposited me in bed and tucked the duvet under my chin. Then, almost as an afterthought, he bent and pressed his lips to my forehead.

"Sleep, Dee. I'm sorry."

Well, at least naked Zander didn't bother me again that night. No, all I saw in my dreams was his bleak expression as he rejected me.

Until that night, I didn't realise it was possible to cry in my sleep, but I woke with a damp pillow and a crushed heart. All I wanted to do was sneak a bottle of wine upstairs, quaff the lot, then hide under the duvet until I repeated the action tomorrow.

But with less than two months until the party and Ivy wanting me to make the vegetable garden presentable, I needed to get back to clearing weeds that grew taller every day.

When I got to the kitchen, Zander carried on staring into his mug of tea.

"I made you a cup," he said.

"Thanks."

"Look, about last night…"

"Don't. You made your feelings quite clear."

"Yeah, I did."

Silence followed, and I'd sat down and begun spreading Marmite on my toast by the time he spoke again.

"I'm going into the office today. More results from the background checks have come in, and it's easier to see patterns if I can print everything out and pin it up on the wall. Vince'll be around all day if you need him."

The excuse was flimsy, and we both knew it. "You don't need to justify yourself to me."

"Still…"

"Just go, Zander."

He pushed his stool back and stood, then bent as if to kiss me on the cheek. Well, he didn't have the right to do that. Not after the way he'd knocked me back. I got up myself and stared out the window.

"Go."

"If I don't come back tonight, I'll send someone else to stay."

The way he said it, I was pretty damn certain I'd be opening the door to a stranger this evening. Maybe not a complete stranger—it could be Max or the Incredible Hulk—but it wouldn't be Zander.

"Just go."

I took my anger out on the semi-frozen ground, attacking it first with a spade and then with a pickaxe. Who knew heartbreak could be so productive? By lunchtime, I'd got more done than in the last two days combined, even if my hands were raw with blisters.

"I'm going to get something to eat," I said to Vince. "Are you coming?"

"In a bit. I want to take the rest of this tree down first. Save me a slice of cake, will you?"

"If there is any."

My stomach grumbled, and I figured it was time to mend bridges with Amber and Lars. Otherwise, the Arndale estate would turn into a very lonely place to be.

"Hey," I said as I walked into the main kitchen.

The pair of them looked up from the remains of their sandwiches, first at me, then at each other. It didn't exactly scream "welcome."

"We're on our way out," Amber said.

"I can leave if you want. I just wanted to say I'm sorry about all of this. You know, the whole situation."

"It's fine."

Lars softened infinitesimally. "You like Zander. We get it, okay? It's only natural for you to side with him."

"We should be on the same side."

"I know. But sometimes it's not so straightforward." He let out a long sigh. "If you're hungry, there's lasagne in the fridge you can heat in the microwave. We're going to the DIY store if you want us to pick up anything."

"No, I've got what I need."

"We'll see you for dinner?"

"I'd like that."

He looked over at Amber. "Be nice."

"Fine." Her smile was more of a grimace. "See you later."

Lars's lasagne tasted delicious as always, the perfect

balance of moist beef, tomato sauce, and pasta, but as I ate, I couldn't help wishing for Zander's grilled cheese instead. He'd probably picked up his lunch at a fancy cafe, or one of those burrito places that seemed to be springing up on every corner in London at the moment.

My phone rang, making me jump. Zander? I fumbled it out of my pocket only to be disappointed. It was Carrie calling.

"Dove? I really need your help." She sounded breathless.

"Why? What's happened?"

"Auntie's in the bath, and usually I lift her out, but I bent over and pulled a muscle in my back. Would you be able to lend a hand? I tried Amber, but she didn't answer."

"She's gone out with Lars."

"I see. Otherwise I could call Vince or Hal, but Auntie doesn't have any clothes on, and this is embarrassing enough for her as it is."

"Don't worry, I'll be right over."

"Thanks, you're a lifesaver. I'll leave the side door unlocked. Can you come up to the bathroom? I don't want to leave Auntie."

"Sure."

"It's the third door on the right at the top of the stairs."

"I'm leaving right now."

The fastest way to Fernleigh House was through the woods at the back, and now the police had taken the crime scene tape down, I could use the half-finished path as a shortcut. Trees whispered in the wind as I stepped into the darkness, and for a moment, I considered turning back. How much longer would it take to go by road?

Too long.

The thought of Mrs. Hearst lying in rapidly cooling water made me hurry forwards, through the gloom and past the chapel. A bird shot out of the undergrowth and nearly gave me heart failure. Maybe I could go back for Vince? Where was he, anyway? He hadn't come in for lunch, but I couldn't hear the sound of his chainsaw either.

The open grave yawned on my right, and I quickly looked away as memories of the girl who once lay inside came flooding back. I quickened my steps, almost running as I burst out into daylight. *Whew.* I'd made it, even if I was panting like Bear after he'd been chasing a particularly energetic rabbit.

As promised, Carrie had left the door open, and I slid my wellies off before I went inside. No sense in creating extra mess.

"Carrie? I'm here," I called.

No answer, but the hairs prickled on the back of my neck as I felt a presence behind me. *Turn, Dove. Turn!*

Or better still, run.

Time slowed, and the message didn't make it to my legs before I heard the rustle of clothing, then a thin whistling noise, an object being swung through the air.

Stars burst behind my eyes, and the hallway ahead with its polished side table and colourful arrangement of silk flowers faded to black.

Chapter 36

WHY COULDN'T I move? I tried lifting a leg, but nothing happened. The same with my arms. And my head felt heavy, so heavy, with a steady throb behind my eyes that grew more intense every time I flexed a muscle.

The smell told me I wasn't home—a vague hint of flowers with an undertone of pine. I'd come across that somewhere recently, but where? The photos. While we looked at the photos. I must be at Carrie's house, but where was Carrie?

Had whoever attacked me hurt her too?

I attempted to open my eyes again, and this time I got one lid halfway. What was that around my waist? Something silver? Duct tape?

Panic welled up inside me as I realised I'd been taped to a chair—wrists, ankles, and stomach. And that ache in my head? I'd been knocked out.

"Carrie?" I tried to shout, but it came out as a croak. Was she all right? Or had she managed to escape?

Footsteps sounded behind me seconds later. "You're awake, then. I wasn't sure if you'd come round or not."

Wait a second. That was Carrie's voice. But she sounded so calm?

It took every bit of my strength to raise my chin,

and I saw I was still in the hallway, but at the back by the door to the dining room. Mrs. Hearst's photo albums lay scattered across the floor, some with pages ripped out, others bent in half by somebody in the throes of rage.

"What's happening?"

"You and your boyfriend fucked everything up. You just couldn't leave it alone, could you?"

"Zander? He's not my…"

"Yeah, yeah, whatever."

"I don't understand."

"Always were a bit dense, weren't you? I dropped enough hints, and you still kept messing around in the woods."

"That was you? The tools? The knife? But how did you know about the body?" Oh shit. Carrie was right. I really was dense. "You buried her there?"

"It seemed like the perfect solution. The Arndale estate had been abandoned for years. *Years*. Then Marlene turned up with her piles of cash and big ideas. She deserved everything she got."

"So you *did* push her down the stairs?"

"She didn't need a lot of help, seeing as she was already pissed. That dog's not much of a guard, by the way. He takes bribes way too easily."

"So, what now? You're going to kill me too?"

Carrie's footsteps came closer, and she stroked my hair, a gentle caress at odds with her demeanour. I jerked my head away as the little bit of lunch I'd eaten threatened to escape.

"Get off!"

"Don't be so touchy. It's nothing personal. I just need another girl in the house to confuse things, and that left you or Amber. By the time the police realise it wasn't me who died in the fire, I'll be long gone."

My heart raced, and every beat sent a shock wave through my head. "Fire? You're going to start a fire?"

More footsteps, and she came into view. Gone was sweet Carrie and her shy smile. This woman's grin was pure evil as she pointed to a mess of duct tape attached to the bannister with wires coming out of the top and bottom. Boy, she really loved that stuff, didn't she?

"It's going to be spectacular, believe me. I'm almost sorry I won't be around to see it, but an old friend messaged me to say your boyfriend's colleagues in Australia are sticking their noses where they shouldn't."

"Where are you going?"

"A tropical paradise somewhere. A beach, palm trees, cocktails."

"But what about your aunt and uncle? And Neil?"

"Neil? Why would I want to stay with that gronk? I don't even go for men, but he made a good cover story." Her face creased into a happier smile, but one still tinged with madness. "Auntie's still in the bath. Every day, I had to pander to her fucking needs. Cook this, clean that—what kind of freak spends their life taking care of a pair of geriatrics without adequate compensation?"

"A kind one?"

"You're kind and look where that's got you. You dig holes to earn a few quid, and that's all you'll ever do."

"It makes me happy."

"And money makes me happy."

"But—"

"Shut up. You've talked enough, and I'm bored

now."

She picked up a roll of tape from the side table, tore off a length, and walked towards me. I realised her plan and twisted away, begging like the pathetic fool she believed me to be.

"Please, don't. Please—"

She slapped the tape over my mouth anyway. "I'd rather you didn't start screaming. It hurts my ears."

I could do nothing but watch as she wheeled a pair of matching suitcases out of the lounge, carried them down the front steps, then loaded them into her Honda Jazz. Such a nice, normal car, totally at odds with the monster about to get behind the wheel.

"Forty minutes," she said as she pressed a button on the bomb she'd made. A digital display flashed into life and began its emotionless countdown to my death. "Sweet dreams."

The front door slammed behind her, and once the car had crunched over the gravel, the only sounds left were the ticking of the grandfather clock and the beeps from the timer. And when I listened harder, a quiet hiss coming from the kitchen. What was that?

I worked it out a couple of minutes later when the smell of sulphur tickled my nostrils. Gas. The bitch had left the gas on. Now I understood her comment about my death being spectacular.

My bonds didn't give an inch as I struggled against them. Carrie had taken the chair from the dining room, a solidly built Edwardian affair that would most likely withstand the apocalypse, let alone the helpless attempts of an eight-and-a-half-stone woman to break it.

The faintest sound of a chainsaw started up, and I

wondered when Vince would notice I was missing. Probably not for a while, seeing as he thought I'd gone inside to get lunch. And Zander. When would he realise? A tear ran down my cheek as I thought back over our relationship, if you could call it that. The highs —our comfortable lunches, the camaraderie on the case, even our good-natured bickering. And that day in London where he'd got me out of a jam with my parents, even at the wrath of Laura.

Then there were the lows. Zander's history with his parents, his inability to commit to anything, and worst of all, the way he'd made me feel last night. But at least I'd die knowing what love was, because I'd fallen for him, even if he didn't reciprocate or even know.

But dammit, I wanted him to know! Even if he only knocked me back again, I wanted him to know that he wasn't the unloveable cad he thought he was.

My tears seeped under the edge of the duct tape and loosened it a little, but no matter how much I rubbed it on my shoulder, I couldn't get it off. And even if I could, what good would it do? Who would hear me scream?

Thirty minutes. I looked around the hallway for something sharp, a jagged edge or a rough corner, but the polished wood gave me nothing. Unless I could get to the kitchen? I hop-shuffled the chair sideways, an inch at a time, closer, closer, until a leg caught on the edge of the rug and the whole thing tipped sideways.

Fireworks burst in my head again as I hit the floor, and a bolt of pain shot through my shoulder, but even then the damn chair didn't break. If only Mrs. Hearst had bought her furniture from IKEA rather than an antique shop, I might have stood a chance. I twisted to see the timer above my head, still beeping away.

Ten minutes.

I'd been hoping for a miracle, that someone would come and rescue me, but with so little time left, I prayed for the opposite. If anyone came now, they could end up in the explosion with me. Better to die alone than in company.

Or was I alone? Carrie had said her aunt was upstairs, but I hadn't heard a whisper. And where was her uncle?

With five minutes to go, my ears began ringing and I felt strangely euphoric, like the finish line was in sight. I snorted in gas-filled air in the hope that it might knock me out before the counter got to zero. The reaper might be coming, but I'd rather not be there to greet him.

Four minutes, and my thoughts returned to Zander. I hoped he'd find someone to make him happy in the end. He deserved that much. He deserved everything.

Three minutes, and I closed my eyes, remembering that last kiss with him, but blocking out the ending. Why not sneak one final morsel of happiness into what was left of my life? It would be over soon enough.

Two minutes, and I...heard voices?

CHAPTER 37

"ON THREE," A female voice said from outside the door.

"One. Two. Thr—"

A splintering crash tore through the air as the front door flew open, and Vince stumbled inside with two women I'd never seen before, one blonde, and the other with hair as black as Carrie's soul.

Vince rushed towards me while the strangers paused by the bomb on the bannister.

"Control from Emmy," the blonde said. "Count me down two minutes."

"What do you think?" the dark-haired girl asked.

"Look at those wires. The whole place could be rigged, not to mention the gas. I vote we don't touch it."

"Agreed."

Vince ripped the tape off my mouth, and I gulped in the air drifting through the open door.

"We need to get out of here. She said it's going to explode," I choked.

"Are you alone in the house?" Emmy asked.

"I don't think so. Carrie said her aunt's in the bath, and I don't know where her uncle is."

She looked at the other girl, who nodded. "Get Dove out of here," she barked at Vince. "Right away from the house."

"You need to leave with us."

She grinned at him. "We've still got a minute and a half."

With that, the two girls sprinted for the stairs, leaving Vince to pick me and the chair up and jog towards the door.

"Third door on the right," I yelled before we got outside. That was what Carrie had said, wasn't it?

Instead of heading down the driveway, Vince turned left for the woods, his pace increasing as he hopped over the low wall at the edge of the patio and got onto the lawn. Once we reached the trees, he set me on the ground behind a sturdy oak and stood to the side, watching.

"Come on, girls," he muttered. "Get the hell out of there."

"Who are they?"

"The blonde's Nye and Zander's boss. The other one, I don't know, but she scares the shit out of me."

I craned my neck to the side, trying to see the doors and muttering a prayer. How long left on the timer? Thirty seconds? Twenty?

They were still inside when Vince shoved me further behind the tree and used his body to shield mine as we waited, and waited...

Carrie was right about one thing—the explosion was spectacular. Even with my eyes closed, the flash of light was blinding, and the noise made my hearing go all funny. Chunks of wood and masonry fell around us as Vince pressed me against the tree trunk, and when the *boom* turned into the crackle of flames, he leaned back and stared at me.

"Fuck me." His words, but I shared the sentiment.

"Did you see them leave?"

He shook his head. "I could see both doors, and they didn't come out either of them."

"Then they..."

He took a deep breath, drew a penknife out of his pocket, and crouched beside me. "Let's get you free, okay? Are you injured?"

"My head hurts. Carrie knocked me out and I still feel a bit fuzzy."

"Carrie did all this?"

"She's insane. I didn't have a clue what she was really like."

"Me neither, and I met her a few times."

"Then how did you know to come here?"

"I didn't. Those girls turned up looking for you, but you'd disappeared, and your phone was turned off."

Hands now free, I reached into my pocket and pulled out the mangled remains. "It must have broken when I fell."

He pulled me into a hug. "It'll be okay."

"It won't. Four people just died in there."

Vince took a deep breath and let it out in one puff. "And one of those people was Emerson Black. I can't believe it. Really, I can't. She knew what that timer said, and she wouldn't make a mistake like that. Are you up to walking?"

"How far?"

"I want to check the other sides of the house."

I looped my arm through his, and we set off as fast as I could go. Even this far back, the ferocious heat seared my skin as the fire leapt into a darkening sky, the wind blowing the smoke and flames towards the woods we'd just come out of.

"Okay?" Vince asked. "Do you want me to carry you?"

"Don't mention that word."

"Huh?"

"Carry."

We'd got to the far corner of the house when Vince picked me up anyway and broke into a run.

"What is it? What have you—"

Then I saw it too. The smoke cleared for a second, and I glimpsed two figures crouching over a body on the far side of the swimming pool. A wave of relief flooded through me. No, a tsunami of relief. Carrie hadn't claimed as many victims as she'd hoped.

All three figures were soaking wet—the blonde, her friend, and Mrs. Hearst lying on the ground between them.

"Where's Mr. Hearst?" I asked.

The dark-haired girl looked up as she carried on with the chest compressions. "The old man was dead in bed with half a face missing. This one was still warm, so we threw her into the pool."

Her accent wasn't British. Eastern European, Russian maybe? Whatever, it only made her blunt words sound harsher, and bile forced its way into my throat as I thought of what Carrie did to her own uncle.

"Will she live?" Vince asked.

"We'll find out when the ambulance arrives with a defibrillator," the blonde said before breathing into Mrs. Hearst once more. "Sorry, we haven't been properly introduced. I'm Emmy Black."

She held out a hand to me, and I shook automatically. How could she stay so calm?

"Dove Hallam."

"I know. Zander's girlfriend."

"I'm not—"

"Trust me, it's only a matter of time."

A shout came from the driveway, and I looked across to see Nye racing towards us. The sight of another familiar face made me feel a tiny bit better, but truthfully, there was only one man I wanted to see.

Nye skidded to a halt in front of us and looked me up and down. "Are you okay?"

"I will be."

"Can you take over from Ana?" Emmy asked him, only it came out as an instruction. "She needs to move the car. The police'll be here soon, and there's no easy way to explain the MANPADS in the boot."

"What the fuck?"

"Don't look at me like that. It's almost legitimate."

"What's a MANPADS?" I asked.

Nye shook his head. "You don't want to know. In fact, forget you ever heard that part."

They swapped places, and Ana sauntered off down the drive, nonchalant, as if she hadn't just leapt from a burning building or seen a dead person up close.

"Who is she?" I asked.

"You don't want to know that either."

Sirens sounded, close, and underneath the high-pitched wailing, I heard a deeper noise—a throaty roar that I recognised.

"Zander's here?"

Emmy glanced at her watch. "He made good time. Wonder how many speeding tickets he got?"

The R8 skidded to a halt behind the ambulance, and Zander was running across the gravel before the paramedics even got their doors open. I disentangled myself from Vince and stumbled towards him on shaky legs.

Zander didn't say a word, just hugged me tight against his chest and rained kisses on my head as I burst into tears. Tremors ran through me as the events of the afternoon sank in properly—Carrie's betrayal, waiting for my own death, the explosion, the Hearsts.

"Did Carrie hurt you?" Zander asked.

"She h-h-hit me on the head, but I'm feeling better now you're here."

He flagged down a second ambulance coming along the drive. "Over here—we need some help." Unless I was mistaken, his voice shook too.

"I'm okay. It's Mrs. Hearst who needs the help."

"And she's getting it. I'm worried about you."

A pair of paramedics helped me onto a stretcher, and Zander didn't let go of my hand while they poked and prodded me and shone lights into my eyes.

"She's got a slight concussion. We'll take her to the hospital for a scan just in case."

The first time I went to A&E, when I put a fork through my toe at college, I'd waited for three hours before I saw a doctor. It was much faster after the car accident, and today, when Emmy and Nye followed us in, they held a brief conference with a man in scrubs and I got wheeled straight through for tests. An hour later, the doctor told me I could go home as long as I had somebody to keep me company for the next forty-eight hours.

"That'll be me," Zander said.

"Is there any news on Mrs. Hearst?" I asked.

"She's alive but unconscious. Looks like the woman we know as Carrie walloped her with a hammer."

"What do you mean, the woman we know as Carrie?"

"It's a long story, and one we're still unravelling. Do you feel up to having a chat with the police this evening?"

"What time is it?"

"Half past six."

"Really? I thought it was much later. Yes, if it'll help to catch that madwoman, I'll do anything."

Zander wrapped an arm around my waist and picked up my bag of painkillers with the other hand. I didn't want to scare him off, but at the same time, I needed his closeness, so I gingerly put an arm around him too. He didn't flinch.

"Where do we need to go? The police station?"

"They can come out to Arndale House. That way you can take a shower and change into something comfortable first."

"Have you got money for a taxi?"

"My car's outside, which is a bloody miracle since Emmy drove it."

"Vince said she was your boss?"

"Not my direct boss, but she part-owns the company."

"She's kind of intimidating."

"There's no 'kind of' about it."

"She's not as bad as Ana."

"Ana's a she-devil with added make-up, but for the situation you were in today, you couldn't have asked for two better people to get you out of it."

"I know." Them being nearby was the first piece of luck I'd had in ages. "What's a MANPADS?"

"A Man-Portable Air-Defence System."

"In English?"

"A surface-to-air missile, but what's that got to do with anything?"

"It doesn't matter."

Nye was right—I really didn't want to know.

CHAPTER 38

ZANDER PLACED MY hand on the gear stick as we drove back to Arndale, his hand wrapped over the top, a gesture I wasn't sure how to interpret after our conversation last night.

Last night.

That moment seemed a decade ago, not less than twenty-four hours. I hoped his touch meant we could go back to being friends again, proper friends, and not have to do that weird dance we'd partnered in over breakfast this morning.

And then he confused me even more when we stopped at a red traffic light and he brought my palm to his lips, followed by a flickering smile. Was he nervous? Why?

I was still trying to sort through my jumble of thoughts when we pulled up next to a police car outside Arndale House.

"At least we don't need to worry about putting the car in the garage anymore," Zander said.

"Because the police are here?"

"No, because Carrie isn't."

"You think that was her as well? The brakes?"

"Yeah, I do. If she could rig the house to blow, I bet the braking system wouldn't have given her a problem." He moved to open his door, and then stopped. "Dee..."

"Yes?"

"Shit." He closed his eyes and leaned back in his seat. "I've been an idiot."

Was this about last night?

"It doesn't matter. I just want to go back to how things were."

"I don't. Fuck. I don't know how to do this."

I reached for his hand and held it tight. He'd given me his strength earlier; now I owed him what was left of mine.

He cleared his throat. "Yesterday I said I was scared, but I was talking bullshit. I didn't know what it was like to be scared until I worked out Carrie was a problem, and then you wouldn't answer your phone."

"I'm sorry, I—"

"I need to finish. Please?"

I nodded.

He turned to me, his eyes wide as they searched for mine and locked on.

"I think I broke rule four."

"What's rule four?"

His voice dropped to a whisper. "Never fall in love."

My pulse raced and that light-headed feeling from earlier came rushing back.

"Are you saying—"

A *thump* on the roof of the car startled both of us, and Emmy grinned through Zander's window.

"Hurry up, would you? The police are waiting, and I've got a flight to catch."

"She always did have a superb sense of timing," Zander muttered.

Perhaps, but I didn't have any complaints earlier when she turned up with two minutes to spare.

"We're coming."

I didn't get the chance to take a shower or even change before the two policemen started with their questions. They'd wanted us to go to the station so they could talk to us separately, but Emmy said if they wanted to talk to all of us, they'd have to do it then and there. Phone calls were made, and the cops' boss obviously caved to her demands. Wow.

In the lounge, Zander wrapped a blanket around my shoulders and settled next to me on the sofa while the detectives took an armchair each. Emmy and Nye sat on the floor in the corner, legs outstretched.

"Miss Hallam, can you tell us your side of the story first? I'm sure you'll agree we've got quite a mess next door, and we need to get to the bottom of it."

I talked through my version of events, from Carrie's phone call to the bomb going off. As I spoke, Zander's hand crept around my back until his fingers curled around my opposite hip, distracting me so I kept stumbling over my words.

"Would you like some water?" the older of the two cops asked.

"Yes, please."

Nye walked through to the kitchen while the policemen scribbled down notes, but the water did me no good at all when Zander's fingers slid up and stroked my side for a few seconds, then found their way under the waistband of my jeans. My mind went completely blank.

"So, this Ana, she left?" the cop asked. "Do you

know why?"

"I have no idea."

"She had a meeting to get to," Emmy cut in. "She'd done her bit, and there was no point in her sticking around. I'm on a schedule too, so if you'd hurry things up, I'd be grateful." In other words, stop dithering.

Both policemen gave her a dirty look before they focused on Zander.

"Mr. Graves, I understand you were the one who requested Mrs. Black's presence at the scene?"

"Yes."

"Why was that?"

"She was closest, and I had a bad feeling about it."

"Could you elaborate on 'it'?"

"As I'm sure you know, we found a body buried behind the house recently. Marlene Grande, who owns this place, hired Blackwood to look into that as well as a series of vandalism incidents that happened on her property. Part of our investigation involved running background checks on everyone connected with the case. The Hearsts next door were three of those people."

"Frederick, Maude, and Carrie?"

"That's right. Carrie arrived here just over a year ago from Australia to care for her aunt and uncle, right around the time the body got buried. Nothing but the timing aroused my suspicion, and the background check took longer than most due to her having moved around over the last few years. Our Perth office tracked her last home to a small town two hundred miles inland. The initial checks came through clean—criminal record, financial history, media reports—but someone suggested we pay closer attention to people who didn't grow up in the village. I pushed for more, and today I received a photo of Carrie. Only it wasn't her."

"Could you explain?"

"The photo Blackwood's Perth office sent through of Carrie Hearst wasn't the girl I knew as Carrie Hearst. I thought they'd made a mistake at first, but I got the investigator out of bed, and he confirmed her old employer gave him the photo. He took it at the office Christmas party the year before last."

"So somebody's had the wool pulled over their eyes?"

"Looks that way. I had a photo of our Carrie in my phone from a party here, and I sent that over to double-check. Whoever was living next door, it wasn't Carrie Hearst."

Realisation dawned. "The body. That's the real Carrie, isn't it?"

Zander's fingers slipped under the edge of my knickers, and I gasped.

"I suspect so."

"I still don't understand the sudden rush to get here?" the policeman said.

"Because pseudo-Carrie was unravelling. She'd murdered one person, vandalised Dove's tools, left a knife as a gift, caused a car accident, and possibly tried to kill Ms. Grande."

"Yes, she did," I said. "She told me she did. She said Bear wasn't much of a guard dog."

We all stared over at him, asleep in his basket near the radiator. He'd taken to this home life a little too well, which had clearly led to him slacking on the job.

"No more steak for him," Zander murmured, moving his fingers down another inch. How could he do that and still concentrate on the conversation?

"Is there anything else you've forgotten to tell us about your time with Carrie?" the younger policeman asked.

"Uh..." I tried to shift away, to escape Zander's heated touch, but he smirked and moved with me. "Uh..." What did she say? Something I couldn't quite grasp... "Ah! I remember. We were discussing Neil, her boyfriend here, and she said she didn't normally go for men. I wonder if she was more than friends with the real Carrie? After all, she knew enough about her to fool everyone, including her family."

"Nice work, Dee," Zander said, his lips so close they brushed my ear.

Dammit! I adored the closeness, but did he have to start this in the middle of a police interview?

"And Mrs. Black?" Both policemen swivelled their heads, and I breathed a sigh of relief. "Could you enlighten us on your part in this?" the older one asked.

"Like Zander said, I happened to be in the area, so I agreed to stop by and check up on Dove."

"Why Dove in particular? Why not..." He checked his notepad. "Amber Stark?"

"Mr. Graves doesn't have the same relationship with Ms. Stark."

"Ahhh." The cop nodded to himself. "Please, carry on."

"Zander asked me to find Dove and keep an eye on her until he could get back, only when I got here, she'd disappeared. Vince last saw her heading towards the house for lunch, and there was a half-eaten sandwich on the table. Something made Dove leave in a hurry."

"And how did you know Carrie called her?"

"We didn't. But we figured if we cut the head off the monster first, we could find Dove afterwards. I'm using a metaphor, by the way."

"I'm not so sure about that," Zander muttered under his breath.

"And when you got to Fernleigh House, you found Dove incapacitated in the hallway and the Hearsts upstairs?"

"Indeed."

"Mr. Holmes? Could you fill in your part for completeness?"

As Nye began to speak, Zander's phone vibrated against his leg, and he fished it out, checked the screen, then raised an eyebrow at Emmy. She winked. Another buzz, and I realised she was the one messaging.

"What?" I whispered, and Zander put a finger to his lips.

The policemen turned back to us. "Right, we've got the outline, and now we need to fill in the details. Miss Hallam, what were Carrie's exact words on the phone? And can you recall the time?"

"No, no, no," Emmy cut in again. "We know what happened. The house blew up. Boom. The part we're missing is Carrie, and you sitting here on your arses isn't doing a lot towards finding her. If you want more waffle for your report, you can speak to Dove and Zander tomorrow when they've had some sleep."

Three jaws dropped open—mine and the two policemen's. "Mrs. Black..." the older one said, visibly struggling to remain civil. "You can't simply walk out of an interview."

"Watch me."

"We haven't finished our questions."

"Then subpoena me."

Zander lifted me to my feet. "Go, while Emmy's got their attention."

"With pleasure."

We'd got halfway down the path when my giggles started. "I can't believe she just said all that. Won't they be mad?"

"Yes, but she doesn't care. She's got a low tolerance for bullshit."

Zander helped me into the car, and he'd got behind the wheel before I realised there was something wrong with the picture.

"Hang on, where are we going? I live here."

He shrugged. "Don't know yet. Emmy messaged me a postcode and an instruction to take you there."

"You didn't ask why?"

"Wouldn't have made a difference. We'd be going anyway."

Zander moved to start the engine, but I put out a hand to stop him. "About earlier. What you said in the car. Are you—"

He sighed. "In love with you? I think so. I don't have anything to compare it to. But every time I close my eyes, you're there, and when you're happy, I'm floating on air, and when you're not, I'm walking through fire. If Emmy hadn't got to you today, a part of me would have died with you, and even now the thought of you suffering because I wasn't there to stop it makes me want to strangle that Australian bitch with my bare hands. So if that's what being in love means, then yes, I do love you."

He pulled a handkerchief from his pocket and wiped away my tears, tears that kept coming no matter how tight I screwed my eyes up.

"Dee, don't cry. It hurts."

"These are happy tears, okay? Just drive, will you?"

"But—"

I started the engine for him. "Go, before the police come after us."

He gave me a doubtful glance but rolled forwards. To set his mind at ease, I wriggled my hand underneath his on the gear stick, to the place where it belonged.

Then we rocketed off to a destination unknown.

Chapter 39

"WE'RE NEARLY THERE." I watched the numbers tick by on the satnav. "One mile left to go." We'd turned off the main road into a quiet lane with no street lights, and curiosity was eating away at me. "Does Emmy make a habit of doing this?"

"No, but I don't make a habit of calling her and asking for favours that involve her nearly dying," Zander said.

"She didn't seem cross."

"No, she's surprisingly understanding about those sorts of things." He slowed to go around a bend, then began laughing when he saw where she'd sent us.

"That meddling bitch. Remind me to send her a bunch of flowers tomorrow."

A sign announcing our arrival at the Kendall Grange Luxury Hotel and Spa stood next to the imposing metal gates, and I was glad Zander had a car that fitted in. Then I glanced at my attire.

"I'm not dressed for this place."

"I wasn't planning on you wearing clothes for long." He gave me a nervous glance. "As long as you're okay with that?"

The sparks in my belly flared into an explosion to rival this afternoon's at the prospect of a second Zander-induced orgasm, especially one he knowingly participated in.

"I'm okay with that."

Inside, the receptionist didn't share his enthusiasm as she looked down her nose at us. Well, me. Mostly me.

"I've got a room booked in the name of Graves," Zander guessed.

She tapped away at her keyboard with long red fingernails. I'd tried painting mine that colour once, but with gardening, the polish lasted less than a day before it chipped away into an ugly mosaic.

"Mr. and Mrs. Graves? I see you've reserved our honeymoon suite." Her surprise rivalled mine. "With the deluxe welcome pack. It's waiting in your room." She handed over a key with a burgundy tassel attached. "Congratulations, and we hope you have a pleasant stay at Kendall Grange."

The lift doors were open and waiting at the end of the corridor, and as Zander herded me inside, I caught sight of myself in the mirrored wall.

"Bloody hell, I look like I've been rolling around in a coal cellar."

"I don't care."

The doors closed, and he bent his head to kiss me as we whizzed up to the second floor. A little tongue, not too much, and the flames inside me leapt higher as he picked me up and carried me along the corridor.

"I can walk, you know."

"I do know, but if Emmy's gone to the trouble of booking us the honeymoon suite, the least I can do is carry you over the threshold."

Aw, sweet Zander made my heart sing. I leaned up to kiss him as he fumbled with the key, and he nearly dropped me trying to keep his balance. In the end, I reached down and turned it for him, and we fell inside.

"Nice." He let out a low whistle, but I barely got a chance to look at the room beyond before he blocked the view. Still, with his kisses, I wouldn't care if we were in a tent, so what did it matter?

When he made his move, I realised two things. One, he'd merely been going through the motions when he kissed me outside the shop, and two, Wes had been substandard in every way that counted. Tonight, Zander made me forget everything with a few of his magic touches.

"How are you feeling? How's your head?" he murmured. "Do you just want to sleep, or are you up to more?"

Headache? What headache? "I'm good. More than good. And I want the full Zander experience before I explode."

Zander had a secret smile, one he'd never hinted at before. A dirty, predatory smile that made me want to tear his clothes off and lick him all over.

Hang on. What was stopping me?

I reached for his shirt, but he got in first and trapped my arms as he yanked my jumper upwards, pausing so it covered my eyes.

"No fair. I can't see you."

He pressed his hips into mine. "Then feel me."

Holy hell, I did, every last inch, and there were a lot of inches. I gave up on the idea of his shirt, and as soon as my hands were free again, I went straight for his belt buckle. That turned into a frantic race to see who could get the other's trousers undone first, which Zander won but only because I wasn't wearing a belt. I hopped about, managing to pull a foot out of one leg until Zander took pity and helped, then he pushed me against the wall again.

"I'm not going to make it to the bed, beautiful."

"Then you'll have to hold me up because my legs aren't working so well."

He slid a condom out of his wallet, and as he rolled it on, I gulped at the size of him.

"It'll fit. Trust me. Now, wrap your legs around my waist."

I hopped up and braced my back against the wall, then he slid inside, stretching me to the point of pain. A delicious pain that intensified every thrust, offset by the way he nuzzled my neck and whispered dirty snippets into my ear about all the things he wanted to do to me later.

A slow burn spread through me, hotter and hotter, until he bit my earlobe and I shattered into a thousand ice crystals, then melted into his arms. One last grunt, and he followed suit.

He turned and sank to the floor with me straddling him, the last tremors of orgasm still washing through me.

"Dee, I love you."

"I love you too."

He dropped his forehead against mine. "I never thought I'd hear anyone but Alana say that to me."

"Then you're an idiot."

"And you're filthy, and not in a good way."

We both burst into laughter. That was my favourite thing about us, now that there was an us—we could laugh through anything, and I knew we would for a long time to come.

"What did you say about taking a shower?"

"Allow me to demonstrate."

The bathroom contained not only a Jacuzzi bath, but also a fancy shower cubicle big enough for two with jets coming out of everywhere and a sturdy grab rail on one side. At least, that's what I assumed it was for, seeing as it was in the honeymoon suite. Zander had the same thought, because he gave it a good shake.

"Seems solid."

He'd stripped off the rest of his clothes on the way, and I reached down.

"So do you."

Zander looked wistfully at the streaming water. "I've got a plan B for the shower. You get to have all the fun."

"But—"

He held up a packet. "I failed as a Boy Scout and didn't come prepared. We've only got one condom left, and I'm saving that for the bed."

I cupped his cheek in my hand, his day's worth of stubble rough against my palm.

"We're serious about this, aren't we?"

"I've never been more serious about anything in my life."

"I'm on the pill, and I never slept with Wes without a condom. He was paranoid I might get pregnant."

"Wes was a prick." He frowned. "Sorry."

"No, you're right."

"I always covered up. Always. I was clean on my last medical, and I haven't looked at anyone but you since then. It's just been me and my hand."

"I know," I blurted. "I saw you in the shower one morning."

His eyes widened. "Fuck me, I take it all back. You're a filthy little bitch in a good way too." His grin widened as well. "Did you jill off thinking about it?"

Oh, hell. My colour must have matched the heritage tomatoes I was trying so hard to grow.

"While I was watching."

He laughed as he yanked the door open and lifted me inside. "Let me show you how to do proper shower filth." He spun me around before I got a chance to agree. "Hold on."

After the shower, the bottle of champagne, and the chocolates from the welcome pack, we finally tumbled into bed, and I got my third version of Zander that night: the sweetheart who kissed and licked his way over every inch of my body before making love to me almost reverently. Two more orgasms and I was done. Spent.

I was also lying in the wet patch, but I didn't even care.

"What are we doing tomorrow?" I asked.

"Reckon we should move in here and live on room service."

"That's not very practical."

"I'm sick of being practical, and I never want to go that long without sex again."

We still needed to find Carrie too, but I didn't want to bring her up tonight, not after Zander had managed to turn the worst day ever into a much better one.

"I don't want you to go without sex either, not if it means I get orgasms like that every evening."

"And every morning."

My only previous experience of morning sex was a dry fumble one weekend before Wes went home to visit his mother, and I couldn't wait to see what Zander brought to the party. But I still had six hours before I'd find out.

"We should get some sleep first."

He kissed me softly on the lips. "Sweet dreams, Dee. My Dee."

I relaxed into him and laid my head on his chest. His heart beat steadily, while mine still raced from his earlier tricks. "My dreams have already come true."

CHAPTER 40

MORNING SEX WITH Zander didn't suck. I sucked, because I figured it was about time I repaid Zander for the efforts he made with his tongue last night.

"Did I mention that I love you?" he asked as I licked the last of the mess away.

"Only twice so far today."

"Once for each orgasm. Want to go for a third?"

I crawled up the bed and took a moment to admire his body in the sun splashing through the window before I kissed him. "Why not?"

A knock at the door, that was why not.

"Who is it?" Zander called.

"Breakfast, sir, and a package has been delivered for you."

We looked at each other, and I shrugged. We'd come to the hotel on the spur of the moment, and the only person who knew we were there was...

"Emmy," we both said at the same time.

"Who sent the package?" Zander asked the man.

"Uh, the Queen Bee? She said you'd know what that meant?"

"Yeah, I do. Give me a second."

I dashed into the bathroom while Zander threw on a robe and wheeled in a trolley filled with covered dishes, a carafe of coffee, and a large gift-wrapped box.

"You open it," Zander said. "I'm looking for the bacon."

Clothes. She'd sent me clothes, and not just any old outfit. I looked at the labels as I pulled each item out of the box—a Calvin Klein skirt, Wolford tights, LK Bennett ballet pumps, a soft-as-a-cloud cashmere sweater from Ralph Lauren.

"This is too much."

"You know Emmy married a billionaire?"

"Are you serious?"

"Yep."

"Does he realise she jumps out of exploding buildings?"

"He trained her to do it." Zander leaned forwards and rummaged in the box, coming up with a pair of wolf-print briefs and an economy-sized box of Durex. "Ah, these must be for me."

"Rowr."

We sorted out orgasm number three in the shower after we'd eaten, and then it was time to check out. The big question was, where did we go?

"Are you heading back to London?" I asked.

"Yes, and so are you. Until we know who and where Carrie is, I'm not letting you out of my sight."

"But what about work?"

"Marlene would understand. Ivy will understand. Hell, I'll hire another gardener to help you once we've caught that scheming bitch."

"Can I stay in your apartment?"

"Which part of this whole 'being in love with you' thing don't you get? We've practically been living together for the last six weeks anyway."

I couldn't help smiling at the thought of going back

to Chelsea, even more so because I'd be in Zander's bed and not on the pull-out in his sister's room. "It'll be nice to see Alana again."

"The feeling's mutual. She keeps asking when I'm bringing you back."

If only so much bad hadn't happened over the past few weeks, I could have smiled a lot more at the good. But my happiness was tainted by two deaths and three injuries. Time was a great healer, my granddad had always told me, and I had faith that in the years to come, I'd find enough joy with Zander to wipe out some of the sad memories. But for now, my goal was the same as his—catch the scheming bitch and make her pay.

"We'd better get dressed. You've got a job to do, and I want to help."

On my second trip to the Blackwood offices, dressed in designer gear and holding Zander's hand as we strode through reception, blondie on the desk did a double take and reached for the phone.

"I think she's going to tell everyone about us," I whispered to him.

"Let her. I want the world to know I'm taken."

It seemed the news had already begun to spread, at least on Zander's floor, because when he opened his desk drawer to get his laptop out, we were showered with condoms in every flavour, colour, and texture imaginable. I caught Nye grinning from a glass-fronted office at the edge of the room before he backed inside and closed the door.

"Do they always do this?" I asked.

"The novelty'll wear off soon, and they'll move on to their next victim. In the meantime, I'll put in a request for whipped cream and chocolate body paint because we don't need all these." He leaned closer and whispered right into my ear. "I love being bare inside you."

"How many hours until you can go home?"

"Too many. Now, let's see what we've got."

Lydia Bowman, that's what, or rather, who. Her mugshot stared out at me from the file emailed overnight from Zander's colleagues in Australia, along with a brief history and a promise of more to come.

"Two years in the army before she got a dishonourable discharge for theft. Guess that explains how she knew about explosives," Zander said.

"And look here—she worked as a car mechanic for the last year, in the same town as the real Carrie."

"Seems like you were right about their involvement —her boss said she and Carrie had a thing going as well as being housemates."

"What kind of freak murders their own partner?"

Zander pulled me into his lap, ignoring the round of applause from the desks nearby. "A sick and very dangerous one. I'll work here until Monday, and when you go back to Arndale, I'm coming with you."

"Then until Monday, I'm your new assistant. What can I do to help? And can I get my own chair?"

Zander kissed me, and we got whistles. "You can have anything it's in my power to give you, beautiful."

A chair was enough for me, and I helped an intern go over surveillance tapes from Heathrow Airport for the rest of the day. Three other assistants got Gatwick,

Luton, and Stansted, and boy was it boring. Only the endless cups of coffee and a big box of chocolates kept me awake.

"We'll carry on tomorrow?" one of my new buddies asked at the end of the day.

"I can't wait."

We walked out of the building the same way we came in, hand in hand, with me questioning what on earth I'd done to snag myself a man like Zander.

"Lanie's making dinner," he told me. "How was surveillance duty?"

"Uh, I prefer being outdoors."

He chuckled and dropped a kiss on my head as he bleeped the car doors open. "Thought you might say that."

"Did you find anything?"

"Her motive. Lydia was in it for the money. She's been draining the Hearsts' bank accounts since the beginning, but we reckon she was hanging in there for the big payoff—once both the Hearsts died, the house and everything else would have gone to her."

"That's cold."

"A couple of million quid for, what, three or four years' work? If I were a betting man, I'd have put money on the pair of them having 'accidents' if they didn't pop their clogs fast enough."

"So you're not a betting man?"

"Fifty quid says I get lucky tonight."

"Oh, please. I'm not a walking cash machine."

Alana was waiting with a bottle of champagne and a hug when we got back to the apartment. Zander popped the cork while I got my face smushed into her hair.

"I'm glad my brother finally met someone he wants to spend more time with, and I'm so happy it's you."

"I promise not to bring Laura over again."

She burst out laughing. "Good grief, if he'd ended up with a girl like that, I'd have thrown them both off the balcony. I made risotto for dinner. Hope you enjoy it."

"I know I'll love it."

She'd also bought us a few gifts, as we found out when we went into the bedroom after dinner. A sexy nightie, a giant box of condoms, furry handcuffs, and... What was that? A vibrating cock ring?

"Lanie!" Zander yelled.

"I bought earplugs too," she shouted, then slammed her bedroom door.

"How did she end up like this?" he groaned.

"Genetics." I opened up the box I was holding. "How does this work?"

He kissed me, long and deep. "Let's find out, shall we?"

"I'm glad I finally bought a car I love driving," Zander said two weeks later. "You were right about the BMW being boring."

We'd settled into a routine for now—Monday to Thursday, Zander either worked remotely from Arndale House or commuted into London. Friday and Saturday nights, I travelled to London and stayed with him and Alana in Chelsea. We got the best of both worlds that way, as well as being able to spend time with each other.

Lydia was always in the back of my mind, but on my second day at Blackwood, I'd spotted her going through passport control, now with a blonde bob and glasses. Zander and his team had traced her to Vietnam, but with no extradition treaty, the British police were at a loss as to how to get her back from there.

At least it meant I could garden in peace.

"Go, before you're late. I'll see you tonight."

"Are you sure you don't mind catching the train?" he asked. It being a Friday, Zander had offered to drive back and collect me, but he spent enough time on the motorway already.

"It's fine. Alana's going out with friends, so I want you stripped and waiting when I get home."

Home. We both smiled when I said the word, although truthfully, it didn't matter whether I was talking about Chelsea or Arndale. Home was wherever we both were.

Except that the day didn't go quite according to plan. With two weeks to go until a party looking less and less likely to be held, Vince had agreed to take a break from chopping down trees and help me make raised beds for the vegetable garden instead, on his same hourly rate of course. We'd just lifted another wooden rectangle into place when my phone rang.

Two words from Nye. "Marlene's awake."

My shriek brought Lars and Amber running from the house, and before long, we were all on our way to the hospital. Nye and Ivy were already in the waiting room when we arrived.

"Apparently, her first words were, 'Did I miss the party?'" he said.

Ivy gave us a smug grin. "Told you she'd be awake in time for her get-together."

The doctors wouldn't let us see her until halfway through the evening, and by then, Zander had arrived with a bag of sandwiches and plenty of chocolate. Ivy went in first and came out smiling.

"Marlene wants the waiters in skeleton outfits, and she's got several ideas for themed cocktails."

Bloody hell. Marlene didn't waste time, did she?

"And she wants a word with Zander and Nye about the photo she found. Dove, you sneak in with them."

Despite three weeks in the hospital, Marlene looked sprightly, smiling in a hot-pink dressing gown as she sipped on a glass of...

"Is that rosé?" Nye asked.

She put a finger to her lips. "Shh."

"I need to have words with my grandma."

"Oh, don't be such an old stick-in-the-mud. Being teetotal doesn't agree with me."

Zander rolled his eyes, and I bit my lip to keep from smiling. The fall didn't seem to have harmed Marlene's personality.

"Ivy said you wanted to talk to us?"

"Yes, about that body in the woods. I found a photo at Maude's of a young brunette beside the old chapel, and I have an odd feeling it's important. Maude didn't recall seeing it before, and neither did Carrie when I asked her, but what if it's the missing girl?"

"You asked Carrie about it?"

"Yes, as I left the house. She didn't recognise her, which is hardly surprising since she hasn't lived in Northbury much longer than me."

Zander pulled out his phone and fetched an image

onto the screen. "Was this her?"

Marlene squinted at the picture, then handed it back. "Sure looks like it. Did you find the photo in my bag?"

Nye and Zander looked at each other before Nye took Marlene's hand. "We've got a lot to tell you."

Chapter 41

BY THE SATURDAY of the party, the Arndale estate had been transformed. With Ivy at the helm and Marlene helping via video link from her hospital bed, a swarm of extra workmen had descended to assist with fixing up the chapel and laying the path from the house. We had thirty feet left to go, and Hal was confident of finishing before the guests arrived.

With the promise of free booze and easy debutantes, a group of Zander's colleagues had come to help, but I did a double take when Emmy and Ana turned up in an Aston Martin, along with a small man sporting lilac hair.

"I'm never riding in the back of that car again," he complained. "It wasn't designed for people with legs."

"There's always the train, Bradley."

He blinked a few times, and his jaw dropped. "You wouldn't..."

"Stop moaning and decorate."

He flicked his hair and marched into the house in sparkly silver boots, no doubt on his way to lock horns with Amber.

"That's my assistant," Emmy said. "He never likes to miss a party."

"What are you doing here?"

"Nice to see you too. We had a couple of hours

spare, so we thought we'd stop off and say hello."

"Sorry, I didn't mean to be rude. I'm just surprised, that's all."

Zander came around the side of the house, and he wore the same expression as me.

"What are you doing here?"

"You invited me, remember?"

"Yes, but I didn't think you'd come."

"Wow, you sure know how to make a girl feel welcome."

"Sorry, it's just..."

"Okay, okay, I get it. Look, we were returning some stuff we borrowed from a guy up north, and Bradley wanted to come to the party."

"Are you staying too?"

"No, me and Ana need to go at five. We could do with a chat before then."

"Sure. Over lunch?"

"Yeah. In the meantime, do you need a hand?"

Zander turned to me. "Dove?"

She was offering to help? I hadn't planned for that. "Uh, I need some holes. For the winter cherry trees."

"Holes?"

"Eight of them. I was going to get Hal to use the digger, but he'll be busy with the path all day."

Emmy looked at Ana, who shrugged. "Okay, holes. We can do holes. Show us where you want them."

I felt their eyes on me from behind as I led the way to the spot I'd picked out on the far side of the house. Emmy made me mildly nervous, but Ana studied me with the lazy intensity of a lioness stalking a gazelle. It was all I could do not to run for cover.

Hands trembling, I pulled a folded sheet of paper

from my pocket and pointed at the two spades I'd left out earlier in the hope I could find a pair of willing volunteers.

"I've marked the positions out on this diagram. Eight holes, three feet wide and deep. I know it's a lot, but..."

"We'll get it done."

"There are tarpaulins to put the spare dirt on."

"Leave it to us."

The morning flew past, and before I knew it, Lars called out that lunch was ready in the dining room. With Carrie out of the way, I'd salvaged the relationship with him and Amber, and it was almost like old times.

"Where's Emmy?" Zander asked.

"Still digging holes, I guess."

"I can't believe you gave them that job. Do you know how much she charges to get out of bed?"

"No, how much?"

"Twenty thousand dollars."

"You're kidding?"

"Nope." He burst out laughing. "And she's digging holes."

Except she wasn't. When we climbed up the bank by the old pond, Emmy and Ana had laid out tarpaulins around the spaces where the holes needed to be and weighted them down with rocks, but the turf was still pristine. Not only that, they were sitting on an ornamental boulder, chatting.

"I don't believe this. You haven't even started."

"Yes, we have," Emmy said.

I glanced down at my diagram. She'd scribbled all over it—numbers and lines. "You haven't dug anything."

Ana glared up at me. "You didn't say anything about digging."

"I clearly said I needed holes."

The spades lying next to her had never even seen dirt. Hang on, why did they have a metal stake and a sledgehammer?

"Good to go?" Emmy asked.

Ana looked at the sheet of paper in her hand. "Yes."

"Far enough back?"

"A bit further."

"Guys, we need to stand over there." Emmy pointed to the bank Zander and I had just climbed over.

"Why? What are you talking about?"

Zander stared at her. "Tell me you haven't..."

She took both our hands and led us away like small children, Ana following. Had she gone quite mad?

"Ready?" Ana asked.

"Go for it."

The shock wave blew me onto my ass and left my ears ringing. Zander picked me up, looking towards Emmy with murder in his eyes.

She'd already climbed the bank with Ana. "Look. Holes. Gardening's so much more fun with military-grade explosives, don't you think?"

"I think you're insane," Zander told her.

"And that's news how?"

Ana smiled, and that scared me more than her resting bitch face. "Our work here is done."

Standing on the bank, I had to agree with all of them. Yes, Emmy and Ana were insane. No, it wasn't a surprise. And I now had eight perfect-sized holes ready for my cherry trees.

"It's a shame you can't stay for the party," I said to Emmy as she prepared to leave at five.

"We're going to a different party."

"Somewhere nice?"

"Yeah. Vietnam."

Wait a minute. Vietnam? "Hold on—"

But I was talking to empty air. Emmy had already slammed the car door and started the engine. I turned to Zander. "Do you think...?"

"I don't ask, and she doesn't tell. It's better that way."

How did I feel about that? Because I bet they weren't flying to Vietnam for a relaxing holiday. Emmy may be beautiful with her perfect figure and Barbie doll hair, but a hardness lurked in her eyes, earned not bought. And Ana? That hardness spread through her entire soul.

But do you know what? Carrie deserved everything that came to her. She was broken inside, and she'd let her evil leach out and poison the whole of Northbury village.

"Yes, you're probably right. I don't want to know."

Bradley and Amber had got their hands on Marlene's wheelchair, and by the time the party started, it sported purple feathers on the arms and a glittery gold crown painted on the back.

Bradley tried to dress Lars up to match, and while

he wore the gold bow tie with good humour, he drew the line at the boa. Undeterred, Bradley wrapped it around his own shoulders and carried on.

"Such a shame Maude couldn't make it," Marlene said.

"It might have been a bit much," Amber told her.

"We need to save her a slice of cake for tomorrow."

Proving her heart was big enough to share, Marlene had offered Mrs. Hearst a place to stay while her home got rebuilt, although I had my doubts she'd ever live at Fernleigh House again. Who would want to be surrounded by those final memories? Mind you, if anyone could help her get through this difficult time, it was Marlene and Ivy—both had lost husbands and maintained a positive outlook on life, and Mrs. Hearst needed exactly that.

The doctors had said she could come home tomorrow, but not before. Marlene accused them of being awkward, but one of them whispered to me on my way out.

"I've heard stories of Ms. Grande's parties. I'm not sure Maude's ready for one of those."

"I agree. Don't worry—as soon as Marlene's drunk a cocktail or two, she'll be fine about it."

And I was right. An hour in, she and Ivy were halfway through the drinks list and voting on which waiter had the tightest ass. I didn't care. I only had eyes, and hands, for Zander's.

"So, this ghost thing..." Alana said. She'd come along in a dress that matched Bradley's hair, although they both swore they hadn't planned it. "Do you think it's real? Or a load of old rubbish?"

"We'll have to wait until midnight and see."

She held up her "Green Lady" cocktail, a vicious mixture of absinthe and lemonade with a little ghost on a stick decorating it. "I'm not sure I'll be able to see by midnight. Or stand." Her attention got momentarily distracted by a waiter walking past with a tray of canapés. "Flipping heck—did you see the arse on that?"

"Marlene and Ivy picked them out from photos."

"Do either of them need a new assistant?"

I left Alana pursuing the object of her affections and went to find the object of mine. It took me a while, but I eventually located him in the study, hiding behind a rack of plants.

"What are you doing in here?"

"I lost you," he hissed. "Where did you go?"

"Marlene wanted her cardigan, but that doesn't answer my question."

"There are women out there. Everywhere. One blonde tried to join me in the downstairs toilet, and when I got away, two others chased me into the TV room."

"Your reputation precedes you." I tried to sound stern, but I couldn't help giggling. He'd brought it on himself with his past habits.

"I swear, I've deleted all the numbers from my phone, and I'm doing nothing to encourage them."

"Come on, Casanova. I promise I won't leave you by yourself again."

He grinned sheepishly as he slunk into full view. "Sorry."

"You've got lipstick on your collar."

"Dammit."

I stepped forwards and kissed him. "Now you've got it on your lips too, but I'm not sure red's your colour."

Or mine, but Amber insisted.

Zander's eyes darkened, and my stomach flipped. I knew that look, and when he used it on me, it usually meant I struggled to walk for an hour afterwards. By the time we'd finished, most of the lipstick was on his underpants and he needed to hold me up.

"This party's got better," he said.

"I can't believe we just did that. Anybody could have walked in."

"All part of the fun, Dee."

By midnight, my tally of dirty looks was well into double figures, and one brazen girl hit on Zander right in front of me. No, I didn't want a threesome, not even if she had a posh title and brought the really expensive champagne.

"Nearly time for me to take you to bed," Zander whispered once he'd sent her packing.

"As opposed to a slightly dusty wall in a dimly lit temporary greenhouse?"

"I do like to spoil you. How long until Marlene's surprise?"

"Anytime now."

Not content to leave the ghostly visit to chance and risk disappointing her guests, she'd called in a special-effects guru her late husband worked with in Hollywood, and he'd spent the past three days installing a hologram to walk its path from the house to the chapel, with dessert canapés to be served on the altar once it arrived. We'd done a run-through once it got dark yesterday, and as the shimmering lady swept through the trees, I'd shuddered even though I knew she wasn't real. With all the wine imbibed tonight, the effect should be wild.

The first screams happened just after midnight, and they covered up my own shrieks as Zander threw me over his shoulder and carried me off to the cottage.

"Put me down! People will see up my dress."

"Nobody's looking."

"You don't know that." I glanced around wildly, checking for an audience. "What's that over there? The flash of pale green in the trees?"

Zander stopped to look, craning his neck in the same direction as mine. "I don't know. It looks kind of...spooky."

"Maybe it's the real ghost."

"Or maybe it's a couple sneaking off for a quickie."

"Or maybe..." Zander's hand slid up my bare thigh, and I gasped. "Maybe I just don't care."

CHAPTER 42

TWO WEEKS ON, and I'd just about caught up on sleep from the party. How did Marlene and Ivy do it? They'd had mani-pedis on the Sunday afterwards, then gone out to a burlesque club on Monday, much to Marlene's doctor's horror.

Still, Zander also had this Saturday off, which meant a lie-in followed by lazy sex followed by brunch. Well, lunch, seeing as it was eleven o'clock already. What was the cross between lunch and dinner? Dunch? Linner?

Zander was still working on the lie-in part.

I kissed him on the forehead then rolled out of bed, focused on the coffee machine in the kitchen and its life-giving properties, but I'd only got halfway across the bedroom when my phone rang with an unknown number.

"Hello?"

"Miss Hallam?"

"Yes. Who is this?"

"Inspector Prescott with the Oxfordshire Constabulary. Have you got a few minutes?"

I sat down on the edge of the bed with a bump, waking Zander.

"Who is it?" he mouthed.

I covered the microphone with my hand. "Police."

"Speaker."

Hand shaking, I pushed the button. "Yes, I can talk."

"Good, good. I just wanted to update you on developments in the Hearst case."

My stomach leapt into my throat, and Zander sat up and put his arm around me. I'd managed to block Lydia out over the last month, although with the real Carrie's funeral coming up next week, that wouldn't last forever.

"What developments?"

"Lydia Bowman walked into the station yesterday and gave herself up."

He sounded surprised, but not half as surprised as me. After Emmy and Ana flew to Vietnam, I'd expected to see a small news story about an unidentified body washing up on a beach one morning.

"She what?"

"Walked right in, she did, and told the desk sergeant she wanted to make a statement. She confessed to everything, even killing Maude Hearst's West Highland Terrier."

"Why would she do that when she'd put so much effort into getting away?"

"Who knows? Said it was the right thing to do, but clearly she's not right in the head. Seemed oddly nervous."

Could Emmy and Ana really make a woman scared enough to fly halfway across the world and beg for a jail cell? I very much suspected the answer was yes, and that made me oddly nervous too.

Still, I forced myself to be positive. "That's good news."

"Isn't it? Saves us a lot of paperwork and a nasty trial at any rate. And she's put back what's left of the money she stole too. Maybe she does have a conscience."

No, she didn't. Not even a shred of one. "So it's over?"

"Apart from sentencing, yes. But don't worry, she won't be getting out anytime soon."

He hung up, and I turned to Zander. "Will you thank them for me?"

"Yeah, for both of us."

The news of Lydia's capture called for a celebration, and Zander insisted on taking me out to a new Japanese place in Mayfair. It had got rave reviews in the *Evening Standard* last week, and the menu on their website listed so many tempting dishes I'd need him to roll me home.

"Tell me if it's good," Alana said.

She'd already planned to go out with friends, and secretly I was pleased to have her brother all to myself.

"I'll sample as many dishes as possible."

Zander had put on a suit, which gave me a problem. I wanted to tear him straight out of it, restaurant be damned.

"Ready to go?" he asked.

"I just need to check my hair." Six months ago, doing my hair meant dragging a brush through it and shoving it back in a ponytail, but Amber and Alana had shown me a handful of simple styles, and while I wouldn't admit it out loud, I kind of enjoyed looking more like a girl and less like a scarecrow.

Except when I emerged from the bedroom, complete with lip gloss and a touch of mascara, Zander and Alana were both sitting on the sofa, ashen-faced.

"What's wrong?"

Zander looked up at me. "Everything."

"No, seriously. You're scaring me."

Alana answered for him. "His mother's on her way. She's on a layover, which gives her precisely..." She checked her watch. "Two hours and thirty-five minutes to eat dinner with her beloved son."

"Do you want to take her to Sobo instead of me?"

He shook his head. "No, because our inevitable argument will be more embarrassing in public."

"So, you're staying here?"

"I'll order something in."

"It's fine. I can go out and come back when she's gone."

"Please, stay."

"Uh, are you sure?" Yes, he'd eaten dinner with my parents, but that was mostly by accident.

"You'll have to meet her sooner or later, and it's best to get it over with."

Alana gave him a worried glance. "I can go though, right?"

"Don't you dare desert me."

If dinner with my family was painful, sharing a table with Zander's mother was like having red-hot needles shoved under my eyelids. The only good part was that after Zander introduced us and she looked at me with disdain, she more or less ignored me.

"Jean-Jaques isn't with you?" he asked, fiddling with his cufflinks. I'd finally given him the pair I bought, and I'd made sure they contained the aspirin he'd surely need when this meal was over.

"Of course not, darling. We got divorced," his mother said.

"You did?"

"I thought I sent an email?"

Wow. She made Ana look positively warm-hearted. What kind of mother didn't pick up the phone over something so important?

Zander spoke through gritted teeth. "No, you didn't."

"Oh, well, never mind. I'm engaged to Gianni now."

"Is Gianni a doctor, a lawyer, or a banker?"

"A hotelier, actually. He owns property all over Europe, and he's been extremely generous in the prenup."

Zander gave his head a slight shake and stabbed at a piece of chicken. "Have you ever married for love?"

I think she tried to crinkle her brow, but most of her forehead was frozen in place. "Why would I want to do that? Love never lasts, unless it's a Chanel 2.55 bag in caviar leather. Those go on for years."

"What if you're wrong?"

Her laughter made me want to borrow Alana's earplugs. "Oh, Zander. I never thought I'd hear you of all people say that."

"I've changed."

"Perhaps for a month or two, if... What's her name again? Quail? If she's looking after you properly, but you'll be playing the field again soon enough."

How dare she?

"I'm sitting right here, and my name's Dove."

She smiled, not kindly, but the superior smile of a woman convinced she's always right.

"I don't mean any offence, darling, but that's just how Zander is. A man like him wasn't designed for commitment."

"Because you made him that way?"

The smile didn't leave her lips, and I longed to remove it for her. "I've seen hundreds of girls like you come and go. You're not worth more than a quick roll in the sack, and certainly not marriage material."

Zander shoved his chair closer to mine. "Wrong again, Mother. We *are* getting married. Next week, in fact."

The shock on her face was the sweetest moment of the evening. Under the table, Alana pulled off her diamond solitaire and slid it onto my finger. A little big, but it would do for this evening's charade. After all, Zander had played along for my parents—the least I could do was return the favour.

The witch recovered her composure. "You didn't send me an invitation."

"Really? I thought I'd emailed, but I must have forgotten."

She narrowed her eyes. "So, where's the ceremony?"

"Vegas," Zander announced, at the same time as Alana said, "Gretna Green."

"You haven't made up your mind with a week to go? What about the guests?"

I coughed nervously. "We're leaning towards Vegas, because of the, uh, casinos." Casinos? I wanted to smack my own head.

Zander gripped my hand. "We wanted something small, just us. After all, money doesn't buy love, no matter how much of it you have to splash around. You should know that by now."

"I'm bridesmaid," Alana put in.

The witch shoved her chair back. "I'm late for my flight, and Jean—Gianni's waiting."

Bloody hell, the woman couldn't even get her own fiancé's name right.

Zander got up too. "Let me show you to the door."

"Don't let it bruise your backside on the way out," Alana muttered.

"I can't believe that woman," I said after Zander's mother had gone.

He'd broken the Scotch out, whether in celebration that she'd left or in misery at being related to her I wasn't sure, and the ice cubes clinked as he took a sip. "It's not funny. This is my life."

"How many husbands has she had now?"

He counted on his fingers. "Gianni will be the seventh, unless there's anyone else she's forgotten to mention."

"Bloody hell." I began giggling. "But her face when you said we were getting married." I twisted Alana's ring off my finger and held it out. "Here, you'd better have this back."

"I'll buy you a proper one tomorrow."

I froze. What did Zander just say?

"Hang on, you weren't serious about that, were

you?"

He leaned over and kissed me softly, just below my earlobe. "Rule five: never get married, and I want to break it with you. Next weekend. Vegas. What do you say?"

Alana shrieked and threw the ring at him. "You can't ask her like that! Do it properly."

"Oh, fuck it." He got down on one knee. "Dove Hallam, will you be my wife?"

It was my turn to shriek. "Yes!"

Zander clutched my hand as we walked into the lobby of our hotel in Las Vegas a week later. Six hours, and I'd be Mrs. Graves, and there was something deliciously illicit about telling nobody but Alana what we were doing. Not my family, not Zander's friends or colleagues. If Marlene and Ivy got involved, the whole thing would turn into a circus, and that was the last thing we wished for.

Just us, Reverend Elvis, two rings, and one bridesmaid. Zander had been sure to book Alana a room on a different floor.

Complete secrecy, that's what we wanted.

"Good afternoon," the receptionist said. "Mr. and Mrs. Graves?"

"Not quite," I said. "Wait a second—how did you know that?"

She smiled at us. "Mrs. Black has upgraded you to the honeymoon suite, and you'll find our deluxe welcome pack in your room. We hope you enjoy your stay at the Black Diamond."

WHAT'S NEXT?

The Blackwood UK series continues with Alana's story in *Indigo Rain*...

Journalism student Alana Graves is having second thoughts about her choice of career when her best friend, Tessa, decides to help her out. Several drunken messages and one gold bikini later, Alana finds herself working as social media coordinator to Rush Moder, one quarter of the world's hottest rock band.

Life on tour isn't quite what Alana expected, and neither are the members of Indigo Rain. Everyone has their secrets, especially the enigmatic lead singer, Travis Thorne. But he's not Alana's only problem. Accidents keep happening, and nobody wants to attend another funeral. Can Alana find out what makes Travis tick before becoming a victim herself?

For more details:
www.elise-noble.com/indigo

And if you'd like to find out more about Emmy, her story's told in the Blackwood Security series, starting with *Pitch Black*:

Even a Diamond can be shattered...

After the owner of a security company is murdered, his sharp-edged wife goes on the run. Forced to abandon everything she holds dear—her home, her friends, her job in special ops—assassin Diamond builds a new life for herself in England. As Ashlyn Hale, she meets Luke, a handsome local who makes her realise just how lonely she is.

Yet, even in the sleepy village of Lower Foxford, the dark side of life dogs Diamond's trail when the unthinkable strikes. Forced out of hiding, she races against time to save those she cares about.

Pitch Black is currently available for **FREE**:
www.elise-noble.com/pitch-black

Want to read about one of the other characters?

Nye's story starts in *Joker in the Pack*, Max appears in *Roses are Dead*, and Ana tries to destroy the world in *Ultraviolet*.

If you enjoyed *Shallow Graves*, please consider leaving a review.

For an author, every review is incredibly important. Not only do they make us feel warm and fuzzy inside, readers consider them when making their decision whether or not to buy a book. Even a line saying you enjoyed the book or what your favourite part was helps a lot.

WANT TO STALK ME?

For updates on my new releases, giveaways, and other random stuff, you can sign up for my newsletter on my website:
www.elise-noble.com

Facebook:
www.facebook.com/EliseNobleAuthor

Twitter: @EliseANoble

Instagram: @elise_noble

If you're on Facebook, you may also like to join Team Blackwood for exclusive giveaways, sneak previews, and book-related chat. Be the first to find out about new stories, and you might even see your name or one of your ideas make it into print!

And if you'd like to read my books for FREE, you can also find details of how to join my review team.

Would you like to join Team Blackwood?

www.elise-noble.com/team-blackwood

END OF BOOK STUFF

The idea for Shallow Graves came when I walked into my friend's flat to feed her (now sadly deceased) goldfish and water her plants while she was on holiday. She had a small plaque hanging on her living room door handle, with the words "To plant a garden is to believe in tomorrow" on it. I thought that was a nice sentiment, and before I started writing books I actually had time to grow things and quite enjoyed it, so I decided to write a book about a gardener.

Sadly, my own garden's more like a jungle at the moment, but every so often, the tree surgeons turn up to make it look more presentable. Although none of them are Vince, unfortunately.

The "graves" part came partly from Zander's name, and partly from time spent at Bradenham Manor, an old National Trust property near where I live. It inspired Arndale House (and even stands in for it on the cover), and has a little pet cemetery hidden in one corner of the gardens—two rows of tiny headstones with faded inscriptions dating back to the 1920s.

Ivy was a character I've wanted to write more about since I introduced her in *Joker in the Pack*, and I figured I'd give her an equally crazy friend, mainly because my mum kept asking when I was going to write a book with "nutty old ladies" in it. Marlene was named after Marlene Dietrich (pronounced Mar-lay-na, the German way), because I love the old movie glamour.

And Carrie? Well, women can be bad apples too.

Alana's up next in the Blackwood UK series, together with a quartet of rock stars, Zander, Max, a best friend who loves to stick her nose into other people's business, and of course Emmy. I've drafted Indigo Rain already, but the editing always takes longer than the writing part!

Thank you as always to my editor, Nikki, and cover designer, Abi—this game would be so much harder without you both. Thanks also to my proofreaders, John and Lizbeth.

Carbon
Rhodium
Platinum
Lead
Copper
Bronze
Nickel
Hydrogen (TBA)

The Blackwood UK Series
Joker in the Pack
Cherry on Top (novella)
Roses are Dead
Shallow Graves
Indigo Rain
Pass the Parcel (TBA)

Blackwood Casefiles
Stolen Hearts

Blackstone House
Hard Lines (2021)
Hard Tide (TBA)

The Electi Series
Cursed
Spooked
Possessed
Demented
Judged (2021)

The Trouble Series
Trouble in Paradise

Nothing but Trouble
24 Hours of Trouble

Standalone
Life
Coco du Ciel (TBA)
Twisted (short stories)
A Very Happy Christmas (novella)

Books with clean versions available (no swearing and no on-the-page sex)
Pitch Black
Into the Black
Forever Black
Gold Rush
Gray is my Heart

Audiobooks
Black is my Heart (Diamond & Snow - prequel)
Pitch Black
Into the Black
Forever Black
Gold Rush

www.ingramcontent.com/pod-product-compliance
Lightning Source LLC
Chambersburg PA
CBHW020237200626
46816CB00001BA/10